I0823958

SUNRISE ON THE REAPING

SCHOLASTIC PRESS / NEW YORK

SUZANNE COLLINS

SUNRISE ON THE REAPING

Library of Congress Cataloging-in-Publication Data available

ISBN 978-1-5461-7146-1

10 9 8 7 6 5 4 3 2 1 25 26 27 28 29

Printed in Italy 208

First edition, March 2025

Book design by Elizabeth B. Parisi

For Richard Register

"All propaganda is lies, even when one is telling the truth. I don't think this matters so long as one knows what one is doing, and why."

— George Orwell

"A truth that's told with bad intent
Beats all the lies you can invent."

— William Blake

"Nothing appears more surprising to those, who consider human affairs with a philosophical eye, than the easiness with which the many are governed by the few; and the implicit submission, with which men resign their own sentiments and passions to those of their rulers. When we enquire by what means this wonder is effected, we shall find, that, as Force is always on the side of the governed, the governors have nothing to support them but opinion. It is therefore, on opinion only that government is founded; and this maxim extends to the most despotic and most military governments, as well as to the most free and most popular."

— David Hume

"That the sun will not rise tomorrow is no less intelligible a proposition, and implies no more contradiction, than the affirmation, that it will rise."

— David Hume

PART I

"THE BIRTHDAY"

"Happy birthday, Haymitch!"

The upside of being born on reaping day is that you can sleep late on your birthday. It's pretty much downhill from there. A day off school hardly compensates for the terror of the name drawing. Even if you survive that, nobody feels like having cake after watching two kids being hauled off to the Capitol for slaughter. I roll over and pull the sheet over my head.

"Happy birthday!" My ten-year-old brother, Sid, gives my shoulder a shake. "You said be your rooster. You said you wanted to get to the woods at daylight."

It's true. I'm hoping to finish my work before the ceremony so I can devote the afternoon to the two things I love best — wasting time and being with my girl, Lenore Dove. My ma makes indulging in either of these a challenge, since she regularly announces that no job is too hard or dirty or tricky for me, and even the poorest people can scrape up a few pennies to dump their misery on somebody else. But given the dual occasions of the day, I think she'll allow for a bit of freedom as long as my work is done. It's the Gamemakers who might ruin my plans.

"Haymitch!" wails Sid. "The sun's coming up!"

"All right, all right. I'm up, too." I roll straight off the mattress onto the floor and pull on a pair of shorts made from a government-issued flour sack. The words COURTESY OF THE CAPITOL end up stamped across my butt. My ma wastes nothing. Widowed young when my pa died in a coal mine fire, she's raised Sid and me by taking in laundry and making every bit of anything count. The hardwood ashes in the fire pit are saved for lye soap. Eggshells get ground up to fertilize the garden. Someday these shorts will be torn into strips and woven into a rug.

I finish dressing and toss Sid back in his bed, where he burrows right down in the patchwork quilt. In the kitchen, I grab a piece of corn bread, an upgrade for my birthday instead of the gritty, dark stuff made from the Capitol flour. Out back, my ma's already stirring a steaming kettle of clothes with a stick, her muscles straining as she flips a pair of miner's overalls. She's only thirty-five, but life's sorrows have already cut lines into her face, like they do.

Ma catches sight of me in the doorway and wipes her brow. "Happy sixteenth. Sauce on the stove."

"Thanks, Ma." I find a saucepan of stewed plums and scoop some on my bread before I head out. I found these in the woods the other day, but it's a nice surprise to have them all hot and sugared.

"Need you to fill the cistern today," Ma says as I pass.

We've got cold running water, only it comes out in a thin stream that would take an age to fill a bucket. There's a special barrel of pure rainwater she charges extra for because the clothes come out softer, but she uses our well water for most of the laundry. What with pumping and hauling, filling the cistern's a two-hour job even with Sid's help.

"Can't it wait until tomorrow?" I ask.

"I'm running low and I've got a mountain of wash to do," she answers.

"This afternoon, then," I say, trying to hide my frustration. If the reaping's done by one, and assuming we're not part of this year's sacrifice, I can finish the water by three and still see Lenore Dove.

A blanket of mist wraps protectively around the worn, gray houses of the Seam. It would be soothing if it wasn't for the scattered cries of children being chased in their dreams. In the last few weeks, as the Fiftieth Hunger Games has drawn closer, these sounds have become more frequent, much like the anxious thoughts I work hard to keep at bay. *The second Quarter Quell. Twice as many kids.* No point in worrying, I tell myself, there's nothing you can do about it. *Like two Hunger Games in one.* No way to control the outcome of the reaping or what follows it. So don't feed the nightmares. Don't let yourself panic. Don't give the Capitol that. They've taken enough already.

I follow the empty cinder street to the hill with the miners' graveyard. A jumble of rough markers spikes the slope. Everything from headstones with carved names and dates to wooden boards with peeling paint. My pa's buried in the family plot. A patch of Abernathys, with one limestone marker doing for us all.

After a quick check for witnesses — no one's here much, and certainly not at dawn — I crawl under the fence into the woods outside District 12 and begin the trek to the still. Brewing white liquor with Hattie Meeney is dicey business, but it's a picnic compared to killing rats or cleaning outhouses. She expects me to work hard, but she works hard herself, and even though she'll never see sixty again, she can do more than a person half her age. There's a lot of grunt work involved. Collecting firewood, hauling grain, taking in the full bottles and toting back the empties to be refilled. That's where I come in. I'm Hattie's mule.

I stop at what we call the depot, a bare patch of ground concealed by the drooping boughs of a willow tree, where Hattie drops off supplies. Two twenty-five-pound sacks of cracked corn await, and I swing one over each shoulder.

It takes about half an hour to reach the still, where I find Hattie tending a pot of mash next to the remains of a small fire.

She offers me her long-handled wooden spoon. "Why don't you give this a stir?"

I drop the bags of corn under a lean-to where we keep supplies and raise the spoon in victory. "Whoa, a promotion!"

Me being allowed to handle the mash is something new. Maybe Hattie's starting to train me to be a partner one day. Two of us brewing full-time would increase output, and there's always more demand than she can meet, even for the eye-watering stuff she makes with the Capitol grain. Particularly for that, since it's cheap enough for the miners to afford. The good stuff gets bought up by disorderly soldiers — Peacekeepers, that is — and the richer folk in town. But bootlegging's illegal ten different ways, and all it would take is a new Head Peacekeeper — one who didn't like a stiff drink himself — to land us in the stocks or worse. Mining's tough work, but they don't hang you for it.

While Hattie packs pint bottles of white liquor into a basket lined with moss, I squat down and stir the mash on and off. When it's cooled some, I pour it into a deep bucket and she adds the yeast. I set the mash in the lean-to so it can ferment. She's not distilling today since she doesn't want to risk the smoke attracting attention if the mist burns off. Our local Peacekeepers may turn a blind eye to Hattie's still and her stall in the Hob, an old warehouse that serves as our black market, but she's worried their Capitol counterparts in their low-flying, cloaked hovercraft will spot us from the air. No hauling in the bottles today either, so I'm tasked with chopping wood for the week. When the pile's replenished, I ask what else needs doing, and she just shakes her head.

Hattie's endeared herself to me by throwing in a tip sometimes. Not with my wages, which she pays directly to my mother, but by slipping me a little something on the sly. A handful of cracked corn I can take to Lenore Dove for her geese, a packet of yeast I can barter with at the Hob, and today a pint of white liquor for my own use. She gives me her broken-toothed grin and says, "Happy birthday, Haymitch. I figure if you're old enough to make it, you're old enough to drink it."

I have to agree and, though I'm not a drinker myself, I'm glad to get the bottle. I can easily sell it or trade it or possibly pass it on to Lenore Dove's uncle, Clerk Carmine, so that he might have a kinder opinion of me. You'd think the son of a washerwoman would be harmless enough, but we Abernathys were known rebels back in the day, and apparently we still carry the scent of sedition, scary and seductive in equal parts. Rumors spread after my father's death, rumors that the fire had not been an accident. Some say he died sabotaging the mine, others that his crew was targeted by the Capitol bosses for being a pack of troublemakers. So it could be my kin's the problem. Not that Clerk Carmine has any love for the Peacekeepers, but he's not one for yanking their chain either. Or maybe he just doesn't like his niece running around with a bootlegger, even if the work's steady. Well, whatever the reason, he rarely gives me more than a terse nod, and he once told Lenore Dove that I was the kind that died young, which I don't think he meant as a recommendation.

Hattie yelps as I impulsively give her a hug. "Oh, enough of that. You still sparking that Covey girl?"

"I'm sure trying," I say, laughing.

"Go bother her, then. You're of no more use to me today." She dumps a scoop of cracked corn into my hand and shoos me away.

I pocket the corn and take off before she can change her mind about her best gift: unexpected time with my girl. I know I should probably head home and get a jump on filling the cistern, but I can't resist the thought of a few stolen kisses. It's my birthday and, for once, that cistern can wait.

The mist begins to thin as I run through the woods to the Meadow. Most people comment on its beauty, but Lenore Dove calls it the friend of the condemned, because it can hide you from the Peacekeepers. She tends to take a dark view of things, but maybe that's to be expected from someone named for a dead girl. Well, half for the dead girl called Lenore in this old poem and half for a shade of gray, which I found out the day I met her.

It was the fall after I'd turned ten and the first time I'd ever snuck under the fence that surrounds our district. I'd been deterred by both the law and the threat of wild predators, which are rare but real. My friend Burdock had finally worn me down, saying he did it all the time and there was nothing to it and there were still apples if you could climb. And I could climb and I loved apples. Plus, him being younger than me made me feel like a big scaredy-cat if I didn't.

"Want to hear something?" Burdock asked as we ventured deep into the woods. He tilted back his head and sang out in that remarkable voice of his. High and sweet like a grown-up woman's but cleaner, nothing warbly about it. Everything seemed to go still, and then the mockingjays began to pick it up. I knew they'd sing for other birds, but I'd never heard them sing for a person before. Pretty impressive stuff. Until an apple dropped smack on Burdock's head, cutting him off.

"Who's squawking at my birds?" a girl's voice demanded. And there she was, about twenty feet up, sprawled out on the branch like she lived there. Crooked pigtails, dirty bare feet, munching on an apple, a small clothbound book in her hand.

Burdock cocked his head and laughed. "Hey, cuz. You allowed out here alone? 'Cause I'm sure not."

"Well, I didn't see you," she said.

"Me you either. Toss us down some, would you?"

In answer she stood up on her branch and began to bounce up and down, showering us with apples.

"Hang on, I've got a sack with my bow." Burdock ran off. She scooted down the branches and swung to the ground. She wasn't one of Burdock's Everdeen cousins, but I knew he had some distant ones on his ma's side. I'd seen her around at school — kind of shy, I thought, but I didn't know her to speak to. She didn't seem in a rush to change that, just stood there looking me over until I broke the silence.

"I'm Haymitch."

"I'm Lenore Dove."

"Dove like the bird?"

"No. Dove like the color."

"What color's that?"

"Same as the bird."

That started my head spinning and I guess it's never quite stopped. Soon after at school, she waved me over to a dog-eared dictionary and pointed. *Dove color: Warm gray with a slight purplish or pinkish tint.* Her color. Her bird. Her name.

After that, I started to notice things about her. How her faded overalls and shirts concealed snips of color, a bright blue handkerchief peeking from her pocket, a raspberry ribbon stitched inside her cuff. How she finished up her lessons quick, but didn't make a fuss about it, just stared out the window. Then I spotted her fingers moving, pressing down imaginary keys. Playing songs. Her foot slipped from her shoe, her stockinged heel keeping time, silent against the wood floor. Like all the Covey, music in her blood. But not like them, too. Less interested in pretty melodies, more in dangerous words. The kind that lead to rebel acts. The kind that got her arrested twice. She was only twelve then, and they let her go. Now it would be different.

As I reach the Meadow, I slip under the fence and pause to catch my breath and drink in the sight of Lenore Dove perched on her favorite rock. The sunlight picks up the hint of red in her hair as she bends over an ancient piano accordion. She coaxes a melody out of the wheezy old thing, serenading a dozen geese grazing on the grass, her voice as soft and haunting as moonlight.

They hang the man and flog the woman
Who steals the goose from off the common,
Yet let the greater villain loose
That steals the common from the goose.

It's a treat to hear her sing, since she never does it in public. None of the Covey do. Her uncles are really more musicians than singers, so they just play tunes and leave the singing to the audience if they're so inclined. Lenore Dove likes this better anyway. Says it makes her too nervous to sing in front of people. Her throat closes up.

Clerk Carmine and her other uncle, Tam Amber, have raised her since her ma died in childbirth, seeing her pa's always been something of a mystery. They're not blood kin, her being a Baird, but the Covey look out for their own. They worked out a deal with the mayor, whose house boasts the only real piano in

District 12. Lenore Dove can practice on it if she plays during an occasional dinner or gathering. Her in a faded green dress, an ivory ribbon tying back her hair, lips tinted orange. When her family performs around District 12 for money, she makes do with the instrument she is playing now, which she calls her tune box.

The law demands that we atone
When we take things we do not own,
But leaves the lords and ladies fine
Who take things that are yours and mine.

This is not a song her uncles let her play at the mayor's house. Or even when she performs around District 12. There's the danger that some people might know the words and start a ruckus. Too rebellious. And I have to say I agree with Clerk Carmine and Tam Amber. Why go around asking for trouble? Plenty to be had without inviting it in.

The poor and wretched don't escape
If they conspire the law to break.
This must be so but they endure
Those who conspire to make the law.

I scan the Meadow. It's secluded, but we all know there are eyes everywhere. And eyes generally come with a pair of ears.

The law locks up the man or woman
Who steals the goose from off the common.
And geese will still a common lack
Till they go and steal it back.

Lenore Dove explained to me once that the common was land anyone could use. Sometimes the Peacekeepers chase her and the geese off the Meadow for no reason. She says that's just a teaspoon of trouble in a river of wrong. She worries me, and I'm an Abernathy.

A few of the geese hiss to announce my arrival. Lenore Dove's was the first face they saw when they hatched, and they don't love anyone but her. But since I've got corn, they'll tolerate me today. I toss it a ways away to call off her bodyguards and lean in to kiss her. Then I kiss her again. And again. And she kisses me right back.

"Happy birthday," she says when we come up for air. "Didn't expect to see you until after."

She means the reaping, but I don't want to talk about it.

"Hattie let me go early," I tell her. "Gave me this, too — a present for my big day." I pull out the bottle.

"Well, that won't be hard to trade. Especially today." Besides New Year's, today's when most people get drunk. "Four kids . . . That's going to hit a lot of families."

I guess we're going to talk about it. "It's going to be all right," I say, which rings hollow.

"You don't really believe that, do you?"

"Maybe not. But I try to. Because the reaping's going to happen no matter what I believe. Sure as the sun will rise tomorrow."

Lenore Dove frowns. "Well, there's no proof that will happen. You can't count on things happening tomorrow just because they happened in the past. It's faulty logic."

"Is it?" I say. "Because it's kind of how people plan out their lives."

"And that's part of our trouble. Thinking things are inevitable. Not believing change is possible."

"I guess. But I can't really imagine the sun not rising tomorrow."

A crease forms between her eyebrows as she puzzles out a response. "Can you imagine it rising on a world without a reaping?"

"Not on my birthday. I've never had one that came without a reaping."

I try to distract her with a kiss, but she's determined to make me see. "No, listen," she says earnestly. "Think about it. You're saying, 'Today is my birthday, and there's a reaping. Last year on my birthday, there was also a reaping. So every year, there will be a reaping on my birthday.' But you have no way of knowing that. I mean, the reaping didn't even exist until fifty years ago. Give me one good reason why it should keep happening just because it's your birthday."

For a girl who's quiet in public, she sure can talk up a storm in private. Sometimes, she's hard to keep up with. Lenore Dove is always patient when she explains stuff, not superior, but maybe she's just too smart for me. Because while it's a fine idea, thinking about a world with no reaping, I don't really see it happening. The Capitol has all the power and that's that.

"I didn't say it was *just* because it was my birthday. I said —" What *did* I say? I can't even remember now. "Sorry, you've lost me."

Her face falls. "No, *I'm* sorry. It really is your birthday, and here I am going on about who knows what." She digs in her pocket and holds out a small package wrapped in a scrap of dove-colored fabric, tied with a ribbon the same dappled green as her eyes. "Happy birthday. Tam Amber made it. I traded eggs for the metal and helped him design it."

Besides playing a crazy good mandolin, Tam Amber's the best hand forger in District 12. He's the go-to blacksmith for new gadgets or broken parts for old machines. Burdock has a dozen of his arrow tips that he treats like gold, and some of the richer folks in town have jewelry he made from actual gold or silver, melted down from heirlooms and refashioned. I can't think what he'd make for me, but I eagerly untie the bow.

The object that slips into my palm doesn't register at once. It's a thin strip of metal, shaped like a C. My fingers naturally grip the curved back as I examine the colorful animals facing off at the opening. The head of a snake hisses at the beak of a long-necked bird. I flatten out my hand and see that their enameled scales and feathers travel around the piece until they merge and become indistinguishable. Two small rings are welded on, one behind each head. For a chain, maybe?

"It's beautiful," I say. "It's to wear, right?"

"Well, you know I like my pretty with a purpose," Lenore Dove replies cryptically, making me work it out myself.

I turn it over in my hand, then grip the C again, this time covering the animal heads with my fingers. Then I see its purpose. The smooth steel edge isn't solely decorative.

"It's a flint striker," I conclude.

"It sure is! Only you don't have to have flint. Any decent sparking rock like quartz will do."

At home, we have a beat-up old striker passed down through my ma's family. Ugly and dull. On long winter nights, she made me practice with it until I could reliably get a fire going, so we wouldn't have to waste money on matches. A penny saved is a penny earned.

I run my finger over the fine metalwork of the feathered neck. "I wouldn't want to ruin it."

"You won't. That's what it's made for." She touches the snake's head, then the bird's, in turn. "It takes a lot to break these two. They're survivors."

"I love it." I give her a long, soft kiss. "And I love you like all-fire."

All-fire is Covey talk, but that expression is ours. Usually it makes her smile but she's dead serious now. "You, too."

We kiss until I taste salt. I don't have to ask why.

"Look, it's okay," I assure her. "We're going to be fine." She nods but the tears keep trickling. "Lenore Dove, we're going to get through today, just like last year and the year before, and eventually move past it."

"But we won't really," she says bitterly. "No one in Twelve will. The Capitol makes sure the Hunger Games is burned into our brains." She taps the bottle. "Guess Hattie's in the right business. Helping people to forget."

"Lenore Dove." Clerk Carmine doesn't holler, but he has one of those voices that carries without needing to. He stands at the edge of the Meadow, fists shoved in his patched overalls. He's a fiddler and protective of his hands. "Better be getting ready."

"I'm coming," she says, wiping her eyes.

Clerk Carmine doesn't comment on her state, just shoots me a look that says he holds me responsible, then turns on his heel. He never paid me much mind until Lenore Dove and I got serious. Since then, nothing I do seems right. I once told Lenore Dove I thought he just hated love. That's when she revealed that he'd been together some thirty years with the fellow in town who replaces busted windows. They have to keep it quiet because loving differently can get you harassed by the Peacekeepers, fired from jobs, arrested even. Given his own challenges, you'd think Clerk Carmine would be a champion of our love — I'm certainly supportive of his — but I guess he thinks Lenore Dove could do better.

She hates us to be at odds, so all I say is, "I'm definitely growing on him." That gets her to laugh enough to break the mood. "I can come by after. Got some chores, but I should be done about three. We'll go to the woods, okay?"

"We'll go to the woods." She confirms it with a kiss.

Back home, I take a cold-water bucket bath and pull on the pants my pa got married in and a shirt my ma pieced together from handkerchiefs from the Capitol store where the miners shop. You have to at least try to look dressed up for the reaping. Turn up in raggedy clothes and the Peacekeepers hit you or arrest your parents because that's not how you show respect for the Capitol war dead. Never mind that we had plenty of war dead of our own.

Ma gives me my birthday presents: a year's supply of flour sack underwear and a brand-new pocketknife, with strict instructions that the latter's not to be used for mumblety-peg or any other knife games. Sid presents me with a piece of flint rock wrapped in a grubby bit of brown paper, saying, "I found it in the gravel road by the Peacekeepers' base. Lenore Dove said you'd want it." I pull out my flint striker and try it out, making some beautiful sparks in the process. And though Ma isn't sold on Lenore Dove, given that she's a distraction, she likes the striker enough to thread a leather bootlace through the metal rings and tie it around my neck.

"It's an awful fine striker," says Sid, touching the bird wistfully.

"How about tonight I teach you how to use it?" I suggest.

He lights up at the promise of doing grown-up stuff combined with the promise that I'm not going anywhere. "Yeah?"

"Yeah!" I ruffle his mop of hair so his curls go every which way.

"Quit!" Sid laughs and bats my hand away. "Now I've got to comb it again!"

"Better get on it!" I tell him. He runs off and I drop the striker down my collar, not ready to share it with the world, not on reaping day.

I've got a few minutes to spare, so I head into town to trade. The air's turned heavy and still, promising a storm. My stomach clenches at the sight of the square, plastered with posters and crawling with heavily armed Peacekeepers in their white uniforms. Lately the theme has been "No Peace" and the slogans bombard you from every side. *NO PEACE, NO BREAD! NO PEACE, NO SECURITY!* And, of course, *NO PEACEKEEPERS, NO PEACE! NO CAPITOL, NO PEACE!* Hanging behind the temporary stage in front of the Justice Building is a huge banner of President Snow's face with the words *PANEM'S #1 PEACEKEEPER.*

At the back of the square, Peacekeepers check in the reaping participants. As the line's still short, I go ahead and get that over with. The woman won't meet my eye, so I guess she's still capable of shame. Or maybe it's just indifference.

The apothecary shop has a flag of Panem in the window, which pisses me off. Still, this is where I'll get the best deal on my white liquor. Inside, the sharp odor of chemicals makes my nose twitch. In contrast, a faint, sweet scent comes from a bunch of chamomile flowers resting in a jar, waiting to become tea and medicine. I know Burdock collected these in the woods. Of late, he's added wildcrafting to his game business.

The place is deserted except for my classmate Asterid March, who's arranging tiny bottles on a shelf behind the counter. A long blond braid falls down her back, but the damp heat has brought out tendrils of hair that frame her perfect face. Asterid's the town beauty and rich by District 12 standards. I used to hold that against her, but she showed up one night in the Seam, alone, to treat a neighbor woman who'd been whipped for back-talking a Peacekeeper. She brought some ointment she'd concocted herself, then slipped away, never mentioning payment. Since then, she's who people turn to for help when a loved one goes under the lash. I guess Asterid has more substance than her pack of snooty town friends suggests. Besides, Burdock's nuts about her, so I try to be nice even though he's got about as much chance with her as a mockingjay with a swan. Town girls don't marry Seam boys, not unless something really goes haywire.

"Hey. You got any use for this?" I place the white liquor on the counter. "For cough syrup or some such?"

"I'm sure I can find one." Asterid gives me a fair price and throws in a sprig of chamomile. "For today. They say it's good luck."

I slide the stem into a buttonhole. "Who says? Burdock?"

She blushes a bit, and I wonder if I'm wrong about his chances. "Maybe it was him. I can't recall."

"Well, we could all use a little luck today." I glance at the flag in the window.

Asterid drops her voice. "We didn't want it there. The Peacekeepers insisted."

Or they'd what? Arrest the Marches? Bust up their shop? Close them down for good? I feel bad I judged them earlier.

"No choice, then." I nod to the chamomile. "You wear some, too, okay?" She gives me a sad smile and nods.

I go next door to the Donners' sweetshop and buy a little white paper bag of multicolored gumdrops — Lenore Dove's favorite — for us to share later. She calls them rainbow gumdrops and swears she can tell the flavors apart, although they all taste exactly the same. Merrilee Donner, who's in my class, waits on me in a crisp pink dress and matching ribbons in her sandy hair. No one's going to arrest the Donners for looking shabby. Fortunately, Asterid paid me in cash, because the Donners won't take scrip, which is what the Capitol pays the miners with. It's technically only good in the Capitol store, but a lot of the merchants in town take it and my ma gets plenty of it in the laundry business.

When I step outside, I smile for a second at the Donners' pretty candy label, thinking of meeting Lenore Dove in the woods. Then I see that it's time. The giant screens flanking the stage have lit up with the waving flag in honor of the Hunger Games. Fifty-some years ago, the districts rose up against our Capitol's oppression, kicking off a bloody civil war in Panem. We lost, and in punishment every July 4th, each of the districts routinely has to send two tributes, one girl and one boy between the ages of twelve and eighteen, to fight to the death in an arena. The last kid standing gets crowned as the victor.

The reaping is where they draw our names for the Hunger Games. Two pens, one for the girls and one for the boys, have been clearly marked out with orange ropes. Traditionally, the twelve-year-olds gather in the front and the kids get older until you reach the eighteen-year-olds in the back. Attendance for the entire population is mandatory, but I know my ma will keep Sid at home until the last possible minute, so I don't bother looking for them. Since Lenore Dove's nowhere to be seen, I head to the section designated for fourteen-to-sixteen-year-old boys, thinking about my odds.

Today I have twenty slips of paper with my name in the reaping. Every kid automatically gets one each year, but I have an additional three because I always take on three tesserae to feed myself and my family members. A tessera gets you a ration of tinned oil and a sack of flour marked COURTESY OF THE CAPITOL for one person, collectible each month at the Justice Building. In exchange, you have to put your name in the reaping an extra time for each tessera that year. Those entries stick with you and add up. Four slips a year times five years — that's how I have twenty. But to make things worse, since this year's the second Quarter Quell, marking the fiftieth anniversary of the Hunger Games, each district has to send twice the usual number of kids. I figure, for me, it's like having forty slips on a regular year. And I don't like those odds.

The crowd thickens but I can see one of the twelve-year-olds up front trying to hide that he's crying. In two years, Sid will be there. I wonder whether it'll be me or Ma who sits him down beforehand and explains about his role in the reaping. How he has to look nice and keep his mouth shut and not cause any trouble. Even if the unthinkable happens and his name gets drawn, he's got to suck it up, put on the bravest face he can muster, and climb onto that stage because resistance is not an option. The Peacekeepers will drag him up there kicking and screaming if they have to, so he should try to go with some dignity. And always remember, whatever happens, his family will love him and be proud of him forever.

And if Sid should ask, "But why do I have to do this?"

We can only say, "Because this is the way things are."

Lenore Dove would hate that last bit. But it's the truth.

"Happy birthday." Someone bumps my shoulder and there's Burdock, in a frayed suit, and our friend Blair, who's inherited a dress shirt three sizes too big from his older brother.

Blair smacks a pack of roasted peanuts from the Capitol store against my chest. "And may all your wishes come true."

"Thanks." I pocket the nuts and my gumdrops. "You two didn't have to dress up for me."

"Well, we wanted your day to be special," says Blair. "What kind of idiot gets born on reaping day anyway?"

"The kind that likes a challenge," says Burdock with appreciation.

"Just playing the hand I was dealt. But you know what they say, unlucky at cards, lucky in love." I arrange my chamomile. "Hey, look what your girlfriend gave me, Burdie."

Our attention shifts to the girls' pen, where Asterid stands talking with Merrilee and her identical twin sister, Maysilee, who's the most stuck-up girl in town.

"Her friends know about you, Everdeen?" asks Blair.

"Nothing *to* know," says Burdock with a grin. "Well, not yet anyway."

The sound system crackles to life, sobering us up. Just then, I see Lenore Dove sidestep a Peacekeeper and squeeze into the pen. She's looking fine in a ruffly apple-red dress she sometimes performs in, her hair pulled up with metal combs Tam Amber made her. Fine and grim.

A recording of the anthem blares over the square, rattling my teeth.

Gem of Panem,
Mighty city,

We're supposed to sing along but instead we mumble whatever. Just keep our lips moving at the right time. The screens project images of the Capitol's power: armies of marching Peacekeepers, airborne fleets of hovercraft, tanks parading through the wide avenues of the Capitol, up to the presidential mansion. Everything is clean and expensive and deadly.

When the anthem ends, Mayor Allister takes the podium and reads the Treaty of Treason, which is basically the surrender terms for the war. Most of the people in District 12 weren't even alive then, but we're sure here to pay the price. The mayor tries for a neutral tone, but her voice leaks disapproval in a way that guarantees she'll be replaced soon. The decent mayors always are.

Next, fresh from the Capitol, comes Drusilla Sickle, a plastic-faced woman who escorts our tributes to the Hunger Games each year. I have no idea how old Drusilla is, but she's been showing up in District 12 since the first Quarter Quell. Maybe she's around Hattie's age? It's hard to tell because she has a line of what look like fancy thumbtacks encircling her face, pulling her skin back and pinning it in place. Last year, each one was decorated with a tiny buzz saw blade. This year, the number 50 seems to be the theme. As for clothes, she clearly struggled to incorporate two fashion trends, military and sassy, and the result is her current outfit, a lemon-yellow officer's jacket with matching thigh-high boots and a tall hat with a visor brim. Feathers fan out from the top of the hat, making her look like a deranged daffodil. No one laughs, though, because here she's the face of evil.

Two Peacekeepers set giant glass balls holding the tribute entries on either side of the podium. "Ladies first," says Drusilla, dipping her hand into the ball on the right and extracting a single slip of paper. "And the lucky girl is . . ." She pauses for effect, twirling the name in her fingers, smirking before driving in the knife. "Louella McCoy!"

I feel sick. Louella McCoy lives three houses down from me, and a smarter, spunkier thirteen-year-old doesn't exist. An angry murmur ripples across the crowd, and I can feel Blair and Burdock tensing up beside me as Louella climbs the steps onto the stage, flipping her black pigtails over her shoulders and scowling hard as she tries to look tough.

"And this year, ladies second as well! Joining Louella will be . . ." Drusilla's hand stirs the slips in the ball and fishes out another name. "Maysilee Donner!"

My eyes find Lenore Dove's, and all I can think is, *It's not you. At least, not for another year. You're safe.*

The crowd's reacting again, but more in surprise than anger, because Maysilee is a purebred town girl and about as highfalutin as they come, what with the Donners being merchants and the general consensus being that her pa will be tapped to succeed Mayor Allister. Town kids are rarely tributes because they don't generally have tesserae like those in the Seam.

In the girls' pen, Maysilee's gripping Asterid's hand while a weeping Merrilee embraces her, their three blond heads pressed in a tight knot. Then Maysilee carefully disengages herself and smooths her dress, which is identical to her twin's pink one, only a shade of lavender. She pretty much always has her nose in the air, but she holds it extra high as she walks to the stage.

Now it's the boys' turn. I brace myself, preparing for the worst, as Drusilla plucks a paper from the ball on the left. "And the first gentleman who gets to accompany the ladies is . . . Wyatt Callow!"

I haven't seen Wyatt Callow around school for a while, which probably means he hit eighteen and started in the mines. I don't really know him. He lives on the other side of the Seam and keeps his head down. I hate myself for the relief I feel watching him approach the stage, his measured steps and vacant expression revealing nothing. I feel bad for him, too. Wyatt has to be closing in on his nineteenth birthday, a big deal in the districts because that's when you age out of the reaping.

As Drusilla's hand dives back into the ball, it seems too much to hope that both Lenore Dove and I will escape this terror. That in a few hours, we'll be far away from the square, locked in each other's arms in the cool shade of the woods. I suck in my breath, preparing for my death sentence.

Drusilla peers at the final name. "And boy number two is . . . Woodbine Chance!"

An involuntary huff escapes my lips, echoed by several boys around me. Lenore Dove looks over, tries to smile, but can't help shifting her attention to the latest victim.

Woodbine's the youngest and handsomest of those crazy Chance boys. They all get so wild when they drink that Hattie won't sell them white liquor for fear it will bring down the Peacekeepers, so they have to buy it from old Bascom Pie, who has no scruples and sells rotgut to anyone with enough coin. If the Abernathys give off a whiff of sedition, the Chances reek of it, and they've lost more family members to the rope than I can keep track of. Rumor has it, Lenore Dove might be related to them on her pa's side. They seem awfully fond of her, even if it's not official. One way or another, there's a connection there that Clerk Carmine discourages.

I can see Woodbine, who's a few rows ahead of me, projected up on the screen. He makes as if to follow Wyatt, but then his gray eyes flash defiantly and he whips around and sprints for an alley. His kinfolk shout encouragement and bodies instinctively block the Peacekeepers. Just when I'm thinking he might make it — all those Chance kids run like greased lightning — a shot rings out from the Justice Building rooftop, and the back of Woodbine's head explodes.

The screens go dark for a second and then the flag reappears. Obviously, they don't want the rest of the country to witness the disorder here in District 12.

The square erupts as some people make for the side streets and some rush to help Woodbine, even though he's long past helping. The Peacekeepers keep firing, mostly as a warning but hitting a few unfortunates at the edge of the crowd. I don't know which way to go. Do I find Sid and Ma? Get Lenore Dove off the square? Just run for cover?

"Who did this? Who did this?" demands Drusilla.

A bewildered young Peacekeeper gets pushed to the edge of the roof of the Justice Building.

"You imbecile!" Drusilla berates him from below. "You couldn't wait until he was in the alley? Look at this mess!"

It's a mess all right. I catch sight of Ma and Sid at the edge of the crowd and take a step their way when a rough male voice booms over the sound system.

"On the ground! On the ground, everybody! Now!" Automatically, I fall on my knees and assume the position — hands linked behind my neck, forehead pressed to the sooty bricks of the square. Out of the corner of my eye, I see almost everybody around me follow suit, but Otho Mellark, a big lug of a guy whose folks own the bakery, seems bewildered. His meaty hands dangle loosely at his sides and his feet shuffle back and forth, and then I notice his blond hair's splattered with someone's blood. Burdock punches him hard in the back of his knee and it's enough to get him down on the ground and out of the line of fire.

Drusilla's hot mic bounces her voice around the square as she screams at her team, "We've got five minutes! A five-minute delay and then we'll have to finish this live! Get rid of the bloody ones!"

For the first time, I understand that when they show the reaping live, it isn't really live. There must be a five-minute hold on the broadcast in case something like this happens.

Peacekeepers' boots tramp through the audience as the soldiers grab anyone marked with gore, including Otho, and push them into the nearby shops to conceal them.

"We need another boy! That dead one's no good!" says Drusilla, clunking down the steps into the square.

There's a high-pitched keening followed by Peacekeepers barking orders. Then I hear Lenore Dove's voice, and my head shoots up like I don't control it. She's trying to help Woodbine's ma, who's latched on to his hand as a pair of Peacekeepers attempts to carry him away. Lenore Dove's tugging on one of the soldier's arms, begging them to please let his ma have him, just let her see him for one minute. But they don't seem to have a minute.

This will not end well. Should I get in there? Pull Lenore Dove away? Or will I only make the situation worse? I feel like my knees are glued to the ground.

"What's the problem there?" I hear Drusilla say. "Get that body off the square!" A squad of four more Peacekeepers heads over.

Having Woodbine referred to as a "body" sets his ma off. She begins to shriek, flinging her arms around his chest, trying to pull her son away from the soldiers. Lenore Dove joins her, grabbing hold of Woodbine's legs to help free him.

Ma's going to lay into me for intervening, but I just can't grovel on the ground while Lenore Dove's in danger. I push myself up and run toward her, hoping to get her to let Woodbine loose. I spy one of the incoming Peacekeepers raising his rifle to knock her out.

"Stop!" I leap in to shield her, just in time to intercept the rifle butt that slams against my temple. Pain explodes in my head as jagged lights cut through my vision. I don't even make it to the ground before iron hands lock on my upper arms and haul me forward, my nose inches from the bricks. I'm dropped flat on my face before a pair of yellow boots. The tip of one lifts my chin before letting it bang back on the ground.

"Well, I think we've just found our replacement."

Lenore Dove's behind me, pleading. "Don't take him — it wasn't his fault! It was mine! Punish me!"

"Oh, just shoot that girl, would you?" says Drusilla. A nearby Peacekeeper trains his rifle on Lenore Dove, and Drusilla snorts in exasperation. "Not here! We've got enough blood to clean up. Find a discreet location, can't you?"

As the soldier takes a step toward Lenore Dove, a guy in a violet jumpsuit appears, laying a hand on his elbow. "Hold it. If I could, Drusilla, I'd love to keep her for the tearful good-bye. The audience eats that stuff up and, as you always remind us, it's a challenge to get them to even notice Twelve."

"Fine, Plutarch. Whatever. Just get the rest of them up. Up! On your feet, you district pigs!" As they lift me, I notice Drusilla has a riding crop clipped to the side of one boot and wonder if it's just decorative. Her dead-fish breath hits my face. "Play this right or I'll shoot you myself."

"Haymitch!" I hear Lenore Dove cry.

I start to respond but Drusilla clamps on to my face with her long fingers. "And she can watch."

Plutarch gestures to one of the crew. "Get a camera on that girl, would you, Cassia?" He pursues Drusilla. "You know, we've got footage of the Peacekeepers controlling the crowd. It could be an opportunity to hit the 'No Peacekeeper, No Peace' angle."

"I don't have time, Plutarch! I barely have time to pull off the status quo! Get the first boy. . . . What was his name?"

"Wyatt Callow," says Plutarch.

"Get Wyatt Callow back in the pen." Drusilla smacks her forehead. "No!" She thinks a moment. "Yes! I'll call them both. It will be smoother."

"It will cost you another thirty seconds."

"Then let's get going." She points at me. "What's your name?"

My name sounds alien as it leaves my lips. "Haymitch Abernathy."

"Haymitch Abernanny," she repeats.

"Haymitch Abernathy," I correct her.

She turns to Plutarch in vexation. "It's too long!" He scribbles on his clipboard pad and rips off a strip of paper. She takes it and reads, "Wyatt Callow and Haymitch . . . Aber . . . nathy. Wyatt Callow and Haymitch Abernathy."

"Why you're the professional," Plutarch says. "Better take your place. I'll position him." As Drusilla hurries up the steps, he takes my elbow and whispers, "Don't be stupid, kid. She'll kill you with a snap if you mess up again."

I don't know if he means with a snap of her fingers or some extra-horrible snappy way to die. Either way, I don't want to die with a snap.

Plutarch leads me to a spot closer to the stage. "This'll do. Just stay here, and when Drusilla calls your name, you calmly walk up onstage. Okay?"

I try to nod. My head throbs and my thoughts tumble around like rocks in a tin can. What just happened? What's happening now? Somewhere inside me, I know. I'm a tribute in the Hunger

Games. In a few days, I'll die in the arena. I know all this, but it's like it's happening to someone else while I watch from a distance.

The remaining members of the audience have regained their feet but not their composure. People whisper urgently to their neighbors, trying to figure out what's going on.

"Live in thirty," someone says over the speakers. "Twenty-nine, twenty-eight, twenty-seven . . ."

"Shut up!" Drusilla yells at the crowd as a makeup person puffs some powder on her sweaty face. "Shut up or we'll kill every last one of you!" As if to emphasize this, a Peacekeeper next to her fires a spray of bullets into the air, and a hovercraft passes right over the square.

It gets quiet fast and I can hear my blood pounding in my ears. I have an impulse to flee, like Woodbine did, but remember the look of his brains hanging out of his skull.

". . . ten, nine, eight . . ."

Everyone onstage has returned to their pre-shooting places: Louella and Maysilee, the Peacekeepers, and Drusilla, who quickly tears the paper Plutarch gave her in two and positions the slips on the pile in the glass ball.

I reach for Burdock and Blair to steady myself, but, of course, they're not there. Just a couple of younger kids who are giving me plenty of room.

". . . three, two, one, and we're live."

Drusilla pretends to draw a name. "And the first gentleman who gets to accompany the ladies is . . . Wyatt Callow!"

In some strange replay, I watch Wyatt, as impassive as before, go by and obediently take his place on the stage.

Drusilla's hand hovers over the ball, then removes a slip with surgical precision. "And our second boy will be . . . Haymitch Abernathy!" I just stand there in case this is a bad dream and I'm about to wake up in my own bed. Everything's all wrong. Minutes ago, I dodged this bullet. I was headed home, then to the woods, safe for another year.

"Haymitch?" Drusilla repeats, looking straight at me.

My face fills the screen over the stage. My feet begin to move. I see them cut to Lenore Dove, who has a hand pressed against her mouth. She isn't crying, so Plutarch won't get his tearful good-bye. Not from her and not from me. They will not use our tears for their entertainment.

"Ladies and gentlemen, join me in welcoming the District Twelve tributes of the Fiftieth Hunger Games!" Drusilla acknowledges us. "And may the odds be EVER in your favor!" She begins to clap and I hear a huge audience response over the speakers, although I can only see a handful of people applauding in 12.

I locate Lenore Dove in the crowd and we lock eyes, desperation setting in. For a moment, everything else peels away and there's only us. She lowers her hand and presses it to her heart as her lips form the words silently. *I love you like all-fire.* I mouth back, *You, too.*

Cannons break the spell. Confetti showers down on me, on the stage, on the whole square. I lose sight of her in the fluttering bits of bright paper.

Drusilla spreads her arms wide. "Happy second Quarter Quell, everybody!"

"And we're out," says the voice on the speaker.

The broadcast has moved on to the District 11 reaping. The canned applause cuts off and Drusilla lets out a groan, dramatically slumping against the podium.

The Capitol TV crew gives a loud cheer as Plutarch appears from the side of the stage, shouting, "Brilliant! Bravo, everybody! Absolutely seamless, Drusilla!"

Drusilla recovers and yanks off her daffodil hat by the chin strap. "I have no idea how I just did that." She pulls a pack of cigarettes from her boot and lights up, exhaling the smoke through her nose like it's a chimney. "Well, it's a great story for dinner parties!"

One of the assistants appears with a tray of glasses filled with a pale liquid. He accidentally offers one to me — "Champagne?" — before he realizes his mistake. "Whoops! None for the children!"

Drusilla grabs a glass and notices the people of District 12 standing mute and miserable while the last bits of confetti drift down on them. "Well, what are they staring at? Filthy beasts. Go home! All of you!" She addresses a Peacekeeper. "Get them out of here before their smell gets in my hair." She sniffs a lock of her hair and grimaces. "Too late."

The Peacekeeper gives a signal and the soldiers begin pushing the crowd back. While I see Burdock and Blair put up a struggle, most people rush to the side streets, only too happy to escape the ordeal of the reaping, to hurry home, embrace their children, and, for those who patronize Hattie's stall, get good and drunk.

I'm panicked by the sight of a District 12 Peacekeeper restraining Lenore Dove. Why didn't I step in sooner? Why did I wait until I had no choice but to defy that soldier? Was I feeling afraid? Confused? Or just powerless in the face of those white uniforms? Now we're both doomed. The Peacekeeper's bringing out cuffs when Clerk Carmine and Tam Amber swoop in. They talk to him fast and low, and I think some money changes hands. To my relief, the Peacekeeper glances around, releases her, and walks off. Lenore Dove makes for me, but her uncles hustle her down a side street.

The other luckless loved ones of this year's tributes remain behind.

Mr. Donner runs up on the stage with a fistful of cash, hoping to somehow bail Maysilee out, while his wife and Merrilee huddle near their storefront. "Don't, Papa!" Maysilee cries, but her father keeps waving the money in people's faces.

There's a family I judge to be the Callows, where a woman weeps hysterically and the menfolk have come to blows. "You jinxed him!" one accuses another. "This is on you!"

Our neighbors, the McCoys, have their arms wrapped around Ma, who's barely able to stand. Sid's hanging on her hand, pulling her forward, as he hollers, "Haymitch! Haymitch!" I'm already so homesick I could die. I know I need to be strong, but the sight of them totals me. How will they manage without me?

What's supposed to happen next is that the tributes go into the Justice Building for a final farewell to their families and friends. I've done this once before. My ma and pa took me when Sarshee Whitcomb, the daughter of Pa's old crew boss, got reaped. She'd been orphaned that year when her pa, Lyle, died of black lung. Ma told the Peacekeepers we were kin and they took us to a sitting room with a lot of scratchy furniture that needed dusting. I think we were her only visitors.

I know I should wait for the official good-bye time, but the only thing that matters now is to hug Ma and Sid. With Mr. Donner and Maysilee making a ruckus, I get to the edge of the stage, crouch down, and reach for them as they run to me.

"None of that!" I'm yanked backward by a Peacekeeper as Drusilla continues. "No good-byes for these people. They've lost that privilege after that outrageous display today. Take them straight to the train, and let's get out of this stinkhole."

A pair of Peacekeepers tosses Mr. Donner off the stage. Midair, he loses his grip on his money, which floats down and mingles with the confetti on the ground. Then they pull out handcuffs.

Louella's been holding it together, but now she looks at me, her eyes wide with fright. I lay my hand on her shoulder to steady her, but as the cold metal touches her skin, she lets out a small squeak, like a baby animal in a trap. At the sound, the families surge forward, desperate to reclaim us.

The Peacekeepers hold them back as Plutarch speaks up. "I don't mean to be a pain, Drusilla, but I'm really low on reaction shots for the recap. Could I just snag a few?"

"If you must. But if you're not on the train in fifteen, you can walk home," says Drusilla.

"I owe you." Plutarch does a quick assessment of our families and points to me and Louella. "Leave me this and this."

The Peacekeepers steer Maysilee and Wyatt into the Justice Building, beating back their relatives with batons when they try to follow. Somehow, Merrilee slips by them, and for a moment the Donner twins become one, arms locked around each other's necks, foreheads, noses pressed together. A mirror image that the Peacekeepers tear in two. I see Wyatt give a final look to the hysterical Callow woman before marching through the door.

Louella and I rush for our folks, but Plutarch intervenes. "Let's get the footage."

The crew sweeps an area in front of the shops clear of confetti. A cameraman positions himself while Plutarch poses Louella's parents and her half dozen brothers and sisters in front of the bakery. "Wait, if you were in the reaping, get out of the picture." Two of the kids move out of range of the camera. "Good," he says. "Very nice. Now, what I need you to do is to react exactly the way you did when you heard them call Louella's name. In three, two, one, action."

The McCoy family stares at him numbly.

"And cut!" Plutarch crosses to the McCoys. "Sorry. Obviously, I wasn't clear. When you heard them call Louella, it was a big shock, right? 'Oh, no!' Maybe you gasped or cried out her name. Anyway, you did something. And now I need you to do the same thing for the camera. Okay?" He backs up. "So, in three, two, one, action!"

If anything, the McCoys are more stony-faced than before. It's not confusion; it's a blanket refusal to put on a show for the Capitol.

"Cut." Plutarch rubs his eye and sighs. "Take the girl to the train."

Peacekeepers whisk Louella into the Justice Building as the McCoys finally crack, crying out her name in anguish. Plutarch motions to the crew to film their reaction. When the McCoys realize he got their distress on tape, they're infuriated, but the Peacekeepers just muscle them off the square.

Plutarch turns to Ma and Sid. "Listen, I know this isn't easy, but I think we can help each other out. If I can get a usable reaction shot from you, I can give you a minute with Haymitch. We clear?"

I see Sid's eyes flicker skyward as there's a low rumble of thunder, which feels like a warning. I look at my ma's pale face, my brother's trembling lips. The words spill out of my mouth unbidden. "Don't do it, Ma."

But Ma overrules me and addresses Plutarch. "No, I'll do it. We'll both do it, if you let us hold him one more time."

"Deal." Plutarch positions them side by side, but Ma moves behind Sid and wraps her arms around him. "Nice. I like it. Okay, so it's the middle of the reaping, Drusilla is picking the boys. She's just said, 'Haymitch Abernathy.' And three, two, one, action."

Ma gasps and Sid, confused, as no doubt he was at the time, cranes his head around to look at her.

"Cut! That was terrific. Can we try it once more, and this time, maybe make the gasp a little louder? Okay, in three, two, one . . ."

But it isn't once. Plutarch keeps calling for more dramatic responses — "Call out his name!" "Hide your face in her dress!" "Can you break into tears?" — until Sid's crying for real and my ma looks ready to pass out.

"Stop it!" I burst out. "That's enough! You've got enough!"

The walkie-talkie on his belt crackles and I hear Drusilla's impatient voice. "Where are you, Plutarch?"

"Just wrapping up. There in five." Plutarch waves Ma and Sid in my direction and they rush into my arms. "You've got two minutes."

I crush them against me for what I know is the last time. But time's a-wasting and we are not a wasteful family. "Take this." I empty the contents of my pockets into their hands, money and peanuts into Ma's, knife and the white sack of gumdrops into Sid's. Bequeathing them the remains of my life in 12.

Sid raises the gumdrops. "For Lenore Dove?"

"Yeah, you see she gets them, okay?" I say.

Sid's voice is hoarse with tears, but determined. "She'll get them."

"I know she will. Because I can always depend on you." I kneel in front of my little brother and hold out my sleeve like I did when he was tiny, so he can wipe his nose on it. "You're the man of the house now. If you were some other kid, I'd be worried, but I know you can handle it." Sid starts to shake his head. "You're twice as smart as me and ten times as brave. You can do this. Okay? Okay?" He nods and I muss his hair. Then I rise and hug my mother. "You can, too, Ma."

"I love you, son," she whispers.

"I love you, too," I say.

Through the static of Plutarch's walkie-talkie, I hear Drusilla's impatient voice. "Plutarch! Don't think I won't leave without you!"

"Got to go, people," Plutarch says. "Drusilla waits for no man."

The Peacekeepers move in to separate us, but Ma and Sid hold tight.

"You remember what your pa said to the Whitcomb child?" Ma says urgently. "It still goes."

I flash back to the Justice Building, and the weeping girl and the sickly scent of decomposing flowers that pervaded the place. Pa is talking to Sarshee, and he's telling her, *"Don't let them use you, Sarshee. Don't —"*

"Plutarch!" screeches Drusilla. "Plutarch Heavensbee!"

Peacekeepers rip us apart. I'm lifted off my feet as Sid begs, "Please don't take my brother! Please don't take him. We need him!"

I can't help it, I should be a good example, but I struggle to get free. "It's okay, Sid! It's going to be —" A jolt of electricity racks my body and I go limp. I can track the heels of my boots bouncing up the stairs, over the carpets of the Justice Building, through the gravel on the drive behind it. In the car, I let them cuff me without objecting. My brain's fuzzy, but I know I don't want to be zapped again. Wobbly-legged, I climb the metal steps to the train, where I'm tossed into some compartment with a single, barred window. I press my face against the glass, but there's nothing to see but a grimy coal car.

For all Drusilla's whining, we go nowhere for an hour. The sky blackens and the storm breaks. Hail clatters against my window, followed by sheets of rain. By the time the wheels of the train begin to turn, my head has cleared. I try to memorize every fleeting image of 12 — the lightning illuminating the dingy warehouses, the water streaming down the slag heaps, and the glow of the green hills.

That's when I see Lenore Dove. She's up on a ridge, her red dress plastered to her body, one hand clutching the bag of gumdrops. As the train passes, she tilts her head back and wails her loss and rage into the wind. And even though it guts me, even though I smash my fists into the glass until they bruise, I'm grateful for her final gift. That she's denied Plutarch the chance to broadcast our farewell.

The moment our hearts shattered? It belongs to us.

After a while, I slide down the wall, cradling my swollen hands, panting. Pain stabs my chest, and I wonder if a person's heart can really break. Probably. The word *brokenhearted* had to come from somewhere. I imagine my heart busted into a dozen glassy red pieces, their hard, jagged edges stabbing into my flesh at every beat. It may not be scientific, but it matches what I feel. Part of me thinks I will die right now, bleeding out on the inside. But it isn't going to be that simple. Eventually, my breathing slows, and a general despair descends.

I will never see Lenore Dove again. Never hear her laugh coming from high above me in the branches. Never feel the warmth of her in my arms as we lay on a bed of pine needles, my lips pressed into the hollow of her neck. Never pull a stray goose feather from her hair, or listen to her play her tune box, or press my finger into the crease that forms between her eyebrows when she's puzzling out a thought. Never see her face brighten at a bag of gumdrops or a full moon or the sound of me whispering, "I love you like all-fire."

It's all been taken away. My love, my home, my ma, my sweet little brother . . . why did I tell him he's the man of the house now? That wasn't fair. It's too much for someone so young and hopeful to shoulder. My mamaw on Pa's side used to say Sid was born looking on the sunny side. I think he's missed a lot of trouble down here on earth, because he's always studying the sky. He's fascinated by the sun, the clouds, the bodies that come out at night. Tam Amber taught Lenore Dove about the stars, as the Covey used to navigate by them long ago, and she taught Sid. On a clear night, he drags us all outside to see the pictures they make. "There's the water dipper, just like ours in the bucket. That over there's the bowhunter. He looks like Burdock, don't you think? That one's a swan, but Lenore Dove says she calls it a goose. And that's yours, Ma. See the *W*? That's yours. *W* for your name, Willamae, and flipped around it's an *M* for Ma!"

And Ma always looks pleased, because when does she get anything nice, let alone something so fine as her own set of stars? It's all about her giving things to us. I pretended not to see her bring in a chicken last night that I'm sure she planned to fry for my birthday. Probably took on extra wash to afford it. Will she be able to make ends meet without my wages from Hattie? She will, or she'll die trying. Ma . . . oh, Ma . . .

Plutarch was right. I did mess up. Big-time. And I will pay for it with my death and with the broken hearts and lives of everyone who loves me.

I stare out at the trees flying by. I always thought if one of us shook free of 12, it would be Lenore Dove. Her people were great travelers once, going from district to district to perform their music. Tam Amber remembers it, as he was about my age when the war ended and the Peacekeepers rounded up the Covey, killing all the adults and confining the kids to our district. Nothing Lenore Dove loves better than those stories of the old days, with her kin rattling around in a broken-down pickup. When fuel got scarce, they resorted to hitching it up to a team of horses. By the time they were herded into 12, the team was pulling an old wagon and most of them were on foot, but they were making it work. Cooking over open fires, rolling into towns, playing in warehouses like the Hob, or fields if none were available, famous in their way to the locals. I'm sure their life had its trials, but she has such a romantic view of it, I never mention that. Returning to it is impossible, since no one can leave 12, and her uncles would never entertain the idea of hitting the road again. But Lenore Dove's convinced there must be people outside of Panem, far to the north. Sometimes she takes to disappearing deep in the woods, and I worry she's not coming back. Not really, but a little. Guess I can let that go now.

Either we outrun the storm or it outruns us. The lingering raindrops on the window make me think about the cistern, and how I ran off to see Lenore Dove instead of going home to fill it. I don't regret that precious final rendezvous with my love, but I wish I could've left Sid and Ma with a full tank, not just the few gallons the rain barrel might provide. Not that I think Ma will be able to do laundry this week. Or, I don't know, maybe she will. She didn't miss a beat when Pa died. Just made a giant pot of bean and ham hock soup, the way we do in the Seam when someone dies, and got back to work. I remember sitting by the stove, my tears splashing on the floor a few inches from a puddle under a miner's shirt. In winter, clothes have to be hung inside to dry. Something's always dripping.

The train keeps rolling on, putting miles between me and everything I've ever known or loved or hoped for. Dreams of one day letting Ma quit the laundry business. Leaning on Sid about his schoolwork so he might get a coveted aboveground mine job — like keeping books or loading trains — where he could always lay eyes on the sky. And a life with Lenore Dove, loving her, marrying her, raising up our kids, her teaching them music and me doing whatever, digging coal or making white liquor — it wouldn't have mattered if she was with me. All gone, all lost.

Woodbine no longer seems reckless since he got to die in 12 and not in some sadistic arena out west like I will. A few years ago, the arena would go darkish without warning, and these giant coal-black weasels would melt right out of the shadows and attack the tributes. I think of those pointy teeth ripping off the face of the girl from District 5 . . .

I should've run. Should've let the Peacekeepers blow off my head on the square. Plenty of things are worse than a quick, clean death. By now, I might be wrapped in white linen, sleeping with my kin under the Abernathy headstone. We don't tend to let bodies ripen in the heat.

Several hours pass before a key's turned in the lock and Plutarch sticks his head in my compartment.

"Feel up to joining the others?"

He says this like I'm recovering from a bellyache, not from being tased and torn from my life. I don't know what to make of this Plutarch. I hate him for forcing Ma and Sid to playact for the cameras. But he did let me hug them when Drusilla said I couldn't. And he probably saved Lenore Dove's life by asking to keep her for the tearful good-bye. He's as unpredictable as lightning. Might be worth staying on his good side.

Besides, I need to check on Louella. I'm all she's got now.

"Sure," I say.

Plutarch orders the Peacekeepers to uncuff me, then leads me down the rocking hallway of the train to another compartment. Molded plastic seats in an array of neon colors line the sides of the car. I slide in next to Louella, across from Wyatt and Maysilee.

"Anybody hungry?" asks Plutarch. No one replies. "Let me see what's cooking." He withdraws, locking the car door.

I nudge Louella with my elbow. "Hey, girl." I offer her my hand.

Hers slips into mine, icy cold. "Hey, Hay," she whispers. "Wasn't fair how they took you."

For the first time, I consider this. Fair? It sure wasn't. My reaping was irregular, maybe even illegal. But the number of people in the Capitol to whom I could plead my case is exactly zero. I'm nothing but an amusing tale for Drusilla to tell between the caviar and the cream puffs.

"For me or anybody else," I tell Louella. Her little face is so pinched that before I really think it through, I ask, "So, are you going to be my ally or what, sweetheart?"

She actually smiles. It's an old joke. When she was five and I was eight, she decided she was my sweetheart and trailed after me, telling anyone who'd listen. It lasted about a week, then she transferred her affections to a boy named Buster who gave her a bullfrog. I think her heart would've moved on anyway, as you're probably not too stuck on someone you have burping contests with, but we're still good buddies. If I had a little sister her age, I'd want her to be just like Louella, and I've harbored the hope that she'd wait for Sid to grow up before settling on a real sweetheart. Now, of course, her chances of growing up are nil. She's frozen forever at thirteen.

"I'll be your ally," she says. "You and me, we can trust each other."

You might think this would kick off a general District 12 alliance, but as I consider the other candidates, I'm not sure that's desirable. I can't get a read on Wyatt. On the one hand, that blank stare doesn't suggest a lively mind. On the other, he's fairly good-sized and I've never heard anything bad about him, which is more than I can say for Maysilee. I have no shortage of information on her, most of it gathered firsthand, and none of it flattering.

Maysilee Donner — where to begin? Right from when we started school, she and Merrilee made an impression on me. Not just because of their town ways, but because my ma had recently lost a set of twins. Two little girls, tiny things that came too early. She grieved them mightily in her way, scrubbing clothes against her washboard until they shredded, and while Pa was never one to show his feelings, I heard him bawling when he thought I was asleep. The Donner twins have always held a certain fascination for me, as I wondered what my own sisters might've been like. Not like the Donners, I hope. I guess Merrilee isn't too bad, except she tends to go along with everything Maysilee does. And Maysilee's been too good for the rest of us from day one. Prissing around in her shiny shoes and nail polish, and never without some kind of ornament. How that girl loves jewelry.

I look at her now, staring out the train window, her fingers entwined in the strands of a half dozen necklaces. Some beaded, some braided cord, some with trinkets hanging off of them, and at least one real gold. While Seam folk might have a treasured ornament or two, nobody has six necklaces. And if they did, they wouldn't show off by wearing them all at once.

Plutarch slides open the door and steps back to admit a Capitol attendant bearing a tray heaped with sandwiches. Each one's loaded with a day's wages of meat — fresh ham or roast beef or chicken cut thin and piled high — and sports a small paper flag of Panem on top. My mouth starts watering and I realize I haven't eaten since breakfast.

The attendant offers the tray to Louella, who hesitates, overwhelmed by the bounty before her. The McCoys can go weeks without meat, and what they do get generally comes from a tin. The attendant registers her discomfort and adopts a patronizing tone. "Is there a problem, miss?"

Louella reddens — the McCoys don't lack pride — but before she can answer, Maysilee snaps, "Of course there's a problem! Do you expect her to eat with her hands? Or don't you have plates and silverware in the Capitol?"

Now it's the attendant's turn to blush. He stammers out, "They're just sandwiches. I mean . . . people pick them up."

"Without even a napkin?" asks Maysilee. "I seriously doubt that."

The attendant turns to Plutarch, thrown. "Do they get napkins?"

"Certainly. They're our guests, Tibby," says Plutarch mildly. "I've got to check on something in the kitchen. Let's see if we can scrounge up a few plates, too. Excuse us."

When the door clicks shut, I can't help laughing.

"Shut up," says Maysilee. "Listen, Louella, if you let them treat you like an animal, they will. So don't let them."

It's a little too much for Louella. Her eyes narrow and she retorts, "I wasn't planning to. Somebody cut me off."

"Fine," says Maysilee. "You don't need my help."

"I don't need help from anybody who said my sister uses coal dust for powder," Louella tells her.

Maysilee smiles a little, remembering. "She got a lot cleaner after that."

This reminds me of when I was six and got chiggers and Maysilee nicknamed me "Itchy Itchy Haymitchy." Nobody would come near me for two weeks, even though I told them it wasn't contagious. That name still makes me cringe ten years later.

Any inclination I had to team up with Maysilee disappears. "She's making this ally thing easy for us," I say to Louella.

"She sure is." Louella crosses her arms. Then something catches her eye and she frowns.

I follow her gaze to Wyatt, who looks as remote as ever, his eyes fixed on a sign on the door that reads WATCH YOUR STEP.

There's a glint in the evening sunlight; he's knuckle rolling a scrip coin in a smooth, practiced fashion. At the click of the key in the latch, the coin vanishes.

Tibby wheels in a cart laden with the dinner stuff. Everything seems to be made of plastic in this train: cart, seats, utensils, cups, plates. Easy to spray down and sanitize after we're out, I guess.

"I checked. And there's a surprise for dessert," Plutarch teases from the door.

Like we need any more surprises today.

Tibby hovers over Louella. "What can I get you? We have chicken, ham, and roast beef."

"Ham," says Louella.

"Sure you won't try a roast beef as well? The chef uses a marinade that makes it rather special," says Tibby.

"Why not?" Louella accepts her plate, napkin, utensils, and a bottle of lemonade.

When Tibby turns to Maysilee, his solicitousness vanishes. "And you?"

Maysilee takes her time considering the platter. "The roast beef, as rare as you have it." She spreads her napkin out to protect her skirt, then arranges her utensils on it. "Trays wouldn't be unheard of, but never mind."

When Wyatt and I have received loaded plates — I order all three sandwiches — the attendant and Plutarch withdraw. I look at Maysilee, who's daintily cutting hers into tiny bites and spearing them with her fork. Believe me, no one else in Panem — not Capitol or district — eats a sandwich like that. I decide to start with the ham and take a big bite. Boy, it's good. Smoky, salty, and drizzled with something that tastes like Ma's chow-chow. I notice Louella peeking under the top layer of bread.

"Go on, eat up," I tell her. My ally could use some meat on her bones. She digs in.

It doesn't take long for me to polish off my sandwiches and drain my lemonade bottle. The food lifts my spirits a bit. Maybe there's a way out of this. Like we make a break for it and jump from the train. As I puzzle over how we might achieve this, Plutarch reappears and invites us to move to the lounge car with him. In the hall, I check for possible escape routes, but Peacekeepers block every potential exit.

We relocate to the back of the train where an area's done up like a sitting room. The plastic-upholstered furniture is softer and stickier than our compartment seats. Capitol News plays on a screen built into the wall, and the recap of today's reaping begins by the time we've settled in.

"I've been working on the District Twelve segment all afternoon," says Plutarch. "Gave it the old Heavensbee spin. You four come off beautifully."

Drusilla totters in the door, a tall red drink garnished with vegetables in her hand. The front of her yellow military jacket, now unbuttoned, keeps flapping open to reveal her undergarments.

Plutarch offers her a chair. "Saved you the best seat."

She collapses into it, pulls a stalk of celery from her drink, and chomps on it. "How old did I look today, Plutarch?"

"Not a day over thirty," Plutarch promises. "Everybody commented on it."

"Well, you get what you pay for," she slurs, gingerly probing her cheekbone with the celery. She points at the screen and laughs. "Ha! There's Juvenia! Little Miss Perfect didn't get any cloud cover. She looks ghastly, don't you think?"

Juvenia, a pint-sized lady in six-inch heels and pink polka dots, begins calling names in District 1. The program moves on, and they air every district's drawing. Besides us, forty-four tributes were reaped today, half girls, half boys, of every shape and size. As usual, the kids from Districts 1, 2, and 4 live up to their nickname as the Careers, which means they seem to have been training for the Hunger Games since birth. Here and there, chance has thrown in some additional brawny kids, but plenty of scrawny ones balance them out. On the brawny-to-scrawny scale, I do okay, largely because of all those bags of grain I haul for Hattie. But some of those Careers could crush me like a bug. And Louella's yet to get her growth.

As a strapping boy mounts the stage in District 11, Drusilla states the obvious. "You lot better be able to run." She doesn't even say this in a mean way, which makes it scarier.

"Other factors besides size come into play. Brains, skills, strategy. And never rule out luck," says Plutarch. "Your mentors will talk you through everything."

Our mentors. Our guides, our masterminds, our protectors in the Hunger Games. Except the District 12 tributes don't have automatic mentors, not even one, because we're the only district without living victors, and that's who the job traditionally falls to.

In fifty years, we've only had one victor, and that was a long time ago. A girl who no one seems to know anything about. Back then, barely anyone in 12 had a television, so the Games were mostly hearsay. I've never seen her in the clips of the old shows, but then those early efforts are rarely featured, as they are said to be badly filmed and lacking in spectacle. My parents weren't born yet, and even Mamaw couldn't tell me much about the girl. I brought our victor up with Lenore Dove a few times, but she never wanted to discuss her.

"Who are our mentors anyway?" I ask.

"They're in the process of selecting them from the pool of victors not tapped to oversee their own district tributes," says Plutarch. "Don't worry, some very talented candidates are in the running."

Yeah. Candidates who would be pariahs if they led a District 12 tribute to victory while their own district's tributes died. Most years, I don't even hear about who ends up mentoring the kids from 12. Let's face it, we're on our own.

Drusilla lets out a gasp. "Daylight is murder!"

They've cut to District 12, where our fates were sealed.

"And yet, you're luminous," Plutarch assures her.

I watch, both fascinated and sickened by the flawless transition from Maysilee's drawing to Wyatt's and mine. Not even a hint of Woodbine's shooting or the turmoil that followed. And there's my name, and there's me, and there's Ma gasping, Sid crying, Lenore Dove with her hand clasped over her mouth.

"That's not what happened," I say.

"None of the footage has been tampered with — not really time to do that properly," says Plutarch. "I just did a little card-stacking to help you out."

"You did what?" asks Louella.

Before he can answer, Wyatt, who hasn't opened his mouth except to eat since 12, weighs in. "He stacked the deck in our favor. He shuffled the shots around to give us an advantage."

Plutarch beams at him. "Exactly!"

A corner of Louella's mouth twists down. "You mean, like in card games. When people gamble. Isn't that cheating?"

"It is and it isn't," says Plutarch. "Look, we need to sell you to the sponsors. If I showed the audience what really happened — the Chance boy's head being blown off, the crowd control, Haymitch attacking the Peacekeepers —"

I object. "I didn't attack anyone. They attacked my girl and I stepped in."

"Same thing," says Drusilla. "You're not allowed to interfere with our Peacekeepers."

"I'm trying to show you in the best possible light," says Plutarch.

Maysilee rolls her eyes. "Like when our shop calls stale marshmallows 'chewy.' And then charges an extra penny for them."

I scowl at her. I've fallen for that "chewy" marshmallow scam more than once.

"Stress the positive, ignore the negative," says Plutarch.

"Instead of four violent district piglets who hate the Capitol —" Drusilla begins.

"You're a quartet of attractive kids who hop right up there on that stage to the cheers of your district, raring to go!" finishes Plutarch.

"You should be down on your knees kissing this man's feet. Maybe you won't get any sponsors, but at least you haven't repelled them. He's given you a total makeover," says Drusilla.

"You mean, he's given the Capitol a total makeover," scoffs Maysilee. "Made you look competent when you couldn't even pull off the reaping."

"I like to think it was mutually beneficial," says Plutarch. "And the audience is none the wiser. I saw to that."

I'm entirely the Capitol's plaything. They will use me for their entertainment and then kill me, and the truth will have no say in it. Plutarch acts friendly, but his indulgences — my family's goodbyes, his fancy sandwiches — are just a method to manage me, because happy playthings are easier to handle than raging ones. To get his footage, he'll indulge me right into the arena.

As if to confirm this, the door to the sitting room bursts open to reveal Tibby, his face aglow with the sixteen candles on a giant birthday cake.

We don't do birthday cakes in my house. Seems wrong on reaping day, and Ma thinks it's unfair for her and Sid to have a cake if I don't. Instead, she makes something nice for breakfast, like the corn bread and sauce, and saves all of her cake energy for New Year's Day.

She starts setting things aside months in advance: the dried apples, the sorghum syrup, the white flour. The spices — ginger and cinnamon and whatnot — are so costly she buys them in little twists of paper from the Marches' apothecary. A couple days before New Year's, she makes the apple filling and bakes the six layers of cake, and alternates them — cake, filling, cake, filling, until it's in one big beautiful stack. She wraps it all up in a towel so it can rest, and that sweet apple filling soaks into the cake. Then, on New Year's Day at suppertime, she pours everybody a big glass of buttermilk and we eat all the stack cake that we can hold.

So the cake in front of me, with its fancy frosted flowers, is all wrong. The candles smack of the Capitol. And the song Tibby leads the Peacekeepers in, while common in 12, is never sung in my house because it would be as unsuitable as a birthday cake.

Happy birthday
To someone special!
And we wish you many more!

Once a year
We give a cheer
To you, Hay-ay-ay-mitch!
Happy birthday!

The cameraman from Plutarch's crew, sneaking his lens over Tibby's shoulder to film my reaction, is the cherry on the birthday cake fiasco. Clearly, Plutarch wants to capture my delight so he can broadcast it all over Panem. *Look how well the Capitol treats the tributes. How forgiving they are to their enemies. How superior they are to those district piglets in their stinkholes.*

I've seen similar clips before of the tributes being treated like pampered pets. Being brushed and fed and flattered, lapping it up. Playing into the Capitol propaganda. Maybe it gets them more sponsors, but if they do win, it's not going to get them a parade back home.

"Don't let them use you, Sarshee. Don't let them paint their posters with your blood. Not if you can help it."

That's it. That's what Pa told Sarshee in the Justice Building. That's what Ma wanted me to remember. Even though — maybe especially because — she had just let Plutarch use her and Sid like puppets. She had failed, but wanted me to be strong.

Plutarch had my family over a barrel when we were desperate for one last embrace, but now he's got nothing I want. I rise as I weigh my options. I could knock the cake to the ground, hawk and spit on it, or just shove it into Tibby's stupid face. Instead, I go all Maysilee Donner, turning my back and walking over to look out the window.

In the reflection, I see Tibby deflate. "It has pineapple filling?" he offers.

I give my head a slight shake.

"A miscalculation on my part," Plutarch says. "Take it out, Tibby. I'm sorry, Haymitch."

An apology? From a Capitol guy? Then I see it for what it is: another way to manipulate me by pretending I'm a human being, worthy of an apology. I don't even acknowledge it.

It makes me feel pretty bad, though. That cake. The last thing I needed was a big Capitol reminder that this would be my final birthday. The same goes for all of us. And while we're not all allies, I appreciate that no one's shouted out, "Well, hold on, I'll take a piece!"

After my cake and Capitol well-wishers have withdrawn, Plutarch continues. "Back to business. Along with your mentors, District Twelve will be assigned its very own stylist."

"And not a moment too soon." Drusilla snorts and gives Louella's gingham dress an appraising look. "Honestly, where do you people find these things?"

"My ma made it," says Louella evenly. "Where did you find yours?"

Louella's holding her own, but Maysilee lands the insult. "I was wondering the same. It's like someone mated a Peacekeeper and a canary and . . . there you are."

"What?" says Drusilla. She rises from her chair but wobbles a bit before she finds her balance on her spiked heels.

"Careful," says Maysilee. She drips sugar as she goes for the jugular. "Might be time to rethink those boots. Wouldn't something closer to the ground be safer for a person your age?"

Drusilla hauls off and slaps Maysilee, who, without missing a beat, slaps her right back. A real wallop. Drusilla's knocked off her boots and into the chair I recently vacated. Everyone freezes and I wonder if we're about to be executed on the spot.

"Don't you ever touch me again," says Maysilee. The color's gone from her face except for the print of Drusilla's hand. You got to hand it to Maysilee, nobody's using footage of her for propaganda.

"Why don't we all take a deep breath?" Plutarch suggests. "It's been a tough day. Everybody's emotions are running high and —!"

Drusilla flies up, rips the riding crop from its boot clip, and begins beating Maysilee, who cries out and raises her arms to protect her head. But the blows keep raining down, forcing her to the floor.

"Drusilla! Stop! Drusilla, we have to put her on camera tomorrow!" Plutarch warns. He has to summon two Peacekeepers from the hallway to pull her off.

"Nasty, disgusting creature," Drusilla pants. "I will destroy you before you even make it to the arena."

The welts have already risen on Maysilee's arms and neck, but she ignores them. I doubt she's ever been hit before, let alone whipped. I haven't much either. Mamaw used to cuff me on the head, but it was more to get my attention than to hurt me. Maysilee slowly pushes herself up from the floor, using the wall for support, before she responds. "Really? How? You're not a Gamemaker. You're not even a stylist. You're nothing but a low-rent escort hanging on by your fingernails to the trashiest district in Panem."

This hits a nerve. Fear flickers across Drusilla's face before she recovers. "And you're headed for a bloody and agonizing death."

Maysilee gives a bitter laugh. "That's right. I am. So why should I care what you say? Unless I win, of course. But even then, who do you think will be more popular? The victor of the Quarter Quell . . . or you?"

Drusilla's expression twists into a leer. "I hope you do win. You have no idea what's in store for you then. You know nothing." She limps to the door.

"I know my grandmother had a jacket like yours, but we wouldn't let her wear it out of the house," says Maysilee.

Drusilla tenses, but tries to make a dignified exit.

There's a long pause, then Plutarch says, "You may find Drusilla ridiculous, but be smart. You four don't have your own district mentor. Your stylist's job begins and ends with your appearance. It might not be fair, but Drusilla may be the best advocate you have in the Capitol. Think about it before you burn that bridge entirely." He leaves, quietly closing the door behind him.

"You okay?" I ask Maysilee.

"Never better." She gingerly touches the welts, bringing tears to her eyes.

I can't help feeling sorry for her and a little impressed by how she stood up to Drusilla. Even though she's rich, she's not trying to cozy up to the Capitol people. We're all equally beneath her. "There I was, trying to be so high-and-mighty about the cake, and then you go all wildcat on us."

Maysilee gives a small smile. "Well, I have strong opinions on fashion."

"I guess you do," says Louella.

"It's high time someone told Miss Matchy-Matchy she looks hideous," says Maysilee. "But you look fine, Louella. Your mother did a nice job trimming your dress."

The girls eye each other. I can feel a slight thaw, but all Louella says is "I think so, too."

A Peacekeeper beckons us from the door and we follow her back through the train to a compartment with two sets of bunk beds built into the walls. A door leads to a small bathroom with a toilet and sink. "Toothbrushes and towels in the bathroom, and you each get your own bed."

She waits, as if we're supposed to be grateful, but the only person who responds is Maysilee. "It smells like cooked cabbage in here."

"In the old days, we used to put you in cattle cars," the Peacekeeper replies, then locks us in.

On the pillows are pajamas, which we sort out based on our sizes. We take turns in the bathroom and retreat to our bunks. Shades automatically slide down over the windows and the bulbs above the door dim, leaving us in twilight. Wyatt falls asleep almost immediately, judging by his snores, and Louella follows suit. Maysilee sits on the top bunk across from me, holding a wet washrag to her welts. I lie on my back, staring at the ceiling, trying to make sense of the day.

My fingers wrap around the flint striker hanging from my neck. The picture of Lenore Dove, drenched and wailing in the storm, overtakes me, and my heart begins to splinter again. I squeeze my eyes shut tight and reach for her across the miles, knowing she is reaching for me, too. I hear her voice singing a piece of her poem, her name song.

Deep into that darkness peering, long I stood there wondering,
fearing,
Doubting, dreaming dreams no mortal ever dared to dream
before;
But the silence was unbroken, and the stillness gave no
token,
And the only word there spoken was the whispered word,
"Lenore?"

I know every word of the song, since I learned it for Lenore Dove's birthday last December. It wasn't that hard, it being what she calls an earworm, meaning it sticks in your head whether you want it to or not. It's true, the thing's addictive, rhyming and repeating in a way that dares you to stop, all while telling you a haunting story. I sang it to her in an old house by the lake in front of a fire. We were toasting stale marshmallows and we'd skipped school, which we both caught hell for later. She said it was her favorite gift ever. . . .

This I whispered, and an echo murmured back the word,
"Lenore!"

"What is that?"

I try to ignore Maysilee.

Merely this and nothing more.

"The thing around your neck?"

The connection has broken. Lenore Dove's gone. I look over to find Maysilee staring at me, her eyes wide in the dark.

"Birthday present. From my girl."

"Can I see it? I collect jewelry."

You don't hear that much in District 12, but Mr. Donner spoils his girls rotten. Lenore Dove told me that, on their thirteenth birthday, he gave them pure gold pins that had belonged to his mother. They'd been fashioned by Tam Amber over thirty years ago. I never saw them, but Merrilee's featured a hummingbird and Maysilee's a mockingjay, birds being one of the Covey's great loves. Apparently, Merrilee wore hers all of five minutes before she lost it down a well. Maysilee threw a fit over hers, saying a mockingjay was an ugly old thing and why couldn't Tam Amber melt it down and make her something pretty like a butterfly?

When he declined, she stuffed the pin in the back of a drawer and never wore it once.

Lenore Dove saw red when she heard about the twins, feeling they neither appreciated nor deserved Tam Amber's craftsmanship, and for a time, she spoke about breaking into the Donners' and stealing that mockingjay pin back. Burdock and I talked her out of it. What with two recent arrests, it seemed unwise. But it still eats at her. I know she would not want Maysilee's manicured paws on my necklace.

"It's kind of personal," I say. "I mean, I'm not planning on taking it off ever again. It's not really jewelry anyway."

She nods and doesn't pursue it. Just hangs her washrag over the bedrail, gets under her covers, and rolls over to face the wall. I'm chilly in the refrigerated train air, so I pull up the Capitol blanket, which is stiff and has a chemical odor. Nothing like my soft patchwork quilt that Ma dries in the sunshine on Sundays, when the mine's quiet and the soot's minimal so it smells like fresh air. Ma . . . Sid . . .

I don't expect to sleep, but the day's been so draining that the movement of the train lulls me into a semiconscious state. A few hours later, I wake with a start and feel someone shaking my leg.

"Hay. Hay!" Louella whispers over Wyatt's snores.

I prop myself up on my elbow and squint at her through the dim light. "What's going on?"

"I don't want Wyatt. I don't want him for an ally, okay?"

"Wyatt? Okay, but can I know why? He looks pretty strong and —"

She breaks in. "He's a Booker Boy. At least, his pa is."

The Booker Boys are miners who cater to those who like to gamble in 12. They take bets on any number of goings-on — dogfights, mayor appointments, boxing matches — and organize gambling events. On Saturday nights, you can usually find them in an old garage behind the Hob, running dice and card games for a cut. If things get tense with the Peacekeepers, like the time someone set fire to a jeep, then they lay low, popping up in back alleys and condemned houses.

Personally, I never gamble. If Ma heard I'd been spending money on cards, she'd kill me, and beyond that, I just don't get the thrill of it. Life in general seems risky enough to me. But if people want to throw away their money, it's not my business.

"Well, I make white liquor, so I'm not one to point fingers," I tell Louella. "We're both operating outside the law. And doesn't Cayson like his dice?"

Cayson's her older brother and, when he's not in the mines, he's chasing some kind of pleasure.

Louella gives her head an impatient shake. "Not just dice. I mean now. I mean us."

Then I get it. Around this time every year, a couple of Booker Boys take bets on the Hunger Games tributes. Like how old will the kids be, Seam or town, the number of tesserae they carry. The betting continues through the Games, with odds on deaths and districts and the ultimate victor. It should be illegal, but the Peacekeepers don't care. It's modeled on their own system of betting in the Capitol. Most of the Booker Boys shun this, it being too blackhearted, but a few make a nice profit. Those are sick and twisted people, and not the kind you can trust in the Hunger Games.

"You sure, Louella?" I ask.

"Near as I can be. I didn't put it together until I saw Wyatt messing with that coin," she said. "Cayson told me all the gamblers learn that stuff, to signal people there's a game on when they can't say so out loud."

"He seemed to know all about stacking the deck. . . ."

"And one time, someone brought up Mr. Callow, and Cayson spit and said he didn't have no truck with people who made money on dead kids."

Well, Wyatt being reaped is the final word in irony. I think of the Callows frantically trying to reach him on the square. Never getting to say good-bye. Hard to feel much pity for them now. "Do you think he took bets on our reaping with his pa?"

"That'd be my guess," she says.

"Mine, too. Booker Boys keep their business in the family. I don't want Wyatt either, Louella. It's just you and me. Try and get some more sleep, okay?"

I don't, though. Around dawn, the shades retract and I stare out into unfamiliar mountains, adding insult to injury. What's happening in *my* mountains? Is Hattie brewing another batch of forgetfulness? Is Ma scrubbing away her grief on the washboard, while Sid fills the cistern under a cloudless sky? Are the geese standing guard over Lenore Dove's heart? As much pain as my loved ones feel now, how long will it be until I am just a memory?

Plutarch sticks his head in to announce breakfast in a cheerful voice that suggests yesterday never happened. We dress and go back to the sitting room car for egg and bacon sandwiches and more lemonade. Maysilee asks for coffee, a rich person drink in 12, and Tibby brings us each a cup. I don't care for the bitter stuff.

The train climbs and climbs and suddenly we're in a pitch-black tunnel and Plutarch says it won't be long now, but it seems like an eternity. When we finally pull into the station, the sunlight streaming through the glass panels dazzles my eyes before I make out another train across the platform.

I recognize Juvenia, the District 1 escort who Drusilla sneered at, tentatively descending the train steps in snakeskin boots.

Behind her come her four tributes, cuffed and chained together, towering over their Peacekeepers. When the car door shuts behind them, the boy bringing up the rear suddenly turns and kicks the window. The glass shatters like an eggshell.

A quiet voice behind me says, "Panache Barker, District One tribute, trained Career, roughly three hundred pounds. His last name suggests he's related to Palladium Barker, who took the crown four years ago. He'll currently have odds of about five to two, which in the arena would translate into an average of two meals a day from sponsors. He looks to be a lefty, which can be a plus or a minus, but he's also a hothead, and that could cost him. Based on the reaping stats — training, weight, lineage — he's a current crowd favorite, whereas we're strictly long-shot material."

We all stare at Wyatt, who keeps his eyes on the competition as he muses, "You might not want me, but it's a sure bet you need me."

"Not just a Booker Boy, but an eavesdropper," says Louella.

"I'm not a Booker Boy," Wyatt replies. "I'm an oddsmaker. I determine the odds on an event people are betting on. That's all. My family are the Booker Boys — they take the bets."

"That sounds just as bad. And you're still an eavesdropper, either way," says Louella.

"Where did you expect us to go, Louella?" says Maysilee, indicating that she overheard our conversation as well. "Maybe Wyatt and I don't want to be your allies either. Thought of that?"

"Then we don't have a problem," Louella says.

Plutarch beckons us from the door. "All right, kids, we're out of here."

Although the train has not exactly been homey, climbing down into the glaring station makes me feel small and vulnerable. The four of us move closer together, even though we're far from friendly. The Peacekeepers cuff us again and I wait for a chain to link us together, but when it's produced, the officer in charge waves it away, saying, "Don't bother."

"Long shots," Wyatt murmurs.

It reinforces what I already know, that we are not victor material. On the other hand, this could be an opportunity to run. But where can an escaped tribute find protection in the Capitol? I think of the smoky mist in my mountains, Lenore Dove's friend of the condemned, and see no equivalent here.

So I just stand there like the puny long shot I am, taking in the banners that deck the station. *NO PEACE, NO PROSPERITY! NO HUNGER GAMES, NO PEACE!* It's the same campaign they used on our square back in District 12, but with slogans geared to the Capitol residents. Seems the Capitol has to convince its own citizens, too.

Drusilla clatters down the steps in platform boots and a skin-tight jumpsuit emblazoned with the flag of Panem. Her hat, a two-foot pillar of red fur, jauntily tilts over one eye. A smear of yellow frosting trails out of the side of her mouth. Someone had no problem celebrating my birthday.

"Enjoy the cake?" asks Maysilee. The girl has not backed down an inch.

Drusilla looks confused until Plutarch taps his face. "A little something right here." For lack of a mirror, Drusilla checks her reflection in the train window and cleans off the frosting with her tongue. Her cheek, where Maysilee struck her, looks slightly bruised under her thick layer of makeup.

"You're beautiful," says Plutarch. I guess she's just another plaything he has to handle, only what controls her are compliments.

"All right, you lot, let's go," Drusilla says before striding down the platform.

Outside, we get about thirty seconds of fresh air before we're loaded into a windowless Peacekeepers van. I've only ever been in an automobile a handful of times, in the car to the train station yesterday and on a truck for a couple of school trips to the mines. Never when I couldn't see out. Never when I was being taken to die. No light, no air. Like they buried me already.

Louella presses against my shoulder and it steadies me. I sense that she's how I'm going to get through the nightmare of the next few days. Looking after her will give me a reason to keep going; her looking after me will stave off the terror of facing death alone. I can only hope we leave the world together.

"Doing all right, sweetheart?" I ask.

"I've been better," she responds.

"We'll just stick together, okay?"

"Okay."

When the van doors swing open, I'm temporarily thrown by the light again. The dryness of the air makes me crave the cold mountain creek water Hattie has me draw buckets of. What will she do now that I'm gone? Get another mule, I guess. A luckier one.

Drusilla and Plutarch are nowhere to be seen. Peacekeepers order us out of the van. My old boots look peculiar on the white marble paving stones of the walkway. It branches out to a wide expanse of imposing buildings filled with people who point and stare at us from a distance. Not grown-ups. People our age, dressed in matching uniforms. School kids.

I feel like a wild animal on display, cuffed and mute, dragged in from the hills for their fun. All of us shrink a bit. Maysilee keeps her head up, but her cheeks burn with embarrassment.

"Still don't think it's a good idea to bring them to the Academy," one of the Peacekeepers mutters.

"This gymnasium's been empty for close to forty years," says another. "Might as well get some use out of it."

"Ought to tear it down," says the first. "It's an eyesore."

The van pulls away, revealing the gymnasium, a looming, dilapidated structure with a banner over the entrance that reads *TRIBUTE CENTER* in metallic gold letters. The Peacekeepers hold the cracked glass doors open and the smell of floor cleaner and mildew hits us.

We're the last tributes to arrive. Our competitors sit around the room in bunches of four at stations marked with their district numbers. The Peacekeepers herd us to the 12 sign at the far end of the gym, amidst catcalls and taunts. They're a mouthy bunch, this year's Careers.

Each station consists of four padded tables separated by flimsy curtains. Pairs of white-coated assistants flank the tables, wearing utility belts filled with grooming equipment: scissors and razors and such.

The Peacekeepers direct the boy tributes to one locker room, the girls to another. I don't like leaving Louella, but there's no choice. Maybe in a pinch, Maysilee will protect her. She looks like trouble, with her welts and her scowl. Like someone who'd hit back, which it turns out she is.

At the locker room door, they line up the boys by district number, so Wyatt and I don't have to watch our backs, just the muscular ones of the District 11 tributes ahead of us. They're a sullen pair, though, uninterested in their surroundings.

Inside we're told to strip, which is easy from the waist down but undoable above the belt with our cuffed hands. Peacekeepers come around and cut away our shirts with knives. If anyone objects, they laugh and say it's all the same to the incinerator. It hurts watching them slice through Ma's careful stitches. I remember her painstakingly laying out those handkerchiefs to make every inch of material count. Now it sits in shreds at my feet.

A Peacekeeper taps his knifepoint against my flint striker. "This your token?"

My token? Then I remember that tributes are allowed to take one item from home into the arena with them, as long as it's not a weapon. My flint striker could be viewed as an unfair advantage, but I'm not giving them any help with that.

"Yes, it's a necklace," I say.

 The Peacekeeper rubs the metal between his fingers and admits grudgingly, "It's nice. They'll take it later for evaluation." I nod. Even if they examine it, they might not recognize its potential. Here, where there are ample matches and lighters and no one needs a spark to make a fire.

We're marched into a large, open room with blue tiles on the floor and showerheads spaced around the walls. I'm no prude — I've skinny-dipped plenty out at the lake with Burdock — but I'm not used to standing around naked eyeballing twenty-three other guys. At first, I just stare at a drain on the floor, then I realize there's no better place to size up the competition, so I do. The half dozen Careers look like they spend their spare time posing for statues. Another dozen of us might stand a chance if we're handy with an ax. And the remaining half dozen are pitiful, all hollow rib cages and matchstick bones.

Panache, who I recognize from the train, struts around thrusting his privates at people and grunting, much to the amusement of the other Careers. He makes the mistake of trying this on one of the District 11 tributes and winds up with a swift kick in the gut. Panache's about to retaliate when the showerheads come to life, soaking us with scalding water.

We all dodge around, trying to evade the streams. Things go from bad to worse when the water's replaced by a noxious soapy spray that triggers my gag reflex and burns my eyes like pepper dust. The water returns, but this time we're fighting for it as we try to get the soap off. When the showers turn to drips, I still feel covered in a stinging slime from head to toe.

A towel might help, but instead a blast of hot air follows, which adds to the misery and bakes the slime into my skin, making it itch like crazy. Whatever fight any of us had in us has been squelched. We're just a scratching, sniveling bunch of kids with runny eyes and spiked hair. Back in the locker room, we're each given a sheet of crepe paper to wrap around ourselves for modesty's sake and directed back to our district areas in the gym.

I hope Louella has been spared this, but when I see her braids sticking out like a broken weather vane, I know she's been through the wringer, too. It must have been agony for Maysilee, with all those welts. We're each directed to a table, ordered to sit, and this time, like the Careers', our cuffs are fastened to chains.

That's all I see of the other tributes for a while, as the Peacekeepers shut off my cubicle with the white curtains. A girl with puffballs of magenta hair and a guy with metal apples studding his cheeks approach nervously. Neither of them looks much older than me.

"Hi, Haymitch," says the girl breathlessly. "I'm Proserpina, and this is Vitus. We're your prep team, and we're here to make you gorgeous!"

"Yes! Yes!" says Vitus. "Gorgeous, but fierce!" He bares his teeth and growls. "To scare the others off!"

"And get you lots of sponsors!" Proserpina's voice drops to a whisper. "We can't send you things, of course, since we're part of your team. But my great-aunt already said she'll sponsor you. And not just to help my grade."

Her grade? "You're students? At this school?"

"Oh, no, we're *University* students, not Academy. I mean, we're not seniors or anything," says Vitus. "They all wanted better districts."

"But we really like you. You're cute!" Proserpina assures me. "And anyway, we have two more years to move up."

So, my team consists of Drusilla, who hates me, a mentor rooting for another tribute, a couple of underclassmen, and . . . "Who's my stylist?"

Their faces fall and they exchange a look. "District Twelve got Magno Stift again," admits Vitus. "But he is NOT as bad as they say."

I groan. Magno Stift's the guy who's been assigned to the District 12 tributes for as long as I can remember. And yes, he's every bit as bad as they say. While the other stylists do new costumes each year for the parade and interviews that happen before the Games, he seems to have a limitless supply of the same crappy coal miner overalls in an array of sizes.

"He's promised a shining new look for the Quarter Quell!" Proserpina reassures me.

"Which is good, because nobody's going to sponsor you in that old stuff," says Vitus.

"And we shouldn't have any accidents today, because they've banned live-reptile fashion backstage," adds Proserpina. "Not just Magno's — everybody's. Although he's the only one who really wears it."

"Last year his belt buckle fell off and bit Drusilla," Vitus whispers. "It was this really angry turtle. And she got so mad she bit him back. Magno, not the turtle. And we saw the whole thing but we're not supposed to talk about it, even though everybody —"

"Well, we won't have a repeat of that!" interjects Proserpina, shooting him a look. "Shall we start with your body hair? All the bugs gone?"

So that's what the chemicals were. Insecticides. If I was going to be around long enough to worry about long-term effects, I might get angry.

"Wait!" yelps Vitus. "We need to do the before shots!"

Proserpina produces a tiny camera and they photograph me from head to toe. "That was a close one. We'd probably get an incomplete without the before shots."

The prep team shaves off all my visible body hair with electric razors. I don't have much facial hair, but they decide to take that off as well. I feel like a skinned squirrel, raw and exposed. Then they trim my nails, honoring my request to leave me enough to fight with because, as Proserpina says, "You might need your claws." I wonder if she thinks of my nose as a snout, my hair as fur, my feet as paws.

Vitus adds a handful of goo to my porcupine hair and massages it until it's no longer in danger of snapping off. He's pretty good with the hair, actually, reclaiming my curls and eliminating the itch. I talk him into letting me rub some of the goo over my body, and I can finally stop scratching.

I'm obliging with the after shots, given that my prep team has been responsive to my requests and I could use a friend or two here in the Capitol. I'm rewarded with a new sheet of paper and a linty peppermint drop from Proserpina's pocket that I'm not too proud to accept. It takes the insecticide taste from my mouth and reminds me of happier days. They run off then, because Proserpina's sister wants to touch up her magenta hair pom-poms in case she ends up on camera, and Vitus promised his mother he'd help her decorate for her Hunger Games party tonight.

I'm relieved they're gone and welcome my white-curtained privacy. Everything seems surreal, like a terrible fever dream that just keeps going. The chemical shower, my bizarre prep team, looking at my bald legs as I await a man who secures his pants with a live reptile.

My fingers find the snake head at my neck and trace the scales transforming into feathers and then the bird's pointed beak. I travel back to an overcast day, deep in the woods, a patch of trees we call ours, arms around Lenore Dove, night falling, neither of us caring. On a nearby branch perches a handsome blackbird.

"That's a raven. The bird from my name poem," she says softly. "It's the biggest songbird there is."

"He's an impressive fellow," I observe.

"*She* is. She's smart as a whip, too. Did you know they use logic to solve things?"

"Got me beat there," I have to admit.

"And nobody tells them what to say. That bird is who I want to be when I grow up. Someone who says whatever they think is right, no matter what."

No matter what. That's the part I'm worried about. That she might be saying something rash. Or even doing something beyond dangerous words. Something the Capitol won't warn but whip her for. The year she turned twelve, she crossed that line twice.

First, on the night before they were to hang Clay Chance in the square, someone shinnied up the gallows and filed halfway through the rope. Next morning, in front of a crowd, the rope snapped and Clay fell to the ground, where a dozen Peacekeeper bullets took him out. As the night had been pitch-black and snowing, the security camera didn't catch much, but someone in the town had spotted Lenore Dove leaving the square and reported her. She was hauled into the base prison for questioning and would only say she hadn't done anything wrong. The Peacekeepers didn't know what to do with her. A little bit of a thing sitting there, her feet dangling inches from the floor, her wrists too skinny for the cuffs. Then Clay's sister, Binnie, who'd been on borrowed time for a year due to a bad heart, confessed she'd done it. Three days later, Binnie died in her cell, and the uncles were allowed to collect Lenore Dove, promising she'd stay home at night.

After that, Clerk Carmine kept her on a shorter leash. But the morning of the Forty-sixth Hunger Games, our first year in the reaping, smoke began seeping from beneath the temporary stage as we gathered. The Peacekeepers pulled out a wad of smoking cloth that turned out to be the flag of Panem. Burning the flag gets you ten years in prison, or likely more if it's broadcast across the nation, but all traces were removed before the cameras rolled. The stage had been assembled only the evening before, and the Peacekeepers hadn't thought to install security cameras beneath it. Under the platform, a grate leading to utility pipes had been disturbed. Apparently, a candle, lit hours before, had burned down to ignite the kerosene-soaked flag. It could have been anyone. With no proof and no witnesses, they rounded up those with a history of suspicious behavior, and Lenore Dove was arrested again. She said she'd been home, writing her will in case her name got called in the reaping. Then she read them said document, seven pages in which most of her worldly belongings went to her geese. Maybe it was overkill, the way she'd prepared. Maybe the Peacekeepers could sense they were being played. They let her go again, but this time with a strict warning that they had their eye on her.

It was her, though. Both times. I know it in my heart, even though she's never quite admitted it to me or her uncles. She says all the Covey girls are a mystery, it's half their charm. When I press her, she just laughs and says if it's true, that information could put me in danger, and if it's false, what does it matter? "Didn't do much good anyway, did it? Clay's dead and the reaping's alive and well."

Since that year, she's had a clean record. Last New Year's, the Covey even played at the base commander's party, though Lenore Dove wasn't thrilled about it. Clerk Carmine said a job's a job, and music can be a bridge to better understanding between people because most everybody loves a good tune. Lenore Dove said most everybody loves breathing, too, and where did that get us? Some loves don't signify.

Comments like that make me feel like she's still got the potential to make trouble, and that side of her is just laying low.

I'm not sure what I'd have done yesterday if the roles had been reversed. I'd have wanted to follow Lenore Dove, maybe stowed away on the train and helped her escape or died trying. Or at least burned the Peacekeepers' base to the ground. But in reality, whatever plans I might have concocted would've been kept in check by the thought of Ma and Sid trying to get by without me. I'd probably just have gone quietly insane. It's different for her. No one depends on Lenore Dove for their livelihood. She can run as wild as the wind.

After an hour or so, Peacekeepers drop off two nut butter sandwiches and my first banana. While I wouldn't call it fruit — too starchy and juiceless — it tastes pretty good. I wash it down with a bottle of water filled with bubbles, which seems like a stupid thing to do to water, since I just burp them all up anyway.

The Peacekeepers pull the curtains back and I can see everybody's been given the same prep. Some of those Careers had full beards earlier, but they look younger and less scary clean-shaven. Losing the chest hair didn't hurt either.

Juvenia arrives with a woman pushing a rack of fancy clothes, and the District 1 prep teams trot after them into the boys' locker room to get ready for the chariot procession that's the centerpiece of the opening ceremonies. The Peacekeepers unchain their tributes and take them in. In a few minutes, the same routine plays out with District 2 and the girls' locker room. A half hour later, the District 1 tributes, looking almost Capitol in green ball gowns and sparkling suits, parade across the gym.

As they pass us, Maysilee says loudly, "Looking good, Silka! I hope we all get to wear snot green!"

Laughter breaks out around the gym. Silka, who must have eight inches and a hundred pounds on Maysilee, starts for her, only to get a swift baton to the ribs from a Peacekeeper. Silka looks at Maysilee and draws her finger across her throat.

Maysilee pouts back. "Now, pretty is as pretty does. How about a smile?"

Louella grins at me from her table. "They did not hit it off in the locker room."

"Not a fan of One myself," I admit, watching them head to their van as District 2 struts by in purple leather and studs.

"Where are they all going?" I hear someone ask.

"To their photo shoots," a Peacekeeper answers. "Then the chariots."

The teams for 3 and 4 appear next, and I know we'll be last. The place slowly empties out. Proserpina, who's sporting freshly dyed puffs, and Vitus, cranky because his mother's turned his bedroom into a bar for the party, return. The District 11 tributes get whisked away by their stylist just as Drusilla comes clacking across the gym floor in her platform boots, fur hat tucked under her arm.

"Where's that idiot Magno?" she asks my team. They shrug helplessly. "He's making us late for one of the biggest parties of the year!"

She's all about the parties, our escort.

Another ten minutes pass. "I need to take a piss," I say.

The Peacekeepers uncuff us and bring us into the girls' locker room, where we get to relieve ourselves. Still no Magno. I sit next to Louella on a bench. They fixed up her braids and gave her dramatic eyebrows. Maysilee's blond locks are in a fountain of tight curls, which somehow suits her, and Wyatt looks exactly the same as before his prep.

"If he doesn't come, do we get to skip the chariot part?" asks Louella. "Or do we just go wrapped up in paper?"

No one seems to have considered that. Suddenly, everybody

panics, including me. As much as I reject all of this, I don't want to make my big entrance in a paper sheet. If I'm to stand any kind of chance, if I'm to get sponsors, I can't go out there with my rear end hanging in the breeze.

"Where's the dress I came in?" demands Maysilee. "I can pin it back together."

"Already burned," says a Peacekeeper.

With the clock running out, Drusilla orders the prep teams to lend us pieces of their own outfits. I'm trying to squeeze into Vitus's blue velvet shorts when our stylist rolls in with a plastic bag slung over his shoulder.

Magno Stift's sun-leathered skin has been tattooed with a snakeskin pattern. He wears a long shirt made of metal diamonds and no visible pants. His sandals lace all the way up to his pelvis, and from each of his ears dangle tiny, living garter snakes that twist and turn in misery.

"You know those have been banned!" steams Drusilla. "I'll report you."

"Oh, Drusie, they'll be dead in a few hours anyway," says Magno. He dumps the contents of his bag on the floor, revealing a half dozen of the same costumes I've seen on District 12 tributes for as long as I can remember. He lifts his arms in mock triumph. "Now, who's ready to knock them dead?"

We're all so stressed that even these hand-me-down outfits are snatched up, which I'm sure is how Magno planned it all along. I climb into a pair of smelly black miner overalls held together with safety pins and strap on a cheap plastic coal miner hat without complaint. The boots pinch my toes, but I lace them up, relieved to have any footwear at all.

Only Drusilla holds him to account. "What happened to their shining new look?"

With a flourish, Magno flips on the light in Maysilee's hat. The weak beam barely registers. "Ta-da! I replaced the batteries."

"And this is what you brought for the Quarter Quell? If this doesn't get you axed, I don't know what will," Drusilla says with satisfaction.

Magno just laughs. "No one cares about Twelve. Especially you. Get these brats chained up and to the stables. My job here is done."

We hightail it out of there and into the waiting van, which speeds through the Capitol streets, horn blaring. It's not enough to drown out a booming version of the anthem, which they must be blasting out citywide. The Hunger Games opening ceremonies have begun without us. As the anthem ends, we screech to a halt and the van doors fly open, revealing the inside of a cavernous stable, its high roof supported by concrete pillars. Handlers are trying to wrangle forty-eight costumed tributes into twelve chariots while harnessing the horses meant to pull us through the streets. Everybody's shouting, and nobody's listening.

Parade music begins, the grand stable doors open, and the District 1 tributes pose for photographers before rolling onto the avenue to the roar of the crowd. A photographer runs up and snaps our picture repeatedly, then vanishes. Was that our photo shoot? Us chained up in the van?

Drusilla appears to boss around the handlers. "Get District Twelve mounted!"

We're unchained, freed of our cuffs, and hauled to a rickety chariot drawn by a quartet of skittish gray nags. My eyes sweep the stable, confirming my suspicions. Everybody looks better than us. The other tributes have new district-themed costumes —

sexy red cowboy suits for District 10, shimmering deep sea–blue mermaid suits for District 4, iridescent gray coveralls with wheel-shaped crowns for District 6. Their chariots are tricked out, some menacing, others elegant, all of them eye-catching. Their glossy horses sport matching plumes and flowers, while ours are bareheaded.

The cart's much too small for the four of us. The horses dance nervously, jerking it around, making it treacherous to climb on. As one of them rears, Louella stumbles backward.

"Easy there," I say, catching her. "You got this."

"I don't think I do." Her knees give way and she sinks to the floor.

Drusilla yells at her. "On your feet, missy!"

I pull Louella up. "Look at me," I say. "In every way, you are a thousand times better than anybody in the Capitol. You are loved better, raised better, and a whole lot better company. You are the best ally I could ever hope for. Okay, sweetheart?"

She nods and straightens up. "You and me to the end. Right, Hay?"

"You and me to the end," I promise.

"Girls in front!" directs Drusilla.

Maysilee and Louella climb in the chariot and grab hold of the front railing. Wyatt and I follow and brace ourselves on the sides. Presentation takes a back seat to preservation as we try to maintain our footing. One of our horses bucks, banging a hoof into the cart and giving a shrill neigh. We're supposed to be moving forward, but it's all they can do to keep our team in check. The District 11 chariot disappears out the door before they finally release us.

We're late, but what can we do? The horses are supposedly trained to cover the parade route at a stately pace without guidance. Ours head straight into the night air without pausing, bypassing our second photo op.

For the first hundred yards or so, the nags get their act together and trot along in time to the music. I look up at one of the giant screens above the packed stands lining the avenue and see myself in my crappy costume, hunched over the railing. *Long shot*, I think, and force myself to stand up straighter.

The crowd looks drunk to a person, hooting and hollering, red-faced and sweating. People chuck bottles and trash at us. Some puke over the barricade set up along the parade route. For all their finery, the audience smells like the gang at the Hob on a rough Saturday night, a mix of perspiration, raw liquor, and vomit.

A guy trying to jab Maysilee with his cane face-plants onto the avenue and loses a front tooth. A near-naked woman makes lewd gestures at me. It's hard to ignore the mob, but District 12 is hanging in there until someone launches a firework that spirals right in front of our chariot and explodes in a burst of blue.

Our horses lose it, plunging to the side and fighting to stay vertical. I'm knocked to my knees, but manage to keep hold of the railing as our team breaks into a run. The crowd's going wild as we veer around the District 11 chariot and narrowly miss colliding with District 10, whose team also goes rogue. I want to protect Louella, but it's all I can do to hang on as we go thundering down the avenue.

Everything's a blur — the audience, the ground, the other chariots trying to clear out of our way. A siren wails, and I catch sight of red lights spinning, but all this seems to do is whip our team into a frenzy. I remember the parade ends at the circular drive that leads to President Snow's mansion, so I know we can't run forever, but how will we stop?

I look down as the spiked wheels of the District 6 chariot close in on ours, and I have my answer. I see the sparks, feel the axles shredding, and lunge for Louella, hoping to brace her. She's reaching for me just as the wheel collapses and we're catapulted into the air. Next thing I know, I'm lying on the ground, my hand in a puddle of blood as the lights of the Capitol flash like fireflies above me.

This is better, I tell myself. *Better than dying in the arena. Better than weasels and starvation and swords.*

I'm embracing that when I realize the blood isn't mine. That fate isn't mine. And the tribute who's escaped the arena is Louella.

A dead mockingjay chick, eyes still bright, feathers blue-black in the sunlight, clawed feet empty, on a bed of moss. Lenore Dove stroked its plumage with her fingertip. "Poor baby . . . poor little bird . . . who will sing your songs now?"

Louella looks so tiny, so still in the chaos around us. A fine job I did protecting her. Dead before we even made it to the arena. Who will sing your songs now, Louella?

I'm winded by the impact of the fall, bruised for sure, but nothing obviously broken. "Louella?" I say as I kneel over her. Knowing it's useless, I attempt to rouse her, try to find her pulse, but she has flown her body. Her vacant eyes confirm this as I slide the lids closed. One of her braids rests in the blood leaking from the back of her skull, which cracked open when she hit the pavement. The penciled black eyebrows jump out from her drained face. I arrange her braids, lick my thumb, and wipe a drop of blood from her cheek.

The shaft that connected our cart to the team apparently snapped, and our horses are long gone, leaving a trail of wreckage. Wyatt and Maysilee, who managed to hang on to the railings, extricate themselves from the ruins of our chariot, beat-up but alive. Wyatt picks up Louella's hat, which must have fallen off when we were thrown. As they join us, neither one has to ask if Louella's dead.

Maysilee pulls off one of her necklaces, a heavy strand of beads woven into purple and yellow flowers. "I was going to give her this. For her token. So she'd have something from home."

She kneels down, and I lift Louella's crushed skull while she places the beads around her neck. Fresh blood seeps into my hand.

"Thanks," I say. "She likes flowers." I can't speak of her in the past, not while she's warm and close.

"They're coming to get her," warns Wyatt.

I see four Peacekeepers making a beeline for us amidst the medics and handlers and dazed tributes. They want to take Louella away, to hide her tidily in a wooden box along with their crimes, and ship her home to District 12. They don't want to feature this death on the Capitol's watch, unplanned and highlighting their incompetence. This is not the blood they want to paint their posters with.

I scoop Louella up in my arms and begin to back away.

"It's no use," Wyatt says. "They'll still take her."

"She doesn't belong to them," snaps Maysilee. "Don't just hand her over. Make them fight for her. Run!"

So I do. And I'm a fast runner. The only kid who can beat me in footraces at school is Woodbine Chance. Well, he used to anyway. I run for Louella, but I run for Woodbine, too, because he'll never run again. I have no idea where I'm going. I only know that I do not want to give Louella to the Capitol. Maysilee's right. She doesn't belong to them at all.

Dodging any white Peacekeeper uniform, I weave past red-streaked bodies, past the wrecked District 6 chariot. Apparently, their horses leaped the barricades and plowed into the crowd. Medics swarm around, shouting and carrying stretchers with Capitol people, leaving the injured District 6 tributes where they fell.

My escape path leads me farther down the avenue toward the president's mansion. Several of the chariots are pulled over along the parade route. It's a clear shot to the mansion, but I'll never make it. The Peacekeepers' shouts get closer. Louella's growing heavy. My toes blister in the tight boots. My chest aches and I haven't drawn a full breath since I hit the ground. What difference does it make, me handing her over now or later?

Some of the big screens over the crowd have gone to the waving flag, but a handful of others still display the parade route. I catch sight of myself on one. Louella looks peaceful, like she's asleep in my arms. If this is still being recorded and possibly aired, at least in the Capitol, maybe it does make a difference if I resist as best I can. Maybe this is where I paint my own poster.

Ahead I spot the District 1 chariot, a glimmering golden thing drawn by snow-white horses. The tributes have dismounted and stand off to the side, except Panache, who's pulling on the bridles of the horses. "Come on," he yells at them. "Move it!" He no doubt wants to continue the parade, to be the only tribute who makes it to the president's mansion by chariot. A grand entrance for a future victor. But the horses resist, stamping their feet and throwing back their heads. Silka removes one of her fancy stiletto heels and begins to beat the flank of the outside horse, drawing blood. The horse neighs in pain and kicks, throwing the team into confusion. Silka's knocked to the ground and Panache has to dive sideways to avoid being trampled.

Peacekeepers on my tail, my arms giving out, I seize the moment and spring into the chariot just as the horses' distress overcomes their training. Panache had a great idea, and now I'm stealing it right out from under him. I want to be the tribute who arrives by chariot, and I want Louella to be with me, for all to see.

As the team jumps forward, I get tossed into the railing, letting it bear some of Louella's weight. I hear Panache's howl of rage behind me but ignore him. The horses resume their normal pace and I manage to straighten up. I lost my cheesy imitation coal miner hat in the accident and, rid of the headgear, our outfits become merely neutral, black and forgettable. Our tokens catch the eye — Louella's bright beaded necklace, my exquisite flint striker. For the first time, in the gorgeous rig, with our fine ornaments, we look like tributes of consequence. Not long shots. Or at least long shots you might consider sponsoring. A shame one of us is dead.

The horses come to a stop directly under the balcony. I look up and freeze, too intimidated to breathe. President Snow. Not on a screen, but in the flesh. The most powerful and, therefore, the most brutal person in Panem. He stands calm and erect, surveying the calamity of the opening ceremony. His head dips slightly and a lacquered silvery blond curl falls onto his forehead. Our eyes meet, and a smile plays on his lips. No anger, no outrage, and certainly no fear. I have not impressed him with my performance. The reckless mountain boy with the dead girl in his arms seems foolish, a trifle amusing, and nothing more.

Something steels inside me, and I think, *You are on a high horse, mister. And someday someone will knock you off it straight into your grave.* I dismount the chariot and lay Louella down, taking a step back so Snow can't pretend he doesn't see her broken little bird body. Then I gesture to him and begin to applaud, giving credit where credit is due.

Spin this, Plutarch, I think.

Suddenly, the president's expression changes. He turns his attention to the screen to my right, which features a shot of me from the waist up, clapping. His fingers move to the signature white rose in his lapel, straightening it as he looks down again. The blue eyes narrow, but he's not focused on my face. Is he looking at the flint striker?

I'm grabbed from behind and dragged away. Medics descend on Louella, but I know there's no bringing her back. I hate leaving her behind, but what would I do with her, even if I held on to her? Did her family get to see her send-off? Did mine? But they wouldn't have shown this in 12. They probably cut out when our horses bolted.

I struggle for a bit, then feel I'm working too hard. Going limp, I make the Peacekeepers tow me down the long road back to the stable. They catch on and flip me around, cuff me, and make me walk myself. That's when I become aware of the crowd, still in the stands, and hear the voices shouting.

"Hey, you, where are you from?"

"Over here, boy! What's your name?"

"Twelve, right? Are you from Twelve, kid?"

That catches my attention. Me? Are they talking to me? My head twists from side to side.

"Speak up, boy! Can't sponsor you if we don't know who you are!"

These people want to sponsor me? Send me food and supplies in the arena? Then bet on me like a starved dog in a fight? Maybe I should be grateful, or at least smart, but it's impossible with Louella's blood coating my hands. I hawk and send spit directly at a man's face, which is bloated and twinkling with tiny embedded mirrors. It lands on his cheek, and the crowd roars with laughter.

"You tell him!"

"I like your style!"

"Haymitch or Wyatt? Which are you?"

That last from some woman who wears a bird's nest on her head. She waves her Hunger Games program, which has a shiny gold *50* against a background of the flag of Panem on the cover. I'm working up another loogie when one of my guards warns, "Enough of that." I spit anyway. He elbows me hard in the side and the crowd cheers, I'm not even sure for who.

Fed up, the Peacekeepers toss me into a chariot filled with the

District 4 tributes, and I get to ride to the stable holding on to some guy's fake trident so I don't get tossed out again. He's not supportive of this, and we barely make it back before he shoves the butt of it into my solar plexus and I'm on the ground again.

"Nice one, Urchin," laughs a girl from 4, flipping her fishtail at me as they walk away.

Doesn't seem to be any particular reason to get up, so I just lie there, not caring if I get trampled or not. The memory of Louella's lifeless body under Snow's balcony has burned itself onto the back of my eyelids. Seems like that's all I'll ever see again.

Things settle down as the place begins to empty out. No one's in any rush to move an unruly District 12 tribute, though. After a while, Maysilee appears above me, her fountain of curls drooping to one side of her head. "Well, you got the last word tonight, Mr. Abernathy."

"Did I? What exactly did I say again, Miss Donner?"

"Don't mess with District Twelve."

Half my mouth manages a smile. "Scared them pretty good, you reckon?"

"I don't. But at least now they know we're here." She helps me to my feet. "I'd rather be despised than ignored."

Wyatt walks up. "Nice work with the crowd. Should bring you a few sponsors. Our odds have improved slightly with the crash. All of District Six is injured. Ten's beat up, too."

I resist the impulse to hit him. "And Louella's dead."

"Yes, but it's unlikely Louella would have killed any of us. And as an undersized thirteen-year-old from Twelve, she barely factored into the rankings anyway," says Wyatt.

I stare at him, amazed by his coldness. "Just what odds do you think your pa's giving on you winning, Wyatt?"

Shame creeps across his face. But he only says, "About forty to one."

"So, if you're the victor, and I'd bet a dollar on you, I'd get forty dollars back?"

"Forty-one, minus the Booker Boy fee."

"Guess you are a long shot, for your pa to hold you so cheap," I say.

"Never pretended otherwise." Wyatt turns and walks over to our van, one of the few still left in the stable.

"Boy, that was mean, even by my standards," Maysilee says to me. "You can't choose your parents."

"You could reject their business," I point out.

"I couldn't," says Maysilee. "I was going to spend the rest of my life behind that candy counter, no matter how much I hated it. And I'm guessing you'd have been wearing miner's overalls to your grave. We never, none of us, had any choices."

She follows Wyatt to the van, leaving me to ponder the possibility that I've out-meaned Maysilee. Not something to be proud of. But neither is factoring Louella's death into our odds. Her body's not even cold, and he's reduced her to a number. But she was not a number, she was a little girl I met on the day she was born when Mr. McCoy, his face alight with joy, held her up at the window for all us kids to see. A terrible, dark grief begins to well up inside me, threatening to drown me, but I force it back down. Swallow the sadness, clamp a lid on it, dam it up. They will not use my tears for their entertainment.

The effort leaves me dizzy, so I sit against a pillar and watch the birds flitting around the rafters. Horses and chariots disappear into the depths of the stable. Tributes straggle in from the avenue and join up with their districts. A couple of

Peacekeepers stroll around, cuffing the strays. They give me the eye but leave me be.

I find myself staring up at an electronic board that lists all the tributes. We don't seem to rate last names.

SECOND QUARTER QUELL
TRIBUTE ROSTER

DISTRICT 1		*DISTRICT 2*	
Boy	*Panache*	*Boy*	*Alpheus*
Girl	*Silka*	*Girl*	*Camilla*
Boy	*Loupe*	*Boy*	*Janus*
Girl	*Carat*	*Girl*	*Nona*

DISTRICT 3		*DISTRICT 4*	
Boy	*Ampert*	*Boy*	*Urchin*
Girl	*Dio*	*Girl*	*Barba*
Boy	*Lect*	*Boy*	*Angler*
Girl	*Coil*	*Girl*	*Maritte*

DISTRICT 5		*DISTRICT 6*	
Boy	*Hychel*	*Boy*	*Miles*
Girl	*Anion*	*Girl*	*Wellie*
Boy	*Fisser*	*Boy*	*Atread*
Girl	*Potena*	*Girl*	*Velo*

DISTRICT 7		*DISTRICT 8*	
Boy	*Bircher*	*Boy*	*Wefton*
Girl	*Autumn*	*Girl*	*Notion*
Boy	*Heartwood*	*Boy*	*Ripman*
Girl	*Ringina*	*Girl*	*Alawna*

DISTRICT 9		*DISTRICT 10*	
Boy	*Ryan*	*Boy*	*Buck*
Girl	*Kerna*	*Girl*	*Lannie*
Boy	*Clayton*	*Boy*	*Stamp*
Girl	*Midge*	*Girl*	*Peeler*

DISTRICT 11		*DISTRICT 12*	
Boy	*Hull*	*Boy*	*Wyatt*
Girl	*Chicory*	*Girl*	*Maysilee*
Boy	*Tile*	*Boy*	*Haymitch*
Girl	*Blossom*	*Girl*	*Louella*

Forty-eight kids. Minus one. I will never remember all of their names. Doubt they will remember mine. There are just too many of us.

A boy in electric-blue coveralls, about Sid's size, comes up to me, his handcuffs jingling a little. Another lamb for the slaughter. "Hi, I'm Ampert. I'm from Three."

I look behind him, but he's unchaperoned. Probably a bigger long shot than I am. I can't imagine what he wants but I hope someone would be friendly to my brother under these circumstances, so I say, "Hi, Ampert. I'm Haymitch. How old are you?"

"Twelve. You?"

"I turned sixteen yesterday."

"That stinks." He squats down beside me and fiddles with his cuffs. "I could open these in a jiffy if I had a hairpin."

I smile at his bragging. "Or a key."

"You sound like my father. He'll laugh when I tell him that."

I could point out that Ampert will never see his father again, but I've already exceeded my meanness quota for the day. It's kinder to humor him. I take a safety pin from my overalls and hold it out. "Try that, buddy."

His face lights up like he just got a new toy. He pops open the pin and begins to wiggle the point in a cuff lock. "They don't really teach us this in school. They focus on the technology we use in the factories. But my mother taught me. She's the mechanical one. I know lots of things that should be useful in an arena. If you'd like to be my ally."

So that's it. His fellow district tributes have rejected him, and he's on the hunt for someone more pathetic than he is. A District 12 coal miner seems a likely candidate.

I tell him, "I had an ally, and she's already dead."

"I'm sorry. I thought she was just knocked out. Louella McCoy, right? She's the one you made President Snow own?"

Well, I'll say this for Ampert — he doesn't miss a beat. "The thing is, Ampert, I don't know that I'm really ally material. I think you can do better. Why don't you go back and ask your district tributes to team up with you?"

"Oh, they already have. But I'm trying to build an alliance to counter the Careers. I've got all of Seven and Eight on board, and Eleven's thinking it over." He gives a final twist and the left cuff falls off his wrist. He holds up the pin in triumph. "Told you!"

"Whoa!" I exclaim. "How'd you do that?"

"I'd teach you if we had more time." Ampert pops the cuff back on before anyone else notices and pockets the safety pin. "If you change your mind, I'll be around." He scampers off, and I can see him reporting back to the other District 3 tributes, who crane their necks to check me out.

I don't know what that kid needs me for. Not my brain. Maybe, like Hattie, he thinks I'd make a good mule. But my ally days began and ended with Louella.

When I'm the last tribute left, a Peacekeeper orders me inside the van. She chains up me, Maysilee, and Wyatt, then looks around and frowns. "Where's your escort and your stylist? Your mentors?"

None of us answer. We don't know, and why should we?

Another Peacekeeper speaks up. "Drusilla took a powder after the crash. Magno Stift never showed." She consults a clipboard. "And I don't even see a mentor listed for Twelve."

"What are we supposed to do with them?" asks the first. "I'm off-duty in ten. There's an after-party for my squad, and I'm the only one who can make a good rum punch."

"Can't leave them here. Take them to their quarters, I guess. Let them figure it out."

The door closes and the engine rumbles to life. In the pitch black of the van, I lean my head back against the wall. All the miseries of the last two days can no longer be denied: the throbbing headache from the rifle butt at the reaping, the terror of the tasing, the heartbreak of my loved ones' good-byes, the toxic shower, the humiliating parade before Panem, the chariot crash, and worst of all, the horror of being soaked in Louella's blood. Everything hurts, inside and out.

We're unloaded on a street lined with candy-colored apartment buildings. The disgruntled Peacekeeper leads us past armed guards into a lobby with fake wood paneling and onto an elevator that smells like old socks and cheap perfume. She turns a key in the slot marked 12 and uncuffs us on the ride up. "We've been told your mentors are waiting for you here. They said no cuffs, but there are Peacekeepers a buzzer away and there are cameras everywhere." She nods to one in the corner of the elevator. No attempt has been made to conceal it. They want you to know they're watching. Or think they're watching, even if no one is.

"No Peacekeepers, no peace," I mutter.

The Peacekeeper gives a sharp nod. "Exactly."

When the doors open, she pushes us out into an entryway. A framed painting of a white poodle in a tuxedo hangs over a small table holding a bowl of wax oranges. "They're all yours!" she shouts, and the elevator doors close.

We stand abandoned, under the poodle's critical eye, waiting for the next round of abuse. In the quiet, I become aware of a familiar scent. It's the bean and ham hock soup my ma makes when someone dies. It can't be, of course. But still, with Louella's loss so new, something begins to unravel inside me. The tears I've been saving up since the reaping fill my eyes. This infuriates me, and I blink hard to hold them back.

Soft footfalls approach and a small young woman appears. I recognize her immediately. The black-haired girl from District 3 who won last year's Hunger Games. "Hello, I'm Wiress. One of your mentors."

It was an arena full of shiny surfaces. Lakes that reflected the sky, clouds that returned the favor, and everywhere, boulders and caves and cliffs overlaid with mirrors. When the tributes were lifted into the arena, they couldn't get their bearings. Every which way they turned, tributes in shimmering tunics stared back at them.

Watching back in 12, Sid had whispered, "I can't hardly look at this. Makes my eyes cross."

If it was disorienting to view from the outside, it was incomprehensible within. A giant silver Cornucopia held a bounty of supplies, but even navigating a path to it proved treacherous. A tribute would reach for a weapon and get a handful of air, leap into a clearing and smack into a wall, or dodge an attacker only to run straight onto their sword.

Most of the tributes went nuts, but not Wiress. She took it all in, then carefully maneuvered away from the Cornucopia, somehow finding packs of supplies where none appeared to be.

Eventually, a clumsy bloodbath ensued, but she was long gone at that point, exploring the arena bit by bit, until she settled on a rock jutting out over a lake, in full view of her competitors. Except . . . they never were able to see her. She'd found a blind spot, and although they'd come raging within a few feet of her, she avoided detection. She just sat there, quiet as a mouse, eating, drinking from the lake, and sleeping curled up in a ball.

The funny thing, if anything can be called funny in a Hunger Games, was watching the Gamemakers attempting to deliver her sponsor gifts, which they repeatedly failed to do. They were as blind to her spot as the tributes. And while they joked about it, you could see they were embarrassed to have a girl from District 3 understand their arena better than they did.

When the field cleared, it was down to Wiress and a boy from District 6. Wiress finally stood up, revealing herself, and the boy leaped for what he thought was her, cracked his head, and drowned in the lake. The victor's hovercraft flew around for about an hour trying to locate her before she walked back to the Cornucopia for a ride. Later, when asked how she'd figured out her strategy, she replied, "I followed the light beams." More than that, she could not, or would not, say. You wanted to cheer for her, given that she'd outsmarted the Gamemakers, but she was just too unnerving.

So, of course, they gave her to us. We always get the leftovers. Filthy costumes, broken-down nags, and now her. I try to roll with it, but it pisses me off. I don't want Wiress for a mentor. She's just another bizarre person to deal with when I'm already scraped raw. How can a girl who follows light beams help me anyway? How can a girl who left the arena without a scratch teach me how to protect myself? How can a girl who has fought no one, killed no one, mentored no one, mentor me? She can't, that's all.

I'm fixing to say as much when a second woman arrives. It takes a moment to place her. She's older, probably near Hattie's age. Then I remember a Games from when I was little, and a hysterical boy dressed in a suit made of seashells, who'd just been crowned in front of the entire nation of Panem. The hysteria had triggered when they'd played the recap of the Games, showing all twenty-three of his competitors' deaths. And this woman had held the boy and done her best as his mentor to shield him from the cameras, which were devouring every awful bit of it.

It's Mags, a victor from District 4. She looks at me sadly, knowingly, and then opens up her arms and says, "I'm so sorry about Louella, Haymitch."

For a moment, I teeter between anger and grief. But the dam finally breaks. I step into her embrace, drop my head on her shoulder, and begin to cry.

I don't cry much in general. Only when people die, and then I cry hard and fast and ugly, which is what I do now. Because Louella is dead and I was supposed to look out for her and I didn't. And while Lenore Dove will forever be my true love, Louella is my one and only sweetheart.

Mags just holds me while sobs rack my body and tears and snot drip onto her shoulder. Wiress takes Maysilee and Wyatt farther into the apartment, giving us a moment. "I'm sorry," I choke out. But Mags shakes her head and just keeps patting my back.

When I calm down some, she leads me through the apartment to a bathroom where a tub of steaming water awaits. She hands me a bag, saying, "Put your costume in here. Magno wants it back. Then bathe and join us."

When Mags goes, closing the door behind her, I throw a towel over the camera for some privacy, not caring at all if they punish me for it. Then I strip off the vile costume and shove it into the bag. Hot baths are a Sunday ritual in my house, cold water buckets doing for the rest of the week since it takes a lot of pumping and heating to fill our tin washtub. This deep porcelain version, nearly full to the brim, the creamy bar of soap, and the liquid shampoo are undreamed-of luxuries. I sink down into the tub, letting the heat envelop my body, as plumes of Louella's blood tint the pristine water pink.

I shut my eyes and try to empty my mind, so there is only warmth, and the murmur of distant voices, and the smell of soup mingled with the light flowery scent of the soap. This is all the world is. Nothing more. I must lie like that for a long time, because the water's cool and my fingertips wrinkly when I open my eyes again. I drain the tub and have a good scrub under the shower, cleansing myself of the insecticide, the road dirt, and the last traces of Louella's life.

After drying myself with the big cushy towel, I pull on the underwear and the plain black shirt and pants left for me, and slide my feet into a new pair of boots. As I open the bathroom door, I try to decide if I should feel embarrassed about my outburst, and realize I don't give a hang what anyone thinks anyway.

The apartment, which has a strange, impersonal quality, has been decorated by someone whose taste runs to fluffy things and burnt orange. The kitten and puppy knickknacks seem at odds with the bars on the windows. I follow my nose to the kitchen, where Mags, Wiress, and Wyatt sit around the table, eating.

"Join us," Mags says. "Your friend's in her bath now." I'm too tired to correct her about the status of my relationship with Maysilee — *classmate* seems more appropriate. She ladles out a giant bowl of what is, in fact, bean and ham hock soup.

"Mags ordered this specially from the kitchen," says Wiress.

"I did. It's comforting, I think." Mags sets the bowl in front of me.

"It is." I snuff up the steam, thinking about my twin sisters, and Pa, and Mamaw. And now Louella. I take a spoonful and let the taste of home course through me, strengthening me for what's to come. "What is this place anyway?" I ask.

"It's an apartment designed for temporary rentals. They've reserved it to hold the tributes this year," says Mags.

"We stayed in barracks last year, all twenty-four of us. This is more private," adds Wiress.

"Wouldn't call the bathroom private. I hung my towel over the camera."

"Those were just installed for the tributes. It's impossible to tell when they're watching," says Mags. "But it will all be recorded."

Wyatt pushes back from the table. "Guess I'll get my bath now."

I want to say, *I'm sorry about what I said earlier. About your pa taking bets on you.* But I haven't got the energy, so I let him go without a word.

My mentors let me eat in silence — soup, white bread and butter, and a big piece of peach pie to finish. I'm afraid they're going to launch into a strategy session, but Mags only says, "Why don't you go to bed now, Haymitch? We can talk in the morning."

She takes me to a room with two beds covered with fuzzy orange spreads, each with a pair of pajamas on it, and bids me good night. I change, slide in between the sheets thinking I'll never fall asleep, and go out like a light.

Lenore Dove says my dreams are like windows into my mind, too clear to need interpretation. Which is a nice way to say *really obvious.* Tonight, they center on fearful things that have happened — blown-up heads and chariot crashes — and fearful things I dread will happen in the coming days. Since I don't know exactly what I'll encounter when the gong sounds to start the Games, my brain borrows from past arenas. Weapons. Starvation. Mutts. The first two are ancient evils, but muttations, or mutts for short, are genetic atrocities created in the lab to entertain the blood-hungry Capitol audience. Like the face-eating weasels or, in Wiress's arena, the shiny silver beetles that swarmed the tributes, suffocating them. My brain fixates on the latter.

As the beetles suck the oxygen from my lungs, I wake up gasping. Wyatt snores in the other bed. That alone makes me think I was right about him not being my ally. How's he going to stay hidden in the arena if he's sawing logs like that? Of course, he was fake-snoring on the train when he eavesdropped on me and Louella. I look at him hard, but he appears to be dead to the world for real.

I could get up but I stay under the covers, grateful for some time to collect my thoughts. Things have unfolded so fast. I still can't completely wrap my head around the fact that Louella's gone. And now I have an offer from Ampert, who I couldn't help but like. I'm intrigued by his idea of a non-Career pack. I wonder if he'd take Wyatt and Maysilee as well. He doesn't seem too particular. The tributes from Districts 7 and 8 are nothing special. He must be going for quantity over quality. Although 11 . . . that might be a game changer. . . .

Still, I don't know about teaming up with them. Maybe I'll ask Mags what she thinks. Funny to have someone from 4 — a Career — as a mentor. Although she must've been a tribute early on and maybe there weren't always Careers. As for Wiress . . . I shouldn't judge her so harshly. If I could outsmart everybody the way she did without lifting a finger, of course I'd do it. But that seems more like something Ampert could pull off.

The smell of fried food gets me out of bed. I pull my clothes from last night back on and head to the kitchen. Mags and Wiress sit like they haven't been to bed, but the food has turned over. Big covered dishes of eggs, bacon, and crusty disks of potatoes set my mouth watering.

"Good morning, Haymitch," says Mags. "Please, help yourself."

I pile my plate high and stack a second with buttered toast and jam, pour glasses of juice and milk, but pass on the coffee. Again, they let me eat in peace, which I appreciate. Food always picks me up, so after a couple of platefuls, I think I might be able to survive the day. It's going to take a lot of energy to face the Careers, especially Panache. Pretty sure he thinks I owe him a chariot.

I'm sipping sugared hot tea when Maysilee comes in, dressed exactly like me, except for her necklaces. All in black, with her hair pulled from her face and her riding-crop marks, there's something tough about her. Or maybe she's always been tough, but the ruffles and bows just made her seem snooty. She'd look out of place behind the candy counter, which she clearly loathed. What did she dream of doing instead?

"Good morning, Maysilee. How did you sleep?" asks Mags.

"Better than the night before." Maysilee pours herself a cup of black coffee and wraps her hands around it.

"Aren't you going to eat?" I ask.

"I'm not a breakfast person."

You can see why she drives people nuts. If there's breakfast available in the Seam, everybody's just pleased to see it. I spread jam on another piece of toast. "That's going to come in handy in the arena. Especially if you're not a lunch or supper person either."

"If you can manage to get a bit more down in the next few days, it would be a good thing," says Mags.

Maysilee thinks about it, then serves herself a strip of bacon and takes a tiny bite. Not with her fingers, of course. I bet the Donners eat popcorn with a knife and fork.

Wyatt joins us, sheet creases in his face, also dressed in black.

"Nice outfit," I say, trying to lighten things up between us a little.

"It's the same as yours," he says defensively.

"Do we have to go around dressed like triplets?" asks Maysilee. "It was bad enough being a twin."

The Donner girls have a wide selection of matching outfits. "Thought you liked that," I say.

"My *mother* likes that," she corrects me.

Huh. Maybe she loads up on the jewelry because it's the only way she can be herself.

"The Capitol provided this clothing," says Mags. "Everyone will be dressed the same in training and the arena. But Magno should provide your interview costumes. Last year, he sent your district's tributes out in their training outfits. He's on probation for that, so, hopefully, he's finding you something worthwhile. You're due in training soon. Shall we begin?"

I try to focus. This will likely be all the help we get.

"I've mentored several times over the years," Mags continues. "In the early Games, I didn't ask the tributes what they wanted because the answer seemed so obvious. You want to live. But then I realized, there are many desires beyond that. Mine had to do with my district partner. Protecting him."

Wiress offers, "I remember I didn't want to die at night. I didn't want to die in darkness. The thought terrified me."

"So we'll ask you now, what do you want?" says Mags.

We sit in silence, each trying to formulate an answer. Yesterday, mine had to do with protecting Louella. Now I mainly think about the people I love, making my death as easy as possible for them.

I say, "I don't want my girl and my family to watch me die some long, horrible death. Like, I keep thinking about those weasel mutts a few years ago. . . . They'd never get over that."

"Yeah, if I'm going, I want to go fast," says Wyatt. "I don't want people who bet on my death being drawn out to make money on it."

It's a shocking thought. "Would your family take bets on that?" I ask.

Wyatt shrugs. "Somebody would. I'm sure somebody already has. On yours, too. That's how it works."

"I don't want to beg," says Maysilee. "Or plead for my life. I want to go out with my head up."

After a pause, Mags asks, "All right. Anything else?"

There is something else gnawing at the back of my brain. Something to do with Sarshee and Pa, with Lenore Dove's rising sun, with Maysilee's welts, and holding Louella up to the president. What was it Ampert said about Louella last night? *"She's the one you made President Snow own?"*

"I want all that, too. What you just said. But if I could, I'd also like to . . ." I glance at the camera in the corner. How do I say it when the Capitol might be watching? That I want to make the Capitol own what they're doing to us? "I want to remind people I'm here because the Capitol won the war and thinks that, fifty years later, this is a fair way to punish the districts. But I'd like them to consider that fifty years is enough."

That sounded sufficiently diplomatic. I wait for them to laugh or roll their eyes, but no one does.

"So you want to make them end the Hunger Games for good. How?" asks Maysilee.

"I don't know yet," I admit. "I guess, for starters, by reminding the audience that we're human beings. The way they talk about us . . . piglets . . . beasts. They called my fingernails claws. You saw how those kids outside the gym looked at us. Like they think of us as animals. And they think of themselves as superior. So it's okay to kill us. But the people in the Capitol *aren't* better than us. Or smarter."

"If anything, they're stupider," says Maysilee, who clearly doesn't give two hoots about the cameras. "Look at the mess they made with our reaping. The chariot parade. Or Wiress's Games last year. They couldn't even get her gifts to her. Show them something like that."

"Yeah, force them to admit we're people, too," says Wyatt. "And they're the beasts for killing us."

"Right. But I'm not as clever as Wiress. I can't outthink the arena," I say.

"Maybe you can," Wiress encourages me. "The arena's just a machine really. A killing machine. It's possible to outsmart it."

Wyatt rolls his coin over his knuckles. "The trick would be getting them to show it on camera."

"If it involves killing someone else, they'd show that," says Maysilee.

"Or killing yourself," adds Wyatt.

"It's something to think over carefully. You could easily put yourself or your allies at risk," warns Mags, nodding at Wyatt and Maysilee.

"Oh, Haymitch doesn't want us for allies," says Wyatt.

Really? That's where he's going? "Nice, Wyatt. So I'm the jerk? Not the meanest girl in town or the guy who sets the odds so scum can make bets on dead kids?"

Mags gives me a worried look. "It's a good thing to have allies. You may find yourselves gravitating toward one another anyway when you go into training."

Maysilee addresses Wyatt. "I could be your ally. If you're not too choosy."

"Okay," he says.

Even though everything I said was true, I regret saying it. It's not like I'm perfect. They both get under my skin, but I'm blaming them for too much. They didn't kill Louella or pick me in the reaping or create the Hunger Games. I need to back off. Besides, if I'm going to paint a decent poster in the arena, I'll need time, which allies could buy me.

"Okay, look," I tell them. "There's this kid from Three, Ampert, who wants me to join his alliance. He's got Seven and Eight. Eleven might be in. I don't know if I'm doing it, but I can ask if they want you guys. I can tell him you're both smart."

Maysilee gives a little shrug and Wyatt nods, saying, "Pack members have better odds. At least in the beginning. Someone to watch their backs."

I wish he'd shut up about odds. "I'll keep that in mind. So, what's training like?"

"They'll be holding it at the gym where they groomed you," Mags tells us. "There will be stations set up to allow you to prepare for what you'll face in the arena. Don't be distracted by what others are choosing; prioritize what you will need to survive."

"Some way to defend myself," I say.

"Or a good way to hide," says Maysilee.

"What's most important?" asks Wyatt.

Wiress breaks into a strange little song:

First avoid the slaughter,
Get weapons, look for water.
Find food and where to sleep,
Fire and friends can keep.

"I made that up for myself. Most important to least. So I would have a plan in the arena. I knew I couldn't fight in the bloodbath, which meant I had to get away from the Cornucopia quickly. I didn't end up needing a weapon except my brain. But you likely will. The Cornucopia might be your chance to grab one. If not, make something, even if it's just a pointed stick. Then find water. Water before food. You'll die of thirst much more quickly than you will of hunger. But then food. Fire can be good for light and cooking and heat if it's cold. But you might not need it at all and it could be dangerous if it reveals your position. Friends, for me, would have been very risky."

"But were at the top of my list," says Mags. "You must decide for yourselves."

"What about building a shelter?" asks Wyatt.

"There's a good chance you'll be on the move," Mags answers. "Your sleeping spot might change nightly. In my experience, allies to keep watch are far more important than a roof."

"You snore," I tell Wyatt.

"No, I don't. I was fake-snoring on the train."

"Bad news. You also real-snore."

"Like a bear," Maysilee confirms. "I could hear you through the wall."

"Try to find someplace loud to sleep," advises Mags. "Next to rushing water. Or muffle the sound in a cave."

"I'll put a blanket or something over your head," says Maysilee. "Or wake you if you're really loud."

"I forgot you'd be there," says Wyatt. "I guess friends top my list, too. What else happens in training?"

"Experts will be there to teach you how to use the weapons, show you how to make a fire," says Mags. "Look for clues to your arena. The Gamemakers sometimes hide little hints about the nature of the arena in their design. Not in the beginning. My Games were so long ago. Training, if you could call it that, was minimal back then. We didn't get any clues, in or out of the arena."

"Last year some of the survival stations had reflective items. Foil blankets. Metal bowls. And at the fire-building station, a little round mirror. I think that was a clue, but I didn't understand it until I saw the arena," says Wiress. "Inside, when I understood the nature of the place, my instinct was to walk toward danger, because, in fact, it was only a reflection of danger, not the thing itself. Trust your instincts."

"That is good advice in general," Mags says.

The intercom crackles to life and a voice announces that it's time to leave for training. Mags pins fabric squares with the number 12 on our backs. We're met by Peacekeepers at the elevator, loaded into the van, and transported to the gym.

As we step out into the sunlight, Maysilee gives Wyatt the once-over. "You need more attitude, Wyatt." He tries to look tougher. "No, that's worse," she says. "Push your jaw out. Stand up tall. Now stick out your chest." She musses his hair and pushes up his sleeves. "You've got some muscle from the mines. Show it off."

"Yeah, that's better," I admit. "The black clothes don't hurt."

"We're from District Twelve. The crummiest stinkhole in Panem," says Maysilee. "We're wild like our chariot horses. I slugged our escort and Haymitch called out President Snow. Nobody pushes us around."

"We're unpredictable," says Wyatt.

"Just a bunch of loose cannons," I agree.

The Peacekeepers open the doors and we head in, sending out our best loose-cannon vibe.

The place has been transformed. The makeover stations have been replaced with survival skills booths — fire building, knots, skinning animals, camouflage — overseen by trainers in fitted white jumpsuits. The far end of the gym has been reserved for various types of weapon instruction. The other tributes swarm around the booths, dressed in the same outfits but in an assortment of colors. I'm glad we got black because everybody looks sickly in snot green — sucks for you, District 1 — and the buttery yellow on District 9 makes them about as threatening as a hatful of baby chicks.

Nylon ropes divide the bleachers to our right into twelve sections marked with the district numbers. Ours sits closest to the door. The tribute bleachers are empty except for the kids from 11, who are gathered in a tight clump of dark green, heatedly discussing something.

"Are we always the last ones to arrive at everything?" complains Maysilee.

"Keep 'em waiting," I say. But we are consistently an afterthought. And no one has been waiting for us.

"Loose cannons," Wyatt reminds us. We straighten up and stride into the thick of it.

Mags is right. Here at the gym, we do stick to one another. We're the only ones we know. And at the Games, we're the least likely to kill one another.

"We should throw knives," decides Maysilee.

It's not a bad idea. Despite what I promised Ma, I'm not a complete stranger to knife games, although a fondness for my toes keeps me away from mumblety-peg. A target on an old shed or a tree — well, that's fair game. Blair's really good and I'm not too shabby myself. I think of my brand-new birthday pocketknife that I didn't get to throw even once, and hope Sid gets some joy from it.

As we weave our way to the knife range, I notice a few camera crews covering training and a smattering of Peacekeepers patrolling the gymnasium. To our left, the top section of the bleachers is full of Gamemakers draped in snowy gowns. They mosey around, drinking coffee and making notes on the tributes below. In a few days, we will each receive a score, one to twelve, which ranks our likelihood of winning the Games. People will use it as a guide on whether or not to sponsor us.

We join a group with the tributes from 7, clad in russet brown. Everybody sizes one another up while a Capitol woman, Hersilia, instructs us in knife throwing. Ampert said 7 had already agreed to join his alliance, and they make a favorable impression. They seem confident, but not full of themselves. One of them — a slim girl with a lot of glossy black braids and a small carved pin of a tree on her shirt — tells me her name, Ringina, so I tell her mine.

Once we all grasp the basics — how to hold the blade, the straight arm motion, no flicking the wrist — we line up to throw. On a stand, there's a basket of about a dozen different knives, but only one tribute can have their hands on a weapon at a time. You throw, then a guy in white collects the knife and returns it. Hersilia selects the model for the next tribute. A lot of knives bounce off the target, although Maysilee hits more than she misses, and, not to brag, I stick it every time. The throwing unwinds me a bit, since all my associations are good ones, hanging out with my friends in the woods and messing around. When Ringina hits the bulls-eye, I forget where I am and give her a "Nice shot."

As Ringina accepts the compliment with a quick grin, the energy shifts. I know I'm never going to kill this girl any more than I'm going to kill Maysilee or Wyatt. So I might as well be 7's ally and join Ampert's team for real.

I open the negotiation with "So, Ampert says you all are —" when there's a blur of snot green to my left, the clatter of knives as the basket's upset, and the sensation of a sledgehammer hitting my ribs.

If you've ever been sucker punched, you know there's the double outrage of the pain and the unfairness of the attack. As I lie gasping on the mat, watching Panache close in, my fingers grip a knife handle. Before I can rise, a Peacekeeper tases him and three more drag him off. Wyatt offers me a hand up as the other tributes gather the knives.

There's this moment, just as I get to my feet, where I look around, and I'm armed, and they're armed. A half dozen of us hold sleek, deadly knives. And I see that there aren't many Peacekeepers here today. Not really. We outnumber them four to one. And if we moved quickly, we could probably free up some of those tridents and spears and swords at the other stations and have ourselves a real nice arsenal. I meet Ringina's eyes, and I'd swear she's thinking the same thing. When Hersilia holds out the basket, it takes Ringina some effort to drop her knife in.

The two of us resume our places at the end of the line, hanging back a little, just out of earshot, as the training continues.

"Raise your arms," Ringina says.

I gingerly reach up, and she feels my rib cage where Panache's blow landed. "Not broken, I think." She steps back, her lips pressed tight in consternation. "We could've taken them."

The more I think it over, the more my dismay grows. Every year we let them herd us into their killing machine. Every year they pay no price for the slaughter. They just throw a big party and box up our bodies like presents for our families to open back home.

"We could've at least done some damage," I tell Ringina.

"At least a little. Possibly a considerable amount," someone says behind me. I turn to see Plutarch. He waves his camera crew over to record the knife training, but his attention stays on me. "The question is, why didn't you?"

Sore ribs and all, I think about punching the question right off Plutarch's face. Because the implication is clear: He isn't just asking why we didn't start a mini rebellion in the gym. He means back in District 12 as well. Why do we let the Capitol brutes rule us? Because we're cowards? Because we're stupid?

"Why do you submit to it all?" he presses.

"Because you have the guns," Ringina says flatly.

"Is it really about the weapons, though? I grant you, they're an advantage. On the other hand, when you consider the sheer difference in numbers . . . district to Capitol . . ." Plutarch muses.

Yes, we far outnumber the Peacekeepers in 12. I think about the weapons we could lay our hands on. Pickaxes, knives, possibly some explosives. But in the face of automatic rifles, aerial bombings, gases, and the Capitol's menagerie of mutts?

"I don't think we 'submit,'" I say.

"It's implied. You accept the Capitol's conditions."

"Because we don't want to end up dead!" I snap. "Do you really not see that?"

"No, I do. I see the hangings and the shootings and the starvation and the Hunger Games. I do," Plutarch says. "And yet, I still don't think the fear they inspire justifies this arrangement we've all entered into. Do you?" We stare at him. He's not taunting or mocking us, he's genuinely asking. "Why do you agree to it? Why do I? For that matter, why have people always agreed to it?" When we don't respond, he shrugs. "Well, it's something to think about."

"You're up, Haymitch." Hersilia offers me a knife. Which I could (a) throw or (b) drive into a Peacekeeper's heart, ensuring my immediate death. I'm a little wobbly but I still hit the target.

Plutarch waits for me at the end of the line. I try to ignore him, but he keeps yapping. "You put on quite a show last night."

"Yeah, well, I bet you card-stacked it right into a compliment for the president."

"No need to. The broadcast to the public ended when that firecracker went off. The Capitol News coverage is presenting the opening ceremony as flawless."

"I doubt that people who take Capitol News seriously will spend much time questioning that," I say. "They don't care what happens to us tributes, dead or alive." I wonder what they did with Louella's body. I hope it's been sent home to the McCoys. Their family plot's right next door to ours, so Louella and I will be reunited soon enough.

I start to turn away, but Plutarch lays a hand on my arm. "I'm sorry about Louella, Haymitch. She was a person of substance. I could see that right off."

Is he actually giving me condolences? "Why do you keep dogging me?" I snap at him. "There's a gym full of people just aching for some exposure. Why don't you spread yourself around a little?"

"I'm assigned to cover Twelve." He raises his hands and backs away. "But I'll try to give you some space."

Aggravated by his probing, I pull Maysilee and Wyatt aside. "Listen, if we join Ampert's alliance, these folks from Seven will be on our team. Now I'm going to introduce you to Ringina over there." I give Maysilee a hard stare. "You have to be nice. Don't comment on her hair, don't comment on her nails, don't comment on how she looks in brown, don't ask to examine her pin because you're an authority on jewelry."

Maysilee sniffs. "I like her hair."

"And, Wyatt, don't be weird. Don't start spouting out the odds on their deaths."

"Can I do other people's deaths?"

"No! Not yet. Maybe not ever. It's creepy! If you have to do odds, do gifts or sponsors or something," I say. "Forget about being loose cannons. We need to seem like people you'd want to be your allies. Like people you'd hope were beside you in a mine accident. Steady. Smart. Trustworthy."

Ampert, glowing in electric blue, runs up, swinging a loop of black cord over his head. "Hey, Haymitch! District Ten is in. They're the ones in crimson. I met them in knot tying. One of the guys, Buck, made me this lariat. I'm thinking of turning it into some kind of token, since I didn't bring one." He wraps the cord in loose bands around his hand, pulls it over his head, and drops his voice. "Then I can unwind it and use it in the arena."

Maysilee's lips twitch. "Well, you can't wear it like that. It's not the least bit ornamental. You look like a weasel caught in chicken wire."

"I do?" Ampert doesn't seem offended but shoots me a curious look.

"What did we just discuss?" I say to Maysilee.

She ignores me and, uninvited, uncoils the cord from Ampert's neck.

"This is Maysilee, from back home. Looking to ally up with you."

Maysilee examines the cord, testing its flexibility and twisting it between her fingers. "You could do a braid necklace. That's a one-strander. It would look something like this." She pulls out one of her necklaces, an elaborate black braided piece. A small, shiny medallion etched with a flower is embedded in it. "No flower, obviously."

"Okay," says Ampert. "Can you make me one?"

"I guess I could, but I don't have any tape, so you'll need to hold it down while I work," she says.

"I'll hold it," he answers.

"And there's nothing to hook it, so we'd have to tie it off, which is never my first choice."

Ampert digs in his pocket and holds up my safety pin from last night. "I've got this."

She considers it. "All right. Just be careful if you take it off or the whole thing could unravel. Come on." She heads for the bleachers, not even checking if he's following her.

"My father wants to meet you. He's at the booth with the potato," Ampert tells me, then scurries after her.

His father? A potato? Doubts crowd in again. What am I doing? Is Ampert just some deluded child who lives in a fantasy world? Before I commit myself, I need to know. So I introduce Wyatt to Ringina — keeping my fingers crossed that he'll act half-normal — and head off in search of a man with a potato.

After making a lap around the crowded booths, sure enough, I find one. A small man with black hair, his back to me, leans against a counter that holds a lone potato, no takers for his skills. I fiddle with a strip of bandage at the neighboring first-aid booth while I examine him. As he turns, I note the pair of steel-rimmed glasses. While he bears a strong resemblance to Ampert, this is not why he looks familiar. It's Beetee, a victor from District 3.

A cold dread washes over me as the puzzle pieces come together. Ampert is neither a lunatic nor a liar. His father has accompanied him to the Capitol because he's a victor. And therefore a mentor, assigned to coach his own child to his death in the Fiftieth Hunger Games.

Why Beetee's been tapped to man a booth with a potato, I've no idea, because he's supposed to be some kind of technological genius. The real question is: How did Ampert end up here with him? Two tributes reaped from one family . . . are they just the unluckiest family in Panem?

I give up on being covert and approach him. "You're Ampert's father?"

"I am. And no doubt you're wondering why I'm here, Haymitch." Beetee removes his glasses and polishes them on his shirt. "It's because I'm being punished for coming up with a plan to sabotage the Capitol's communication system. I'm too valuable to kill, but my son is disposable."

That pretty much answers my question. "That's terrible. I'm so sorry. He's a great kid."

"He is." Beetee's eyes find Ampert, sitting across from Maysilee on the bleachers, chattering away while she weaves the cord into patterns.

"And they made you be his mentor?" I ask.

"It's part of the punishment. Watching what are almost certainly the last hours of my son's life. They even gave me a booth in training, which mentors don't traditionally attend, so I wouldn't miss a minute. If I wasn't here to witness it, there would be no point."

I can't think of anything to say to comfort him, but I try. "This isn't your fault."

"But it is. Entirely. I took a risk. I didn't suspect that I'd been found out until the reaping. The timing was calculated. If I had known, I could have killed myself, and Ampert would be safe at home. That is how Snow works." He drops his head, resting his fingertips on the wooden counter to steady himself. I wait for him to disintegrate, but he only says, "Would you like to learn how to turn a potato into a battery? Light can be important in the arena."

Not really, Beetee, I think. *What I'd really like to do is run away from the raging pit of fire that is your life.* But that seems cowardly. Like what people back home are probably doing to Ma and Sid right now. So I say, "Okay. Will there be potatoes in the arena?"

"I don't know. I suspect this assignment was meant to demean me, which it doesn't. That may be its whole purpose. But if you can't find a potato, other things — a lemon, for instance — could work as well. Just don't eat anything after it's been used as a battery." He pulls out a small tray with little plastic packets. Each contains a couple of nails, a pair of copper coins, mini coils of wire, and two tiny light bulbs. "Two potatoes would provide more power."

"I guess if I can find one potato, I stand a good chance of finding two."

"If not, you might try cutting one in half." He produces a second potato and slides it in front of me, then offers me a thing that looks like a pencil with a small blade on the end. "For now we'll use both. Follow along."

Beetee tears open a packet and dumps the contents on the counter. His eyes flick up for a second. A Peacekeeper hovers at my shoulder. The slender knife twitches in my hand. Here I am again. Armed and with access. *"Well, it's something to think about. . . ."*

"Now, this battery is made up of copper, zinc, and the phosphoric acid in the potato juice, which is an electrically conductive solution. It makes it possible for ions to travel between the two metals. Our goal is to create a circuit and illuminate this bulb."

He's lost me already, but I nod like he's making sense.

"First, we need a space for the coin." Beetee cuts a coin-sized slot into the side of his potato and I copy him. "Then we wrap one of the copper coins in wire and insert it, leaving the long tail out."

I sink my wire-wrapped coin into my potato. "Does this mean it will be dark in the arena?"

"Oh, I have no actual knowledge of the arena. They say if you boil the potato, you can increase your output, so that's something to keep in mind."

"But if I could boil a potato, I'd already have successfully made a fire. So . . ."

A smile plays on his lips. "So you'd have achieved an alternate light source, and this whole potato exercise would be a waste of your time."

"I didn't mean that. Sorry."

"You needn't apologize for being astute. I'm just glad you're paying attention."

I feel the Peacekeeper move on. "Wiress said there would be clues about the arena in training."

"Well, I would listen to her. Having been her mentor, I know how clever she is." He holds up a nail. "This is galvanized. Coated in zinc. Don't let it touch the coin. These needn't be a coin and a nail. What you need is copper and zinc. Strips of metal work just as well. You might be able to forage some in the arena, if you get beneath the scenery." He sticks the nail into the potato, a few inches from the coin. I follow suit.

"She also says every arena is just a machine."

"Yes, they're all machines of a sort."

I think back to our conversation in the kitchen, when I said I wanted to outsmart the machine and make the Capitol look stupid. Now that just seems like an empty gesture. Wiress spent a whole Games doing that, far better than I ever could, and what did it get us? Besides, whatever little thing I might manage, it'd be too easy to keep off camera. The real coup would be to . . . "So, if it's a machine, it can be broken, right?"

Beetee eyes Ampert. "Yes, in theory. Practice is always a bit trickier. Now let's connect our potatoes." He attaches the wire from his coin to my nail and links a third wire to his nail.

Suddenly, I remember a clip of Beetee's Games. He somehow scavenged parts from his arena and electrocuted all his remaining competitors. I realize if I'm serious about breaking the machine, I will need this man who once not only outsmarted, but hijacked his own arena. Because even if I'm naturally smart enough, I'm still just a poorly educated boy from the hills, who had no idea you could turn a potato into a battery.

"How, Beetee? How can I break it?" I say under my breath. "I don't know anything about machines."

"I'm sure you do without realizing it. A screw is a simple machine. A wheel and axle. A lever. Are you familiar with a water pump?"

"Too familiar."

"That's a lever. It helps create a partial vacuum and water is drawn upward. Some machines take more know-how than others."

"I know how a white liquor still works. Does that count?"

I catch a ghost of a smile. "I don't see why not." Beetee takes the wire from my coin and the one from his nail and attaches them each to one of the little wires poking out of the base of a tiny bulb. "And here we go." It emits a faint glow.

Ma would love this. Think of the money we could save on candles. But this will not destroy an arena.

"What would break it, Beetee?" I press.

Beetee leans over, lifts his glasses, and peers under them as he scrutinizes the battery. "The circuit? Well, you'd only need to disconnect one piece — say, remove a wire — and the whole battery goes dead." I realize there's another Peacekeeper behind me, and Beetee's words are for her benefit. "Remember, we're converting chemical energy into electrical energy to illuminate the bulb. You need to keep the circular path intact."

The Peacekeeper moves in closer, her nose inches from the battery now, her interest attracting a quartet of tributes in peach outfits. District 8. My unofficial allies, if things work out.

"Can we try that?" one asks.

"Of course," says Beetee. "Well, thank you for dropping by, Haymitch. Come back if you'd like to practice. And happy belated sixteenth birthday." I guess Ampert told him. He holds out his hand for me to shake. "That's funny. I was reaped the day you were born."

As I grasp his hand, I feel something, palm it, and conceal it in my pocket. "Thanks, sir," I say before walking away, my fingers probing the plastic packet, bumpy with coins and nails. A little birthday present from Beetee. If I can find some way to smuggle it into the arena, convince people I scavenged the stuff — the coins might be tricky but I can maybe dig up some other copper — and find a potato, I'll be halfway to a really dim bulb. I'm pretty sure my flint striker's a faster route to light, but possibly those kids from 8 could use it.

Up on the bleachers, Maysilee puts the finishing touches on an expertly woven braided necklace. Truly, it could pass as anyone's token from home. She holds it up for inspection.

Ampert strokes it in admiration. "It's beautiful. And perfectly symmetrical. I wouldn't believe it's all one strand. You're really clever!"

"And you have good taste," she says, slipping it over his head.

"I wish you were my sister," he says simply.

A funny look crosses her face. Bet she's never heard those words before. I wait for a cutting remark, but she only says, "I'll be your sister."

"Great. I'm going to show my father!" Ampert gives her a hug, which she stiffly returns, then runs off.

Her brow wrinkles. "His father?"

"It really is his pa," I tell her. "Remember Beetee, the victor from District Three? Got out of line. They're punishing him by making him mentor Ampert."

"That's a special kind of vicious. Would you want your family to be here?"

"I can't think of anything worse."

A Gamemaker announces lunch and we're directed back to our assigned bleachers, where a Peacekeeper delivers four boxes. I'm still full of breakfast, my gut hurts from Panache's attack, and the sight of Louella's unclaimed lunch box kills my remaining appetite.

A parade of blue, brown, peach, and red uniforms makes its way to the foot of our bleachers. I sort out 3, 7, 8, 10.

"Can we join you?" asks Ampert.

"Sure," I say. If they're going to be our allies, be good if we can bond a little. They clamber up beside us and everybody shares their names, most of which I immediately forget. The kids from 10 are bruised and scabby from the chariot debacle but look like a sturdy enough bunch.

From the next section, District 11 pretends to ignore us, but as they've all gone quiet, I guess they're eavesdropping. Trying to figure out what kind of allies we'd make.

"Ampert, this is your show," I say. "Why don't you tell us what you've got in mind?"

I like how even though he's only twelve, he jumps right in. "It's like this. A disproportionate amount of the time, the Careers win. But they're only one quarter of the tributes. We've got three times their numbers. So the idea is, we get the rest of us together and, for a change, we hunt them down instead of letting them hunt us."

"Can we do that, do you think?" asks a girl from 10.

"Why not, Lannie?" replies Ampert.

Why not? I think about how the districts outnumber the Capitol by far more than three to one.

"We don't have to buy into their mind game, that somehow they will always defeat us," Ampert declares. "Everyone acts like the odds aren't in our favor, but I'm sure we can beat those odds!"

At the word *odds*, Wyatt seems to blink awake. "Well, we'd have to factor in their stature, training, temperament, and sponsor gifts. But even given that, if there are enough of us . . ." His eyes get a faraway look.

"Yeah, this is normal for him," I tell the group. "He's working out the odds of the twelve Careers against the rest of us." Everyone waits respectfully.

"Yes, it can be done. We could do it. It's still not a probability, but it's a solid possibility," reports Wyatt. "Especially if we can get all nine districts to agree."

"If we kill all the Careers," asks Ringina, "what do the rest of us do then?"

"Have another meeting," says Maysilee. "At least this alliance gives us something to do besides freak out."

"Right now, we don't have nine districts, though," Wyatt reminds us. "Just five."

"I've asked the others, but not everybody wants to join," says Ampert. Our attention turns to the bleachers stretching across the gym. At the far end, the Careers mirror us, having assembled for lunch. Snot green mixed with the purple of 2 and 4's deep-sea blue. Districts 11, 9, 6, and 5 remain unattached. We watch as a few members of the Careers toss their empty lunch boxes to the gym floor, then walk down to where District 6 sits and steal a couple of the kids' lunches. Games or no Games, if you've got a decent bone in your body, you hate a bully.

 District 6 is composed of four puny kids whose rickety limbs suggest they've never seen sunlight. Victims of last night's chariot episode, they're bandaged in enough gauze to choke a horse. One has a twisted foot, and I remember another collapsing on the shower floor, wheezing from the insecticide. I'm tempted to write them off entirely—what could they possibly bring to the alliance except neediness? But I snag on the shade of their outfits. Dove color. Seems like a sign.

"Six said no?" I ask Ampert.

"They said they want to remain neutral so the Careers don't target them."

"We can see how that's working out," I say.

A bone-thin little girl in Lenore Dove's color collapses on the bleachers, sobbing. I grab my untouched lunch box, scoop up Louella's, and make my way down the bleachers. The crying girl recoils as I approach, and I hold out Louella's lunch. "Here. We had a couple extras." She hesitates, then takes the box with a shaking hand. The wheezing boy accepts the other. "You all managing after the accident?"

The girl nods. "We're sorry our chariot hurt your friend."

Frail she is, but considerate. "Not your fault. Never thought for a minute it was."

"Thanks for not blaming us," she says.

"Blaming you? Seems like we're all in this together," I say. "You know, we've got a pretty good alliance in the works. I understand you're trying to stay neutral, but really that just makes you a target for everybody. Anyway, the invite's still good."

By the time I make it back to my gang, four broken doves are on my tail. They perch on the seats, whisper their names — Wellie, the crying girl; Miles, the asthmatic boy; Atread and Velo, the remaining boy and girl. Then they dig in to their lunches.

"Six makes six," says Wyatt.

"We need a name," says Ringina. "If they're the Careers, who are we?"

People toss out ideas for names. Now that we're allies, District 12 offers Loose Cannons, 10 comes up with Dark Horses, and 7 volunteers Invaders.

"No," says Wellie, intensely. "Those all sound like we're trying to be tough. But we're not tough compared to the Careers. What we are is inexperienced, not trained from birth to win the Games."

"Is that a good selling point?" asks Lannie.

"In a way," says Ampert. "For one thing, it means we haven't spent our whole lives buying into the Games as something we aspire to."

"We're not collaborators," says Ringina.

"Right. But we'll fight if we have to," says Ampert. "We need a good name for people who are just starting something hard. A district name."

"Like Neddie Newcomer," I say without hesitation. The others laugh. "No, it's a real thing. In the mines, if you've just started, they call you Neddie Newcomer. My pa used to call me that whenever he'd teach me something new. Like, 'Come on, Neddie Newcomer, let's learn to tie those boots.'"

"I like it," says Wellie, a smile transforming her tear-stained face. "We're the Newcomers."

Ringina thinks it over, then grins. "And proud of it."

Everything feels better after lunch. It's less that I don't have to fear half the tributes than that I don't have to think about killing them. The latter is much worse. Now I can join my allies at the booths and know they've got my back as we learn to make snares, throw axes, and set a broken leg.

The four tributes from 6 stick to me like glue. My own little dove-colored flock. I hope they don't all think I can protect them when we hit the arena, because I can't.

Wyatt seems to have found his people. Ampert's co-tributes from 3 have a fascination with his odds system, and he seems happy to share it with them. Number freaks find one another, I guess.

It's Maysilee who surprises me. Back home, she isn't popular, she's known. She's not respected, she's feared. Not deferred to, but avoided. Here, following Ampert's lead, kids bring her their district trinkets and ask her to make them special, and she agrees. The girl must know fifty ways to braid, twist, and loop a cord into a piece of finery. She sets off their humble offerings from home with her fancy patterns. District pride runs deep. From 6, which covers transportation, Wellie has an old bicycle bell, Miles a tin train whistle. Livestock-loving District 10 brought horseshoes; the lumberjacks of 7, carved wooden trinkets. The girls from District 8 have little dolls in beautifully sewn outfits. A kid from 3 has a doorknob, but I'm not sure how that reflects technology. Whatever they present her with, Maysilee gives dignity to their tokens, and even though she still offers a fair amount of unsolicited fashion advice — two girls change their hairstyles and a boy promises to stop biting his nails — our allies adore her.

By the end of the training session, District 11 hasn't said yes, but they haven't said no either. If they're in, I wish they'd say so. We could use more brawn. I saw Hull, the guy who kicked Panache in the shower, fling a pitchfork and decapitate a dummy. Why pretend that's not what we're here for?

All of us Newcomers stand a little bit straighter by the time we head back to our vans. Even locked in the dark, Maysilee, Wyatt, and I continue to make plans, sharing information about our allies and working on a strategy. In no time at all, the van pulls to a stop.

"That was quick," says Maysilee.

The door swings open, and a Peacekeeper gestures for me to get out. Wyatt makes to follow, but the Peacekeeper holds up a hand. "No, just Abernathy."

This isn't good. I slide out of the van in front of a white marble building, far more imposing than our tribute apartment. It stretches the length of the block, a single structure accessed by a huge pair of wooden doors inlaid with a pattern of golden stars. I catch a glimpse of Wyatt's furrowed brow as the door slams shut and the van speeds away. What's going on? Where am I?

Two men in violet uniforms stand in silent attendance at the entrance. As if responding to some unheard signal, they haul open the doors to reveal Plutarch Heavensbee. He approaches me, his face unreadable.

"Hello, Haymitch. I'm afraid there's been a last-minute schedule change."

"Just for me?"

"Just for you. It seems the president had second thoughts about your . . . performance."

Louella under the balcony. Snow up above. While I applauded for all the Capitol to see.

Plutarch doesn't need to explain further. This is where I pay for painting my poster.

A fragile collection of muscles and bones, a few quarts of blood, wrapped up in a paper-thin package of skin. That's all I am. As I pass through the doors of this marble fortress, I have never felt more breakable.

My eyes travel up the walls to the lofty ceiling over the entryway. No poodles or oranges here. Just more marble and huge urns filled with bunches of flowers the size of bushes.

A servant in a starched apron runs a feather duster over a naked statue. She catches my eye, her lips parting in pity. Her tongue's missing. She's an Avox, one of the mutilated prisoners forced to wordlessly serve the Capitol for life. Will they take my tongue? The thought turns my mouth bone-dry. Dying at the end of Panache's sword now seems like a mercy.

"This way," says Plutarch.

The carpet has the soft spring of a bed of moss, and it absorbs my footsteps as if I'm already gone and beyond making a sound. One of the ghosts that inhabit Lenore Dove's songs. She once told me about being arrested by the Peacekeepers back home, how frightened she was at first. Then she remembered she'd read that sometimes the only thing you can control is your attitude to a situation. "Like I could decide whether I was scared or not, no matter what happened. I mean, I was still scared, but it helped having that to chew on."

I try to chew on it, but there's too much adrenaline pumping through my veins. *Help me, Lenore Dove*, I think. But she can't. No one can.

Plutarch leads me down a long, arched hallway lined with life-sized paintings of haughty people in fine, old-fashioned clothes. Each holds an object — a scale, a harp, a ruby-studded cup — that seems meant to define them.

Plutarch gestures indifferently. "Meet the Heavensbees," he says.

Wait . . . the Heavensbees? Is this his family? And could this actually be his house?

There's no shortage of Heavensbees; they watch over us through several halls, flaunting their signature possessions — a leafy branch, a glossy white bird, a sword, is that a turkey leg? Dripping in wealth, every last one of them. We pass doorways, some tightly sealed, some flung open to reveal roomfuls of elegant furniture and twinkling crystal lights. Other than an occasional Avox slinking in the shadows, it's deserted.

I think about how many people spent their lives building this place, how many died before its completion, so that the Heavensbees could have somewhere to hang their pictures. Their smug, satisfied, ridiculous pictures. Well, the joke's on the Heavensbees. Now they're dead, too.

Finally, we turn into a room where an old man with a white beard holding out an open book smiles down from his portrait above the fireplace.

"Trajan Heavensbee," says Plutarch. "I'm his great-, great- — I can never remember how many greats. Anyway, he was one of my grandfathers. The only one who's been of any use really. This was his library. It's a good place to talk."

Talking isn't torturing, so I calm down a little. The walls come into focus. They're not lined with instruments of pain but towering shelves of books. Thousands and thousands of volumes, floor to ceiling. In the corner, a golden staircase spirals up a column of white marble and leads to a balcony that runs around the room. A gold eagle perches on the railing at the top of the stairs.

This room is Lenore Dove's dream come true. A world of words to wrap herself up in. Each book's as precious as a person, she says, as it preserves someone's thoughts and feelings long after they're gone. The Covey have a collection of them, ancient things with cracked leather bindings and paper delicate as moth's wings. The family treasure.

Although most of us learn our letters in school, there aren't a lot of books in 12. Sometimes one appears at the Hob, and if I've got anything to trade with, I snatch it up to save for Lenore Dove's birthday, regardless of the subject, since they're so hard to come by. There was a paperback guide to raising poultry once, and even though it mostly talked about chickens and she's a goose girl, she loved it. Another time, I found a collection of maps from long before the Dark Days, pretty useless now. But I really struck gold last year with a small volume of poems by the long dead. Some of those made it into songs.

I remember the joy on Lenore Dove's face when I gave her the poetry, the kisses that followed, and feel stronger. They can't destroy what really matters.

"Do you read, Haymitch?" Plutarch asks.

"I can read."

"No, I meant, do you like to read?"

"Depends on what."

"I'm the same," says Plutarch. "Reading in general isn't a popular pastime in the Capitol. It's a shame. Everything you need to know about people is right here in this room." He turns a knob shaped like a goat's head on what I took to be a desk built into the bookshelves. The top splits in two and a tray full of sparkling bottles rises in its place. Plutarch pours himself a glass of amber liquid. "Can I offer you something?"

"I don't drink." Professional curiosity wins out, though — I'm a bootlegger, after all — and I cross to examine the booze. What we call white liquor's as clear as water, but his bar boasts every color of the rainbow. I don't know if these have been dyed or aged or mixed with other things, like herbs. It's all white liquor, only dressed up. The bottles have little silver nameplates on chains. Vodka. Rye. Cognac.

Then I spy a name I recognize, even though I've never seen the stuff. I lift the bottle and let the light dance off its rosy depths.

"It's called nepenthe," says Plutarch. "You probably haven't heard of it."

You'd be wrong there, Plutarch. Not only have I heard of it, I know it from the poem that gave my love her name. I'm tired of being patronized, so I decide to put him in his place. "You mean, like '*Quaff, oh quaff this kind nepenthe . . .*'?"

Plutarch's eyebrows shoot up in surprise. He completes the line. "'*. . . and forget this lost Lenore!*'"

Now I'm surprised, and a little unsettled. I guess, with all these books, her poem could be here. But for him not only to have read it, but memorized it, unnerves me. I don't like her name in his mouth.

"Of course, it's unclear in the poem if nepenthe's the liquor or the drug added to the liquor," he continues.

I remember having this same discussion with Lenore Dove. She said *quaff* means *to drink*, usually something with alcohol. And the guy telling the story in the song is trying to stop thinking about how he lost his true love.

"I think the important part is it makes you forget terrible things," I say.

"Exactly. I'm sure this is just a poor imitation. Grain alcohol colored with berries. In the old days, it actually contained morphling, but the stuff was so addictive it was banned. May I ask how you know that poem, Haymitch?"

"Everybody knows it in Twelve." That's a big lie, but I want him to think we all learned it in a book, like he did.

"Really? Huh. Well, I've got something you'll want to see. It's in the conservatory."

Sure, the conservatory. Whatever that is. He leads me out a side door, down a narrow hallway, and into a room whose domed ceiling frames a piece of the evening sky. Glass curves around to form the walls as well, revealing a garden of bright flowers and trees outside. Seems like overkill, since the room's already filled with plants that glisten in the humid air. Birds fly freely among the overhead beams, chirping their heads off. Little tables and chairs covered in curlicues surround a fountain that splashes water into a pool. One table holds a telephone shaped like a sleeping swan, its head and curved neck forming the receiver. Something buzzes near my ear and I swat it away.

It's like they've tried to bring the whole outdoors indoors. Why? Is opening a door and walking through it too much trouble? Fools and their money are soon parted, Ma would say.

"Come, look at this." Plutarch waves me over to a plant that hangs from a beam in a basket near the swan phone. From the long, shiny green leaves dangle pinkish pods, each equipped with what looks like a little lid. A small pool of liquid has collected at the bottom of each pod. As I inhale the faintly sweet, faintly rotten smell, Plutarch points to one. "They put out a nectar. Insects adore it. But the surface is slippery, and they fall into the pod and can't get out. They drown and are consumed by the plant."

"I think I'm missing something."

He taps an engraved nameplate on the side of the pot. Somebody in this place must have a full-time job labeling things. It reads *NEPENTHES*. I have to think this over.

"Well," I conclude, "that's one way of drowning your sorrows."

Plutarch chuckles. "You're the first person who's ever gotten the joke."

There he goes again. Trying to make me feel human.

"Why am I here, Plutarch?" I ask.

Before he can answer, someone else interjects, "For me."

I don't recognize the voice at first because its smoothness has deteriorated into a raspy growl. I turn and see President Snow leaning against the doorway, wiping his brow with a handkerchief. Once again, I'm rattled by being in his presence. The power of his position. The record of his cruelty. Evil in the flesh. Was my crime really so great that it requires a personal meeting? Especially when, on closer observation, he's clearly unwell. Perspiring and breathless and white as a sheet. His regal bearing abandoned as he hunches over his gut. For once, despite his cosmetic treatments, he looks his fifty-eight years.

"Oh, Mr. President," says Plutarch. "Are you feeling all right? It's the heat. Let's find you a seat." He hurries over and repositions a chair by the fountain. "I meant for you to use the library. It's cooler in there. Would you prefer that?"

The president seems too preoccupied to respond. He takes uneven steps toward the fountain and his whole body seizes up for a second. Blood trickles from the corner of his mouth onto his white shirtfront as he drops into the chair.

"Can I get you anything? Maybe an icepack?" asks Plutarch. "There's a powder room just over —" Snow leans forward and vomits a foul mess into the fountain. "Oh, okay."

Glad I don't have to clean that up.

Sweat streams down Snow's waxy face. But there's no embarrassment or apology. No effort to disguise this moment of weakness. It's almost like he wants us to see it. I'll probably be dead soon. Is it for Plutarch's benefit?

The president slumps back in the chair, panting. "Too hot."

"Right, let's get you back in the library." Plutarch hoists the president to his feet and gets his shoulder under an armpit. "Haymitch." I'm not being asked, I'm being ordered. I secure Snow's other side, holding my breath to avoid inhaling the noxious smell of puke and flowery perfume that rises from him. Bodily contact with him in this state makes me a little braver. He's just a man, as mortal as the rest of us. For all I know, he's on his way out right now.

Plutarch and I haul the president back into the library, where we deposit him on an embroidered couch.

"You need a doctor, Mr. President," Plutarch advises.

"No doctor," croaks Snow, grasping Plutarch's arm. "Milk."

"Milk? Haymitch, check the bar. We keep some for milk punch. The refrigerator's on the right."

I take my time, playing the confused district piglet who doesn't know left from right and, even when he's worked that out, can't figure out how to spring the paneled door that conceals the fridge. When I finally open it, I spot the milk in a pint-sized white china pitcher. A golden staircase wraps around the cylinder, and an eagle perches on the lid. A replica of the steps in the corner of the library.

I glance around the refrigerator door as Snow goes into a coughing fit while Plutarch hovers over him.

This is probably the best chance I will ever have to fight back against Snow directly. *Here's to you, Louella.* I tip open the eagle lid, down the milk, and wipe the moustache from my lip. Then I close the door, holding out the pitcher helplessly. "It's empty."

Plutarch's eyes widen in disbelief; he knows full well what I've done. I wait for him to rat me out. Instead, he murmurs in exasperation, "Those servants!" and disappears out the door, shouting for more milk to be brought. Like I said, unpredictable as lightning.

I'm left alone with a retching Snow. It's scary watching him possibly die. It's even scarier that I can resist helping him. Before the reaping, I bet I would have been right in there. Louella's death changed me. Maybe I'll end up being victor material after all.

Snow gags, empties a crystal bowl of waxed pears onto the table, and vomits a new wave, more blackish than bloody, into it. I wonder what old Trajan Heavensbee thinks of that. Keep smiling, Trajan — he's the president, after all. Snow's breathing calms. Ridding his body of that last batch seems to have improved his condition. He takes in the room, the portrait, me. Swabs his mouth out with the handkerchief and stuffs it in his pocket.

"Sometimes the cure is worse than the disease," he muses.

"What disease?"

"Incompetence. You can't ignore it, or it spreads."

Plutarch comes back carrying a second pitcher of milk. "There was some in the billiard room."

Snow chugs the milk and holds out the empty pitcher. "Another. And some bread."

Plutarch looks at the reeking bowl. "Are you sure, Mr. President? Sometimes with stomach illnesses, it's best to —"

"Not an illness. Food poisoning. A batch of bad oysters. But I've fared far better than Incitatus Loomy."

"The parade master?" asks Plutarch, a funny look crossing his face.

"Was he?" Snow hands him the bowl. "Bring what I've asked."

When Plutarch goes, Snow peruses the wall of books before him. "Look at them all. Survivors. During the Dark Days, people burned books to stay alive. We certainly did. But not the Heavensbees. They remained stinking rich, even when the best families were reduced to squalor." He removes a small bottle from his pocket, uncorks it, and swallows the contents, shuddering as it settles. "Classmate of mine, Hilarius, was one of them. Useless whiner." He blots his puffy lips on his cuff. "At least Plutarch comes in handy occasionally, don't you think?"

Plutarch handy to me? What does Snow know?

"I think he believes you catch more flies with honey than with vinegar," I respond.

Snow snorts. "Ah, the homey aphorisms of District Twelve are alive and well."

I don't know what an aphorism is — some sort of saying? Lenore Dove would know. But I can tell my way of talking is being sneered at, even if I don't know exactly what he means.

"I'd be surprised if anything much has changed there," he continues. "Nothing but coal dust and miners soaked in rotgut liquor from the Hob. Everybody just waiting to be subsumed by that ghastly wilderness."

His insult disturbs me less than his familiarity with District 12. Miners soaked in rotgut liquor from the Hob — that's us, all right. The worst of us, anyway.

"Come sit down, where I can see you."

Again, not an invitation, an order. I set the milk pitcher next to the nepenthe on the bar and circle around to sit on a sofa across from the president. The embroidered pillow at his elbow features the same image of the golden staircase as the pitcher. Matchy-matchy, as Maysilee would say.

Snow's eyes zoom in on the flint striker, as they did last night. "That's a striking necklace."

Striking . . . flint striker . . . perhaps he's recognized its true purpose and will have it banned from the arena.

He holds out his hand. "May I have a look?"

I could brush Maysilee off, but not the president. I untie the knot in the leather shoelace, give the flint striker a good squeeze in case this is good-bye, and pass it over.

Snow rubs his thumbs over the bird and snake heads. "There's a pretty pair." He flips it. "And an inscription."

An inscription? I must've missed it in the whirlwind of reaping day. Without asking for permission, he pulls a pair of specs from his breast pocket and tilts the striker to catch the light. "Ah, very sweet. From L.D. Who might that be?"

Lying to conceal her won't help. Even though they didn't air it to the country, I bet they showed Snow what happened during the reaping. Me trying to save a girl from the Peacekeepers. Her reaction to my reaping. Twelve's a small district. If he has a mind to, he will track down my girlfriend.

"Lenore," I say.

"But Lenore what? No, no, don't tell me. Let me guess. D . . . D . . . That's a tough one. None of the usual suspects, but they so rarely are. I can think of plenty prefaced by *deep* or *dark*. Deep blue. Dark green. But that's not how they work. Perhaps something in nature? Like amber or ivory. Daffodil . . . dandelion . . . diamond? No, that's no color at all, really. All right, I'm stumped. Lenore what?"

The milk has soured in my stomach at his musings and what they reveal. He knows Lenore Dove is Covey; only they name their children this way. First name from a ballad, second a color. Amber and Ivory are actual family names. How has he unearthed this obscure fact about a pocket of musicians in the throwaway district of 12? Capitol informers?

"Dove," I tell him.

"Dove!" He smacks his forehead. "Dove. I have always heard 'dove color,' though. It's a bit of a cheat. But who could resist when you get both the color and the bird? And we know how they feel about their birds."

He returns the striker. On the back, in minuscule script, are the words I'd missed. *For H. I love you like all-fire. L.D.*

"Do you know much about doves, Haymitch?"

"They're peaceful."

"If they are, they're outliers. All the birds I've encountered are vicious." A dribble of bloody spittle leaks from Snow's mouth. "Bet I know a thing or two about your dove."

"Like what?"

"Like she's delightful to look at, swishes around in bright colors, and sings like a mockingjay. You love her. And oh, how she seems to love you. Except sometimes you wonder, because her plans don't include you at all."

Not exactly, but too close. I think of the misty look she gets when she talks about the open road, the life of the Covey, and a kind of freedom that has nothing to do with me. Worse, I think of Clay Chance and the fire under the reaping stage and how there's a part of her she refuses to share with me. She'd say it was to keep me safe, but maybe she just doesn't trust me with her secrets.

"She loves me," I insist.

"No doubt she says so. But believe me, romantically speaking, you're dodging a bullet with these Games."

"So I should be thanking you?"

Snow laughs. "You should. Although perhaps not for that."

"For what? You're sending me to my death in the Games."

"Yes, your behavior has guaranteed that."

There it is, in case I had a shred of hope left. Straight from the horse's mouth. Allies or no, I am a dead man walking.

"On the good side," he continues, "with you out of the picture, Lenore Dove and your family should be free to enjoy long and happy lives."

Even though their safety is my greatest concern, his reminder that their future will not include me is, as Maysilee would say, "a special kind of vicious."

Snow dabs at the spittle with his shirt cuff. "But there are many different ways to die in the arena. You might get stabbed, or strangled, or die of thirst. Death by mutt tends to be the most memorable. We have some beauties this year. Programmable to serve individual tributes. And far scarier than the weasels."

He watched it, then. Our tribute session in the kitchen where we revealed our final wishes. "I have no say in that."

"No, but I do. And I will orchestrate your death based on your behavior from here on out. You decide what you want Lenore Dove and your mother and that dear little brother of yours to see. You can die clean and fair, or we can open the Games with the slowest, most agonizing death ever to befall a tribute. And yes, you should be thanking me for giving you the option."

I meet those pale blue eyes. "I guess you've got me."

"Don't feel too badly. You're in good company. You know, my family has its own little aphorism."

"What's that?"

"Snow lands on top." Without shifting his focus from me, he calls out, "Hide-and-seek is over! You can join us now!"

Who is he summoning? My torturers, brought in to reinforce his threat?

"So, no more unauthorized chariot rides, I think. No mocking me on or off camera," he continues. "And I have a belated birthday gift for you. I want it treated with the gratitude it deserves." He inclines his head in the direction of the conservatory.

Standing in the doorway is Louella McCoy.

PART II

"THE RASCAL"

My heart leaps, then sinks like a stone. I feel Louella's crushed skull leaking hot blood into my hand. See her vacant eyes. She was good and dead in a way that defied return. So who is this girl in the doorway?

She sure looks like Louella. Same size, same height. Heart-shaped face, big gray eyes, long dark braids. Her fingernails are bitten down and there's a scar on her forehead that matches the one the real Louella got falling off our cistern. She wears the District 12 training outfit, as if she'd dressed at the apartment with us this morning. Maysilee's purple and yellow flower bead necklace hangs over her collar. She checks every box.

But this isn't Louella. In the same way you instinctively know the waxed pears on the table lack juice, this girl lacks Louella's essence.

"Come in. You know Haymitch," the president says.

Fake Louella crosses to the end of the table. "Hello, Haymitch."

The accent's only slightly off, but the greeting's a dead give-away. Louella is a "Hey, Hay" or "How you?" kind of girl. Her cheekbones look funny, too. Like they've shot something into her face to make it fuller. Most of all, she won't look me in the eye, which my sweetheart never failed to do.

"Who are you?" I ask her.

She stares at the mess of pears on the table, her eyes unfocused. "My name is Louella McCoy. I'm from District Twelve."

"You're not," I tell her, then address Snow. "She's not. Anyone can see it."

"I doubt it. Her family, maybe a few close friends. No one outside of the drunken audience at the parade even witnessed the accident. People will believe she's Louella. Especially since you'll be there by her side, coaching her, like the good ally you are. A perfect pair in what I am determined to make a perfect Quarter Quell."

I understand now. The people who saw the crash in person will be told Louella recovered. Incitatus Loomy, the parade master, has been killed for his incompetence. Poisoned by a plate of oysters that Snow somehow survived. And it is up to me and Fake Louella here to cover the worst casualty of the evening.

Plutarch hustles into the room with a glass of milk and a plate of rolls. He pulls up short at the sight of Louella. "Is that —?"

"Louella McCoy," says Snow. "Ah, my bread." He takes a big bite of a roll and grunts in approval. "Fresh. I think we're done here, if you'd like to return our tributes to their accommodations. Louella, this is Plutarch."

"Hello, Plutarch."

"Hello." He can't stop staring at her.

"She's a good body double. We were lucky," says Snow.

"Yes, Mr. President. She certainly is. This way, kids." Fake Louella and I follow Plutarch down a few halls of ancestors before he speaks again. "I did not know about any of this. He just said he wanted to talk to you."

"Right," I say. "Who is she?"

"Best guess . . . child of traitors. Could be either district or Capitol. She might not even know herself. No question they've programmed her. Probably drugged her as well."

Fake Louella chimes in. "Hello, Plutarch. My name is Louella McCoy. I'm from District Twelve."

"So, he's going to send her in, whoever she is, and get her killed in the Games?" I ask.

"That seems to be the current plan," admits Plutarch. "I don't approve of this."

"You're my hero. I hope I'm just like you when I grow up. Oh, wait a minute, that won't be happening."

A Peacekeeper van idles at the entrance. I climb in before they can cuff me. Fake Louella crawls into the van and sits on the floor. "Hello, Haymitch. My name is Louella McCoy. I'm from District Twelve."

"She's going to knock 'em dead at the interview," I say to Plutarch, then slam the door shut myself.

The whole way back, in the dark, I'm terrified she's going to touch me. I hate her, and I hate what her presence will require of me, even though I know none of this is her fault.

Back at the apartment, Maysilee, Wyatt, and our mentors wait for my return in the living room. When I walk in with Fake Louella, a general gasp goes up.

I point them out. "This is Maysilee and Wyatt. And those are our mentors, Mags and Wiress."

Fake Louella fixates on the toes of her boots. "Hello, Maysilee, Wyatt, Mags, and Wiress."

"But they couldn't have —" Wyatt begins. "Who are you?"

"My name is Louella McCoy. I'm from District Twelve."

After a long pause, Maysilee says, "That's not sleeping in my room."

Mags shushes her. "Where did she come from?"

"President Snow introduced us in Plutarch Heavensbee's library. She's been drugged or programmed or something. We're supposed to pretend she's real for the cameras. I have no idea who she is."

"She's a stale marshmallow," says Maysilee. "We're supposed to sell her."

Mags touches Fake Louella's shoulder. "Are you hungry?" The girl shrinks away, then looks up at her, confused. "Let's all have something to eat."

We gather around the table in the kitchen, where Wiress ladles stew into our bowls. Mags places a spoon in Fake Louella's hand. She grasps it in her fist, wraps her arm protectively around her bowl, and begins shoveling in the stew while little whimpering sounds escape her lips.

"They've starved her," says Wiress. "Among other things."

She's right. While Louella's wrists were lean, Fake Louella's tend toward bony. No wonder they had to plump up her face. The irrational anger I've held against this girl dissolves into pity as she lifts her bowl to lick it clean like a dog.

"Would you like some more? We have plenty," says Mags.

"Bread?" Wiress holds out the basket of assorted rolls to her.

Fake Louella stares in fascination at the offering, then her fingers close on a dark crescent-shaped roll dotted with seeds. She holds it to her nose and inhales the scent, her breath coming in short gasps.

Wiress and Mags exchange a look. "Are you from District Eleven, child?" Mags says softly. Fake Louella begins to cry, pressing the roll against her lips and pawing at her ear. "It's all right, little one. Come with me." She wraps an arm around the girl and leads her out of the kitchen.

"Whoever she is, I guess she's ours now," says Wyatt.

I'm surprised to hear something this kindhearted coming out of an oddsmaker, but we all feel it. We can't pile any more hurt on Fake Louella. I guess I'll do my best to look out for her, just think of her as another District 6 dove.

"You're right," I say. "But I can't call her Louella."

"Something too different may confuse her further," warns Wiress.

"How about Lou Lou?" suggests Maysilee. "I used to have a pet canary by that name."

I know this about Maysilee because Lenore Dove caught wind of it and was infuriated that anyone would ever cage a bird, in particular a songbird. But that doesn't seem a reason to reject the name. "I think I can handle that," I say. Louella McCoy was definitely not a Lou Lou.

Mags returns, troubled. "I put her to bed. There's some sort of device attached to her chest, pumping a drug into her, I think. I was afraid to remove it. That might kill her. I've seen something similar before."

"Why did you ask if she was from Eleven?" says Maysilee.

"The roll she chose. With the seeds. It's theirs."

The arrival of Lou Lou has steamrolled the boost we got from joining the Newcomers. A couple of hours ago we had a clear direction, but Snow's gift has reminded us of our frailty and the futility of opposing him. I can't remember what our feeble plan was, or why it mattered. We eat supper in silence, each occupied with our own dreary thoughts.

Dreary. Lenore Dove taught me that word. It's in the first line of her song. What I wouldn't give to see her one more time.

There was a moment, when Snow said he had a gift for me, that I thought he meant Lenore Dove. The way he was going on about the flint striker and the Covey. Glad it wasn't, though. She's much safer in that "ghastly wilderness" around 12.

Mags and Wiress try to get us back on track. After supper, we gather in the living room and talk through our day. Mags seems pleased with the alliance and encourages us to pursue it. I feel better about teaming up with Wyatt and Maysilee as well. Wyatt's more honorable than he has any right to be, given his family, and Maysilee won a lot of points by helping the other tributes with their tokens.

Wiress asks if there are any clues about the arena we might have picked up in training.

"Tarps," says Wyatt, without missing a beat.

"Like . . . sheets of plastic?" I ask.

"Yeah. Did you see that one lady's booth? All she did was show you different things to do with a tarp. Make a poncho, collect rainwater, turn it into a pack. Made me think it was going to be wet in there. Because in the mines, we use them to keep things dry."

"I think you may be onto something," says Wiress. "What about you, Maysilee?"

"I didn't get to many booths. I was too busy making tokens. Trying to complement people's outfits. But you know how we're all in different colors? They're the same colors we were wearing last night in the chariots. Red for Ten, peach for Eight. And if they end up dressing us like that in the arena, which they might do to help the audience keep us straight, then being in black could be a real plus. Especially at night. We may be able to move about to gather food or whatever, while other districts have to hide."

"Also very good," says Wiress. "Haymitch, did you notice anything?"

"Well, right about now I'm noticing how good Wyatt and Maysilee are at noticing things. I need to pay more attention. But there's this." I tell them about Beetee and the potato, fudging the science part. "All I can glean from that is it could be dark and root vegetables might come in handy."

"If it's wet, like Wyatt thinks, then there may be no dry wood and building a fire for light won't be an option, so we'll have to plug into potatoes," says Maysilee.

Wyatt considers this. "Or maybe we'll have to dig for food."

"That's an interesting connection," says Mags.

He shrugs. "It's no great shakes. I dig for a living."

At bedtime, we stand outside the girls' room, watching Lou Lou sleep, unsure what to do.

"I can take your bed," I tell Maysilee.

"No," she says. "It's okay."

"We could come sleep on your floor," offers Wyatt. "Probably closer to what the arena will be like anyway."

So that's what we do. Mags helps Wyatt and me haul our bedclothes and some sofa cushions in and we make up pallets on the floor.

"Do you think we should practice being on watch?" asks Maysilee when we're all ready for lights-out.

"Good idea. I'll go first." I settle in cross-legged with a blanket over my lap.

Mags checks on Lou Lou one last time, tells us good night, and turns out the lights as she closes the door behind her.

After a time, Wyatt falls asleep and starts up the chain saw. Maysilee's so buried in her covers I can't tell her status. My ribs ache and I lean back on Lou Lou's bed, stretching out my arms and letting her mattress take their weight.

Lou Lou stirs fitfully, and I hear her murmuring something but can't make out the words. Don't really want to know. It won't be good. Dog-tired, I start to doze off but startle at the feel of frigid little fingers clutching mine. In her sleep, Lou Lou's rolled over onto her side. She holds on to my hand for dear life, her pulse beating fast like a baby bird's heart.

I remember Louella's hand taking mine on the train, and resist the impulse to pull away. "It's okay, Lou Lou," I whisper, sort of patting her side. "No one here will hurt you."

I could try a lullaby to soothe her, but I don't want to wake the others. Not much of a singer anyway, and I'm supposed to be practicing keeping watch for the arena. I think how Lenore Dove sings to me sometimes. Lonely for her, I close my eyes for a moment and let her voice find me. . . .

While I nodded, nearly napping, suddenly there came a tapping,
As of some one gently rapping, rapping at my chamber door —
"'Tis some visitor," I muttered, "tapping at my chamber door —
Only this and nothing more."

I jerk awake. Was that a tapping? Or did I dream it?

The strip of light under the door, the numbers on the bed-table clock, even the blinking green light of the device on the wall — a camera? A smoke detector? A temperature controller? — have all vanished. Only the faint glow of the Capitol city lights through the window blinds keeps the dark at bay. The humming of the apartment has been stilled; no purring machines or soft currents break the silence. Far away, a car honks. Then nothing. Under my blanket, I sweat. The warm, stagnant air smells like the inside of the cistern and stale supper.

And someone's definitely rapping at my chamber door. Gently. I hear the turn of the knob, the brush of the wood against carpet.

A figure comes around the door, holding something that emanates a thin beam of light. It's a pair of boiled potatoes, connected to a pea-sized bulb. Beetee raises a finger to his lips, then tilts his head for me to follow. Careful not to wake anyone, I detach my hand from Lou Lou's and slip out of the bedroom. Moving away from the door, Beetee and I speak in hushed voices.

"What are you doing here?" I ask.

Beetee's slightly short of breath. "I came up the utility steps from the third floor. Wiress knocked out the power in the building. The surveillance cameras are down. She estimates we have about ten minutes left. Are you serious about breaking the arena?"

"Yes! Just tell me what I have to do. What breaks a machine?"

"Time, usually. With it comes fatigue, wear and tear, erosion, creep. But we don't have the luxury of time, so we'll need a different approach. You saw Wiress's arena last year. Did you wonder how they ran it?"

"From the Capitol, right? They show the control room during the Games. . . ."

"Yes, they show the commands being issued, and some can be triggered remotely. But these days, there's also a Gamemaker level at the actual arena to carry out certain orders. An entire subterranean floor, nicknamed Sub-A, that they never show the audience. It destroys the illusion of the arena being controlled from afar. On Sub-A they manage manual tasks, like unleashing the mutts or stocking a feast. You'll be launched from there in a few days. But all of that is secondary to the real job of managing the onsite computer system that's essential to the running of the Games. That's our team's target. The arena's brain."

My whole life I've watched the Games without even questioning how the arenas actually worked. I don't know what I thought breaking the arena meant — me chopping at some cable or something with an ax? Anyway, it didn't involve an underground computer that, even if I could reach, I wouldn't know how to break . . . unless I could go at it with the aforementioned ax.

But Beetee mentioned a team. Maybe I can be the brawn, and Ampert can do the breaking.

"So we're going to try to find this computer and pull its plug? Enter bad commands?"

Beetee shakes his head. "It would be virtually impossible for one of you to reach it. The computer's in a restricted area with high-tech security systems in place. But the brain can't operate unless other parts of the body are sound. Like this building tonight. When the electricity is cut off, the place goes dead."

"We're going to knock out the power?"

"Oh, no, Haymitch. Even if we happen to, they have an enormous backup generator at the top end, just outside the arena itself."

"So what, then?"

"We're going to drown it."

“Drown it?” I guess Wyatt was right about the arena being wet. “How?”

“The arena has the capacity to drown itself. Creating the tribute ecosystem requires electricity, plumbing, heating, cooling, ventilation, everything your house would have,” says Beetee.

“My house doesn’t have half those things. Does yours?” I ask.

“I live in the Victor’s Village now, so yes, it does.”

We have a Victor’s Village in 12, too. A dozen fancy houses you get to live in for the rest of your life if you win the Games. Burdock and I used to steal over there and peek in the windows on a summer’s night. In the moonlight, we could see enough to tell they had furniture and hanging lights and bathtubs like the ones here. The village was built after our lone victor, though, so no one’s ever lived in it.

Beetee continues. “My point is that, for at least a few weeks, the arena has to be capable of sustaining the tributes and supporting the set pieces. I haven’t seen the plan for the actual arena, but over a year ago, they had me look over the Sub-A design. In the northern part of the arena, there’s an enormous water tank that sits just below the surface. Arenas can require a lot of water to sustain lakes, create rainstorms, quench fires. This reservoir seems especially large.”

“Then if the computer is the brain, this would be the bladder,” I say.

He laughs a bit. "Yes. Exactly. And once the bladder has ruptured, it will flood the brain, leaving it inoperable."

My brain's starting to get flooded as well. "But . . . if I can't reach the brain, how will I reach the bladder?"

"Throughout the arena, there are hatches that connect the surface to the utility corridors below. You'll enter through one yourself. The hatches are used by the Gamemakers to introduce elements into the arena. You'll access the utility corridors by way of a mutt portal."

"A mutt portal," I repeat.

"Yes. The plans showed dozens of these. It must be a mutt-heavy program."

I try not to think about the weasels. "Okay, so I find a mutt portal, climb down to the utility corridor . . ."

"Locate the tank and blow a hole in it, releasing the water. Gravity should take care of the rest. It will naturally flood Sub-A."

I feel overwhelmed. "Okay, hold on. This is a lot. How am I supposed to blow a hole in the tank? Are you sending me in there with explosives?"

"It won't be just you. You'll have Ampert." At the mention of his son's name, his voice catches and a spasm of pain crosses his face.

"This plan sounds . . . pretty dangerous," I venture. "Maybe I can do it without him."

For the first time, his agony breaks through his restraint. "They reaped him to kill him, Haymitch! To punish me! I can think of no realistic scenario in which he does not die. I can only hope that his death is quick and not in vain."

I know he's right. Even without this wild plot to break the arena, Ampert's marked for death, like me. If the Careers don't take him out, the Gamemakers will. "I'm so sorry. I'll try to look out for him in there."

"Don't let him suffer," whispers Beetee.

"I'll do my best," I promise.

"That's a great comfort to me. Thank you." He wipes his glasses and settles them firmly back in place. "So, do you know how to use explosives?"

Oddly enough, I do a bit. We have classes in coal production. Dull as dust usually. But since we're the future miners of Panem, they do show us how coal gets mined, which can involve placing explosives in a hole in the rock, inserting a blasting cap with a length of fuse attached, and then lighting it. We practice this with fake stuff. Inert, they call it. The real stuff can kill you.

"I know the basics," I say. "For the coal mines. But where am I going to get the fuse and —"

"We're working that out now. How to smuggle the materials past security. But unlike the components used in your mines, which as I'm sure you know can be deadly, I have specifically designed these to be safe. Both chemically and structurally. They cannot be set off unintentionally by you or anything else. To set them off, you will need to fully assemble the bomb correctly and light the fuse with fire."

That makes me a little calmer. I don't need a blasting cap exploding on me before it's time to blow a hole in the tank. My fingers find my flint striker. Lenore Dove's voice floats in from the Meadow. *"Only you don't have to have flint. Any decent sparking rock like quartz will do."*

"Will there be rocks in there, do you think? Flint or quartz?" I ask.

"Possibly. I can try to find out. Why?"

"If there are, I can handle that last one." I lift my chin and display my gift. "Flint striker."

Beetee looks impressed. "Very clever. Never underestimate Twelve, as I always say."

"You do?" Be nice if someone said something approving about us for a change.

"I do. You don't think like the rest of us. You've done a better job of holding on to yourselves, despite the Capitol."

"They think we're animals, so that helps."

Wiress appears, startling us. "You better finish. A repair crew just pulled up out front. It could be any time now."

"More to come. Don't tell anyone what we've discussed." Beetee vanishes in the dark.

"Best get to bed," Wiress instructs me.

I return to my watch in the bedroom. After a few minutes, the power surges back with a gush of chilled air and a constellation of lights. A jumble of Beetee's instructions fills my brain. What did I just agree to? Mutt portal . . . bladder . . . explosives . . . ? How on earth am I going to pull that off? Doubt consumes me. Probably I should just be the fire maker and Ampert should set the explosives. But does he have the physical strength to manage the mutt portal and the climb? And what if I do pull it off? What if I break the arena?

How Lenore Dove would love it if she knew I'd bested the Capitol and stopped the Games, at least for this year. There's glory in that. Dignity. And if I did it using her flint striker? It'd be like we did it together. Painted a poster that no one could ignore. Outsmarted the Capitol and forced their citizens to see us as something other than mindless animals.

"Haymitch?" Maysilee stirs. "I'll take over now."

"Okay, thanks." She doesn't sound drowsy. Either she woke with a start or she's never been asleep.

"Everything all right?" she asks.

I wonder if she saw me leave and tried to overhear my conversation with Beetee, but I can't talk about it. The fewer people who know about the plot, the better, and while I like her more in the Capitol than I did in 12, we're not exactly confidants.

"Well, there was a power outage, but they seemed to have fixed it," I tell her. "'Night." Curling up in my blankets, I pretend to drift off until I actually do.

In the morning, I find myself tempted to share Beetee's plan with the others. Doesn't feel honest not to. Lou Lou's enough of a distraction to keep me from blurting it out. We decide the simplest way to manage her appearance is to pretend that while the Capitol miraculously managed to patch Louella up, she's no longer right in the head. We're counting on none of the other tributes having spent enough time with her to distinguish the difference between our real Louella and her body double.

Lou Lou's gone from averting her eyes to watching us constantly, as if she's trying to piece together a puzzle. She tugs on her ear a lot, which makes me wonder if it hurts, because that's what Sid used to do when he had an earache. When she goes to the bathroom, Wiress says, "I think she has an audio implant. Probably a two-way transmitter."

"Why?" asks Wyatt.

"So they can tell her what to say. Direct her behavior."

"Hear what she hears," says Mags.

She doesn't have to explain the ramifications of that. Don't tell Lou Lou any secrets. There's a flip side to that, though. We can gain an advantage by telling her lies. During the Dark Days, the Capitol spied on us with jabberjays, mutts that looked like regular birds but could record the rebels' conversations and play them back word for word. We figured this out and fed them false information. The Capitol released the jabberjays at the end of the war, thinking they'd die off, which they did, but not before they'd sired a whole new species by mating with female mockingbirds, creating Lenore Dove's precious mockingjays. Now I guess Lou Lou is our own little jabberjay.

When we join the other Newcomers in the gym, Lou Lou draws some questioning looks, but they seem to buy that she's our girl, only brain-damaged. None of them knew Louella or had more than a passing look at her, after all.

"You have to be careful what you say around her," Maysilee warns them. "She's not herself, and might repeat it to anyone."

When we break up to practice, Wyatt agrees to take her. Which is helpful, as I don't need a jabberjay at the moment.

Ampert catches my eye and we shake off the rest of the group. I don't know how much Beetee has told him about the arena plot. But before I can broach that, he says, "My father says we need to get Nine to join our alliance."

We spot the yellow-clad tributes nearby at the shelter-building booth. "Any specific reason why? I mean, Five and Eleven are still uncommitted, and they look a lot stronger."

"He just said they were essential. I tried the first day, but they brushed me off. I wonder if they think I'm stuck-up."

"You? Why would they think that?"

"Because I'm from Three. Because I know the tech stuff, maybe. Nine's in the fields a lot. I don't think they get much schooling out there, and everybody knows we do. People call us eggheads."

"Egghead's not so bad."

"It's not a compliment. Anyway, I couldn't get anywhere with them. They're not big talkers."

Like my pa, I think. He was plenty smart, just didn't feel the need to share every thought that traipsed through his brain. Nor did he much trust people who did. A lot of the miners are like that.

"I'll give it a shot," I tell Ampert. "Why don't you have another go at Eleven?"

Halfway to the booth, Maysilee intercepts me. "What's going on?"

This could mean one of several things, especially if she was eavesdropping last night. I decide to play it straightforward. "Just going in for Nine."

"Do they need help with their tokens?"

We turn to assess their token situation. They each wear a necklace of braided grass with a fist-sized sunflower hanging from it.

Maysilee answers her own question. "Oh, my word, yes. Those are hideous. But you have to give them credit for trying, poor things. I guess salt dough clay's all they could get their hands on."

I know the stuff. Once, over at Burdock's, his ma mixed up some white flour, salt, and water into dough, and all us kids made little animals and stars and things. Too wasteful for my family, but the Everdeens could afford it on account of being hunters and having a little more disposable income. Nothing like the Donners, though.

"Yeah," I say, "I guess they ran out of gold."

Maysilee starts for 9, but I step in front of her. "Stop. We need them, Maysilee. And I can't risk you insulting them when you think you're being helpful. Anyway, their tokens aren't so bad. Just kind of . . ." I struggle to describe the lumpy, overly bright yellow flowers.

"Gaudy. Clunky. Shoddy."

"Uh-huh. And that's why I'm going in alone."

She shrugs and walks away, but not far. Just to a nearby

food-preparation booth. Skinning squirrels, making bread on your campfire coals, roasting stuff on a stick. Like we're all going to a cookout.

I get to the shelter booth in time to participate in a session with the four District 9 tributes. I can't help thinking about what Mags said, that we'll likely be on the move. But maybe I can throw something together quick in a rainstorm.

While this booth isn't dedicated solely to tarps, they're certainly featured. You can make a shelter by tying one between trees. Or tying a rope between trees, draping the tarp over it, and anchoring your tent with rocks. Or finding a fallen tree, leaning branches against it, and covering it with the tarp. Or building an A-frame from branches and throwing the tarp over it. Two tarps? Use one for the floor. If there are no tarps in the arena, they're going to have some mighty disappointed tributes.

Other tips include using your weapon, preferably an ax or a knife, to cut brush and branches, and finding a flat surface to build on so if it rains, the runoff doesn't soak you.

We're supposed to work alone, so we each get a tarp and have at it. A half dozen upright posts and a thick column lying on the floor stand in for trees. I build a tent by fastening a rope between trunks and arranging a tarp over it, while quietly observing District 9. Their faces still healing from their last sunburn from home. Their calloused, capable hands. Their lean, muscled arms. Their quiet efficiency. Even without Beetee's directive, I can see they'd make good allies.

Just as I'm joining a couple of them at the rock pile, who saunters up but Panache. He's all full of himself, grabbing a tarp and some sticks — like he's even been at the lesson — and taking over the middle of the fake forest. The instructor frowns, because she automatically hates him, too, and I can feel District 9 shifting, so he's not directly in any of their sight lines.

I ignore him, carry my rocks back to my site, and start pinning the tarp edges to the ground. Panache singles out the biggest guy from 9, since, of course, he thinks he'll be their leader, and corners him against the fallen log. "We've been thinking about letting you guys join the Career pack."

The guy's face shows no emotion. "No."

Not "No, thanks" or "No for now but we'll talk it over." Just a flat, definitive "No." Then he goes back to laying branches against the log.

This doesn't land well with Panache, who clearly thinks he's offered them the moon. "No?" He takes a threatening step toward the guy, then notices a Peacekeeper, hand on his taser, and stops. "What're you looking at?" he says to the smallest girl from 9, who's not looking at him, just making a bed from pine needles. She refuses to meet his eye, which makes him nuts. He snaps, "Fine. We'll kill you first, then!" Stepping forward, he yanks her sunflower from its grass braid and hurls it to the floor. The token shatters into a dozen pieces. Panache plows into the crowd before the Peacekeeper can respond.

A small, pained cry escapes the girl's lips as she crouches over the bits. The sunflower mattered, I think, even more than being her last handful of home. I bet someone close to her made it. Her ma or pa? Her sister or brother? Someone she loves. They made it to protect her and remind her how precious she is, to give her something to hold on to at the end, if the unthinkable happened and her name got called at the reaping. And now it's chunks of salt flour dough dabbed with yellow paint. The other tributes from 9 gather around her, viewing the wreckage as silent tears roll down her cheeks.

I don't know what to do. I wish I could comfort the girl, but I don't even know her name. And I can hardly make my move now, even if Beetee says 9 is essential. I'm racking my brain when suddenly there's Maysilee, kneeling across from the girl, mixing up some white gooey stuff on a leaf with a twig. She doesn't ask permission, she just carefully arranges the broken pieces into their original form, then begins to smear goo on the edges and glue the sunflower back together. And all of 9 just stands there, speechless, letting her.

I notice a little piece of yellow by my boot and retrieve it, then cross to add it to the sunflower puzzle. Squatting down next to Maysilee, I ask, "What is that stuff?"

"It's glue. I made it with flour and water and salt from the food booth. It's the best I could do." She addresses the girl. "After it's mended, you'll have to be very careful with it, since I couldn't heat this up. Maybe your mentor can find you some proper glue at the quarters, but for now this should hold."

The girl wipes her tears and nods. Given the lack of communication, I take that as an opening. "That a sunflower?" She nods again. "I love those things. My ma tries to grow them in the garden every year. Guess yours are finer, though, with all that sun you have in Nine."

There's a pause long enough to make me think I've failed, when she quietly offers, "We have big fields of them."

"Yeah? Bet that's a pretty sight." I spend a minute as if contemplating it. "My girl back home? She sings a song about sunflowers. An old-timey song." Since the four tributes look somewhat interested, I give it a go, even though it's a little weird.

Ah Sun-flower! weary of time,
Who countest the steps of the Sun:
Seeking after that sweet golden clime
Where the travellers journey is done.

Okay, maybe too weird. Maysilee has her lips pressed tight together, like she's trying not to laugh. Nothing from the rest of the group. Ampert's right, these Niners are not a chatty crew. I forge on. "Well, it sounds better when she sings it." The girl laughs a bit, but not mean. "I'm Haymitch, by the way. And she's Maysilee."

"Kerna. You're with Ampert."

"Oh, yeah," I say, like it's been the farthest thing from my mind. "A bunch of us are teaming up. Calling ourselves the Newcomers." I don't reissue the invitation to join. Let them come to us.

"He asked us, too," Kerna says. "We said we didn't want to."

"I said the same at first, then I thought, many hands make light work." Okay, thanks for that homey aphorism, Mamaw. I'm worried it sounds idiotic given the circumstances, but they all think it over.

"There," says Maysilee, fitting the last piece in place. Looks good as new. She reknots the grass braid and carefully places it around Kerna's neck. "Remember, see if they can get you some real glue at the apartment and reinforce it."

"Thank you, Maysilee," says Kerna.

The instructor tells us we have to make room for a new group. We're running out of conversation anyway. I know if they're reconsidering, they'll have to discuss it before they accept.

Maysilee and I join District 11 at the knot-tying booth, where I struggle with my square knot while she replicates everything they show her on the first try, even the snares. "Now you're just showing off," I say.

She rolls her eyes. "Yes, I'm sure the Careers are quaking in their boots at my clove hitch. Let's go throw some axes."

At lunchtime, without another word, the four baby chicks from District 9 sit among us. Ampert has brought in 11 as well. We're now eight districts strong. At the far end of the bleachers, the orange-clad District 5 has teamed up with the Careers. The lines are drawn. They've got more trained fighters, but we outnumber them two to one. Wyatt can barely contain himself as he calculates the odds. The Gamemakers buzz with this new development, gesturing at us, deep in conference, factoring the dual alliances into the Games.

When we've finished our sandwiches, District 12 reunites at the edible-food section, which seems heavy on the poisonous mushrooms. Lou Lou keeps sticking them in her mouth, confounding the trainer.

"I don't know what she's going to do in her private session with the Gamemakers," Wyatt says. "But I guess they won't be expecting much. Not sure what I'm doing either."

"You're an expert on the Games, what with your oddsmaking and all. You could talk about that," Maysilee suggests. "It's more impressive than anything I've got."

"You should show them all the things you can do with a piece of cord," I tell her. "You underrate it because it's easy for you, but I think it's pretty impressive."

"Hm, it's a thought. At least it would make me unique. What are you going to do, Haymitch? Throw knives?"

"I could, I guess. Or axes."

Everyone's sent back to their respective locker rooms while the Gamemakers begin the private sessions. This will be our last chance to influence how they score us for the general public. Heavy Peacekeeper presence monitors the tension between the Careers and the Newcomers, but I have to say I feel a lot more secure with my alliance than I did in the shower.

Lucky I'm slated to go last, because I have no idea how to handle the Gamemakers. Surely, they have footage of what went down at the reaping. Me "attacking" the Peacekeeper and being punished with a trip to the Games. And they witnessed my subversive act at the opening ceremonies live. No telling if they know about President Snow's ultimatum in Plutarch's library. I've avoided thinking about that encounter and how he threatened me with a slow and agonizing death for my loved ones to witness at the Games opening. I'm not planning to do anything else to call him out before the Games begin, now that I'm part of the plot to break the machine, and I can only hope that will keep me alive long enough to carry out my part of the plan.

So, what can I show the Gamemakers that will reassure them that I'm now harmless to the Capitol? A dramatic shift to being a compliant tribute will be hard to sell. Another wrinkle is Lou Lou. They must know that I know she's a fake. Especially since Louella mattered enough for me to carry her lifeless body to the president.

Maybe she's the key. Maybe I can say that Louella was the one thing I cared about protecting in the Games and now I'm all about myself . . . that I'm using the alliance for one purpose and one purpose only . . . that I'm determined to win these Games and get back to the girl I risked everything for and the family I had a touching good-bye with. I'll convince them I want to be the first tribute from 12 to live in the Victor's Village. I'm just a punk kid who tried to escape the Peacekeepers, confronted Snow, and spat on the audience for good measure. A guy who's only out for himself. This is the one way I might be able to sell myself to the Gamemakers without rousing suspicions about my greater ambitions. To paint myself as a selfish troublemaker who's determined to get home and live out his life as a rich and famous victor.

The gym's deserted when I walk out, my footsteps echoing off the walls, except for the neat rows of Gamemakers in their bleachers. The Head Gamemaker, Faustina Gripper, a short, ample woman with close-cropped metallic silver and gold curls, is distinguished by the purple fur collar on her snowy robe. She appraises me, then commands, "Tell us about yourself."

I cock my head, look her dead in the eye, and say, "I'm Haymitch Abernathy from District Twelve. I shouldn't be here. I was reaped illegally, but no one cares. My neighbor, Louella McCoy, was the only person here I gave a hang about, but you killed her and brought in a body double. So, that kind of frees me up to win these Games."

"And what makes you think you can do that? We haven't noticed that you possess any outstanding skills," the Head Gamemaker says.

"Really?" I smirk. "Because from where I'm standing, looks like I came up with thirty-one people who've promised to defend me. But maybe that strategy's a little too subtle for you."

Her mouth tightens. "And you're willing to let them die?"

"Why not, lady? You are."

They dismiss me. I'm hoping I pulled off unlikable but focused on winning the Games. If I can score in the midrange, maybe I can still get a handful of sponsors.

On the way out the door, the Peacekeepers collect my token for inspection. I run my fingers over the inscription and press my lips against the bird before placing it in a little basket marked with my name. It kills me having to let it go, knowing they may tag it as unfair and dispose of it. And besides the heartbreak, losing it means I will have to find another way to make fire to carry out Beetee's plot. On the other hand, it's the

Capitol, and all they may see is a pretty necklace. Either way, my neck feels naked without it.

None of us talk much on the van ride home. After a dinner of roasted chicken and mashed potatoes, we gather around the television in the living room for a special announcement of our individual scores. On a scale of one to twelve, the Careers mostly land in the eight-to-eleven range. With the exception of District 11, who bring in similar numbers, the Newcomers generally manage between four and seven. We're announced last. Maysilee and Wyatt each get a six, Lou Lou pulls a three.

And me? I get a one.

I don't remember anyone getting a one before. Ever. In fact, I'm hard-pressed to remember a two. Even threes are rare and reserved for extreme long shots like Lou Lou. How will the audience interpret this? That I'm weak? Friendless? A coward? Any way you slice it, it will not result in my getting sponsors. I'm going to be entirely on my own in the arena when it comes to supplies.

"You must have gotten to them," Maysilee says with satisfaction. "Between the reaping and Louella and spitting on the crowd. You really caught their attention."

"Well, that's a sunny interpretation," I reply.

"Perhaps she's right," says Mags. "If nothing else, it's distinctive. People will be gossiping about it. With forty-eight tributes, just becoming recognizable is a plus."

Wyatt shakes his head. "I don't even know how to factor that into your odds. What'd you do anyway?"

Good question. "I guess . . . not in so many words but . . . I accused them of murdering us."

"Yes!" says Lou Lou, her eyes boring through me. Then she winces and swipes at her ear. We can hear a faint but piercing tone that must be deafening in her head. When it eases, tears stream from her eyes and she's gasping. Wyatt presses his finger against his lips and then hugs her tightly.

I take the first watch again at bedtime, my mind swimming with strategy. The Gamemakers, no doubt under Snow's direction, have made an example of me, and that displeasure could follow me into the arena. I may have doomed myself to a gory opening death. My hand seeks my flint striker for comfort, but finds only bare skin. They couldn't even leave me that last token of Lenore Dove's love. What did she think when they announced my score tonight? Since she didn't get to witness all my reckless behavior here, she probably blames herself for me getting called out in the reaping. But how will she ever know that was only a teaspoon of trouble in my river of wrong?

I feel like I'm a big risk now to the plot to disable the arena, but I'm sure Beetee's figured that out. I stay awake through three watches, thinking he might pay me another visit. Eventually, my eyelids get so heavy I wake Wyatt to take over.

Our mentors let us sleep in late, and I feel better when I find my precious necklace awaiting me at the kitchen table. All four of our tokens cleared, and we reach for them with eager hands.

"Can I see yours now? Since it's already off?" Maysilee asks me.

What can I say? *No, because my girlfriend hates you?* We're supposed to act like allies now, and I figure Lenore Dove will never know, so I pass over my token.

Maysilee studies it meticulously, going over every bit of engraving and reading the inscription, which does not escape her notice as it did mine. "Well, the Covey have an eye for beauty, that's for sure."

"Heard you have one of Tam Amber's pins," I say.

She wrinkles her nose. "Oh, that. It's well made, but I don't care much for mockingjays. Something unnatural about a bird that's half-mutt."

Never thought of it that way. "Some people think that's a victory in itself. Way they escaped the Capitol and survived."

"Do they?" says Maysilee. "Well, if I escape the Capitol and survive, maybe I'll give that pin a second chance."

"If you don't, I'm sure Lenore Dove would be happy to take it off your hands," I say.

"Lenore Dove . . ." Maysilee gives me a knowing smile. "She doesn't like me, your girlfriend. And it's not because of any pin."

"Because you're so mean, you think?" I ask innocently.

Maysilee laughs. "Partly, maybe. But mostly because I know her secret and she hates being at my mercy."

Her secret? "What's that mean?"

"It means how come she's got orange paint on her fingernails when she shows up to play for the mayor's birthday party?" She hands me back the token. "You ask her that if you get home."

I look down at the necklace in confusion. There's orange on some of the feathers. She was probably just helping Tam Amber. Or maybe she tried painting them to match her lipstick. I guess Maysilee made some crack about Lenore Dove having ugly nails. But why is that a secret that would put her at Maysilee's mercy? Nail polish is pricey — is Maysilee suggesting Lenore Dove stole it?

"Tell me now," I say.

"I told you, it's a secret. Those should be respected." Maysilee carefully arranges her necklaces — apparently, the Gamemakers viewed her collection as a single token — and hooks the purple and yellow flowers around Lou Lou's neck. "Unless, of course, you've got one to trade? Then we'd have something to talk about."

"Some girl thing," Wyatt comments as he puts on his token. "They never make sense."

"You said a mouthful," I agree. The scrip coin Maysilee wove into Wyatt's cord distracts me. She designed it so it's easy to pop the coin in and out of the weave because flipping it through his fingers helps Wyatt think.

"Hey, what's that coin made of? Nickel?" I ask.

"Zinc, I think," says Wyatt.

"Potato battery," I remind him. "Keep an eye out for copper."

Maysilee fishes the flower medallion from the display at her neck. "Already on it."

"Of course you are, Miss Donner," I say. "If the Gamemakers cleared those, maybe they're hoping you'll use them."

Just then, Drusilla shows up and calls us into the living room so she can help with our interview prep. After the reaping and chariot fiascos, she's feeling some heat. Our training numbers aren't doing her any favors either. This is her last big event for the Quell and she needs it to go well.

"Listen, you lot, there are always softhearted dolts who will send supplies to losers like you, *if* they can find some way to relate to you. The only one who's got any name recognition right now is Haymitch, because people are trying to figure out why his score's so abysmal. He also got some attention for his appalling behavior toward the audience at the parade. But the rest of you are basically nonexistent. This interview will be your last chance to make some sort of impression before the Games begin. Anything that makes you stand out is a plus. Make me remember you. So, who are you? Why should I want to lay my money on you? What are you selling?"

With an audience of Drusilla, Mags, Wiress, and ourselves we clear a space and try to simulate our upcoming interviews. Drusilla plays Caesar Flickerman, the smooth-talking host of the event. She loses patience with Lou Lou almost immediately, given that the child can't do much more than repeat, "My name is Louella McCoy. I'm from District Twelve."

"That's absolutely dreadful," says Drusilla. "Flickerman will eat you alive. What's wrong with you anyway? Snap out of it!" She gives Lou Lou a shake by the shoulders.

The contact triggers something in Lou Lou, who begins to scream, "You're murdering us! You're murdering us!"

Drusilla gasps and raises her hand to slap Lou Lou, but the rest of us intervene, and Mags takes Lou Lou into the bedroom.

"That isn't Louella McCoy," Maysilee tells Drusilla. "She's dead. That's a body double. Some little girl the Capitol has tortured until she can't even remember her real name. But even she can see the obvious. You're murdering us."

Drusilla looks around for backup, but the Peacekeepers remained downstairs and Wiress isn't giving any. So there's just her and us district piglets, including Maysilee, who slaps back. She composes herself. "That's not my department. Your interviews are." She points to Wyatt. "You're up."

After they exchange niceties, she asks Wyatt what makes him special.

"I'm an oddsmaker," he says without hesitation.

"An oddsmaker? What's that?"

"I set the odds for gambling events back in Twelve. I give odds on who will win the Hunger Games."

"You do?" asks Drusilla skeptically.

"I do."

"So, who do you recommend our audience bet on?"

Wyatt takes a deep breath and rattles off his projections. "Well, it's tempting to go for the low-hanging fruit. The odds will always look good for most of the Careers. Like Panache from District One, the largest tribute, trained, high score, I'd give him eleven-to-five odds, which means he has a thirty-one-point-two-five percent chance of winning. Or Maritte from Four, she's obviously a contender, with her physique and an eleven from the Gamemakers, probably an indication that she's exceptional with a trident. I'd say six to one, or a fourteen-point-two-nine percent."

"Hmph. Fancy math, but nothing new there," says Drusilla. "Everybody knows the Careers are a good bet."

"Obviously," returns Wyatt. "But what's made these Games a novelty is that all forty-eight tributes have locked into alliances before the start. Nothing like this has ever happened before. The Careers are powerful, yes, but the Newcomers outnumber them two to one. If I was betting, sure, I'd take a look at the Careers, but if the alliances really hold, if the tributes really defend each other to the death, anyone has a shot. And if you're not afraid of some risk, it's better bang for your buck if you back a more obscure Newcomer because the odds are not in their favor, so they'll pay off higher in the end."

"Give me a name," says Drusilla.

"Haymitch Abernathy," says Wyatt.

"He scored a one."

"Exactly. With no apparent handicaps. He's physically fit and his behavior suggests a boldness that disturbs the Gamemakers."

Thrown, I interject, "You don't have to do that, Wyatt."

"I'm not doing anything, Haymitch. This is my honest assessment of your chances. Maysilee's not a bad bet either."

"What about yourself?" asks Drusilla.

"Oh, I wouldn't bet on me," admits Wyatt. "I simply —"

"No!" cuts in Wiress. "Don't underrate yourself, Wyatt. No other tribute can do what you just did. Play up how intelligence matters. Reference me. Say Wiress won the Games last year without shedding a drop of blood. Brains matter."

Wyatt thinks this over a moment, then turns to Drusilla. "Here's the thing. At any given moment in the Hunger Games, I will know everybody's odds, how they stack up against each other, and how likely they are to receive gifts. It should keep me from making a lot of stupid mistakes. That's my advantage. It's up to you if you're smart enough to see it."

"Good," says Wiress. "Yes. Position yourself as the smart choice for bettors. People who pride themselves on being smart will respond to that."

When it's Maysilee's turn, she and Drusilla stare daggers at each other, but refrain from exchanging blows.

"So, Miss Donner, what do you think of the Capitol?"

"I think I can't believe people with so much money have such bad taste. Here you are with mountains of cash, and this is where you wound up?" She gives Drusilla's outfit — a red-and-white-striped jumpsuit with a matching beanie — the once-over. "You look like you jumped right off our candy counter back home. Just a peppermint-stick nightmare, you are."

Drusilla's hand goes to her collar. "You're not going to make any friends with this approach, you little shrew."

"Who said I wanted friends? I'm here to make people remember me, 'member? It's not just you, it's everyone I saw from the chariot. Garish color, unflattering lines. And there are some fashion choices you people are going to regret. Why you'd want to resemble a barnyard animal is beyond me, but I hope those goat horns are removable. And to the woman with the diamonds implanted along her teeth? People age, there's no shame in that, but I think those stones are going to make eating a trial when those gums recede."

"So, we should be emulating what — District Twelve?" sputters Drusilla.

"Heavens, no. People who don't have two cents to rub together can hardly be expected to dress well. Although there's not a miner in Twelve who doesn't have a better physique than the people I witnessed in that crowd. All the surgery in the world won't change that."

"What —?"

"And all the money in the world won't buy good taste. Clearly. Some people in Twelve have a lot more than what I'm witnessing here."

"Are you done?" Drusilla says.

"Honestly, I have barely warmed up."

"Sit down."

It's Wiress who concludes, "It's a risky strategy, but yes, they'll remember you."

Mags comes back, holding a handkerchief dotted in blood. "She's drifted off. I don't know what they've got in her ear, but it's starting to bleed."

Drusilla waves her off. "Again, not my department. You're up, Abernanny. So, Twelve has a lunatic, a computer, and a shrew. What are you?"

"Bad news, apparently," I say. "Else how'd I get a one in training?"

Mags coaches me. "Yes, that's good, highlight it immediately. Own it."

"Well, how did you?" asks Drusilla.

"Earned it. The Gamemakers don't like me. It probably started when I messed with a Peacekeeper during the reaping."

"You can't say that!" Drusilla protests. "You'll spoil the brilliant work I did covering up the riot!"

"What riot? Woodbine ran and your people shot him."

"I know a riot when I see it! Never mind. That's forbidden. It won't win you any points with the audience anyway. They'll respond to a bad boy, not a rebel. You need to be naughty, not dangerous. For instance, last winter, one of the University students dyed all the fountains pink when there was a face cream shortage. So saucy! Everyone loved it!"

I sense she's actually trying to help, but . . . "Yeah, okay. But I'm going into the Hunger Games. I don't think a face cream statement is going to cut it. Can I talk about spitting on the crowd?"

"Absolutely not! What will people do with that?"

"Well, if I can't do the reaping, and I can't do the spitting, what am I supposed to talk about?"

Drusilla thinks a moment. "You must be mysterious. Allude to radical behavior without being specific. The ones who witnessed the opening ceremony have already been gossiping. Let the audience use its imagination."

"Naughty, not dangerous," I repeat.

"That's it. Be a rascal. A charming, naughty rascal."

A rascal. That's what Mamaw used to call a squirrel who'd sneak up on the porch to steal nuts she was shelling. Right from under her nose. Bold as a stump, but funny, too. "Well, I can try."

I don't get a chance, though, because right then, Proserpina and Vitus burst into the apartment in a state of agitation.

"It's Magno. We went to his apartment to see the interview costumes so we can plan tonight's makeup and hair —" begins Proserpina.

"We're allowed to do that. Required to, actually, on our syllabus. So it's not like we're brownnosing or anything —" interjects Vitus.

"And the door to his apartment was wide open and he's reeling around, he's sick —"

"He's puking all over the place and talking like a crazy person and —"

"We think the toad venom rumors might be true!" Proserpina claps her hands over her mouth as if she's let some monster cat out of the bag.

"Rumors?" rants Drusilla. "That man's been licking toads since the war. I can't believe that even he would risk it during the Games. Oh, what am I saying? Of course I can. If for no other reason than to end my career!"

"Why would he lick toads?" asks Wyatt.

"Because he's a reptilian freak! And he'll do anything to take me down."

"They say some kinds make you hallucinate or something. If they don't kill you," explains Vitus. "Some people do it for fun, but ugh, nasty."

"I'm going to issue a formal complaint with the Gamemakers!" Drusilla grabs her handbag and storms out, effectively ending my interview practice.

"Do you two, perhaps, have any black clothing they could wear?" Wiress asks our prep team.

"Us?" asks Vitus in disbelief. "We don't wear black!"

"It's too depressing!" Proserpina bursts into tears, her magenta hair puffs bobbing wildly. "I need to call my sister." She throws herself into a chair next to a table holding a burnt orange telephone, presses some buttons, and begins to wail into the receiver, "I'm going to fail! I'm going to fail!"

Mags corrals the rest of us, including Vitus, into the kitchen to eat bowls of strawberry ice cream.

After a few minutes, Proserpina joins us. "My sister says it isn't our fault and to just do the best prep we can." She slurps a big spoonful of ice cream, a last trickle of tears sliding down her flushed cheeks. "She says if they try to fail us, we can appeal to the University Board. My sister knows everybody on the University Board on account of how she used to be the student social planner and had to get everything approved."

"Her sister's amazing," says Vitus.

"She is," says Proserpina. "She was the president of the Capitol Cohorts Chapters. And she basically created the Spring Saturnalia her freshman year."

"It's the best party of the year," Vitus tells us. "So much better than that tired old fling."

"So much better," echoes Proserpina. "Anyway, she thinks we're going to be all right. Like she says, a positive attitude is ninety-seven percent of the battle."

It's so astonishingly self-absorbed, in the face of our impending deaths, that I don't even know how to respond.

Maysilee, on the other hand, doesn't miss a beat. "I'll try to keep that in mind in the arena. More ice cream?"

Mags catches my eye, her smile barely suppressed.

Proserpina just holds out her bowl, oblivious. "I really think it will help you."

Maysilee, Lou Lou, and Wyatt's prep teams arrive, and we take turns in the bathrooms and bedrooms being groomed. I try to negotiate a few extra minutes floating in the tub so I can work out how I might come across as a rascal, but all I can think about is stealing nuts. I have a bad feeling I'm just going to come off as annoying.

Since they're not trying to counteract the insecticides from the gym shower, the prep teams get better results with less effort, but they can't compensate for our clothes. We were given a few changes of socks and underwear, but aside from that, we've been wearing our training outfits for three days straight. Lou Lou's is as wrinkled as a raisin from her napping in it, Wyatt spilled mashed potatoes on his and scraping it off made it look worse, and I have a tear at my shoulder from when Panache attacked me. Even Maysilee, who looks the least crumpled, has a spattering of her homemade glue from working with tokens. On top of that, the cheap fabric really holds the smell of fear sweat that we've been pumping out, and that's demoralizing even if the cameras won't pick it up.

I try to keep a positive attitude, since that's ninety-seven percent of the battle, reminding myself that at least we have black clothing that fits us and we have our tokens. But the truth can't be denied. We look like what we are: neglected, no-account, not-worth-a-professional-stylist long shots from District 12. Who's going to sponsor that?

On top of this, we have eight prep team members, half of them in tears, totally preoccupied with how this will affect their grades and, consequently, their future job prospects. Drusilla returns, pissed because she was unable to file a complaint until after the Games. As an afterthought, she went to see if she could rouse Magno, but he didn't answer his door and she thinks he might be dead, which is the only thing that's keeping her going. Except maybe that quart bottle of rum she's knocking back in the kitchen. Wiress and Mags try to focus our minds on our interviews, but the general commotion makes that impossible.

The noise drowns out the ping of the arriving elevator, so she seems to appear out of thin air. A young woman with lavender hair, a dress like a grape gumball, and green checked stockings. Four black hats stacked on her head, clothes bags draped over her arms, she wheels a cart of spiky shoes into the center of the living room and announces, "Who's ready for a big, big, big day!"

"Effie!" cries Proserpina, flinging herself into the newcomer's arms.

Effie pats her back. "Well, I'm not going to let my baby sister — or her friends! — fail because some slackard didn't do his job!"

All the prep teams break into cheers or tears or both as they crowd around her. She accepts the adulation, but then gets serious. "Listen, everybody. There is something bigger than you and me happening here. As we all know, the Hunger Games are a sacred ceremony of remembrance for the Dark Days. A lot of people lost their lives to guarantee peace and prosperity for our nation. And this is our chance — no, it is our *duty* — to honor them!"

Well, she's swallowed the Capitol propaganda hook and took the line and sinker with it, but at least she's brought us some decent footwear. She begins unzipping bags. "When you called, Prosie, at first, I didn't know what to do, and then I thought, *Great-Aunt Messalina!*"

"Great-Aunt Messalina!" crows Proserpina. "She never throws anything out!"

"A lot of it's really old, but fortunately all the war-era styles are back in fashion," explains Effie. She holds up a black lace dress with matching gloves. "And there's loads of black because there were so many funerals."

"You — are — brilliant — Effie — Trinket!" sputters Vitus.

"I confess to having a moment," says Effie. "Don't worry, boys, Great-Uncle Silius was no slouch in the threads department either."

He certainly wasn't, and even better, he seemed to be roughly the same size as Wyatt and me, with a few adjustments. We find a tuxedo for Wyatt and a three-piece suit with a rakish vest embroidered with cocktail glasses for me. Just the thing for a rascal. Or a bootlegger. By the time I've added a roomy pair of patent leather shoes and eight-ball cuff links on my white silk shirt, I look slick as a whistle.

"Clothes make the man," says Effie with satisfaction, giving me an approving pat on the shoulder. At least the Trinkets aren't mean, just clueless, which makes for a big improvement over Drusilla and Magno. The girls look sensational, too, with Lou Lou in the black lace dress, expertly pinned up to fit her, and Maysilee in an off-the-shoulder velvet gown, a boa, and the black lace gloves. I know we're being prettied up for slaughter, but at least we might have some sponsors now.

"Who could believe they're from District Twelve? It was really nice of your great-aunt to let you borrow everything," says Vitus.

"Well, she owes us after all the disgrace she brought to the name of Trinket. We'll be recovering from that for years," Effie says, crinkling her brow. "If even only half the stories are true . . ."

Vitus puts a consoling arm around her and says, "You don't pick your ancestors." Then his voice drops to a shamed whisper. "My grandfather was a rebel sympathizer."

"You win," concedes Effie. "But look at you now!"

When Drusilla swings out of the kitchen, she does a double take at our outfits. "What happened here?"

"My sister!" beams Proserpina, nudging Effie forward.

"Oh, it was a privilege to dress them for Panem," says Effie modestly.

Drusilla's face twists through a range of expressions — confusion, relief, admiration, with bitterness ultimately winning. "These cannot be credited to Magno. You." She grabs Effie by the arm. "You're coming with us, and I'm telling everyone you're responsible."

"But — I don't even have a backstage pass," objects Effie.

"That, at least, I can remedy." Drusilla waves us toward the door. "Come on, you lot, let's try to make it to at least one event on time."

Proserpina shoves a makeup box into Effie's hands. "Touch-ups!"

"I'm on it," promises Effie. "For everybody!" She gives Lou Lou, who's baring her teeth, a worried look. "Maybe a lighter shade of lipstick for you."

"And tone down the blush," says Maysilee.

"Exactly," agrees Effie. For a moment, they're just two girls on a mission to beautify the world. Effie holds up a compact for her opinion. "I'm thinking maybe a peach?"

"Much better."

"Hold on." Effie reaches over and removes a broken feather from Maysilee's boa. "There. You're perfect."

"Is my mascara okay?"

"Yes, but I can see it'd be a problem with those long lashes of yours." Effie digs in the makeup box and hands her a little pad. "Take this in case it smudges."

Drusilla starts to haul Effie to the elevator, sending the makeup box to the floor. It cracks open and tubes of color roll across the burnt-orange carpet. I lean over and collect them, returning it all to Effie, who looks slightly surprised.

"Thank you, Haymitch," she says. "That was very considerate, especially given your circumstances."

"Well, thank you for bringing us some dress-up clothes."

"You deserve to look beautiful tonight," Effie replies. "And I think you're all being very brave."

We don't have much choice, but it's nice to have someone recognize it.

In the van, inspired by Great-Uncle Silius's taste in fashion, I decide to double down on the bootlegger angle. I imagine brewing up illegal booze falls into the category of what the Capitol would consider naughty, not dangerous. Judging by the opening ceremony crowd, most of these folks drink like fish, so there should be a fair amount of sympathy for a kid who goes outside the law to keep his district pickled. Anyway, it's the best rascally angle I can come up with, and it's founded in truth. I don't want to get Hattie in any trouble, though, so I decide to pretend it's something I do on my own.

I'm starting to get antsy about the breaking-the-arena plan, given that I still don't know the timeline or how the explosives are being smuggled in. Mags and Wiress were allowed to accompany Drusilla, so Beetee should be with his tributes tonight, too.

The interviews are televised from an auditorium that seats a couple thousand people. Drusilla tells us there won't be a delay, since there's no potential for an uprising in the Capitol audience, so don't mess up and expect her to cover for us. That's rich. After she gets the official lineup, she slips off to have a word with Caesar Flickerman, so he can know how to approach our interviews. As she walks away, she mutters, "Shrew, calculator, lunatic, rascal."

We're taken to a waiting room backstage called the greenroom, although it's painted white. It's already crowded with mentors, escorts, and stylists hovering around their tributes, who are all polished up and dressed in chic evening wear in their districts' signature color. Even District 1, who wore ball gowns and suits to the parade, have upped their game, and their snot-green ensembles with flowing trains and plumed coattails require three times the space of any other district.

Effie eyes them critically and whispers, "Thank goodness your color is black! Can you imagine trying to outfit everyone in peridot? That was a flash in the pan."

Honestly, 12 comes off a lot classier and somehow potentially deadlier. Maybe I'm projecting. My jacket and vest have hidden compartments and my belt some extra loops that Effie told me were for decorative weapons. Hm, decorative. And Effie quickly ruled out the first shirt I tried on because of something that looked suspiciously like a bloodstain that hadn't come out in the wash. I can't help wondering if what Great-Aunt Messalina and her husband did to disgrace the family was connected to some lifeless bodies. Makes me feel a little more dangerous, slipping into their skins tonight.

Beetee catches my eye from a cluster of electric blue and gives a quick nod toward the buffet. Drusilla's busy making sure everybody knows Effie did our clothes, so I'm able to plead thirst and make a beeline for the punch bowl. The table's spread with delicacies, like candy high-heeled shoes and caviar in seashells and miniature pigs made of ham salad. I don't recognize half the food, but I follow a lady's example and smear a dollop of goat cheese on a square of peanut brittle. Surprisingly good.

I'm ladling myself some punch when Beetee sidles up beside me. He picks up a large pair of silver tweezers and begins to meticulously choose tiny vegetables from an arrangement shaped like a bunch of flowers. It's ridiculous.

"Those work better than your fingers?" I ask.

"Trying not to draw attention to myself," he says quietly.

I glance around and see several Peacekeepers have their eyes on us. A couple begin to close in when there's a commotion at the door. Magno Stift lurches into the room, holding a cage of reptiles above his head and shouting, "The party animals are here!"

As the Peacekeepers redirect toward my stylist, Beetee plucks off a minuscule radish and speaks rapidly under his breath. "Head north. Ampert will do the same after he has the explosive. Do your best to locate a mutt portal by tracking returning mutts after an attack. After you and Ampert meet up, take one to access Sub-A, where the tank is located. We've replaced the black cord in Ampert's token with fuse, the blasting cap's hidden in the weave."

I take a deep pull on my punch, checking out Ampert's token over the rim of the cup. It's indistinguishable from the one Maysilee made, with no sign of the blasting cap in the braided cord. Beetee doesn't say where it came from, but the rebels must have someone on the inside who smuggled it through security and swapped it for the original.

"All four of District Nine's sunflowers are now composed of explosive," he adds.

"But their sunflowers are hard. Kerna's shattered on the floor."

"Yes. These are coated with a shellac. Wet them with water and rub them between your palms. The friction will help dissolve the shellac and leave the explosive malleable."

"Does Nine know the plan?" I ask.

"They do not. Ampert will scavenge one from their persons." From a dead body, he means. Probably at the bloodbath. "Or more if he can get them. It never hurts to have a spare. And if Ampert fails to show" — Beetee's voice breaks slightly on this last bit. We both know why Ampert might not be able to reach me. For a moment, he examines a pea-sized tomato under his glasses — "we've also replaced the —"

A flutter of chiffon at my elbow alerts me to the arrival of all four District 6 doves, who shimmer in their iridescent gray finery. Beetee moves down to a meatball pyramid without further clarifications, a good-bye, or a good luck.

Wellie whispers, "Ampert says, when we get to the arena, we're supposed to band together as soon as possible."

Is that by design? Probably. If Ampert bands with the others, he'll have access to the tributes from 9 when they die. Meanwhile, I have my own mission, which does not involve protecting this flock.

"That sounds like a good plan," I agree.

"He says maybe some of you bigger tributes can grab weapons first," Wellie tells me.

"I'll give it a shot." But I will not be able to look after them in the arena — I will have to devote my abilities to blowing up the tank or die trying. "Listen, I'm going to be a real jerk in my interview. It's something my team worked up, but I will never hurt you, okay? Or any of the Newcomers. That's a promise."

"We know that," says Wellie, eyes full of trust.

Too much trust. I need to distance myself from them for the good of everybody.

"There's another thing, though," I say. "You saw my score, that I only got a one. The Gamemakers may be targeting me. It's dangerous for any of you to be around me. So I'm thinking of going it alone."

Wellie's face falls. "But they're targeting all of us. We need you."

"You don't if I'm drawing packs of mutts or being chased into the Careers. You don't. And you all have to understand that. Tell the others, okay?"

Across the room, a glassy-eyed Magno has backed into a corner but managed to clear some space by freeing a six-foot snake from the cage and waving it around. "Where are my tributes? I need to dress them!"

People are shrieking, and the Peacekeepers form a huddle to confer over their plan to subdue him. Drusilla looks overjoyed, shouting, "Take him down! Take him down!"

But before the Peacekeepers, tasers pulled, can do the job, Lou Lou steps up, hands extended for the snake, and says, "Mine."

Magno grins, bypasses her hands, drapes the snake around her shoulders, then loops the tail end around her neck. "You wear her like this."

Lou Lou entwines her arm with the snake's neck so its head rests on the back of her hand and holds it up. Magno leans over and kisses the snake on the mouth. It's the very picture of madness, this damaged little girl and our debauched, drugged stylist. Wyatt goes to collect her, putting an arm around her to guide her back to the District 12 crew. The snake seems to have given Lou Lou a sense of power, and she walks by tributes three times her size, brandishing the snake and hissing.

I rejoin my district just as the television at the end of the green room comes to life. On-screen, an invisible hand writes a big curlicue *50* over a shot of the auditorium stage as a booming voice announces, "Ladies and Gentlemen, welcome to the Fiftieth Hunger Games Night of Interviews. And here's everybody's favorite host, Caesar Flickerman!"

Caesar descends from the ceiling perched on a crescent moon, stars shooting behind him. He's a young guy wearing a suit so dark blue it's almost black, embedded with tiny light bulbs that make it twinkle. The suit never changes, but every year he dyes his hair a different color, tonight a deep pine-forest green, and paints his eyelids and lips the same color. Maybe you could make an argument for the hair and eyes, but green lips suggest a man in the process of decomposition. He just looks ghoulish. The gleam of his overly white teeth as he flashes the audience a knowing smile only reminds you that he's got a skull under all that glop. As he deftly dismounts the moon, he opens his arms and says, "Hello, Panem! Shall we get this party started?" The audience roars in approval.

Here in the green room, a young Gamemaker lines up Districts 1 and 2, reading out their order of appearance. They file out the door after her to wait in the wings.

On-screen, Caesar launches into a brief retrospective of the other forty-nine Games, starting with the no-frills version of the early years directly after the war, when the tributes were thrown into an old, bombed-out sports arena with weapons and little else. I watch carefully when he talks about the Tenth Games being a turning point, as that was the year District 12 had a victor, but they only feature the introduction of betting, the sponsors, and the rickety drones that dropped food and water to the tributes.

From this point on, the Games evolved from pure punishment to unapologetic entertainment. The original sports venue was abandoned as the Gamemakers began to use existing settings in the wild or bombed-out towns and such, introducing an assortment of mutts and a variety of weapons.

The Twenty-fifth Games, the first Quarter Quell, proved particularly heinous, as the districts were forced to choose their own tributes rather than relying on the reaping. Another Flickerman named Lucky hosted with commentary from a relic of a woman named Gaul, who was credited with coining the phrase "May the odds be EVER in your favor" for the anniversary. That phrase has caught on as a way to wish someone good luck, but if you think about it, it's a sadistic thing to say to a tribute, given that survival's an impossibility for twenty-three of the twenty-four kids.

For this first Quell, the Gamemakers had the tributes kick off the Capitol portion by riding chariots through the streets in district-flavored costumes. Rather than scout a location for the Games, they built an arena for a single use. Also, the Cornucopia made its first appearance, loaded with weapons and supplies, triggering a heated bloodbath when the opening gong sounded.

For the last twenty-four years, they've unveiled a brand-new arena each year based on a different environment or theme, from a desert to a frigid landscape to Wiress's reflective puzzle, which they called the Nest of Mirrors. Caesar teases the audience about the second Quarter Quell arena. He's heard a rumor it puts all the previous arenas to shame. Can they imagine it? No, they can't. Will it be fabulous? Yes, it will.

My stomach feels sick and I'm glad I don't have to go first. I'm also glad District 1 does. When Caesar introduces Silka, she strides onstage dragging fifteen feet of a snot-green train behind her.

"Ugh. Just like a snail," comments Maysilee loudly, getting a round of nervous laughter in the green room. What everybody's really thinking is about how Silka's over six feet tall without the heels and can throw an ax into a dummy's heart at fifteen feet. And that is not something you can laugh off.

Since there are so many of us this year, we're limited to two-minute interviews and after every four districts, there will be some sort of break that Caesar calls a "palate cleanser."

Silka wastes no time in bragging about her size, her strength, her ax-handling, and her scoring a ten. She doesn't even bother mentioning her alliance with the Careers, and when Caesar brings them up, she just says, "Sure, it helps to have someone to clear the field."

Panache swaggers onstage next, stopping three different times to pose and flex his muscles for the audience.

"Panache from District One!" Caesar bellows. Then asks him, "So, Panache, in addition to your obvious assets, why should our audience back you?"

"Because I'm the biggest, the beefiest, and the best!" Panache hits another pose.

"My word, it sounds like we should barbeque you!" quips Caesar.

"That's right. I'm all meat, little man," says Panache, giving Caesar a patronizing pat on the head.

He's just so easy to loathe. You can see the cut landing with Caesar, but he lives for this stuff. "Even your brain?" he asks in wonder.

The audience titters. Confusion crosses Panache's face, then anger at the teasing. "Not my brain! Obviously, it's . . . gray stuff."

Caesar nods, straight-faced, as if digesting this, while the audience cracks up. Panache begins to burn and I remember the train window, which was only an innocent bystander. For a minute I think he might destroy Caesar, but he catches himself and just shouts at the audience, "What does it matter?"

"Matter?" Caesar sputters. "I think brain matter . . . matters quite a bit!"

The Capitol citizens lose it and so do I, until I remember the joke's not just on Panache. It's on all of us stupid, clawed district piglets. Animals for their entertainment. Expendable for their pleasure. Too dumb to deserve to live.

Caesar settles the audience and tries to get back to the interview. "All in good fun, Panache, all in good fun. Personally, I failed biology. So tell us, what's your weapon of choice?"

"My fists," says Panache, holding one right up to Caesar's nose.

Caesar takes a delicate step back, turns his head to the audience, and stage-whispers, "Also meaty."

It's all over then for Panache. They show shots of people overcome with hilarity, tears streaming down their cheeks, gasping for breath. Caesar pretends he's trying to continue his questions, then jumps back every time Panache looks at him, mugging in terror for the cameras. I can't stand Panache, but it's unfair. A bell signals his time's up, and he has no choice but to leave the stage, steaming and humiliated.

The rest of the tributes from Districts 1 and 2 seem to realize they're in danger of being classified as stupid beasts, too, so they make an effort to play up their prowess with weapons and the benefits of the Career pack. But Panache has done some damage, and any attempt to boast about muscle comes with a comic side-eye from Caesar that tickles the audience. I remember my pa saying, if you can get people to laugh at someone, it makes them look weak. He meant the heavies in the Capitol, but it seems to be true here as well.

Up until this point, no mention has been made of the Newcomers, but Dio kicks off the District 3 interviews with news of our alliance, generously laying out the entire team by name, every one of us, and touting our skills. Ampert follows with his whole theory of previous tributes being brainwashed, the disproportionate number of Career wins, and how it will only take numbers to bring a different result. He doesn't even mention his own attributes, but he doesn't need to, because he's clearly so whip-smart that Caesar remarks on it with approval. In fact, all of District 3 comes off as brainy, collaborative, and composed, in high contrast to the Careers, and they get plenty of applause.

District 4 came prepared to showcase their trident and netting skills, not to strategize about the Newcomers. They fumble when confronted with Caesar's line of questioning. "Those kids seem pretty bright, don't you think?" "What else do you think they have up their sleeves?" "What about their numbers?" "What plans have the Careers discussed to counter the Newcomers?"

By the first palate cleanser, the Capitol's buzzing about the Newcomers. While the audience is treated to highlights of fashion through the Games, District 5 calls an emergency meeting in the green room. As the sole remaining Career district, this will be their alliance's last chance to present their case against the Newcomers. The rest of the evening will belong to us.

District 9, despite their commitment to the Newcomers, tends to remain exclusive. Shy, maybe, or just not very social. I go over to say hey, which also gives me an opportunity to covertly examine their sunflower tokens. I see the replicas have been approached just as seriously as Ampert's token. The little cracks in Kerna's flower look so convincing I worry they haven't actually replaced it. I don't want to go to the trouble of getting to that tank only to be caught trying to detonate a lump of salt flour dough. But either I trust Beetee or I don't. He's certainly going out on a limb trusting me.

After the break, District 5 does their best to highlight our shortcomings. They focus on our size and dearth of training, but they lack a cohesive plan to eliminate us, probably because the smugness of Careers made this seem unnecessary, and they end up contradicting each other. Will they stay in one pack or break up? Will they share food and water? Who is the leader of the Careers and will they follow them? Basic questions clearly never discussed. And when they're not sure of the answers, the temptation to promote themselves wins out.

I'm a little worried since my doves are next, swimming in chiffon ruffles, but once Wellie steps up to Caesar's mic, it's pure Newcomers for the rest of the night. Her diminutive size becomes secondary as she assuredly answers the same questions that tripped up District 5 without hesitation:

"We'll always be one pack, as you call it. But we'll divide up as necessary to defeat the Careers."

"Oh, we're going to share our provisions. It just makes sense."

"We don't have one leader, as such. The Newcomers are more committed to the alliance itself, which is better, you know, because we will lose kids. But Ampert came up with the idea and brought us all together, and we've all sworn to follow his plan and protect one another to the end."

I don't know, maybe Ampert left me out of the loop when it came to our interview strategy because he knew I'd be preoccupied with sabotage, but the Newcomers have their ducks in a row. Nobody talks too much about themselves, they stress the power of the group and the advantages the Newcomers will exploit in the arena. How small size can be a plus for climbing trees or hiding or needing less food, how being able to trust your teammates means you'll get better sleep — so the Careers won't be catching any zzz's — and how brain power, which we have in spades, comes in handy for everything from strategy to building things to catching food. In the brief moments when they pitch their personal skills, it's about how they'll use them to help one another.

Maybe we'll lose, but we're sure making a lot of people proud back home.

Even with the interruption of the second palate cleanser, a terrifying review of the deadliest mutts in Games history, the Newcomers keep building our case, and before you know it, District 12 is up.

As admirable as the Newcomers may be, I think we've begun to wear on Caesar. Selflessness and quiet resolve don't really make for rollicking entertainment. So, after a quick confirmation of our Newcomer commitment, he's more than ready to go with District 12's sauce.

Caesar eggs on Maysilee, who garners a lot of laughs when she machine-guns the midsection of the front row for their poor taste. To a man dressed in a suit made of hundred-dollar bills, she says, "That's sweet. You wore all your friends tonight." To a lady with surgically implanted cat ears. "And is that purse for your flea powder?"

Wyatt spouts off complicated odds that a Gamemaker with a calculator confirms. When he correctly figures the amount of sponsor dollars it would take to send a tribute a stuffed pheasant two weeks into the Games, given rising inflation of thirty-eight percent a day, he genuinely blows Caesar away. "I wasn't so hot in arithmetic either!" he exclaims. "I don't know if the odds are in your favor in the arena, Wyatt, but if you win, you and me are heading to the casino!"

Lou Lou's a sensation, wielding her snake, baring her teeth at the audience. As usual, she states her name and district, but then resorts to hissing at Caesar when he asks a question. When the audience snickers, she crouches down and holds out the snake, causing some people to jokingly recoil, and the bolder ones to stroke its sinewy body. She's winning them over, until, for the first time this evening, perhaps inspired by her ferocity, Caesar asks, "Now, Louella, what will the Newcomers do if they kill off all the Careers? What will happen with you kids then?"

As if on cue, the snake hisses in a woman's jewel-studded face and Lou Lou growls, "You'll murder us. You'll murder us."

If the sight of this strange little girl wrapped in a snake amused them, her attack on the Capitol does not. Gasps and sounds of disapproval rise from the audience, but she persists.

"You'll murder us! You'll murder us!" Her pitch gets higher and higher and the effect is chilling. "You'll murder us!"

The facade of fun vanishes. She begins to crawl along the edge of the stage, singling out front-row ticket holders and shouting, "You! . . . You! . . . You! . . . You! . . ."

Even Caesar's famous cool is blown as he dances after her, trying to recapture the magic. "Okay, Louella . . . Louella! It's unfortunate, but the Games can only have one winner. Louella! She's certainly determined! A little help here, please!"

Mid-accusation, Lou Lou falls silent. Her eyes roll upward and she collapses to the floorboards.

"She's fainted from exertion, and not a moment too soon!" exclaims Caesar. I'm certain the Gamemakers had a hand in it, probably drugging her through her pump. They let Wyatt return to carry her offstage as Caesar immediately segues into introducing me. "And now our final tribute of the evening, Haymitch Abernathy from District Twelve!"

I take my time crossing the stage, because I don't think a guy with cocktail glasses on his vest would hurry. Caesar, in recovery mode, jumps right in. "So, Haymitch, what do you think of the Games having one hundred percent more competitors than usual?"

This is the first time they will hear me speak, and I want to make a lasting impression. But suddenly I'm not thinking of Great-Uncle Silius — I'm thinking of Woodbine Chance, who should have been standing here in my place. He was always walking a line of trouble, but people liked him. Especially the girls. Too young to be considered a real danger yet, but certainly a rascal.

I give a shrug and let a little of that Chance attitude slip in. "I don't see that it makes much difference. They'll still be one hundred percent as stupid as usual, so I figure the odds will be roughly the same."

An appreciative chuckle runs through the audience.

I give them half a smile. "I'm speaking of the Careers, of course."

"Well, it isn't common knowledge, but I heard you've had some run-ins with one of the Careers. Panache maybe?" Caesar asks.

I come back with, "Heard you did, too." Caesar laughs along with the audience. "Yeah, I'm not on good terms with any of the Careers. But the Newcomers are plenty smart and one hundred percent safe with me."

"Well, judging by your Gamemakers' score, everybody's safe with you," observes Caesar, drawing an *ooh* from the audience. "I hear you got a one in training?"

"Not so easy!" I tell him. "I consider that one a badge of honor. I mean, I've got thirty-one sworn allies, this rock-hard body, and a brain five times smarter than any Career's. Know what else I've got? Guts. Because clearly . . . I'm not afraid to piss off the Gamemakers!"

I open my arms to the audience and pace along the front of the stage while they hoot in support. "Shoot, a ten? A ten? Anybody can get a ten! You have to be a special kind of trouble to get a one, am I right?" Cheers of affirmation. "I can tell some of you know just what I mean." I point out a man in the second row who wears a glass cube of live bees on his head. "This gentleman right here, for instance." He nods vigorously. "And you, darling?" I lean over the lady with the cat ears. She covers her face in gleeful embarrassment. "Sure, you been there."

"So let's make a list of everyone you've pissed off," says Caesar. "There's Panache . . . and the other Careers . . . and the Gamemakers. That's just in the few days you've been in the Capitol. Anybody back home?"

"Well, there's the Peacekeepers." The audience quiets a bit. "They can get out of sorts if I don't deliver their white liquor on time." Shocked laughter.

"'Their white liquor?' Just exactly what do you do after school, Haymitch?"

I'm careful to keep this as removed from Hattie's still as I can. "Well, let's just call it my science homework. Turns out, I can make hooch out of just about anything, Caesar. District Twelve can't brag about much, but we've got the finest shine in Panem. And I'm pretty sure the base commander will back me up on that!"

"But . . . isn't that illegal?"

"Is it? For real?" I turn to a moustachioed man holding an oversized brandy snifter. "You'd think the commander might've mentioned that."

The bell rings and Caesar gives me a slap on the back. "This one's a real rascal, ladies and gentlemen! Haymitch Abernathy from District Twelve! May the odds be EVER in his favor!"

Half the audience gets to their feet to applaud me off. I wink at the lady with the cat ears, much to her delight, and exit the stage. I'm pretty sure Drusilla planted the label *rascal* in Caesar's head, but even so, I feel I've earned it.

Backstage, Mags and Wiress await me. Mags gives me a hug, Wiress a quick nod, saying only, "You've got some sponsors."

I can hear Caesar wrapping things up for the evening as we rejoin the rest of the team and hurry down the halls to our exit. I think we must be headed back to the apartment, but when we reach our van, Plutarch's waiting.

He addresses Drusilla. "Great job! You know, these kids never got a proper photo shoot. What say we swing by my place and get some high-quality pictures, maybe even a little footage? Be nice to have for cameos if they hang in there. And it might seem like you and I weren't doing our jobs without it."

Drusilla considers this. "Just so long as Magno Stift is never mentioned."

"Magno who?" says Plutarch, and Drusilla flounces off to her private car.

Under her breath, Effie says, "Some marriages should never have happened."

"Drusilla and Magno were married?" I ask in disbelief.

"Still are, technically," says Plutarch. "Thirty years and counting! She says it's a tax thing, but who really knows? Shall we go?"

Mags and Wiress weren't invited, but the rest of us land in Plutarch's library with Trajan Heavensbee watching over us. Everybody almost looks at home in the Trinkets' wardrobe. Effie touches up our makeup and even adds a flower to my lapel from an arrangement in a replica of the golden staircase.

Plutarch suggests he take us off one at a time to the conservatory to practice for the video footage. "District Twelve's gone from nobodies to a hot commodity among the more daring sponsors," he says brightly. "That's a breakthrough. But let's try and get everybody to jump on that bandwagon." I go with him first, while Drusilla oversees Maysilee's photo shoot and Wyatt keeps an eye on Lou Lou, who stares in fascination at a candelabra while she cuddles her snake.

We left the Peacekeepers at the entrance, since Plutarch said his private security team would be sufficient, so we're as unguarded as on my earlier visit to the mansion.

Plutarch seems in a hurry, and I'm practically jogging to keep up with him. "I was thinking, like you said, about people who think we're too risky, and I —"

He cuts me off. "Listen, Haymitch, I know you don't like me, and you certainly don't trust me, but you should know that, despite appearances, a desire for freedom is not limited to the districts. And your misfortune does not give you the right to assume so. I hope after tonight you'll consider this."

I have no idea what he's talking about. "What?"

The warm air of the conservatory hits my face. He crosses over to the swan telephone, lifts the receiver, and says, "Ready on this end." He listens for a moment more, then hands it to me. "Someone wants to talk to you." Then he walks a discreet distance away.

Oh. Now I get it. President Snow. I overdid it in the interview and I'm about to hear about my gory demise. And Plutarch, who likes to think of himself as a decent guy, is upset about throwing me to the wolves again. Figures. With trepidation, I lift the receiver to my ear, brace myself, and manage to get out a "Yeah?"

"Haymitch? Is that really you?" The breathless voice, rough with recent tears, cuts right through to my heart.

Lenore Dove.

I grip the phone, eyes shut tight. I am back in the mountains. Arms wrapped around her, the scent of honeysuckle in her hair. She'd been crying then, too. Not at anything I did, but because they'd hung a man that morning and made the rest of us watch. But there we were, high in the hills, with not one but two rainbows arching across the sky. Sometimes she cries because things are so beautiful and we keep messing them up. Because the world doesn't have to be so terrifying. That's on people, not the world.

"Haymitch?"

"Yeah, it's me. I'm here. Where are you calling from?"

"I'm on the Peacekeepers' base. They arrested me."

This jolts me back to the conservatory. It's not honeysuckle I'm smelling, but the faint mix of roses and decaying meat drifting off the nepenthes. My arms can't protect her, only embrace the empty air. "Arrested you? When? What for?" Is this because I just joked about the Peacekeepers buying white liquor? Are they taking out my waywardness on her?

"Last night. For playing music. I guess I went a little crazy when they gave you that one in training. I took my tune box over to the Justice Building. They hadn't pulled the stage down yet, and I did a few songs."

She doesn't have to tell me which songs. "The Goose and the Common." "The Capitol Store." "The Hanging Tree." All the ones she's forbidden to play in public. Clerk Carmine and Tam

Amber must be going nuts right now. And I share their exasperation and fear. "Oh, Lenore Dove . . . are you all right? Did they hurt you?"

"No. Just hauled me in. Less about what I played, more about how it drew people. Everybody's real upset this year, so many kids. They needed a place to be together, to raise their voices. Sometimes the hurt's too bad to bear alone."

So it wasn't just her, playing her heart out in front of the Justice Building. A crowd had gathered. Sung the forbidden songs. "Did they say the charges?"

"Disrupting the peace or something. And you know, 'No Peace, No Anything.'"

My mind races. Disrupting the peace isn't sedition. They can lay that on you for getting drunk and busting up a few bottles, which happens all the time in 12. It's not like she's part of some big conspiracy, so, hopefully, they won't use methods to force her to talk. Just view her as an emotional sixteen-year-old whose boyfriend got reaped. Maybe take away her tune box for a while or keep her locked up until after the Hunger Games when things have died down. I hope they don't put her in the stocks on the square, which is what they threatened to do when she was twelve. But that was four years ago, and the Covey have some Peacekeepers among their fans, so that could work in her favor. A lot will depend on how rowdy the audience got and how the base commander views it. I sure didn't do her any favors by bragging about selling him white liquor tonight. Now he may feel obliged to come down harder on her.

"Was there fighting? Did anything get broke?" I ask.

"Oh, who cares? They're letting me out tomorrow morning, but you're going into the arena." Relief surges through me. They're letting her out. Just a slap on the wrist. "None of my stuff matters a whit," she continues. "And I sure don't want to spend our last moments talking about what's broken. Except my heart . . . how about that?"

She's mad and probably near tears again. "Oh, Lenore Dove . . . I'm so sorry I messed everything up." And I did, too. The Peacekeepers wouldn't have targeted her just for trying to help Woodbine's ma. At least, not as a rule.

"You? It's entirely my fault you're there! And I know I'm why you got that score. I as good as killed you, and that's not something I can live with."

And so she's doing what she can to get herself killed? Now *I'm* mad. "That's just a lie you've got to stop telling yourself! If I'd kept my head, you might've gotten a few bruises, but we'd both still be in Twelve."

"No, darling, that's not how it went down at all. I overstepped, just like my uncles always warn me about. I lost my temper and started hollering and now you're — oh, Haymitch . . . I don't want to be on this earth without you."

"So now you're trying to get them to hang you? You do, and I swear I'll — I'll —" I'll what? I'll be dead and gone is what, in no position to do anything. But I feel so helpless now, I've got to try whatever I can to change her mind. I have no idea what happens when we die, but Lenore Dove believes nothing ever dies, and we just move from one world to the next like the Covey did from town to town. "Like in one of your songs, my ghost will hunt down your ghost and never give it a moment's rest."

"Promise?" She sounds a little more hopeful. "Because if I could count on that, I think I could bear it. But what I can't bear is . . . what if we're never together again?"

"We will be together always," I say with conviction. "I don't know how, and I don't know where, I don't know anything, but I feel that in my heart. You and me, we will find each other, as many times as it takes."

"You think?"

"I do. But not if you do something stupid like getting yourself killed on purpose. I feel like that could throw the whole thing out of whack. You stay alive, play your songs, love your people, live the best life you can. And I'll be there in the Meadow waiting for you. It's a promise. Okay?"

"Okay," she whispers. "I'll try. That's my promise back."

Plutarch waves his hand to get my attention, taps his watch. Time has run out.

"Lenore Dove, I love you like all-fire. That's for always."

"I love you like all-fire, too. You and no one else. Just like my geese, I mate for life. And then some. Forever."

I need to say, no, don't spend your life grieving me, love whoever you want. Only I just can't bear the thought of it at the moment. Her kissing someone else. But I'm trying to be noble, to pull myself up to say those words, when the line goes dead without warning.

"Lenore Dove? Lenore Dove?"

She's gone. Truly for good, this time. But she is safe. I set the swan head back in the cradle like I am laying down a sleeping child, slow and gentle-like. Good-bye, my love.

Only now do I wonder how this call has occurred. I've never even heard of a tribute getting to talk to someone back home from the Capitol. I meet Plutarch's eyes. "You set that call up?"

He shrugs. "I have an old friend in Twelve."

"Why would you do that for me?" I say, genuinely perplexed. "I bet it could get you in real trouble."

"Yes, you're right. If it gets discovered, my next meal will probably be a large platter of poisoned oysters. But I risked it because I need you to trust me, Haymitch. More importantly, I need you to trust the information I'm about to give you."

I'm completely lost. "What information?"

"About how to break the arena."

This pulls me up short. Plutarch? Plutarch knows about the arena plot? He's right. I don't trust him, or the whole forsaken plan now. Were Beetee and I being recorded somehow during the blackout, even if the cameras were out? It would be easy enough to bug the place. Were there microphones in the vegetable bouquet tonight? If that's the case, Plutarch could be working for the Capitol, trying to get more info out of me and kill anyone involved. He set up the call with Lenore Dove so I would trust him, so I would confide in him.

"I have no idea what you're talking about," I say.

"Fine. That's smart. Don't trust me. Only hear what I have to say and, when you're in the arena, see if it comes in handy."

I lift my hands in bewilderment. "You sure you got the right guy?"

"Okay, just listen. I don't have any real security clearance, but my cousin knows a Gamemakers' apprentice, barely out of the University, who wants to quit the program and work in television. I spent a fortune the other night getting him drunk. The most useful piece of info I got was that the arena's sun is in sync with our own."

I look at him, baffled. "Isn't it always?"

"Sometimes. Depends on the arena. You could have multiple suns or none at all. The reason this will be of importance to you is that since the sun rises in the east, you will be able to tell direction."

Beetee said the tank was in the north. If it's true, this is essential information, but I act blasé. "Guess I would've assumed that anyway."

"Another thing: About a year or two ago, a committee of Gamemakers asked to tour our conservatory and gardens. The Heavensbees are known for their collection of rare flowering plants. I gave them the tour and then stepped out of the room to order tea. I overheard them discussing opening the berms."

"Berms?"

"It's what our gardener calls those mounds of earth." He points out through the window where hanging globes illuminate a little knoll covered in flowers. "She plants shrubs and flowers on them. And if the Gamemakers are planning to open them in the arena, then something's either going in, coming out, or both."

Mutts. He's trying to tell me the mutt portals are going to be concealed by berms of flowers. But I just say, "You have completely lost me, sir."

"Of course I have. One last thing. From the Capitol's perspective, the Games are the best propaganda we have. You tributes, you're our stars. You carry it out. But only if we control the narrative. Don't let us." Plutarch grasps my shoulders and gives me a little shake. "No more implicit submission for you, Haymitch Abernathy. Blow that water tank sky high. The entire country needs you to."

I can't help but think of Pa's directive to Sarshee Whitcomb. Seems like a lot to lay on my doorstep. Fix this mess for us, or else.

Effie hurries in the door. "Mr. Heavensbee? Oh, there you are. Drusilla wants you to help with Louella's photos. The snake's stealing focus."

Plutarch chuckles. "Never work with children or animals, Miss Trinket. Come along, Haymitch."

"And maybe it isn't my place to say," continues Effie, "but she's being awfully hard on Maysilee."

"Well, Maysilee's sixteen years old with great cheekbones — two things Drusilla can never achieve."

"I know, it's sad. But I give her points for trying." Effie's hands go to her face. "I guess it's time for me to start trying myself."

"Oh, I think you've got a few years."

"All my friends have begun maintenance. It's just, I hate needles."

While Plutarch reassures Effie, I follow them back to the library, trying to make sense of his position. If he's working for the Capitol, I don't think I've given him anything to use against us or copped to any involvement. But if he's not Snow's lackey, and he knows about the plot, and he's trying to help us . . . what is he after?

His words from a few minutes ago echo back. *"You should know that, despite appearances, a desire for freedom is not limited to the districts."* Was he suggesting that he, with all his wealth and privilege and power, lacks freedom? Freedom to do what? Maybe to not have to live in terror of Snow poisoning his oysters, for one thing.

I think about Vitus's shame over his rebel-sympathizing grandfather. That seems to be the norm here, but who was his grandfather? A Capitol citizen who sided with the districts. And somebody here must have helped Beetee switch out the tokens. It's possible that Plutarch could be on the level. I won't really know until I'm in the arena and get a good look at those berms, if they even exist.

Back in the library, Lou Lou's blowing out the candles and greedily inhaling the smoke curling off the burned wicks. The smell takes me home for a moment, dark winter nights, your last impression as you snuggle safe beneath the quilts. Does smoke conjure up the same memory for Lou Lou? Like the roll with the seeds did? Something deep and long ago, a home in District 11 where she was cherished and cared for? Wyatt talks her into sitting for the camera and then I pose for a couple of shots. They show us the results, and the photos are miles better than the ones of us in the coal miner costumes, chained up in the back of the van. Again, like the reaping presentation, we have Plutarch to thank for that.

He decides he can just direct us all at once for the propos that will air throughout the Games, so he doesn't have to repeat himself. "Let me catch you up on what Haymitch and I have been discussing."

Yes, I think. *Better catch me up*.

"Let's start with the basics. Public opinion is driven by emotion. People have an emotional response to something, then they come up with an argument for why it logically makes sense," says Plutarch.

"I don't think that's smart," says Wyatt, looking uneasy. I'm sure his calculator brain's appalled by the idea.

"Oh, I didn't say it was smart — I just said it was true. Make the audience feel for you, they'll figure out intellectually why you're the right tribute to support," Plutarch explains.

"But they hate all of us," Wyatt counters. "They're watching us kill each other for entertainment."

Plutarch waves this away. "They don't see it that way. Supporting the Hunger Games is their patriotic duty."

"Whatever. We're all their enemies," says Maysilee.

"Sure, but they have to root for someone. Why not you? You Newcomers have done a terrific job setting yourselves up as worthy adversaries to the Careers tonight. In fact, I think the Capitol audience finds you much more engaging, oddly enough, because you're not trying to appear to be like them."

"You mean, because we don't seem like Capitol suck-ups," concludes Maysilee.

"Exactly. There's been a lot of concern in the Capitol lately that district citizens are aspiring to break in here. It's not entirely unfounded, particularly with people from One and Two who work closely with us. Luxury and military, you know. There are Capitol-born folks assigned out there who've got mixed families they want to bring here now. But you're unapologetically district. And any way you can drive home that the Careers are buying into the Games and trying to be more Capitol than the Capitol itself will increase the social disapproval for them."

Once in a blue moon a Seam girl falls for a Peacekeeper and ends up with a baby, resulting in plenty of social disapproval in 12 as well. But there's never any talk of the kid going to the Capitol. Most are simply disowned by the father, who's then shipped off to another district.

"Calling them the Careers still makes them sound like they're better than us," says Maysilee. "We need to give them a stupid nickname."

"Name-calling! Excellent!" exclaims Plutarch. "Cheap but effective."

Itchy Itchy Haymitchy. Yep. Cheap but effective.

"But the nickname should call them stupid without being stupid itself," Plutarch goes on. "We need some wordplay. Something clever or rhyming or catchy. But not crude — this is a family show."

We toss around words. *Suck-ups. Bootlickers. Turncoats. Pretenders. Backstabbers. Wannabes.* Nothing quite works.

"We need an image that comes from real life," says Maysilee. "That's why Neddie Newcomer stuck with us. We need something that's a poor copy of something else. Like that artificial sweetener we have to use in our candy when real sugar's too dear. But worse."

"Powdered milk," says Wyatt.

"Fake leather," chimes in Effie.

I think of the beer they sell in the Capitol store, thin, sour, and feeble. The joke is a barrel of it wouldn't get your mamaw tipsy. "Near Beer," I pitch.

Everybody laughs. The name itself is the joke.

"Hey, Near Beer Career!" says Wyatt. "It even rhymes."

"I think we might be onto something," says Plutarch. "Haymitch, why don't you kick it off? You've already got the bootlegger angle going. People loved it. It was one of the most memorable bits of the evening."

We work up a little piece where Plutarch asks me about our opponents and I answer, "Well, back in Twelve, where we know our libations" — I brush off pretend dust from my cocktail glass vest and continue — "we just call them Near Beer Careers. You know, because they're all foam and no beer."

We play with it and change "no beer" to "no kicker" so as not to repeat the first "beer." Then we make up some similar sayings for variation. Maysilee does "All brag and no britches," since she's about fashion, and Wyatt comes up with a gambler's "All bluff and no aces." Lou Lou's really not in a position to write her own, being curled up with the snake now, so we decide on the old standby "All bark and no bite." Wyatt gets her to say it, just once, for the camera. The snake shows its teeth on "bite," so it's really all we need.

Plutarch seems genuinely happy, saying he's going to be able to edit the clips together into some fine propos. He sighs when he mentions the tools that were abolished and incapacitated in the past, ones deemed fated to destroy humanity because of their ability to replicate any scenario using any person. "And in mere seconds!" He snaps his fingers to emphasize their speed. "I guess it was the right thing to do, given our natures. We almost wiped ourselves out even without them, so you can imagine. But oh, the possibilities!"

Yeah, it's amazing we're here at all. Given our natures.

Lou Lou's snake comes up missing, and we're about to hunt it down when Plutarch notices the clock on the mantel and waves us toward the door. "Never mind, never mind. We've got to get you to bed. Tomorrow's the show." As he escorts us past the Heavensbees, he starts talking about getting everybody to jump on the bandwagon again, which he says is about people being eager to join a popular thing, but it makes me think about the Covey riding around on their wagon, which was an actual bandwagon. When we reach the waiting van, Plutarch wishes us all well.

I still don't know what to make of the man, but maybe he really did risk his life to give me a last, few priceless moments with Lenore Dove and maybe, in the arena, his information will prove true. Who knows if he might be able to aid us in some other way once the "show" begins? Yet again, it's better to stay on his good side.

I offer him my hand. "Thanks for all your help, Plutarch."

Gratified, he takes it. "Well, I'm despicable on many levels, but in this I'm on your side."

I guess we'll see.

Back at the apartment, Mags and Wiress have a big dinner awaiting us — pot roast with all the fixings — but there's not much room in my stomach due to the butterflies. They compliment us on our performances and the wonderful work we've done with the Newcomers, although I feel like most of that credit goes to people other than me. At least I didn't mess things up.

I'm feeling okay until bedtime, when Maysilee says to me, "Is it true? That you're going off on your own?"

Wellie apparently got the word out. "I got a one, Maysilee. They're gunning for me. You and Wyatt have a much better chance without me." I don't mention Lou Lou because I don't think she stands a chance at all.

Wyatt nods, factoring odds, no doubt. "My head says you're right but . . ."

"Trust your head. I'm a bad bet for you." I wonder, if I wasn't part of the flooding plot, would I be so selfless? Or would I cling to the safety of the group? It doesn't make me happy to break from them. "Look, who knows what will happen in there? We may end up crossing paths. But I can't make you pay for choices I've made."

"Okay," says Maysilee. "So we're back to where we were on the train. You don't want us for your allies."

"I don't want *anybody*," I clarify.

It's lonely going rogue. I wish I could tell them everything. About the plot. About speaking to Lenore Dove. About Snow's warning and Plutarch's rising sun. But all that would do is invite questions and ultimately cause trouble, so that's where I leave it. I don't want anybody. Lights off.

Lou Lou's immediately dead to the world and the rest of us toss and turn a lot. I keep dreaming about Lenore Dove, then snapping awake. Her name song's hitting way too close to home. In it, a guy loses the love of his life, Lenore, and he's going crazy for missing her. Then this big old raven shows up at his house and won't leave and whenever he asks the bird anything, it just says "Nevermore" — which, as you can imagine, just makes him crazier.

> *"Tell this soul with sorrow laden if, within the distant Aidenn,*
> *It shall clasp a sainted maiden whom the angels name Lenore —*
> *Clasp a rare and radiant maiden whom the angels name Lenore."*
> *Quoth the Raven "Nevermore."*

Angels, Lenore Dove told me, are humans with wings, who live in a place called heaven. Some people believe, she said, it's a possible destination after death. A good world for good people to go to. But Lenore Dove is the winged being on my mind at the moment. If there is anything after the life I'm about to lose, will I be with her again? Like the guy in her song, I'd sure like to know. But the Raven isn't giving the answer either of us wants to hear.

The night seems both endless and way too short. I'm awake but exhausted when Mags comes to rouse us. We wash up and put on our old training outfits, since they won't dress us until we're in the holding pens at the arena. I know Maysilee's unhappy with me for abandoning the Newcomers. As a peace offering, I slip Beetee's birthday gift, the turn-a-potato-into-a-light packet, into her hand as we head to the kitchen. Although she doesn't acknowledge me, it disappears into her pocket.

There's a big hot breakfast, but it's all Wyatt and I can do to swallow a few bites, the stuff sticks in our throats so, and Maysilee only wants coffee. Lou Lou, on the other hand, eats a stack of pancakes as high as her head and fistfuls of bacon, confirming that she's too far gone to know what the next few days hold for her. That's a blessing, I guess. She looks so defenseless without her snake.

Wiress gives us last-minute pointers and then seems to shut down. Mags hugs each of us and says that whatever happens, we have been remarkable. She knows at least three of us won't be back. What else can she say?

All pretense is over. We are being propelled forward, faster and faster, to the inevitable moment when the gong sounds. All the tribute preparation — the costumes, the training, the interviews — was just a distraction from the real agenda. Today some of us will die.

Drusilla drops by the apartment to complete her last official escort duty, seeing we're searched and loaded into the van. I don't know where Maysilee stowed the packet, but she comes up clean. Once we're chained in, a woman in a white coat and carrying a set of syringes shoots something into each of our forearms. She doesn't have to tell us it's our tracker, an electronic device that allows the Gamemakers to find us in the arena.

"What happens if we win? Do they take it out?" asks Wyatt.

"We collect all of them from the tributes, dead or alive," says the woman. "They're reusable. Of course, this year we needed twenty-four extra."

Thanks for reminding us.

Drusilla stands at the back of the van. "All right, you lot," she says. "Try not to embarrass me."

Maysilee rallies one last time. "As if you needed our help."

Drusilla slams the door shut on us.

We're taken to some sort of runway where a half dozen hovercraft await, then loaded into a windowless compartment and strapped into our seats across from District 11. They look as terrified as we do. Only Lou Lou seems unbothered. She catches sight of the token that one of the girls, Chicory, wears — a flower woven of grass — and fixates on it. Then she begins to make little hand motions as she sings in a breathy voice:

Flower there beside my feet
Growing up between the corn
Combine's here so duck your head
Duck your head
Duck your head
Combine's here so duck your head
To see another morn.

Chicory reacts with surprise. She addresses the rest of us, since Lou Lou's mental state precludes answering. "How does she know that song? You sing it in Twelve?"

As something of an authority on songs in 12 by virtue of time spent with Lenore Dove, I shake my head.

"That's a harvest song for kids," Chicory continues. "That's our song." She peers at Lou Lou's face, exchanges a look with her 11 tributes, then sings:

Mockingjay up on the branch —

Lou Lou takes over the song at once.

Nesting in this apple tree
Picking time so fly away
Fly away
Fly away
Picking time so fly away
Fly away with me.

"How do you explain that, then?" Chicory asks us.

"We don't," says Maysilee. "She's not ours. Ours is dead and she's the replacement they sent us. Like as not, she's from Eleven. Our mentors think so anyway." She never seems to care if the Capitol's listening.

Tile, the largest of the 11 tributes, speaks in a tight voice. "You didn't think that was worth mentioning?"

"We didn't know for sure until now," says Wyatt. "We've just been trying to look out for her. Does it matter where they took her from, Eleven or Twelve? Aren't we all on the same side?"

Lou Lou ignores us all as she tries to wriggle out of her safety straps.

"Do you know who she might be?" I ask.

Chicory shakes her head. "We're a big district. And who knows how long she's been with them." She leans toward Lou Lou as much as her straps allow. "Little girl? What's your real name? If one of us makes it back, we can tell your family."

Lou Lou hesitates, attempts to speak, then grabs her ear and lets out a shriek. Wyatt catches her free hand and tries to soothe her.

"We think they put something in her ear to control her," Maysilee tells them.

"That's why you wanted us to be careful what we say," says Chicory, putting it together. "They're listening." She sits back in her seat, her face sorrowful. "Maybe her people will recognize her."

I don't say so, but I've got a feeling her people are long dead, and if they're alive, how tragic for them to see her only to lose her again. There's no good ending to Lou Lou's story.

We lift off, which would be amazing under other circumstances but here only adds to my queasiness. Everybody shuts up for a while, which gives me a chance to mentally prepare. I should be planning my strategy in the arena, but I just keep thinking about Lenore Dove, and how much I love her, and wondering if she's home by now and how she's doing. And Ma. And Sid. Burdock and Blair. Hattie. Before I know it, we're descending.

When we arrive at the arena, we're escorted directly from an interior landing pad to a hallway. I can't look out, but it feels underground, and I'm certain I'm on Sub-A. I turn my head from side to side, trying to take in every detail of the place as we walk along a curved concrete floor. There are some sort of pipes to my right and doors spaced out to my left, which begin with four marked with the number 6 and go up from there. Four of the same number each time. 7, 7, 7, 7, 8, 8, 8, 8 . . . It's a bit of a hike until we get to an 11 and they direct Chicory inside. We lose the rest of our 11 allies and then a Peacekeeper opens the first door marked 12.

I hold out my arms. Without a word, Wyatt and Maysilee join in a group embrace. Lou Lou wiggles into the center of the hug and we tighten our hold, feeling one another's pulses and sweat and skin. Ten minutes from now, who will even still have a heartbeat?

After a minute, a Peacekeeper says, "Let's go."

We peel off into our rooms, me last of all. Before I go in, I catch sight of the next door down the hall, which has a 1 on it. A ring of tributes for the opening ceremony.

I'm alone in a circular room with a transparent tube in the center of it. My launchpad. A neatly folded set of clothes sits on a lone chair. Black, like Maysilee suspected.

The intercom crackles to life. A voice greets me: "Welcome to your launch room." At home we call it the Stockyard. The place where animals wait to be slaughtered. The voice instructs, "The tributes are to change into their new outfits, courtesy of the Capitol." Courtesy of the Capitol. My flour sack shorts. Ma. Sid.

I strip, tossing my training outfit in a pile on the floor. All the arena clothes — underwear, long-sleeved shirt, pants — feel like one of the old silk scarves Lenore Dove uses to accent her costumes. Thin and cool, the fabric runs through my hands like water. There's a belt but no loops on the pants, only on the flowing shirt, so I fasten it around my waist. It's made of stretchy material, and instead of a buckle, it's secured with two metallic circles that interlock and then unfasten with a quick twist. When I finish dressing, my knees feel wobbly and I drop into the chair, listening to the pounding of my heart. The arena's minutes away. I can't remember what to do. I hear Wiress's voice. . . .

First avoid the slaughter,
Get weapons, look for water.

Water. Right. I'm supposed to drown the brain. What?

More instructions. "Tributes, please enter your tubes."

I rise shakily to my feet as the door handle turns and Effie Trinket flies into the room. "Wait, not yet! I have to check him!" She's white as a sheet. "I only found out I was supposed to do this at breakfast," she says in a hushed voice. "No one could find Magno." She quickly goes over my outfit, adjusting the belt. "Did you see this?" She shows me my pants have a handkerchief in one of the pockets, which I leave in place.

"Thanks," I manage.

"Tributes who are not in their tubes in thirty seconds will be disciplined," says the voice.

"Come on!" Effie guides me to the tube and centers me on a glass plate. She arranges my token so it's outside the shirt.

The trembling of her hands allows me to ask a favor. "Will you make sure my token gets home to my girl?"

Effie nods and lays a hand over it solemnly. "I will do my absolute best." She steps back and the door begins to slide shut. "Remember, Haymitch, don't step off your plate for sixty seconds!" As the door clicks shut, she pumps the air with a fist and adds, "And keep a positive attitude!"

I rise up, locking my eyes on hers until things go black, making me lose my bearings. My sweaty palms swipe the sides of the glass tube as I try to steady myself. Then the tube runs out and I'm teetering on my plate when a gust of air hits my face and the light blinds my eyes. As they adjust, my brows shoot up in disbelief as I get my first look at the arena.

The beauty takes my breath away.

"Ladies and Gentlemen, let the Fiftieth Hunger Games begin!" proclaims an announcer.

A scowl contracts my face as suspicion sets in. It's just too attractive to be good. The smooth green meadow stretching for miles in either direction. The array of colorful songbirds overhead that match the tufts of cheerful flowers underfoot that match the outfits on the tributes' backs. Sky so blue it hurts your eyes, clouds so fluffy you want to bounce on them. And the smell! Like they bottled the best day of spring and uncorked it just for us.

I block my nose and begin to mouth-breathe to avoid the dizzying scent. I try to examine the shiny gold Cornucopia in its nest of weapons and supplies that rests in the center of the meadow fifty yards away, but a gentle breeze caresses my face, and the birdsong distracts me with thoughts of Lenore Dove. There are woods here, too, like our woods in 12, far off to my left. To my right, a small mountain with a crown of snow. Is that where the tank is? Under the mountain?

A fluffball of a bunny rabbit hops up to my foot and nibbles the grass next to my plate, its pale gray fur tinted lilac and pink. A shade of dove. I'm reaching for the silken coat when suddenly the rabbit startles and speeds off, bringing me to my senses.

Focus! my brain orders. *What are you supposed to be doing?*

First avoid the slaughter,
Get weapons, look for water.

Right. I have to get weapons and get out of here. But which direction do I need to run? North. Beetee said go north. And Plutarch said the arena sun is positioned like our sun. Do I believe Plutarch? I think of getting to say good-bye to my family and how he covered for me with the milk pitcher and the call to Lenore Dove. . . . Okay, what the hell, I do! Wiress said to trust your instincts and mine say he was telling the truth. If I don't locate any berms, maybe I'll reconsider. But for now . . .

It's nine o'clock in the morning and the sun's rising up behind the Cornucopia directly across from me. Okay, that's east, west to my back, that makes north to my right. No! My left. North to the left. Where the woods are, not the mountain. That's good news because the tributes fanned out to my right are mostly Careers, Silka on the next plate, then Panache and the other girl and boy from District 1, then District 2, while to the left it's nothing but Newcomers. In general, District 1's too close for comfort, but they'll want weapons and kills more than they'll want to chase me down, especially if I'm armed, and there are such easy pickings. I spot Ampert and the other District 3 tributes sandwiched between Districts 2 and 4 and have to squelch the impulse to run in to protect them. Ampert wouldn't want me to. He'd want me to clear out and find a mutt portal and rendezvous with him as soon as possible. He'll be headed north soon, too.

I home in on a spring-green backpack near the tail of the Cornucopia. I can run at a diagonal directly at it, grab a few weapons on the way, or at least a knife, and hopefully be gone before anyone notices. It might work — people look pretty confused. I see Panache's head twist as a daffodil-yellow bird perches on his shoulder and twitters.

Then the gong rings out and the treads of my new boots grip the meadow grass as I sprint for the backpack. Barely breaking pace, I scoop up a spear in my left hand and a knife in my right, which I use to hook the strap of the backpack. I allow myself one quick glance over my shoulder, which is enough to reassure me that the Careers are late to the party, some still on their plates, others slow on the uptake and just reaching the weapons. As I make for the woods, I lock eyes with Kerna for a second, clock her sunflower as she heads for a weapon. And then I just run for those distant trees.

It's only moments before the screams begin, but I force myself to stay on course, knowing that seeing a District 12 tribute or any Newcomer at death's door could pull me into the fray. Was that Lou Lou's shriek? It was a girl's, a young one's certainly. *Don't look back*, I tell myself. *Don't you dare look back.*

My right arm aches from the weight of the pack, so I take a moment to secure it on my back and slip the knife safely in my belt. Spear in my right hand now, I settle on a jog I think I can sustain for the long haul to the north. The meadow grass, which was short and even at the Cornucopia, increases in height as I progress, until it's tall enough to tangle my boots if I don't step high, so I step high and keep an eye out for snakes. I only spot flowers, songbirds, and the occasional bunny. Nothing venomous or deadly.

I revisit Wiress's checklist.

First avoid the slaughter,

Doing it.

Get weapons,

Got them.

look for water.

I can't yet. Not until I'm safely in the woods and then it will have to be on my way north. Say I find it quick. Then what?

Find food and where to sleep,

Nope, way too soon. Still slaughter avoidance going on. Then I have to get as close to the tank as possible and find a mutt portal. But I feel okay about my progress.

I run as long as I can, then slow to a hike and use my spear for a walking stick. The grass now reaches my waist. Up ahead, the forest borders the meadow in a smooth arc. The lush trees, a mix of greens with bursts of gold and orange, laden with bright blooms and ripe fruit, promise everything I seek. Shade from the hot sun, food to fill my belly, concealment from the Careers. The heady scent of pine and blossoms wafting from the woods calms my racing heart. Charming . . . enticing . . . these words don't do it justice. There's something almost magical about it, as if once inside those leafy arms, nothing bad could ever befall you. This must be how insects feel in the nepenthes plant, right before they drown. Which may well be my fate when the tank explodes.

When I reach the tree line, I judge I've covered about two miles. I climb on a big rock to check for tributes, but the expanse of grass seems empty of both allies and enemies. The cannon shots begin, letting me know the bloodbath at the Cornucopia has ended. Normally, they fire to confirm any death, but those come on so thick and fast at the beginning that the Gamemakers wait until the initial killing spree has ended. The booms keep coming, resonating in my backbone, until I count eighteen of us dead. I won't know who until tonight when they show the faces of the fallen tributes in the sky. But there are only sixteen

Careers, so the Newcomers have not been spared. Probably, many are Newcomers.

I try not to think about who, but it could be Maysilee or Wyatt or Lou Lou or Ringina or Ampert. . . . What if Ampert has already been taken out? What happens to the plan then? He was an easy target in that big patch of Careers. . . . *No!* I tell myself. *No. He's too smart. He will find you. Just do your part of the job.*

I take a seat on the rock to catch my breath and examine my backpack. After years of hauling grain for Hattie, I can confidently judge it to be around twenty-five pounds. It's made of a nice tough canvas with padded straps. The spring green should blend well with the trees. I hesitate before I open it — my life may well depend on the contents — then flip back the flap and begin to lay out my supplies.

A mesh hammock, same color as the pack, cushions a fancy pair of binoculars. Two plastic gallon jugs full of water. That accounts for much of the weight. A dozen apples. A dozen eggs in a cardboard carton, which I determine are hard-boiled by spinning them. And finally, six large potatoes, which excite me until I remember I gave the light bulb kit to Maysilee. Well, she and Wyatt stand a better chance of not getting caught cheating with Beetee's stuff, given they've got a zinc scrip coin and a copper medallion between them. Hopefully, they got some potatoes, too. For me, these will probably be dinner.

To be honest, given the size of the pack and its proximity to the Cornucopia, I was hoping for better. I scrounge around inside to make sure I didn't miss anything. An outside pocket adds a generous packet of coin-sized black tablets to my haul. I'm thinking maybe if you drop them in water, they turn into a steak dinner or something, but a cautious nibble blows that theory. If I'm not mistaken, these are the same charcoal tablets Mamaw used to buy from the

Marches' shop for her indigestion when she overate. A bad joke on the Gamemakers' part, given that no tribute's in danger of overeating. They're probably all having a good laugh at my reaction now. Whatever. Maybe I can use them for camouflage or something.

I take a big swig of water and reload my pack. No food allowed until I get a better sense of what's available in the woods. Then I make sure the mountain's squarely at my back and head into the trees.

It's a relief to get off the meadow grass and onto a forest floor made of dirt covered in pine needles. Scattered patches of emerald moss and a rainbow of ferns add a decorative touch. In a few minutes, I spot my first berm, smooth and symmetrical with a glorious layer of buttercups. Plutarch was right about that much anyway. Does it conceal a mutt portal? No time to check now, and anyway, I'm not northerly enough.

The woods are as picture-perfect as the meadow, full of sweet colorful things, but the farther I press on, the madder I get. That tree? Groaning with apples. Those nests? Full of eggs. And streams burbling with crystal-clear water abound. If it's in my backpack, it's easy pickings. Probably I could dig anywhere and find potatoes. Was my entire pack just a big joke?

Here I am, hauling twenty-five extra pounds around like a saphead. Part of me feels like dumping the contents on the ground but then I'd just have to waste time collecting it all again, so I keep trudging on, noting the berms along the way. I hear two more cannon shots. Twenty dead now. In a usual Games, only four tributes would be left alive. This year, twenty-eight of us remain.

When my thirst begins to get to me, I stop by a stream. Propping my pack against a tree, I scoop up a few handfuls of icy water. It's a little metallic, but not so much as our well water back home. I slow down, though, because guzzling cold water on a hot day can give me a bellyache.

As I lean against my pack, a dove-colored rabbit hops up across the stream from me and helps itself to a good, long drink. It sits on the bank, ears twitching, reminding me that I've helped Burdock set snares on occasion. I don't have any wire, though. And could I possibly kill a creature that brings to mind my girl?

I'm pondering this when the bunny starts squealing like a baby bird, goes stiff as a board, then falls over dead. A trickle of red stains the fur on its chin.

Poison. That's what's running in this stream. I press my hand against my stomach, registering that what I took for cold-water pangs are too sharp and burning. I immediately stick my finger down my throat and manage to gag up some acid before I remember that's not always the best way to deal with poison. It can hurt you as much coming up as it does going down. An antidote's best, like the one President Snow carried in his pocket. But I have no antidote.

I dig through my pack for something that might soak up the toxic fluid. Something spongey like bread, but there's nothing of the kind. Would that even be the right thing to do? The pain intensifies, so I swallow some clean water from the bottle, hoping to dilute the poison, to no avail. My breath comes in gasps and perspiration beads my face. This is it, then. How I die. Not ending the Hunger Games, just curled up in the dirt, poisoned like a rat. I dump out all my supplies and reach for a potato, the most benign thing I have, and have just taken a bite of its hard, crisp flesh when my eyes land on the charcoal tablets.

It's a fall day a few years back and we've overdone it on the hot pepper soup. Mamaw's chomping on her tablets, saying, *"Good for whatever ails your belly. Fire, wind, or poison."* I thought the Gamemakers meant them as a joke, but maybe they are the antidote?

Without hesitating, I spit out the potato, tear into the packet, and stuff a handful of tablets in my mouth. I grind them to powder with my teeth, wash them down, and gauge the condition of my stomach. No change. I send another half dozen down my gullet. This time, I think I can begin to feel some relief. Without warning, I spew everything since yesterday's lunch into the stream. I kneel on all fours, panting, dripping sweat and saliva. I'm still queasy, but the pain has ebbed. For good measure, I put a tablet on my tongue and let it dissolve. My back finds a tree trunk and I collapse against it, waiting for my heartbeat to slow.

I might not die. I can't die. Not just yet. Not before I blow that tank sky-high. As I step back from death's door, I try to get back on track. My supplies lie in a jumble at my feet. My stupid, redundant supplies that I could find anywhere —

Suddenly, I sit upright as I remember Mags's advice: *"Look for clues to your arena. The Gamemakers sometimes hide little hints about the nature of the arena in their design."*

If the contents of my backpack are clues, what are they revealing? Why would all of my food and drink be easy pickings in the arena, unless . . . I take in the rabbit carcass across the stream . . . unless they aren't. Unless every mouthful is precious, because their counterparts are poisonous.

The minute I conceive of this possibility, I know it's true. That the luscious apples on the boughs over my head are as deadly as the crystal water. And if that is true, what other food and drink in here will kill you? Everything, probably. It isn't safe to sample anything that didn't come from the Cornucopia.

As I brush off my supplies and carefully repack them, I think about the two cannon shots that fired after the bloodbath. Did one Career and one Newcomer die, thereby alerting the rest of their alliance to the poisonous nature of the arena? Reminds me of the canaries we take down to the coal mines in 12. They are the first to die when there's deadly gas around, warning the miners of imminent danger. Maybe both were Careers, because I bet Ampert and Wellie would've figured out pretty quick that the food in the packs is a clue. Probably, if we hadn't formed such tight alliances, far more tributes would be dying now. Were the Gamemakers counting on that, and have we thrown them?

Every bite of clean food is priceless. I consider the rabbit again, fur color or no. While I've no appetite now, I know I'll be famished later, but its bloody beard puts me off. The last thing I need is to be ingesting more poison. What I need is to be moving north. Unfortunately, when I rise to my feet, a wave of nausea hits me and I clutch my spear to stay upright. How long will the toxins take to leave my system?

I take deep gulps of the finely crafted air, which no longer charms me. It's not deadly, but it's not fresh either. Something unwholesome hides under the perfume. I remember the dazed looks on the tributes' faces as we awaited the gong. Did the air drug us? And is it contributing to how weak and sick I feel now? Or is the water to blame for that? I guess I can't stop breathing, though, so I wobble off into the north.

It's no good. After a few hundred yards, I slide to the forest floor, throw up my latest charcoal tablet, and scrunch back into a ball. The chills begin, racking my body and causing my teeth to chatter so hard I'm in danger of breaking them. All I want is to be home in my bed in 12, with Ma there to take care of me. To spoon me sips of chicken back broth and pile every quilt on my shaking body and put a goose feather pillow under my head. The thought of Ma watching, unable to get her hands on me, makes me try to look less pathetic. I force myself to sit up and dry my dripping face on my handkerchief.

I'm nothing but a sitting duck. I need to hide, but since there are no real paths in the woods, I can't get off of one. Over there looks no safer than right here. If a Career followed me across the meadow, I'm not just a sitting duck, I'm a dead one. Muddled, I reach for Wiress's song:

Find food and where to sleep,
Fire and friends can keep.

Heading north takes a distant second to finding a safe place to recover. Fire and friends will have to keep. I hoist myself back onto my boots and consider climbing a tree, but I'm so woozy I'm sure to tumble out. What I really need to do is lie down somewhere hidden. I totter around for a bit, veering a little to the east, and come upon a large blueberry patch laden with fruit the size of cherries. Obviously, I can't eat them, but the dense bushes, free of thorns, offer a refuge. I lay on my belly and burrow deep into the thicket, dragging my pack behind me. At what I judge to be the center, I arrange my hammock on the ground and collapse onto it, pulling the meshy skin around me for warmth. I can't see out, so I'm hoping no one else can see in. Doesn't matter, I'm going nowhere.

For several hours, I alternate between violent chills and drenching fever sweats. Pain spikes my muscles, and my head feels like it's trapped in one of Tam Amber's vises. I vaguely wonder if some of my fellow tributes are experiencing the same misery. No cannons have fired since the two I attributed to the poisoning. Possibly others now lie helpless like me, waiting for the rest of the poison to work its way out. Whatever has happened, the Gamemakers don't appear to be unleashing mutts or driving us together. After twenty opening-day deaths, we're rewarded with a lull in bloodshed. Our performance has been satisfactory.

Nightfall brings the anthem blasting through the arena. I rally enough to pull myself to the edge of the berry patch and look up to see the flag of Panem projected on the sky. It's time for the memorial photos of the dead tributes, a rare hint into our standing in the Games. Twenty today. I splay my fingers on the dirt, pressing down one for each death. After I've run through them twice, it'll be over and I'll know how the Newcomers have fared.

When the first fallen tribute appears, I register the outfit, snot green, and know it's a District 1 girl. Carat, I think her name was. Then we jump to Urchin, the boy from District 4 who knocked me from the chariot with his trident. I'm relieved to see District 3 has been spared, particularly Ampert. A boy and a girl in District 5 orange bring the Career death count to four. One of my doves, Miles, the kid who couldn't breathe in the shower, appears next, and my heart sinks. The Careers are all through by District 5. That means that the other sixteen deaths today are all Newcomers. I watch as they unspool. A second dove, Velo from 6. Both boys from 7. All four kids from 8. All four from 9. Both girls from 10. Tile, the boy from 11. The pinkie on my left hand remains lifted. One tribute left. Is it another kid from 11 or one of my own?

Wyatt. Wyatt Callow whose luck just ran out. I can't believe how hard it hits me, how much it hurts. A few days ago, I didn't even want him for an ally. But he wasn't a bad guy, really. He just came from a rotten family. District 12's sympathy will be in short supply.

How's the betting going, Mr. Callow? You make some money on your boy today?

Most people wouldn't say this to him, but they wouldn't stop another from doing so, as repellent as his behavior has been.

I wonder how Wyatt died and immediately feel certain he was protecting Lou Lou, the way no one had ever protected him. Including me. I ran off and left all the Newcomers to fend for one another. I know I had to if I was going to carry out Beetee's plan, but it sure doesn't feel good.

A fury rises up in me at the thought of Wyatt's sacrifice and how the Capitol has pitted us tributes against one another in this poisonous beauty of an arena. The Games must end. Here. Now. Every death reinforces the importance of the arena plot succeeding. *Focus*, I tell myself, and struggle through the brain fog. I remember that all four of the kids from 9 are dead. Did Ampert manage to scavenge a sunflower before the hovercraft collected their bodies? If he didn't, what could we possibly do? We're useless without those explosives. Maybe even with them, but certainly without them.

The sky goes dark. Show's over. I crawl back to my hammock, wrap my arms around my backpack, and shiver myself to sleep.

When I wake late in the morning, I find myself staring into a pair of limpid green eyes. One of the gray bunnies has taken cover in the brambles and has hunkered down a few feet from me. Maybe it's just a normal rabbit that got thrown into this creepy place and feels as frightened as I do. It could be accustomed to human keepers and found me because it's hungry and has figured out all the plants and grass and everything are as poisonous as the water. I could use a smart companion. I take out an apple, bite off a small piece, and gingerly set it in front of my new friend. After a bit, it scoots forward, wiggles its nose, and begins to nibble. I realize this is a way to double-check if the apples in my pack are toxic, which makes me feel kind of lousy since I sort of owe the rabbits. The one that woke me up at my plate, the one that sacrificed its life at the stream to warn me. Wait, am I saying it knew the water was poisonous and chose to protect me? That this bunny here would do the same? Okay, okay, I know I'm over-crediting the bunnies. But still. I don't want one of my last acts to be taking out an ally, especially a dove-colored one.

Fortunately, it doesn't die and I plow into my apple, which tastes amazing and helps me assess my situation. So, twenty died yesterday. Four Careers. Sixteen Newcomers. Those aren't good numbers. Even though I'm no Wyatt, I can figure out we used to have twice as many Newcomers as Careers, and now we're almost even. We may be smarter, but they're mowing us down with brute force. I'm afraid Ampert's theory isn't holding up too well in practice. Although maybe now that the bloodbath's over, the Newcomers' brain power and unity will give them an advantage.

"Find Haymitch."

"Aa!" My head bashes into a tangle of berry branches at the whispered voice.

"Find Haymitch."

A pair of little hands wrap around my boots and Lou Lou's face, splattered in dry blood and dirt, materializes over them.

"Found him," she says.

The rabbit bolts, and I have to resist the impulse to follow. Lou Lou? She is not part of the plan. How did she find me? Is she being tracked?

Suddenly, my bushes don't seem safe at all. "Hey there, Lou Lou," I say, trying to sound calm. "You alone? Are the others with you?"

"Mountain."

Just us, then? Everybody else went to the right after I ran to the left?

Lou Lou tugs on my boots for me to follow her, then back-crawls out of the bushes. Not knowing what I will find, I emerge, knife and spear at the ready, but our surroundings seem quiet and deserted. Maybe both packs did go to the mountain.

A quick appraisal of the immediate area solves the mystery of her finding me. I broke off several branches digging my way into the thicket and, most embarrassingly, my handkerchief snagged on one and hangs there like a welcome sign. The illusion that I'd successfully camouflaged myself is silly. I'm just lucky no Careers came along. Even Lou Lou's appearance presents a problem for a rascal bent on winning. But I said in my interview that the Newcomers were "one hundred percent safe with me." And she's supposedly from my district. I guess I can look after her, at least until Ampert shows up and I have to blow up the tank. Then that will be my sole priority.

Lou Lou stares up into an apple tree and quietly sings to herself:

Mockingjay up on the branch
Nesting in this apple tree
Picking time so fly away
Fly away
Fly away
Picking time so fly away
Fly away with me.

She reaches up for an apple and I grab her hand. "No, no, not those. Those are the bad apples. I've got a good one here." I pull a nice shiny red one from my pack and settle her on the ground with it. She carries no pack or supplies of her own. As usual, she attacks her food ravenously. It's going to be a full-time job keeping her away from the deadly fruit. It's a wonder she made it this far. I guess the meadow was safe, and perhaps she didn't notice the fruit in the dark. Judging by the dirt on her clothes, she spent some time sleeping on the ground.

I peel a couple of hard-boiled eggs for us. I consider asking her about Wyatt, but there's a real likelihood she witnessed his death, perhaps even wears his blood, and I don't want to set her off. "Who told you to find me, Lou Lou?"

She taps her bad ear. "Find Haymitch."

That pulls me up short. The Gamemakers? Why would they send her to find me? It can't be for any good reason.

"Murderers," Lou Lou adds, picking at the dried blood on her cheek.

She finishes her egg and, without asking, finishes mine, too. She starts rooting around in my pack and comes out with a potato. I gently pry it from her hand. "For later. For supper." But I let her drink her fill of the water, afraid she could dive for a stream at any time. She's already drugged and brainwashed — I don't need her sick as well. No question, her arrival has thrown a wrench in my plans. I don't know if I can manage to do my part with her tagging along, but I can't just dump her alone in the woods for the Careers to slaughter. Like Wyatt said, she's ours now. For better or worse, she's part of the flood mission.

I wet her handkerchief and wipe her face clean. "Come on," I tell her. "Let's find your snake."

This suggestion perks her up and she bounces to her feet. Using the sun to get my bearings, I lead her north. I've got two jobs to accomplish before I meet up with Ampert, which could be at any moment. First, I need to find a sparking rock and confirm that I can make fire with my flint striker. Then I have to locate a mutt portal, probably under a berm, that will serve as an entrance to the tunnels.

As we walk along, I keep an eye peeled for likely rocks. Flint would be best, but Lenore Dove said any kind of sparking rock would do. The floor of the forest proves devoid of rocks, but I feel like I've seen some . . . the pattern of colorful stones . . . glistening in the sunlight . . . the stream! That's it. When I was retching into it, I remember the shiny rocks winking up at me. But the water — it will be poisonous. Could I risk dipping my hand in to snag one?

When Lou Lou shows too much interest in a raspberry bush, I distract her with another apple and slip off to a nearby stream. With the tip of my spear, I dislodge several rocks from the bed and slide them onto the bank. I wipe them with leaves, pour on a bit of clean water, pat them off, and scoop them up. I get back to Lou Lou just in time to stop her from raiding the bush. I go ahead and give her chunks of the raw potato I bit into yesterday, and eat a few pieces myself to calm my rocky stomach. Doesn't take long for us to finish it off.

The rocks dry quickly in the midday sun, and I give them to Lou Lou to hold, emphasizing the importance of the job, but really to keep her occupied. After untying the flint striker from my neck, I cup it in my hands, letting the sunbeams play off the bird and snake heads. I allow myself a moment with Lenore Dove, imagining her in the Meadow among her flock of geese or watching me on the ancient television Tam Amber manages to keep functional. Not on the square, where anyone can gather to see huge projections of the Games, but privately in the Covey's funny, crooked house. Forbidden by her uncles to leave. Distraught, but unbruised, unbeaten, unbroken, and safe at home.

I consider faking a moment of discovery that I've brought a flint striker into the arena, but since I've already collected the rocks, that seems stagey. Instead, I decide to double down on the rascal angle and admit I've pulled a fast one on the Gamemakers. A rascal, not a rebel. Just a trickster who's trying to win the Games.

"See this, Lou Lou?" I say. "This is our ticket to a hot meal. Let's start with that pink rock."

Lou Lou plucks out the rosy stone from our stash and sets it in my open hand. I grip the flint striker in the other, and take a crack at it, bringing the steel edge of the striker across the surface of the stone. Nothing. After three more attempts, I know it's a dud. “Green,” I instruct Lou Lou. But it’s as sparkless as the first. As we work our way through the pile, my heart begins to sink. What if there isn’t a sparking rock in the whole arena? When I’d mentioned it to Beetee, he’d said there “possibly” was. But he’d never come back and said there weren’t any, leading me to assume I’d find one. If not, the whole gig is up, and I’m left to wait for Snow to kill me.

She sets the final rock, a long, muddy-gray crystal in front of me. Quartz, maybe? I take a vicious swipe at it, drawing the rock back for good measure. A spray of sparks flies, letting me know we’ve found a live one. Lou Lou claps and I let out a huff of relief. “Baked potatoes tonight,” I promise her with a grin.

Since we’re not immediately attacked by mutts, I figure the Gamemakers have decided to let my rascally behavior ride. It adds a little harmless spice to the Games. Bet my sponsors are sending some dollars my way, too. Since Mags and Wiress know I’ve got Lou Lou to feed now, I hope it’s enough for something to complement our potatoes.

Lou Lou gives a tremendous yawn and, just like that, she curls up like a kitten and falls asleep. It’s so fast, I wonder if the Gamemakers are drugging her again, but maybe she just hasn’t gotten much rest in here. I try to rouse her, giving her shoulder a little shake, but she only frowns and mutters something. What now? I can’t carry her, not in this condition, and I can’t abandon her. Now’s as good a time as any to bake those potatoes, I guess. . . .

First, I’ll need to build a fire. I wander around, never straying far from Lou Lou, collecting the driest pine needles, kindling, and small branches I can find. This is a strategy Hattie taught me: Steer clear of green or wet wood to minimize your smoke. No use in pointing out you’re breaking the law, even if everybody knows it full well.

Along the way, I have a chance to examine some of the berms. The mounds appear uniform, about eight feet in diameter, two feet at the crown, and perfectly circular. However, each features its own flower, identified by a small brass plaque at the base, much like the labeling in Plutarch's mansion. Since this is the Gamemakers' garden, probably isn't wise to trust it, but I read the plaques anyway, hoping for clues. Crocus, tiger lily, pansy. I try not to think what lies beneath some of them, waiting to attack me.

One catches my attention: GAS PLANT. The Covey's yard has a wondrous hodgepodge of flowering plants, dug up from the woods over the years and bedded down in front of their house with no apparent rhyme or reason. From late March to November, you can count on at least one flower or bush being in bloom, and Lenore Dove generally wears a few blossoms in her hair when she performs. Never from the gas plant, though. "Too dangerous," she told me, and then demonstrated why, touching a lit match to a stalk of pale purple flowers. A whoosh of flame followed, and then disappeared just as quick, leaving the flowers unharmed. "Imagine if that happened on my head!" she said with a laugh.

Using shreds of cardboard from my egg carton, I get a small flame going pretty quick. I coax it along by feeding it pine needles and twigs until I've got a proper fire. Almost no smoke, so I keep it alive with infusions of dry wood. About an hour passes before I have enough ashes to bake the potatoes. I lay three in the coals and settle down to wait.

A distant boom alerts me to the fact that another tribute has died. Twenty-one gone now, twenty-seven left. Career? Newcomer? I've no way of knowing until tonight.

When the potatoes get soft, I wake Lou Lou, and we make quick work of them and a couple more eggs. I feel loads better, like the rest of the poison has been absorbed, and she's bright-eyed after her nap. I consider dousing the fire but decide my water's too costly, so I leave it to smolder, a thing Hattie would never allow. Fire is catching, she'd say, but if this one burns down the arena, I say good riddance.

I'm more optimistic after my success with the flint striker. Now on to find my berm. They're so numerous that I can't imagine every single one of them conceals a mutt portal that connects to a Sub-A tunnel. Beetee said, "Do your best to locate a mutt portal by tracking returning mutts after an attack." Since I haven't identified any mutts yet, I keep working my way north to find likely candidates.

Lou Lou thinks we're looking for her snake, which holds her attention and keeps her trotting ahead of me at a reasonable pace. As we move north, I almost forget about her, preoccupied with checking our surroundings for dangers and reviewing my bomb-setting techniques from 12. Fire to fuse, fuse to blasting cap, blasting cap to explosive —

Her squeal of delight snaps me back to the arena. She darts for a nearby berm covered with scarlet flowers. I don't know why this one, since she's viewed the others with indifference. I chase after her, but she reaches the hillock first, plowing into the greenery, crushing handfuls of the leaves and burying her face in the red blossoms. I spot the nameplate and relax a bit. I know this plant, recognize the faint minty scent. I've even helped Burdock gather some for Asterid to make into medicines at the apothecary shop. Bee balm. A healing plant. It grows wild in our mountains and Lou Lou clearly recognizes it as well.

The seeded bread, the candle smoke, and now these flowers — all of them must transport Lou Lou back home somehow. Mamaw said that smells stick in your memory the strongest, more than sounds or sights. Didn't the bean and ham hock soup take me back to 12?

Lou Lou's breathing so deep she's starting to gasp and, good memories or no, I decide it's time to pull her out of there. I drop my stuff on the ground and I've just wrapped my arms around her middle when the coughing begins. After I haul her off the berm, she sits back on her heels and makes a choking sound. A yellow pollen coats her from head to toe and, thinking she's allergic to the bee balm, I dampen her handkerchief and begin to wipe her down.

"Just breathe, Lou Lou," I say soothingly. "They're only flowers." But nothing's only anything in this arena, and when the blood begins running from her eyes, her nose, her mouth, the last reminding me of our dear president, I know I'm wrong.

"Lou Lou?" I cry. "Lou Lou, hold on!"

She collapses against me, and I cradle her in my arms as the convulsions begin. There is nothing I can do but watch, helpless again. Just as I was to save Louella. For a moment, the two merge, Lou Lou and Louella. She's just one pigtailed kid I've known her whole life, and I would do anything to spare her this.

Her skin begins to turn blue. "Enough," I beg the Gamemakers. They could end this with a touch of a button. Knock her out as they did at the interview, this time sending a lethal dose of sedative through her pump. Spare her this torturous death. But her agony continues, filling me with fury. "Enough!" I scream. "She is not your plaything!"

My fingers find the pump hidden under her shirt and lock around it. With one powerful yank, I free her.

The cannon fires to confirm her death as her body goes limp. Whoever Lou Lou was, she's moved on. Her slight, starved frame lies quiet, finally beyond the Capitol's reach. I lean down and whisper into her bad ear. A personal message to the Gamemakers. "You did this to her. This is who you are." And then for Lou Lou, I say the thing she no longer can. "Murderers."

In answer, a hovercraft appears, waiting for me to step aside so it can collect her body.

Lou Lou won't be on the hill with me and Louella. They can't send back two bodies to District 12 without exposing their incompetence. So where will you go, little girl? Back to 11? Into Capitol soil? Or will they incinerate your body and leave no trace of you behind? Either way, mine will be the last touch of someone who cares about you.

The thought of Capitol hands disposing of her infuriates me. And like my Louella, I cannot give her up without a fight. I lift her into my arms and head into an area of the densest trees I can spot. Are they showing me to the audience? Can they witness my refusal to hand over Lou Lou? Do I have the Capitol viewers glued to the screen? The rascal has run off with his district partner — again! The rascal will make the Gamemakers chase him down! Delighted laughter, phone calls to friends, are you watching this?

Lou Lou's body's noticeably lighter than Louella's. The ferocity that gave her weight has vanished. I locate a clump of willows and hunker down in the center, catching glimpses of the hovercraft overhead. A claw descends, tangles in the treetops, withdraws, and makes a second attempt. They can't reach us. For the moment she's safe.

As my breathing calms, I realize I'm playing right into Snow's hands. This is exactly the behavior I've been forbidden to engage in, and there will be repercussions. Deadly ones. Soon. And I will have lost my chance to blow up the tank. How to salvage this moment? Take Lou Lou out and give them a rascally "just kidding" wave? Set her down and run and hide? Just stay put and wait for the claw to break through and then helpfully place her in its jaws?

Indecision immobilizes me. The Gamemakers seem immobilized as well. The hovercraft remains static, claw retracted. A standoff. We are waiting each other out. It would be peaceful if not for the looming sense of danger.

It comes in the form of a brilliant blue butterfly. Almost the same electric blue of District 3's outfits. It navigates the willow tree branches and lights on a nearby bough. I can't seem to tear my eyes from the pattern of tiny golden lightning bolts decorating its wings. Then another lands over my head. And a third, on the back of the hand that cradles Lou Lou's blood-streaked face. As if in slow motion, a stinger descends, a tiny spark jumps off my flesh as it makes contact, and a jolt of pain blinds me. An involuntary scream parts my lips, Lou Lou has tumbled to the ground. My vision returns in time for me to see a second butterfly come for my face. My cheek explodes with what I can now recognize as an electric shock, as if the butterflies have mini tasers in their stingers. One of Snow's beauties.

Raw panic consumes me; all I know is I never want to be stung again. I burst out of the willow bower, leaving Lou Lou to the Gamemakers. Hundreds of butterflies, dotting the trees, come to life and target me. I sprint into the woods, oblivious to all but escape, but they swarm after me. Not with the drunken motion I associate with the butterflies back home, but in a straight line. I'm bobbing and weaving, trying to evade them, but they keep landing stings, each one momentarily freezing me. It isn't enough to have left Lou Lou; these things are bent on torturing me. This is about punishment. As public as possible.

I'm not really sure how long this goes on, seems endless, like I'm losing my sanity, when I fall face-first into a berm of flowers. Afraid of Lou Lou's fate, I spring up, toppling into a heap beside the berm, frantically wiping my face. But it's not the bee balm, it's the gas plants. As a cloud of butterflies descends, I get an idea. After retrieving my flint striker and rock from my pocket, I start making some sparks of my own, sending showers of them into the blossoms. Five-foot flames erupt off the plants, engulfing the butterflies and lapping at my chest, before disappearing. My shirt front glows for a few moments, like a bed of coals, then returns to black, apparently fireproof. A few crispy skeletons float down, but the attack has ended. The stragglers loopily fly away, the picture of innocence.

I lie gasping on the ground, examining my body for wounds. There's absolutely nothing — not a blister, not a scratch. Only the memory of the terrible pain. I press my lips to the flint striker, hoping Lenore Dove sees me, knows this is a thank-you to her for saving me from the mutts.

The mutts! This is it! This is my chance to follow them to their berm! However, I don't jump up; the recent attack has zapped some sense into me. *For once in your life, be smart*, I think. *Do this, but do not jeopardize the arena plan.* Why would I possibly be chasing mutt butterflies? Only one answer: retaliation.

A nearby branch caught fire when the gas plants blazed. I break it from the tree and take off in the general direction of the butterflies. When I catch a glimpse of blue, I know I'm on the right course. Another twenty yards of charging through the woods brings me to a berm covered in flowering bushes. It has slid open as if on tracks, leaving a six-foot-wide gulf right down the middle of the circle. The butterflies make their lazy way into it. For the benefit of the Gamemakers, I rage at them, swinging my torch around madly, incinerating a half dozen or so when I notice the berm beginning to slide closed. As if in a last-ditch effort, I lunge at the final mutt and succeed in wedging the branch between the lips of the hatch. It clamps shut, crushing the wood but leaving an eighth-of-an-inch opening in the seam. I pretend not to notice and slump down next to the berm. The sign reads BUTTERFLY BUSH. Well, I won't forget that one.

I think about going back to look for Lou Lou, but I know she's long gone. Instead, I make my way back to the bee balm, careful not to inhale too deeply, and collect my things. Still no sign of anyone else.

My skin may be as smooth as a baby's behind, but I'm twitchy from the multiple shocks and done in for the day. I've achieved my two tasks, though: making fire and finding a mutt berm. The shadows are growing long, which means I need to start searching for somewhere to sleep, conscious that my piss-poor hiding place from last night must be improved upon. I'm not dizzy now, so I pick a sizable tree with thick foliage near the butterfly bush and climb about thirty feet into the branches. I pitch my hammock between two sturdy limbs, making sure that if one side gives way, I'll have a fork to catch me. This wasn't recommended in the class, but I don't feel secure enough to sleep at ground level again.

Famished, I eat three eggs and a couple of apples. Surely, sponsors will enable my mentors to replenish my pantry soon. Through the trees, the sunset glows golden, then the orange of burning coal, before fading out, leaving me in darkness.

At the sound of the anthem, I position myself to get a clear view of the sky. The first tribute. More snot green. The boy from District 1 who isn't Panache. Then Lou Lou, pictured with her snake. I wonder if, anywhere in Panem, a family member or playmate recognizes her for who she really is. The McCoys must know she's a fake. Surely, they do. Right now, they must be weeping and wondering where their own darling girl has gone. At least that's one terrible conversation I've been spared.

Five Careers gone. Seventeen Newcomers. Twenty-six of us left.

The woods quiet down. A clear yellow moonlight filters through the trees. Honestly, I think I'm the only one on this side of the arena, but you never know. I wonder how Maysilee's doing — just the two of us left from 12 now — and if there's any chance I might see her again. Funny missing Maysilee Donner, but there it is.

Grateful I don't snore, I let myself fall into a dreamless sleep.

Something startles me awake, and I see a parachute with a good-sized bundle caught in the sunlit branches above my head. My first sponsor's gift. I untangle it, set it on my lap, take a deep breath — right now it could hold anything! — and then open it. A dozen white rolls still warm from the oven, a block of orange cheese, and what looks like a bottle of wine, complete with its own long-stemmed glass goblet. This actually coaxes a smile from me. I uncork the bottle and take a sniff. Grape juice. Bet this cost someone a pretty penny. Water would've been more sensible, since I'm about through my first gallon, but I'm not complaining. Grape juice is a big treat back home, reserved for birthdays and wedding punch. Who sent it? The lady with the cat ears? The man I spit on? Great-Aunt Messalina? Right now, I don't even care.

I tip the bottle over my elegant glass, admiring it as the juice fills the stem, then the bowl. Giving the audience a knowing grin, I raise it in a toast and say, "Thank you, my fellow rascals from the Capitol!" Then I take a slow sip, easing my parched mouth. It's so full of goodness, not just the taste but the happy memories it conjures up, that I have to keep myself from gulping it down. Accompanied by a couple of fresh rolls and a chunk of fatty cheese, it restores me enough to face the day.

While I breakfast, I review why, from the Capitol sponsors' perspective, I think I've earned this expensive gift. I evaded the bloodbath with supplies and weapons, I survived poisoning, I made fire, cooked food, torched some butterflies, and found a tree to sleep in. Conclusion: I'm fairly resourceful and clearly selfish enough to win.

I'm worried that the districts have a low opinion of me for abandoning the Newcomers. Trying to save Lou Lou might've helped. And if I blow up the arena, I guess I'll be welcome back in 12 again. Not that going home is a possibility. Still, I want Sid to be able to hold his head up, not be ashamed of me forever.

Since I've made camp near my berm, there's no point in traveling anywhere. Nothing to do but wait for Ampert to arrive with his token fuse and the District 9 sunflower explosive. I'm pretty worn out from Days 1 and 2 of the Games, so I just hang out in my hammock, keeping an eye out for butterflies. By early afternoon, I begin to get restless. We should have worked up a better rendezvous plan. The woods are deep and wide; we could easily miss each other. Far north could still be miles away. Something to remember when I get down in that tunnel. I may still have a long way to go before I reach the tank.

I decide to go look for Ampert.

As I pack up my supplies, carefully wrapping my goblet in the hammock, I come upon the binoculars and try them out. That inspires me to climb higher and get a better sense of the lay of the land. Near the tippy-top of the tree, which towers over most, I can see a great distance. I'm again struck by the beauty of the place, the idyllic woods, the uniform sweep of meadow, the snow-capped peak which now sits under the arch of a shimmering rainbow. I judge the mountain to be about five or six miles away. That's where the rest of the kids are presumably hunting one another down. So different from here, where I'm purely up against the Gamemakers. The sea of trees continues behind me, but seems to narrow to a point in the distance. It's impossible to tell exactly how far away that is, since everything starts to look a little blurry. Does that indicate it's the end of the arena?

I twist back around to view the meadow again and catch sight of a bit of electric blue near the Cornucopia moving toward the woods. Ampert? Worried I will miss him among the trees, I climb down and head for the meadow, hoping to intercept him. Along the way, I cut small, discreet notches in the bases of trees with my knife, leaving markers for my return. Backtracking takes me farther from my target, but I'll need Ampert with me, one way or the other.

When I reach the tree line, I climb onto a rock and survey the meadow through my binoculars. It's Ampert, all right, about a mile away, tromping toward me. The expression on his face, so grim and sad, forged by the last few horrific days, reminds me that I've had it easier than most. Around his neck I spy two sunflower tokens, one stained with blood. At least he's been spared watching his own district mates' deaths, since none have appeared in the sky. I bet he hasn't had much to eat and I'll need him on his toes for the tank bombing. . . . Should I make some sandwiches?

Wait a minute. . . . Once again, what am I doing? Why has the rascal, after running away from the Newcomers, caught sight of Ampert and returned to the edge of the woods? This is different from Lou Lou; she found me. My behavior sure seems suspicious. Like I've been waiting for him the whole time. I don't think this will matter to the audience, but what are the Gamemakers going to make of it? I told them I was only out for myself. What could have drawn me back to Ampert? The answer can't be explosives. What would extend my survival? I've got my own food and water and charcoal tablets and weapons — what can Ampert offer me?

The one thing I don't have much of is information. I know who's dead . . . but who killed them and how? What weapons arm the Careers? Have they discovered anything to eat and drink in here that isn't poisonous? Except for Lou Lou, I've been alone, and she wasn't exactly a wealth of information.

Okay, then. This rascal wants an update.

Cocky. Out for myself. Sarcastic. Nice to the other Newcomers. I'm channeling all these things so I can present a consistent character to the audience, but when Ampert arrives, he throws his arms around me and I just hug him back and say, "Hey, buddy." I'm surprised by how small he feels, because he's such a take-charge kind of kid. But he's only about Sid's size and plenty scared. Even the brightest brain can't think its way out of being trapped in the arena.

"The Newcomers need you back," he says. "They sent me to find you."

Good. That's why the Gamemakers will think he's here.

"We talked about this. My scoring a one makes me dangerous to be around," I say for the audience's benefit. I don't want my gifts to dry up because I'm shirking my Newcomer duties. Also, Sid needs to hear my motive for ditching them.

"Lou Lou ran off. Then we saw her in the sky."

"Case in point," I say, stepping back from him. "She found me, and she's dead now. We didn't see the poison flowers coming."

"Those are poisonous, too?" he asks.

"At least the bee balm. The gas plants came in handy when I needed to barbeque some butterfly mutts. The Gamemakers sent those after me. You hungry?" He nods vigorously. "How about a trade? Some lunch for a mountain update?"

I spread out a big picnic on the rock: rolls, cheese, eggs, apples, and a wineglass of grape juice for him. I don't interrupt as he wolfs the food down, pretty sure he hasn't eaten much in here. He doesn't even have a pack of supplies, just an ax in his belt and a sunhat made of leaves. When he finishes, he wipes his mouth and sighs. "I wish I could've shared that with the others. The Careers got most of the food."

"How are you guys holding up?" I ask.

"It's tough. We've lost seventeen now. All but Lou Lou at the bloodbath."

"Nobody got poisoned?"

"Oh, several of us did. But Wellie figured out about everything being poisonous almost immediately. And Hull's pack had a big bottle of the syrup antidote. None of us died from poison."

"Syrup? I had these." I pull out the tablets and show him. "Else I'd be gone, too."

"Must've been bad. No one to look after you."

I shrug. Then I have to ask. "Wyatt?"

Ampert reaches into his pocket and passes me Wyatt's token. "Panache killed him. And five others. With a sword. Maritte's wicked with the trident. Silka used an ax, it's sharp as a razor, and I saw . . ." His voice chokes off.

"I get the picture. Maysilee's okay, though, right?"

"I don't know. She got separated from us during the bloodbath. Haven't seen her in the sky, though. I'm guessing she's still on the mountain, same as the rest of the Newcomers. We've been trying to stick together, like we planned. The Careers followed us there."

A despicable thought crosses my mind, that Maysilee has somehow joined up with the Careers. Then I remember how combative she was with Silka from the first encounter and feel ashamed of myself. I examine the necklace she wove to securely carry Wyatt's scrip coin. She spent most of her training hours helping the Newcomers display their tokens with pride, when she could have been learning skills to protect herself. Whatever else she may be, Maysilee Donner is not a turncoat.

I tell Ampert, "Wherever she is, she's making trouble for the Careers. You can count on that." When I hook Wyatt's token around my neck, it's like having both him and Maysilee with me.

For a while, Ampert and I just sit there, letting the breeze cool us, staring at the ridiculously pretty, flower-scented meadow, listening to the songbirds. I pour another glass of juice, which we pass between us. Every sense is being catered to, every element designed to soothe. We're cocooned in soft pleasures as we face our deaths.

"So you won't come back?" Ampert asks.

"It wouldn't help. I'm a mutt magnet. And clearly no judge of flowers."

"Can you show me around the woods at least? We need to get off that mountain, but no one knows if it's worse here."

"If that's what you want. But I can't promise to keep you safe from the Gamemakers."

Ampert laughs a bit. "What a funny thing to say. Who could?"

When we finish the juice, I lead him into the woods. My giving him the tour is the perfect cover story, really. Not that he gets much information besides "Watch out for the stream — it's poisonous. And the fruit. And those flowers over there, too." Basically, I could've just said everything's poisonous and left it at that. But I play the guide. I show him the berms with the bee balm and the gas plants, saving the butterfly bush for last. "This here's where the butterflies went. The ones I didn't burn to a crisp."

I see him eye the branch, but he only says, "Do you think it's safe to be near their home?"

Home. He calls it their home. Is it because he misses his own so much? Twelve years old . . . barely five feet tall . . . his voice still hasn't even changed. If I'm homesick, what must it be like for him?

"Well, I don't really think anybody much is at home," I say. "There weren't many left. No more than we can handle. And they don't kill you when they sting, just give you a nasty shock. I had dozens and I'm fine. So it's probably safer than a lot of places, since they tend to space the mutts out." Do they? Maybe. But at least it explains why we should hang around the berm.

"Could I rest here a bit, do you think?"

I look at his puffy eyes. "Sure. I don't really have any plans this afternoon." I make him a bed out of my hammock and he tosses a bit, then drifts off to sleep. Looking at him, I can't help thinking that all the little ones seem to end up with me. Louella. Lou Lou. Ampert. I can't keep a one of them safe. Why do they flock to me?

When Ampert's settled into a deep slumber, I begin my preparations for the bombing, gathering double the wood and pine needles I did yesterday. This will be a nighttime job, and the fire's my responsibility, both for illumination and ignition. Since my butterfly torch held up pretty well, I make sure and break off a few more branches from what I judge to be the same kind of tree. Not wanting to waste my fuel, I set up the fire site, but hold off on lighting it. No potatoes tonight. I'll leave them for Ampert, who stands a better chance of surviving our mission.

If I do this thing right, blow open the tank and set off a flood, likely it will take me out. I mean, six feet of fuse does not allow for much of an escape window. If the explosion doesn't finish me off, surely the water will. I console myself with the thought that either of those deaths will be far kinder than anything the Capitol will devise for me if I somehow make it out of Sub-A alive.

Hoping for something better could be dangerous; it could blind me to the reality of my situation. I remember how Mamaw always said, *"Where there's life, there's hope."* But from where I'm sitting, hope seems a lot like white liquor. It can fool you in the short run, but like as not, you'll end up paying for it twice.

When evening falls, I go ahead and start the fire. Ampert wakes and we toast bread and cheese, then eat it with apples. He says he doesn't want to go back to the Newcomers in the dark and we plan for him to stay the night. In the flickering flames, I remember how my shirt didn't so much as char in the gas plant blaze. Ampert pulls off one of his socks and dips it in the fire, where it glows for quite a while before the toes begin to melt. Seems like a clue. Perhaps it's protective, but from what? I've only encountered one gas plant berm. The clothing suggests any number of things could burn.

As if inspired by the cookfire, Ampert says he'd like to try and catch something to eat to repay me for the food. His token has gotten tangled up with the two District 9 sunflowers, so he removes all three at once and lays them on the ground. He separates his fuse and says, "I might be able to fashion a snare from this. But do you think the animals are poisonous?"

"Maybe not the rabbits," I tell him. "I watched one die from drinking water — it seemed as susceptible as we are. Of course, they could be carrying rabbit fever."

"What's that?"

"Sickness. You don't want it. But if we cook it through, it might be safe." All of this is just chatter meant to mislead the Gamemakers. We're not trapping rabbits. Or cooking their meat. Or even counting on being here for breakfast. "Worth a try."

Ampert begins to unweave his token, simultaneously winding the black fuse around his hand. When he reaches the end, he surreptitiously tucks something that must be the blasting cap in the coils. "I'll give it a go in the morning. You can keep anything it catches." His eyes fall on the sunflowers. "Do you want a sunflower? I bet Nine would like you to wear one. You're the reason they were in the alliance."

"It was really Maysilee who won them over," I respond. "You should've seen them stand up to Panache. Thought he was doing them some big favor letting them join the Careers, and they shut him down like that." I snap my fingers and smile at the memory. "Yeah, I'll wear one. They were good allies." I hang the blood-stained sunflower around my neck.

The anthem begins, but no faces appear tonight.

"Still twenty-six of us," I say.

Ampert wraps his arms around his knees. "Can we stay by the fire awhile? I don't like the dark."

Even though we need the fire for the plot, this rings true. Ampert puts on a brave face, but I can imagine what images haunt him after the bloodbath. "We can sleep here if you want. I don't think the tree will work for both of us. We can take turns being on watch," I tell him. "Go ahead and rest some more."

"Can I have some water?"

I give him the full jug and he downs a few swigs.

"Wake me when you've had enough," says Ampert. "I'll be ready." He takes a final mouthful of water and lies down.

He's leaving it to me to call the shots. "Okay," I say. "Sweet dreams." In a few minutes, he's either sleeping or making a good show of it. I keep guard, my spear resting on my knees, waiting for its big moment when I use it to pry open the berm. I'm glad that's its job, instead of taking someone's life. If I make it out of the Games without killing anybody, that will be a victory in itself.

I say my good-byes to those I love. Burdock and Blair. Hattie. Ma and Sid. And finally, Lenore Dove, my rare and radiant girl. I try not to be scared. I tell myself that everybody has to die sometime, and my number's up. In a way, it's a comfort that a bunch of people I know have gone before me. Pa and Mamaw and the twins and Louella and Wyatt and Lou Lou and a lot of the Newcomers. Maybe Lenore Dove's right, and I will meet up with them, and one day with her, in another world. Or maybe there's just nothing, in which case, it won't hurt any. Mostly, I just don't know.

The darkness deepens, the air cools, and when I think it's past midnight and the audience has gone to bed, leaving a handful of Gamemakers to mind the show, I light a torch branch. Crouching down, I tap Ampert on the shoulder and say softly, "Hey, buddy, let's beat those odds."

Ampert jumps to his feet immediately, thrusting the coiled fuse into my hand. "You'll have sixty seconds," he whispers. This is followed by the explosive, which feels soft and sticky like putty and has been shaped into a block. That last mouthful of water was put to good use. I pocket the materials and without further conversation, we cross to the berm. He holds the torch while I drive the tip of my spear into the crack held by the branch that I left behind yesterday. Using my full body weight for leverage, I pry the sides of the berm apart. The mouth yawns, then begins to slide closed, but not before I wedge the spear between the lips, holding the hatch open wide. To one side, a utility ladder runs down into the depths.

A mechanical buzz of protest comes from below.

Ampert passes me the torch. "I'll be here."

He looks so young, standing there in the flickering light, armed only with an ax I doubt he's strong enough to wield. I slide my knife into his belt, muss his hair like I do Sid's, and say, "Best ally ever." He gives me a lopsided grin and I hop onto the ladder. Torch in one hand, I begin my descent. My feet feel stiff and clumsy on the thin rungs. "Right, left, right, left," I instruct them. Five, ten, twenty feet down and I land on concrete in a narrow hallway and turn to my right, which seems in the northerly direction. I trot along with the help of my torch and the dim utility lights that glow along the side of the floor.

I haven't gone far when I realize the internal wall on my left is not a wall at all. Metal . . . ribbed . . . every few feet, a water droplet, shaped like a tear, has been stamped at about eye level. This must be the side of the water tank, and it's indeed massive, running from the concrete floor twenty feet up to the ceiling. The droplets stretch as far as I can see in either direction. What could they possibly need this much water for? Do they intend to turn the entire arena into a lake? I hesitate, trying to assess the most effective point to place the explosive. Then I give up and slap it a few feet below the droplet right in front of me. What does it matter, really, where the tank is damaged? With a flick of my wrist, I unfurl the fuse and slide it through my fingers, smudging them with black, until they find the blasting cap. Lucky I paid attention in class. I place the cap in the explosive and steel myself. No time like the present. I dip my torch to the end of the fuse, watch the flame eat through the first inches, leaving only the faintest trace of ash, and run like hell. Sixty seconds and counting.

One hundred one, one hundred two, one hundred three . . . I track the time in my head as my feet pound down the concrete. The ladder comes into view and I fling my branch aside, as it's slowing me down and I trust that Ampert will be waiting at the top with a second torch. I know it might be wiser to embrace my death now, but there's something in a person that wants to live. Even if it's only for a few more hours. *One hundred twenty, one hundred twenty-one* . . . Besides, there is Ampert to think about. I may still be able to offer him some protection.

I hear them before I see them. A delicate chirping sound, not unlike a bird, overlaid with occasional squeaks. Whatever they are, they don't sound threatening. I'm more perplexed than alarmed. Perhaps a flock of songbirds has escaped and flies free in Sub-A, like the birds do in the rafters of the chariot horse stable. As my hands hit the first rung of the ladder, I look up in time to catch sight of Ampert's face lit by torchlight. Then a swirl of color obscures his image and spirals down at me.

Transparent wings tinted every color of the rainbow flash above me. They catch the firelight, making them shine like the hard candy in the Donners' shop window on a sunny day. It'd be something to admire, except each three-foot-wide pair of wings carries a vicious face and two back feet sporting four-inch curved claws. Genetically engineered bat muttations. Designed to shred me to slaw.

These creatures haven't broken out of a cage; they're a gift from the Capitol.

One hundred thirty-six, one hundred thirty-seven —

"Haymitch!" I hear Ampert cry out. "Catch!"

He releases the torch, which scatters the bat formation for a second, and I somehow manage to grab it. With my free hand, I begin to scale the ladder, waving the fire above my head. But these are no butterflies, simple to ignite and destroy; they are sinewy mammals that can turn on a dime. They evade my torch and begin to claw me, taking painful swipes at my shoulders and back, causing blood to flow. Climb I must, though, because the clock's ticking and if I'm not aboveground, I'll be drowned for sure.

I'm not going to make it. I've lost count, but I'm thinking at any moment that tank will blow and there will be nowhere for that water to go but into this hallway. I take a final swing at the bats, solidly connecting with the one with its claws sunk into my thigh, and hurl the torch at their evil faces. My fingers fumble for my belt, unhook the interlocking rings, wrap the belt around a ladder rail, and secure the clasp. I throw my arms around the ladder, brace my legs, and hang on for dear life, filling my lungs with deep breaths. About five seconds and three bat scratches later, deafened by squeaks and hisses, I think I've made a mistake. I've bungled setting the explosive, or the cap was a dud, or a Gamemaker has arrived in time to yank the fuse from the putty—

An earsplitting blast almost knocks me off the ladder and I'm totally submerged in water. Icy-cold blackness engulfs me, rips one arm free. Without the belt, I'd be a goner, but somehow, I regain my grip and cling to the bars with every limb, eyes closed tight against the flood. After what seems like forever, the current eases enough for me to pop open my belt and continue my ascent. By this point, the burning in my lungs has pushed all other fears into the background. Legs floating free, I drag myself up the ladder. I'm about to black out when my face breaks through the surface. Between great gasps of air, I choke and gag up the bucket of water that managed to force its way in, despite my best efforts.

The good news is that the bats have disappeared, hopefully drowned in the initial wave. Also, the water lacks the metallic taste of the stream. I'm thinking they didn't bother to poison that colossal tankful, but targeted the streams individually, so my mutt wounds have been washed clean safely. Glass half-full.

When I get my breathing and shivers in check, I call for Ampert. Above me, in the dim light of the fake moon, I can see the spear still propping open the berm, but no sign of him. Something isn't right. He wouldn't leave me to fend for myself. When the wave came, did the bats have time to escape through the berm and attack him? It seems unlikely that even they could fly that swiftly, as the water came almost simultaneously with the boom. Then what has happened to him? Careers? Gamemaker attacks?

I scale the ladder as fast as my frozen muscles will allow. As I reach the surface of the arena, I survey the woods, softly glowing in the mix of moon and firelight. Our campsite remains as we left it, with my pack and the rumpled hammock on the ground. No sign of Ampert, but no sign of a struggle either. What has led him to abandon his post?

I wrench the spear from the berm. The lips try to close, but damage has occurred, and they end in a sort of floral leer. I call softly, "Ampert? Ampert?" No response.

My hearing's funny from either the water or the blast, but a sound reaches my ears, only just distinguishable from the usual nighttime hum of the forest. Animal, but distinct from the bats. Not chirping but chattering, coming from multiple mouths. I grab the hammock, wrapping it around my left forearm, thinking a net might come in handy, and creep toward the chatter. The sound intensifies, making my skin crawl, but I push forward until I break into a small circular clearing.

The trees buzz with life. I make out the hundreds of squirrel-like creatures, swarming around in their gorgeous golden coats, their eyes shining as if lit from within. Cute in a way, but too hyper, bouncing from branch to branch, gnashing their long rectangular front teeth in agitation. Mutts. They only pause to emit piercing rodent screams at a mound of their comrades in the center of the clearing. The boldest are fighting viciously, throwing themselves onto the heap, kicking one another away with powerful hindquarters. One flies through the air and lands at my feet. Before it springs back up, I spy a bloody scrap of electric-blue fabric snagged on its incisors, and everything becomes clear. Carnivorous mutts. Tearing Ampert apart.

I promised Beetee I would not let him suffer. Flinging my hammock to its full length, I holler and lunge for the pile. The hammock snares the furry bodies, and I jerk it toward me, succeeding in unseating a layer or two of mutts. Then I flip around my spear to use as a club and swing it across the mound again and again, sweeping the squirrels away. I prepare myself for their attack, for the inevitable tearing of my flesh, but nothing happens. The moment one's knocked free of the mound, it dives back in. These are programmed for Ampert, and Ampert alone. His look, his smell, his taste.

I am losing, I am losing the fight, I am losing him. I know this, but there's nothing to do but keep swinging. I never even get a glimpse of Ampert, just writhing furry bodies fighting for a piece of him. Finally, as if someone blew a whistle, audible only to them, hundreds of heads pop up and turn in unison toward an unseen master. A mad dash ensues, and in seconds the squirrels have vanished into the foliage.

Panting, I watch them fade away. Then I turn back to what I am meant to witness. A small white skeleton, stripped clean to the bone. No flesh or clothing remains, only an ax at its right side, my knife at its left. My lips move, but no sound comes out. "Buddy?" I stumble forward, spotting his tracker, wedged just below his elbow. There is no one to comfort, to ease out of this world. Ampert's been swallowed up by the Capitol, and his coffin will hold only these pearly white bones.

A cannon fires.

Somewhere, Beetee's heart breaks into fragments so small it can never be repaired. Mine pounds like a drum as a wave of rage surges into it. My head drops back and I emit a howl that bounces off the fake sky and echoes around the arena. I want to kill them all, Snow, the Gamemakers, every person in the Capitol who has been party to this atrocity. But they are safely out of reach, so I drop my spear, grab the ax, and begin to chop away at the arena, determined to take it apart, piece by piece — the trees, the berry bushes, the birds' nests — as inhuman sounds roar out of me.

I am hacking a berm of bluebells to bits when the earth begins to shake so violently that I'm thrown from my feet onto a bank of moss. My fingers dig into the stuff, and I hold my position as branches and debris rain down on me. When the earth settles, I scream at the sky, "Ha! You missed!" I spring to my feet and start careening through the trees like a wild man. "I'm still here! I'm still here!"

When I stagger onto our campsite, I catch sight of the berm and realize that something much bigger than targeting me is happening. The mouth opens and closes spasmodically, sending bursts of blossoms into the air. In the trees behind it, a herd of adorable baby deer runs around in a frenzy, rearing up to show spiked hooves slashing viciously at the air. An apple tree has transformed into a fountain of blue sparks, and clouds of steam rise from a nearby stream. Everything's taken on an eerie, dream-like quality. Either the arena's malfunctioning or I've been licking toads.

Half afraid to hope, I slowly raise my eyes upward to see the night sky, which cuts in and out like bad television reception. A burst of static dazzles, then suddenly, I'm looking straight up at the real sky. A gush of fresh air fills my lungs, and moonlight illuminates the chaos. It worked! We have done it! Me and Ampert and Beetee and District 9 and a slew of people I've never heard of — we have drowned the brain! We have broken the arena!

This is my poster. Right here. I give a wild victory cry and spin around shouting, "Did you all want a party? I'll give you a party!"

Lightning flashes, a clap of thunder booms. I dance around the berm, bellowing the first thing that comes to mind for all of Panem to hear. A song too dangerous to sing —

They hang the man and flog the woman
Who steals the goose from off the common,
Yet let the greater villain loose
That steals the common from the goose.

I extend my arms to the stars, Sid's stars, all of our stars.

The law locks up the man or woman
Who steals the goose from off the common.
And geese will still a common lack
Till they go and steal it back.

I jump up and down hollering, "We got it back! We're getting it back!"

Finally, I drop to my knees, arch my back, stretch out my arms, and embrace the sky. Only it goes pitch-black, as suddenly as if someone threw a switch. A low humming emanates from the forest floor. What's causing that? I get a bad feeling. To my horror, I see the arena sky flicker back into focus.

"No . . . no!" I cry out. The berm's still going at it, and sparks still spray from the apple tree, but the woods as a whole seems to have quieted. Maybe that's okay, maybe that's just part of it shutting down. To be sure, I dig in my pack, sling the binoculars around my neck, and fly to my sleeping tree, scurrying up the trunk like a squirrel mutt. When I reach my lookout position, I sway in the branches, peering through the lenses for an answer. Have I truly broken the arena? Are the Games finished?

Far in the distance, beyond the meadow, the mountain erupts in a fountain of lethal gold, and I have my answer. For me, the party is over.

PART III

"THE POSTER"

I have failed. The arena has been damaged, but not incapacitated. The Games continue.

In District 12, we learn about mountains but predominantly the ones that cover the seams of coal that will provide our livelihood. Volcanoes barely get a mention. I know just enough to connect the name to the dazzling bursts of lava, the glowing streams, the cloud of ash flowing down the mountainside, enveloping everything in its path. I picture the tributes . . . Wellie . . . Hull . . . Maysilee . . . gasping for air . . . suffocating . . . and drop the binoculars. I can't see them, but I can see enough to imagine their terrifying ends.

A blast of air hits my face, thick with stinging grit and a scent so cloying I begin to gag. I lose my footing for a moment and scramble for purchase. If the tree branches below didn't catch me, I'd be dead on the forest floor. I squinch up my eyes against the howling, toxic wind. When I pull the collar of my billowy shirt up over my face, it provides a pocket of protection from the swirling particles. As I've learned at the gas plant berm when my shirtfront refused to ignite, and again when Ampert experimented with his sock in the campfire, our clothes provide a shield. This volcano is why. It has to be why. But I doubt our outfits are of much help to those caught on the mountain.

Am I it, then? The last tribute left alive? The victor of the Quarter Quell? Even if the Gamemakers are firing cannons, there's no way I could hear them between the aftereffects of the explosion and the roar of the wind. From what Ampert said, everybody else was over on the mountain. Perhaps some, if they'd bedded down near the base, could've fled to safety. I don't know, though. They might outrun the lava, but not that cloud. It isn't a real volcano, but how closely did the Gamemakers try to replicate one? Could the lava set everything on fire? What if that ginormous water tank was built so they could quench the aftermath of the volcano? In bombing the tank, I may have destroyed any hope for those who survived the eruption.

I'm too exposed up in the tree. As soon as I'm able, I shinny down and collapse on the pine needles, using the trunk to block the wind. I retreat inside my shirt; there's nothing to see anyway with the cloud erasing the moonlight. Besides, even if I could see, what would I do? Where would I go? If the fire comes, it comes.

The full force of my failure hits me. Who do I think I am? Why did I think I could change anything? That I could take on the Capitol, with all its might, and bring the Hunger Games to a standstill? Me, a sixteen-year-old kid from the trashiest district in Panem with little schooling and no outstanding skills. I've got nothing but a big mouth and an inflated sense of my own self-importance. All foam, no beer, that's me. Near beer.

Plutarch's words echo through my head, mocking me. *"No more implicit submission for you, Haymitch Abernathy. Blow that water tank sky high. The entire country needs you to."*

Well, bad call, Plutarch! Turns out I was built for implicit submission, head to toe, through and through, inside and out.

I grind my palms into my face. What an idiot I am. What a stuck-up, self-centered, incompetent idiot I am. I don't even know if Plutarch was on the rebels' side. Like as not, he's just another Capitol monster who's laughing his head off now.

But no, that doesn't make sense. Because even if the Games continue, his advice helped me throw a real wrench in the works. The Capitol's gorgeous arena's gone haywire. It isn't enough, though, just a minor disruption with no real consequences. Nothing I've done is enough.

Ampert's lopsided grin in the torchlight . . . surely his last smile . . . how he trusted me . . . and now there's not even a body to return to Beetee . . . although Beetee could be dead, too. . . .

I find I'm crying, or maybe it's just my eyes trying to wash out the biting bits of ash. The scratches from the bat claws burn like all-fire and ooze blood into my clothes, which are no star in the absorbency department. Tear-soaked, blood-soaked, misery-soaked, I lay on my side and curl myself around the base of the tree trunk.

Oh, Lenore Dove, how did it all come to this? The moaning wind conjures up the cabin by the lake last winter, her birthday, the best gift ever . . . me singing her song, which I am beginning to hate . . .

Ah, distinctly I remember it was in the bleak December;
And each separate dying ember wrought its ghost upon
the floor.
Eagerly I wished the morrow; — vainly I had sought to
borrow
From my books surcease of sorrow — sorrow for the lost
Lenore —
For the rare and radiant maiden whom the angels name
Lenore —
Nameless here *for evermore.*

Nameless *here* in this world. Dead and gone as I am about to be. Will I be her lost one for evermore? Will she be haunted by me for the rest of her life?

"Just let me go!" I cry out. I'm furious at myself for not telling her to move on after my death when I had the chance. I pound my head into the tree bark until blood runs, and then go limp as I await my end. All yours, President Snow . . .

Sleep? No, I don't sleep, but I'm so exhausted by the night's exertions and the crushing weight of my despair that I achieve a sort of stupor. Hours and hours pass, I guess, because the wind quiets, the ash settles.

Lenore Dove said there's no guarantee the sun will rise, and I wish today proved her right. Nothing good awaits me. I'd rather hide in the dark. But eventually a faint daylight shows through my shirt. I don't want to come out, so I don't. Why am I even still alive? What cruel jokes are the Gamemakers playing on me now?

The humming I noticed last night still radiates from the ground. I remember it directly preceded the return of the fake sky, and I put two and two together. It must be coming from the generator Beetee mentioned. The one just outside the arena. At the top end. Despite whatever disruption the flooding caused to the energy supply, the generator is keeping the arena running. Well, the energy supply was never our target: The brain was. Though it was damaged, enough of it's still functioning to entertain the audience.

"Oh, shut up! Who cares now?" I tell myself. I'm sick of wallowing in my failure. Enough. It's all over.

I try to go back into my stupor, but I'm too antsy. Scratching at the back of my brain are the words Mags spoke when we were about to begin our training. *"In the early Games, I didn't ask the tributes what they wanted because the answer seemed so obvious. You want to live. But then I realized, there are many desires beyond that. Mine had to do with my district partner. Protecting him."*

We had wanted to die quick and proud with a minimum of suffering for our loved ones. I had wanted to outsmart the arena. But Mags had been concerned about her district partner. I don't know if Maysilee's still out there, but if she is, she might need me to help her die with her head up. And maybe some other Newcomers could use a hand as well. Multiple cannons must have fired after the volcano, but I didn't hear them with everything going on. I haven't been declared the victor, though, so someone else is alive. I won't have a clue who until nightfall.

Instead of giving up, maybe I'll see if I can't be of some tiny use to someone else. Throw myself in front of an attacking Career. Bring a Newcomer some food or water. I'm pretty hungry and thirsty myself, come to think of it, and I can't afford to get weak. I might as well see if my supplies survived.

When I pull back my shirt, I'm once again shocked by the beauty around me. I'd imagined the ash to be gray and dingy but, in keeping with the arena's design, they've made it clear and sparkling, so that everything seems to be coated in a layer of rock candy. Sunlight bounces off the crystals, throwing tiny rainbows around the forest. I rise, stiff and sore, and knock the stuff from my clothes. I'm tempted to put a chunk of it to my parched lips, even though I'm pretty sure where that would land me.

The ash disorients me, but after a while, I manage to crunch my way back to the butterfly bush berm, where the blossoms look preserved in ice. The berm's ajar, although the mouth has gone still. No more sparks shoot from the trees, no baby deer rampage around, but I do see a few dead ones under the ash. Damage was done, for sure. Probably throughout the arena. The Gamemakers are going to have to be very careful about where they point their cameras.

Everything looks frozen, like I should be shivering, but the air's warm and perfumed. I kick the ash from my backpack, retrieve my water, and take a deep drink, leaving about half a jug. My remaining food consists of two potatoes, two rolls, one egg, one apple, and a final glass of grape juice. My belly's hollow so I smush the egg between the rolls for a sandwich and wolf it down. I savor my last apple, then retrace my steps to the scene of Ampert's death. His skeleton has been removed, but I find my hammock and shake it out. When it's free of ash, I fold it neatly and return it to my pack.

Now what? I consider going to find survivors, then realize I'm as likely to run into Careers as Newcomers. I dig around with my feet, trying to locate the spear I abandoned, but to no avail. Did the Gamemakers take it with his body? I uncover my knife, however, and try to retrace my steps to Ampert's ax. It takes a while before I can remember I dropped it when the earth shook and I was flung to the ground. I hunt it down and slip it into my belt. I want to carry mementos of my allies with me.

My fingers go to the sunflower at my neck and find its shellac coating has dissolved in the flood, leaving it firm but impressionable. The paint job holds up, so it still looks as good as new. Too bad I don't have a blasting cap; the stuff isn't much good without it. It needs another explosion to set it off. What would I blow up anyway? We succeeded in messing up the brain, but either it's partially working or they've been able to run the arena from the Capitol. Probably some of both. Anyway, no chance I could get to it. At this point, the generator's also essential to continuing the Games, but the only way to reach that would be to break out of this place.

A tiny ray of light penetrates the gloom of my mind. Perhaps it would be possible to escape the arena and try to break the generator. All I've got is a knife and an ax, but that's not nothing.

Of course, it's an incredible long shot . . . but so am I. Maybe I'm just the guy for the job.

Doubts swamp me. *You can't do it! It'll never work! You're just a loser with an ax, trying to chop down the Capitol again. Have you really learned nothing?*

Maybe I haven't learned anything and there's no chance of success and I should double down on my implicit submission. But the truth is, what have I got to lose? Nothing, that's what. And I owe it to Ampert to try.

What would Beetee do? For starters, he'd get me to the generator. He said it was at the top of the arena, and I must be close. The first thing will be to make it all the way north and find some way to break through the arena wall. I don't even know if that's made of cement or metal or some kind of force field, but I guess I'll deal with that when I get there.

After consulting the sun, I get my bearings and head north. My whole body's stiff and sore and the straps on my backpack rub my bat scratches raw. I'd be quite a sight if District 12 had been dressed in yellow, but the black conceals the bloodstains fairly well. Even though I'm still starving and thirsty, I can't afford to use any more of my meager supplies. If I find the generator, maybe I'll celebrate with a slice of potato.

The woods have patches of life — songbirds singing and insects buzzing — and sections of complete silence. I don't see any sign of the other tributes, and it's quite likely that I'm the only one who's traveled this far north. That means the mutt berms will be fully loaded, but they might also be disabled. Nothing to do but keep putting one foot in front of the other.

After a couple of miles, I hear a pattering in the trees and a gentle rain begins to fall. I open my mouth and catch a few drops on my tongue. It tastes clean, like the fresh water, not the poison.

Where did the Gamemakers find it with the tank blown wide open? Do they have a reserve tank? Pipes that reach this far from the Capitol? I placed the explosive chest-high; maybe the bottom foot or two of the tank remained intact and they're accessing that. At any rate, I've got fresh water and I better not take it for granted.

Quickly, I unscrew the caps of my water jugs and set them in the center of a clearing. I know it's not ideal, catching stray drops, but it's the best I can do at the moment. Then I strip down to my skivvies and wash off the blood. I notice the grit under my fingernails dissolving like sugar crystals, and survey the trees. Sure enough, even the light shower melts the volcanic ash off the branches, and the runoff soaks into the ground. In a half hour, the rain stops, leaving the forest as fresh and pristine as the morning I entered it.

It's a relief to have the ash gone, but I can't have caught more than a couple of tablespoons of water. A wasted opportunity. One of Wyatt's tarps would've come in real handy — a mesh hammock isn't worth diddly for rain collection. You work with what you get.

What I get when I reach the end of the forest is not a brick or a steel or an electrified barrier, but a tall hedge that comes to a point like a V and stretches as far as the eye can see in both directions. On closer inspection, the plants appear to be some kind of holly, loaded with clusters of red berries and sporting prickly green leaves. It's not unlike what people in 12 use to decorate at New Year's, although these berries have little black dots on their skins. Even the regular ones are poisonous, so I ignore these. I walk along the hedge, pondering how to approach it. The boughs don't look like they'd support my weight and digging under the mulch at the base doesn't seem like an option. Then I spy a slight opening, turn sideways, and manage to slip through the foliage without getting scratched. A narrow path leads about ten feet in, then curves farther into the hedge, which appears to be quite deep. Cautiously, I begin to weave my way through the greenery on the twisty-turny path, feeling I'm headed north but sometimes forced to diverge right or left out of necessity. *It can't go on forever*, I think. *Eventually, I will reach the end of the arena.*

But I don't. The path winds this way and that, sometimes reaching a dead end or coming to a fork, which requires me to make a choice. Too late, I realize I should have been notching trunks or making little piles of mulch or something to mark my path because I'm hopelessly lost. I try to use the sun to orient myself, but I swear the Gamemakers are shifting the thing around in the sky just to confuse me further. Trapped in a dense maze of holly, I start panicking, plowing down paths recklessly, without any real plan but with a rising sense of claustrophobia. Forget the northern wall — I just need to get out of this place. Perspiration pours down my face and I'm dying of thirst, but I certainly don't think I deserve a drink, given how easily I've been duped into this predicament. If the Gamemakers decide to unleash a mutt on me, and why not, I won't stand a chance of escaping. This is not how I want Ma and Sid and Lenore Dove to see me die. So very foolishly.

This goes on for hours, with me driven by a fear of taking my last breath in this spiky holiday hallucination, desperate for any change of scenery. Finally, exhausted and frazzled, I sink down onto my knees and try to collect my thoughts. The hedge has muffled the forest sounds, so just the faintest notes of birdsong reach my ears. A breeze is too much to hope for, but if I sit very still, I can catch the slight movement of air. I weigh my options: give up, continue to bumble around, or try to hack my way through the hedge with the ax. The last seems to have the most potential, but there's something almost sinister about the hedge that stays my hand. With it towering about me, at least several feet thick, I feel diminished by its size, frightened by what it might harbor. Resigned to my fate, I rise to my feet and reach for the ax.

As I do, a movement ahead of me catches my attention. I look up to see a gray rabbit watching me. I don't know if it's really the same one I shared the apple with, but it comforts me to think it is.

"Hey, my friend," I say. "How you doing?"

After a few ear twitches, it turns and darts away from me. Without thinking, I follow. Maybe it can use its nose to get us out? I stay on its trail, tracking that white cottontail at every turn, and after a minute or two, I see the forest at the end of a stretch. I give a whoop and sprint for the trees. The rabbit shoots out the opening and I'm a few yards behind it.

As I barrel out of the hedge, a sword blade whistles by my head, just catching the tip of my ear. I cry out and trip backward over a dead branch. After days of isolation broken only by allies, I've all but forgotten about the threat of the Careers. Now they've caught me completely off guard.

Nothing that happens in the next minute is premeditated, only reflexive. As a girl tribute from District 4 lunges with her trident pointed at my neck, I clumsily deflect it with my left arm and whip out my knife just in time to drive it into her gut. Rolling to the side, I encounter a leg and hamstring it, leaving her district partner writhing on the ground. Scrabbling to my feet, I pull out the ax and cleave open his neck with a single adrenaline-fueled blow, then turn to take on the owner of the sword: Panache.

For a moment we face off, me, my knife, and the ax against him, his sword, and his shield. With the terrible groans from the wounded girl accompanying us, we circle each other slowly. I take in the burns along his arms and legs, the cracked lips, the mad-dog look in his eyes. A sense of dread fills me. He's much bigger, better armed, and crazed with pain. My eyes flick to the nearby woods, seeking an escape route.

"Uh-uh," says Panache.

With a single swoop, he knocks the ax from my hand, his blade drawing blood, and then slams the shield into my chest so hard I lose my grip on my knife. Gasping for breath, I back away, hands lifted, with only my words to defend me.

I start talking fast. "Whoa, whoa, whoa, whoa, Panache, think about this. Looks bad, killing an unarmed man. Especially me being from Twelve and all. I mean, I got a one in training. Seems cowardly. On your part. Think about your image. You don't want to do something *stupid*." I am not making the world's strongest argument, but the word gives him pause; I guess I have Caesar to thank for that. I jabber on, saying anything, trying to buy time. "Listen, I know you're not a meathead — that chariot idea was brilliant, sorry I swiped it — but you need to play this smart, am I right? Else it could affect your sponsor gifts. How you making out with those anyway? Me, I've been doing pretty well. Turns out, some people love a loser. But you, everybody knows you're going to win. You always win. Come on, at least slide my knife over here so we can give the people a show."

Panache gives his head a shake, like he's clearing my words from his brain. "No! We already fought. You lost. Now you die!" He draws back his sword, eyes locked on my throat, and I brace myself for the blow, trying to look brave and defiant and proud, staring him down so hard he has to admit that even if he kills me, he hasn't defeated me. In my last moment, I need to see recognition of that.

What I see instead is the surprise that transforms his face as the dart pierces his throat.

Panache's sword thuds to the earth and he collapses, senseless. I whip around to see Maysilee emerge from behind a tree. A blowgun balances delicately in her fingers, the mouthpiece attached to a braided vine around her neck. Her latest necklace. Emotionless, she watches Panache expire.

"We'd live longer with two of us," she says.

"Guess you just proved that." I rub my neck where the dart entered Panache's. "Allies?"

She thinks it over, nods, and pats a pouch at her hip. "But I've got a dozen poison darts left if you're still feeling exclusive."

"Noted. It sure is good to see you, Miss Donner." The cannon fires three times, shutting me up. I take in the dead bodies around us, for the first time recognizing that I've killed someone. Two someones. Brutally. It was self-defense, no question, but I know I can never go back to five minutes ago. Having taken their lives . . . in that way . . . it's undoable. I pick up my weapons. "Let's get out of here."

Maysilee considers the dead Careers and relieves the District 4 girl of her dagger. "Want anything else?"

"No." I can't use a trident and the idea of claiming Panache's sword, stained with Newcomer blood, creeps me out. I'm not his heir, the new leader of the pack, nor do I want to present myself as such.

We walk away from the hedge, deeper into the woods. After a minute, the hovercraft flies over us, en route to collecting the bodies. The giant claw descends, lifting them, one, two, three into the sky as the craft swallows them up. We stop when they've all been retrieved. There's nothing to walk away from anymore.

"You're bleeding," Maysilee points out.

Two gashes. One from deflecting the trident, one from Panache's sword.

"Sit down," she orders. I sink onto a fallen log and she pulls a first-aid kit from her black backpack. "I got this off a dead Career. The burn cream kept me from going off my head." Her shirtsleeves have been cut off at the shoulder, and I note the burn marks on her arms, competing for space with the riding crop welts and a range of cuts and bruises, her skin a map of the abuse she's suffered since the reaping. Who would've ever believed that coddled Maysilee Donner, of the nail polish and velvet bows, would come to this? And face it with such fortitude? Mamaw used to say you never really knew who'd swim in a flood.

"I guess the lava just burned up everything in its path?"

"No, it wasn't even hot. It was some sort of gel that gave you chemical burns if it got under your clothes, then turned hard and slippery as ice on the ground."

Guess that's why there was no smoke and I didn't burn up.

Methodically, Maysilee cleans the wounds and closes them with neat, even stitches. I'm not surprised really, after watching her create those artful tokens out of spit and string. When I'm sealed up again, she sits across from me and clocks my pack. "Any food?"

"Oh, I've got piles of food, but tragically, no silverware."

One side of her mouth curls up. She pulls a pocketknife and a fork twisted out of a piece of wire from her pocket. "We're covered."

"Well, that's a game changer. Are you free for dinner? Because I'm in possession of two very fine potatoes. Raw, but potentially bakeable. You?"

"Three slices of dried beef and half a can of olives. Fifty-fifty?"

"Close your eyes a minute."

Maysilee squints at me. "Why?"

"Just do it." She closes one. "Both of them." When she does, I pull out my glass, which has heroically survived the day, empty the rest of the bottle into it, and hold it out. "Okay, open up."

At the sight of the elegant glass, the rich grape juice, she gives a little gasp. "That's the most beautiful thing I've ever seen."

"It's yours. A thank-you for saving my life."

She grins. "Fifty-fifty or no deal."

"Done." Because really, I want that juice like all-fire. "But you first."

Maysilee takes the glass, sniffs the bouquet like it's a fine wine, and takes a sip. Tears actually come to her eyes. "Oh, my word. Never thought I'd taste home again." She hands it back. "Now you."

Evening falls as we take our time passing the glass back and forth, savoring every drop. I make sure she gets the last mouthful. She wipes out the glass with her handkerchief and tries to return it.

"No, you keep it. It belongs with your table setting."

She carefully stows it away in her pack. I lean back against the log, spent. "So, I've barely seen a soul. What's going on out there?"

Maysilee thinks a minute, fingering a burn on her arm. "Hard to say. The arena's on the blink, but I'm sure you're aware of that. If you mean the other tributes . . . for all I know, we're the last two left."

"Well, if it comes to that, I'm on borrowed time anyway. Don't think twice about using those darts."

"You think I couldn't?"

I look her straight in the eye. I remember all the years of meanness, but I also factor in how she's transformed since the reaping. Defending Louella, helping Ampert, looking out for the Newcomers. "I think you couldn't."

For just a second, a look crosses her face. Young and vulnerable. "Thanks for that. I don't think you could either."

Just before the moment gets too embarrassing, the anthem begins to play. Our heads tilt up.

"By my count, we were at twenty-six last night," Maysilee says.

"Yeah, mine, too. If I keep track of the overall number, can you try to remember who's gone? You're better at details."

"I'll do my best." Maysilee's fingers entwine in her necklaces as she homes in on the sky.

Panache appears first, followed by all four kids from District 2.

The fingers on my right hand press into the pine needles. "Bad day for the Careers."

But then Ampert leads off his entire team. Every single kid from District 3 is history.

"Bad day for everybody," says Maysilee.

Next the boy and girl I just killed from District 4. Seems like the first time I've ever looked at them. I feel sick, thinking of their families. Self-defense, I know. I focus on the head count. "We're up to eleven."

A boy and a girl from District 5. "Five's out now," says Maysilee.

One of my doves, Atread, who's the last boy from District 6. A boy from District 10. The girl from District 11 who isn't Chicory. Blackout.

"Sixteen," I say. "That leaves ten of us."

"Only two Careers left. Silka from One and Maritte from Four. Eight of us Newcomers. You, me, Hull, and Chicory from Eleven." Maysilee takes a deep breath, concentrating. "Ringina and the other girl from Seven, I think her name's Autumn. Two more. Who am I missing?"

"One of my doves from Six."

"Right, Wellie. And someone else. Can't place them right off. A boy, I think. He's dressed in red. District Ten," she concludes.

I remember Ampert swinging his lariat around in the gym. A boy from 10 had made it for him. . . . "Buck?"

"That's it."

"You did great. I don't know how you remembered them all."

"I focus on their colors. No more purple, no more electric blue, no more orange, or peach, or yellow. And just a smattering of the rest of us."

"Only two Careers left, though," I say. "Wyatt would like those odds."

At the mention of our oddsmaker, we both fall silent. Thirty-eight of us dead. Thirty-nine if you count Lou Lou. Forty if you count Woodbine. Just a smattering of us left. It doesn't seem real. Nothing here is real.

The fake moon rises, casting a silvery light over our little clearing. I feel Maysilee a few feet away, sense her pulse, the rise and fall of her chest, but she seems as impermanent as the rest of it. Possibly I have died — by poisoning, in the tunnel, on Panache's sword — and have moved on to one of Lenore Dove's worlds, where I continue to dream of life.

"Have you killed anyone besides Barba and Angler?" Maysilee asks.

Those must be the kids I fought from District 4. "No, just them. You?"

"Panache was my second. I took out Loupe from District One a couple of days ago. He'd broken away from the pack with Camilla from Two. Pretty sure I got a dart into her, but the volcano might have finished her in the end."

The thunk of the pot hitting the ground behind us makes us jump. Maysilee retrieves the gift and detaches the parachute. "I hope it's food." She lifts the lid, and a cloud of bean and ham hock soup steam dampens my face. Mags. Trying to reach us, to let us know we are not alone in our pain, to give us strength to go on. Tears fill my eyes, forcing me to admit my presence in the only world I know. Not an imaginary one. The one where I am in the Hunger Games for real.

"Like when my grandmother died," says Maysilee.

"Mine, too." I don't list all my dead. It's not a competition.

She unclips two spoons from the lid of the pot and hands me one. Silently, we eat our soup. Fifty-fifty.

The night air feels chilly. Maysilee pulls her shirt down over her knees for warmth and hugs herself, but I can still see the gooseflesh on her arms. "I could make a fire if you'd like," I offer.

"That'd be good. If you don't think it's too dangerous," she says.

"Not if one of us keeps watch. In fact, it could be a good thing if the other Newcomers find us."

"We can handle Maritte and Silka. Right?"

"With you and those darts? I don't think we even need me."

I collect wood and put my flint striker to work.

"Aren't you a sly dog," says Maysilee. "Smuggling that in."

"Well, you know I like my pretty with a purpose." My voice catches a bit, remembering where I heard that. I concentrate on getting a fire going.

Maysilee smooths out a small tarp on the ground, settles herself on it, and rubs her hands over the blaze. "You can sleep now if you want. I'm not tired."

The circles under her eyes say otherwise, but I'm fading fast. "Okay, but wake me anytime to take over." I secure my flint striker around my neck, spread out my hammock on the ground, and stretch out, watching the tongues of fire dance.

"Works better if you close your eyes," she says.

"Yeah." I shift positions, but something seems unfinished. Like I never really thanked her for today. No, I did. With the juice. But that doesn't begin to cover it. What do you say to the meanest girl in town who's become your friend? No, more than a friend, really. A Newcomer. Being tributes and not killing each other . . . looking out for each other with no questions asked . . . that's family, I guess.

"You need to sleep while you can, Haymitch."

"I know but . . . what I'm thinking . . . you and me . . . You remember what Ampert said when you made his token?"

There's a long pause before she says, "Sure. I'll be your sister."

Our hands reach out at the same time, clasp, and then release. "'Night, Sis." I roll over and let sleep take me.

My dreams are nothing I want to remember, full of people I must never forget. I visit death after death. It's a relief to be woken up.

Maysilee has let me sleep most of the night. When we switch places, I'm determined to give her the same opportunity. Ax and knife at hand, I keep the fire burning with bits of fuel until the sun rises on our fifth day in the arena. My stomach growls so loud I'm afraid it might wake her. Last night's soup seems a distant memory. I should be watching the woods, but my eyes keep drifting upward, hoping for a sponsor gift. Nothing would be too small, a piece of bread, a bit of cheese, and our water's getting mighty low.

I focus on my plan. Obviously, I was onto something with that hedge. They played me, but they also confirmed what I suspected.

I've found the end of the arena. If I can get through the shrubbery, I'll find the generator and try to hack it to bits.

Time's a-wasting, but Maysilee deserves some shut-eye. To distract myself, I pull her tarp out from under my butt and attempt to fashion it into some sort of gizmo to catch rainwater, in the event any more should fall. My efforts result in a crooked funnel of sorts, that I tie with vines at the point. Seems like something of an achievement, until I hear her laughter.

"Made yourself a hat, did you?"

I'm kind of glad just to hear her laugh. "This, I'll have you know, is a first-class watercatcher. And you will eat those words."

"Will I? Exactly how are all the raindrops supposed to find that tiny opening?"

She has a point. There's very little room for the rain to enter, which is no way to collect water. The water that fills our rain barrel has a roof to catch it before it finds its way down the drainpipe. "More surface area, you thinking?"

"I'm thinking." Maysilee holds out her hand for my funnel. She unwraps the tarp and flattens it out thoughtfully. It's about four by four feet with little rings in the corners for securing it. "First, we'll need some way to mount it." She looks around, then gathers some vines. I help her tie them to the rings. She borrows my knife and punches a small hole in the very center of the tarp. "Now the water can run out there. Wish we had a tube of some kind; it would channel it into your jug."

We take inventory of our stuff, which seems fruitless until I spy the wineglass. I remember how the juice filled the entire stem. "How attached are you to this?"

"Less attached than I am to water," says Maysilee.

Placing the glass carefully on the log, I chop off the base and the bowl, leaving a hollow glass tube. Maysilee slides it into the hole. The jagged glass does a nice job of holding it in place.

"That should work," she says. "Now all we need's a rain shower." She folds the tarp carefully and returns it to her pack. "So, what's the plan? I was thinking we might go back to the Cornucopia to see if we can find any food that got left behind. Then we could go look for the other Newcomers. Or do you think we should find them first?"

"I think we should head north."

"North? Whatever for?"

"I just have a feeling about it," I say, so the Gamemakers won't suspect my next move.

"Haymitch, I need food."

"Thought you weren't a breakfast person."

"Well, in here, I'm a breakfast-lunch-and-supper person. Never really knew what it was like to be hungry before. I mean, really hungry. It hurts." She presses her hand against her stomach. "And it scares me."

"I'm familiar. But I'm bent on heading north."

"Can we at least try to locate the Careers' packs? They must've hidden them somewhere around here before they hunted you."

"Good thinking, but not for too long. Fifteen minutes and we go."

Maysilee gives me a probing look but begins the search. She suspected I wasn't being up front with her back in the apartment. I don't know if she credits me with the arena breakdown, but she knows something's still up that I'm not sharing. Should I tell her? How? When? Those cameras have to be on us.

We go back to the site of the fight and spiral out, looking for any supplies the Careers might have stashed. Sure enough, we find some tucked under a rock shelf, only a short distance away. Three backpacks of various sizes. We dump them out on the ground and take stock of the contents. A hammock like mine. Two empty water jugs. Three handkerchiefs. A bottle of syrupy medicine for when you've been poisoned. A second tarp. A blowtorch, something like the one I've seen Tam Amber use. I press the lever, there's a click, and six inches of flame shoot out.

Maysilee raises her eyebrows. "Starting fires will be a cinch now."

Almost makes me sad, seeing Lenore Dove's gift become obsolete so quickly. "Until the fuel runs out," I counter.

We lay out the food with care. A flat tin of sardines. A banana with brown spots. Four rolls. A jar of nut butter with about an inch left. I add my two potatoes and Maysilee her three dried beef jerky strips and olives. Could be worse.

"Okay, breakfast person, what will it be?" I ask her.

Maysilee takes charge of the food, halving the rolls and spreading them with the nut butter, artfully arranging slices of smushy banana on top. I'm not sure about the combination, but one bite dispels any doubt. "This is prime," I say.

"Well, I am responsible for the more innovative flavor combinations at our shop. Did you ever try our hot pepper cherry taffy?"

"I did! That was Mamaw's favorite!"

She gets out her knife and fork and cuts off a piece of her roll. "That was mine. Also, the cream cheese cinnamon balls and the lavender suckers. The mayor was partial to those."

"Sounds like the job wasn't all bad," I comment.

She sighs. "Ironic is what it was. I don't even care much for candy. So many more interesting things to make."

I wolf down my sandwiches before she's even finished her first and look around for something to do. I take the lids off the

Careers' water jugs, hoping for a few drops. Dry as a bone. "Guess they were thirsty, too." Stripping some vines off a tree, I rig the second tarp for water catching. "No tube for this one."

"We'll make it work," says Maysilee. "With a second hammock, maybe we can both sleep up in the trees."

"Sure. Feels safer up there. If we go high enough, we won't need to be on watch. We'd hear anybody coming."

We pack up our booty, and she gestures for me to go first. "After you."

Trouble is, I don't know where we are. I head off like I do. Trekking through the woods might give me an opportunity to reorient myself. Since I don't entirely trust the sun's position anymore, I'm hoping for a few landmarks to get my bearings. We run into one after about ten minutes: the blueberry bushes with the broken branches where I hid my first night. That hedge really spit me out a long way from where I entered.

"That's where Lou Lou found me," I tell Maysilee.

"Oh. Blueberries." She pulls out a small bowl and begins to gather them by the handful, which alarms me.

"You know we can't eat those, right?"

"'Course I do. But my poison's running low. Need to restock."

I guess the darts didn't come poisoned. Leave it to Maysilee to make them lethal. She mashes the berries into a juicy paste.

"You really need to do all that now?" It's already late morning, and I'm getting fidgety.

"What's the big rush, Haymitch?" That shuts me up. She knows I've got a secret worth telling and she's using it against me. Like she did with Lenore Dove, I guess.

Maysilee drains some of the liquid into a heart-shaped glass vial that hangs from one of her necklaces. "It's designed for perfume, so it's got a good tight lid to prevent evaporation.

Just wish it held more." She twists the tiny lid back on the heart. "How'd she die anyway? Lou Lou?"

"Inhaling bee balm," I say. "Ampert told me about Wyatt."

"He was trying to shield her. When he died, she ran away. I tried to follow her, but I lost her at the mountain." She wipes her bowl with some leaves. "I wonder what they're thinking back home. Bet everyone's rooting for you."

"Maybe before the gong, but not anymore. You're the one who tried to stick with the Newcomers. I know I'd be rooting for you."

"Trying's not doing."

"No, but it sure beats not trying." Of course, I have been trying to accomplish any number of things that I'm sure never made it on air. But trying wasn't doing there either. At least, I know which way to head now. Maybe at the hedge, I'll be able to get some doing done.

We hike along in silence, keeping an eye out for Careers, Newcomers, and mutts, but meeting no one. Sometimes we pass a casualty of the flooding . . . trees that drip blood instead of sap . . . a gaping hole where something exploded, leaving a slimy clear liquid coating everything in its vicinity . . . a stump that belches sulfurous, glowing gas . . . all of which we give a wide berth to.

I stop to examine a trio of dead fox mutts, fur as orange as sunset, who appear to have died eating poisonous eggs.

"What do you think those things were designed to do?" I ask.

"Steal our food probably," says Maysilee.

Or eat us, I think. *Like the squirrels. Who knows? Maybe those were programmed for me.*

Around midday we reach the hedge. "It's a maze." I tell Maysilee. "No point in trying to outsmart it. It'll spin you around for miles."

"What's your plan?"

“My plan is, we cut straight through it and take a gander at what’s on the other side.” I drop my pack to the ground, roll up my sleeves, and pull out my long knife.

Maysilee surveys the hedge — its height, its length — then steps in closer for a look at the holly leaves and speckled berries. “Something’s not right about this hedge.” She looks back over her shoulder, considering what’s behind us. “But that’s nothing new.”

“I was in it for hours yesterday, and the worst I got was lost. I think that’s its purpose,” I reassure her.

She sets down her pack and pulls out the dagger she got from Barba. We slip through the opening and take advantage of the ten feet of straight path, then stop as it begins to curve into the maze. I square my shoulders so I’m facing true north. “Here. This is where we should go in. Probably the faster the better.”

“Gotcha.” Maysilee steps up beside me. “On three?”

I nod and we count together, slowly raising our weapons. “One, two, three!”

We bring down our blades simultaneously, slicing cleanly through the greenery. But we’ve barely finished our first strokes when dozens of the holly berries pop off their stems and swarm up our arms. We both give a holler and begin brushing them off.

“What the hell are these?!” I exclaim.

“Ladybugs!” says Maysilee.

Ladybugs? I lift my hand to examine one. It’s a ladybug, all right, or pretty near. All up and down my arms, the creatures latch on to the flesh. Within seconds, they inflate to the size of acorns and begin exploding, splattering my face with my blood.

Maysilee has already fled the hedge, and I hightail it out after her. Both of us scream our heads off, running in circles as we try to claw the things from our skin. Once they've attached those tiny hypodermic needle mouths, they're stubborn as all get-out.

"Pluck!" Maysilee orders me. "Pluck!" She dances in place but has settled enough to be pinching each ladybug and yanking it straight out.

I follow suit. The suckers are dug in deep, akin to those on a really determined tick. If I get a grip up near the head and pull firmly and slowly, they pop out in a spray of blood. Planting my feet on the ground to steady myself, I mutter, "Bug by bug . . . bug by bug . . . bug by bug . . ." as I pluck away at my arms, my neck, my face. I strip off my shirt and pants, but only a few made it beneath the loose fabric. When I'm largely vermin-free, I go to work on Maysilee, who, sleeveless, has had the worst of it. "Bug by bug . . . bug by bug . . ."

She's trembling all over and, what do you know, so am I. "Bug by bug . . ." we chant together. "Bug by bug . . ." When all the visible ones are gone, she strips down to her underwear, too. "My back?" Yeah, there's another half dozen there. I'm light-headed and want to sit down, but I don't stop until every bug's dead and gone.

"Okay, you're clean," I tell her. "You're all clean." We both slump to the ground, pale and drained in our bloody skivvies.

Parched, I dig in my pack for the water and insist she drink first. "I'm sorry, this was my fault. Talking big like I knew what was in there. I swear, none of them bothered me yesterday."

"I don't think the Gamemakers want us going through that hedge," Maysilee observes.

I nod. "Message received."

"How much blood do you think we lost?" she asks.

"I don't know. Maybe a cup or two?" A rogue ladybug explodes behind my ear, making me woozier. I pull the three beef strips out of the pack and hand them to her. "Here. Get some iron in your blood."

She divides them in half. "Fifty-fifty." As we eat, she comments, "Your plan is not sustainable."

I look at her sawing away at her jerky with her pocketknife and homemade fork, and can't help laughing a bit. "No, it certainly is not." My head's too muddled to come up with a new plan. All I can do is stretch out on my back and stare at the perfect azure-blue sky. "I can't seem to think straight."

"Me either." She rustles in the pack. "Do you like olives?"

"No idea. Never had one."

She holds one out to me. "Suck on it for a bit, get the salt out. There's a pit inside."

I place one on my tongue, assessing the smooth skin, the strange rich taste, tangy and metallic. "Not bad." She deposits two more in my palm. I savor each one, rolling it around my mouth and slowly letting my teeth wear it down to the pit.

Time passes, clouds move in, and rain begins to fall. "The tarps!" I cry. We shakily find our feet and unfold our tarps. Reluctant to place them under the poisonous trees, we drive branches into the ground to form posts and stretch the tarps out, so there's nothing between them and the sky. Almost immediately, we get results, and a slow trickle runs off them into the waiting water jugs below.

The rain intensifies and we stand, heads back, washing the blood from our faces and bodies. When we pass for clean, we hold our clothes in the downpour, laundering them as best we can. After about twenty minutes, the clouds turn off like somebody twisted the faucet.

We dress, letting the thin material dry on our bodies, and pass a water jug between us. "Well, if we weren't before, we're blood kin now," says Maysilee.

"Sure enough, Sis. I think I swallowed enough of your blood to qualify."

"Did you ever want a real sister?"

"I had two for a short time. Twins like you and Merrilee. They didn't make it."

"I'm sorry. I didn't know that."

"No reason you should. It was before school and all."

A sad look crosses her face. "I keep wondering, will Merrilee still be a twin, after I'm gone?"

"Always," I say without hesitation, imagining Sid watching us. I hope he won't think of himself as an only child.

"This is going to be hard on her," says Maysilee.

After the Games comes the fallout from the Games. Spreading out like ripples in a pond when you toss in a rock. Concentric circles of damage, washing over the dead tributes' families, their friends, their neighbors, to the ends of the district. Those in closest get hit the worst. White liquor and depression, broken families and violence and suicide. We never really recover, just move on the best we can.

Sid's still so young, too tender for this world. "I worry about my brother, too."

"He comes in the shop sometimes. Loves his taffy. Sid, right?"

I'm touched she knows his name, remembered this detail about him. "Yeah. Sid."

The cannon sounds twice, startling us.

"I guess it's too much to hope it's Silka and Maritte," I say.

"I don't know what to hope for. That would leave only us Newcomers. And then what?" says Maysilee bleakly.

Then what, indeed. "Another meeting, like you said in the Capitol."

"And if we agree to stay true?"

"More mutts," I say. "Another volcano eruption."

"Hunger." She rubs her stomach. "So, can we go back now to the Cornucopia? Look for food?"

"It's probably a six-mile hike. Should we try to recover a bit more?"

"What food do we have left again?"

I check the pack. "Sardines, olives, and two potatoes."

"We better try for the Cornucopia," she says.

Truth is, I'm so wiped out, I'd rather sit here and hope for food to drop from the sky, but I owe it to her to try her idea. Besides, the longer the Games go on, the pricier it becomes to send us anything, and our sponsor donations may be depleted. We pack everything up and head south.

We trudge along for a couple of miles before Maysilee stops and raises her head. "Listen."

I strain my ears, but they're still not so good as normal, with the blast and all. Things sound kind of muffled and partial, like I've got bits of cotton wool in my ears. "I don't hear anything."

"Shush!" she whispers urgently. "Over there." She points off to our right, to the west.

I cock my head for better reception, and this time I do pick up something. "Is that a baby?" My brain starts spinning images of ravenous babies designed with superhuman strength crawling around the woods, crying for us to help them, but really looking to swarm us and pick our bones clean as a wishbone with their chubby little fingers.

"I thought so at first, but there's an animal sound to it, too. Kind of squealing and mewling . . . like a goat or a kitten."

My mind adds horns and fluffy tails to the mutt babies. "Let's keep clear. Whatever it is doesn't need our help."

An agonized scream echoes through the trees. Definitely from a guy.

"But *he* does. All the male Careers are dead, Haymitch." Maysilee loads her blowgun. "That's either Hull or Buck."

I pull my knife and my ax. "Let's go."

I ditch my pack in a patch of katniss and we take off toward the disturbance. I can't shake the image of those baby mutts from my mind, but I forge ahead, already thinking of protecting my kneecaps. The weird baby noise becomes more distinct and less recognizable, but it's overlaid by some very familiar moans of human pain. Suddenly, Maysilee yanks me to the ground and I'm peering through the bushes down a small slope into a clearing.

About fifteen feet away, Buck and Chicory lie writhing on the ground. Long metallic spikes that resemble knitting needles protrude from their flesh. They paw at them with clumsy hands, as if they've got really bad frostbite or something's disabled their fingers. I'm trying to make sense of the scene — does Silka have a weapon that shoots projectiles? Did they run into a pine tree with detachable poison needles? Is there an army of mutt wasps with wicked stingers? The mutts so far have come in droves, be it butterflies, bats, squirrels, or ladybugs, so I'm thrown when the lone source of the attack waddles into view.

Porcupines inhabit the hills around 12. Lenore Dove has an affection for the ones back home — *quill pigs* she calls them — saying they're misunderstood. They can't shoot quills like people think; you have to come in contact with them, especially their tails, and if you leave them be, they leave you be. But even she would have trouble loving this massive mutant beast. It's the size of a bear — in fact, it might have been crossed with one in the lab, given its claws and teeth. Like everything in the arena, it's striking in its way. The rows of pure gold, silver, and bronze quills adorning its back, sides, and tail gleam in the sunlight. But I'm long over being seduced by the arena's beauty.

Distorted baby sounds continue to stream from its mouth as it snuffles around the clearing. Hull, who has a half dozen quills dangling from his swollen face, hollers as he lunges at it with a pitchfork. The porcupine responds by backing toward him, its deadly rear raised and bristling. Hull could run away, but he's trying to get to his allies. Hoping they might be only injured, instead of dying.

"We need some kind of shield," Maysilee whispers, sliding off her backpack and pulling out our tarps.

I run my fingers over the thick canvas, coated with something to make it waterproof, though not necessarily quill-proof. "Maybe if we double them up?" I suggest. Layered together, they feel a bit more secure. "Okay, what's the plan? I think we're safe if we keep our distance. It has to make contact to quill us."

We weigh our options. Maysilee decides, "I can try the darts if we're a bit closer, but I'm afraid they'll have trouble getting through to its skin. You think you could get a knife in it?"

"Not sure. It does look pretty well protected. Maybe if we flip it on its back? Get the underbelly?"

"Flip it with what?"

I spy a sturdy tree limb on the ground. "Branch might work."

Just then, the porcupine twists its hindquarters and drives a slew of quills into Hull's thigh. He cries out in agony and sinks to the ground. I retrieve the branch and start snapping off the smaller shoots to streamline it into a staff. The sound draws the attention of the beast and it begins to clatter its teeth together. As it shifts in our direction and approaches, a stench of musk and roses washes over us, making my eyes water.

Maysilee hoists the double tarp in front of us and we peer over it. "I don't have a lot of confidence in this flipping thing," she says. "And it's still too far for darts. What about your ax? Can you throw it?"

With the amount of kindling the world's required of me, chopping wood for white liquor and laundry, I've messed around with axes plenty. This one's on the long side and I've never practiced with it, though it's not dissimilar to one I threw with Ringina back in training.

"I can try," I say. "But you better have those darts ready."

I shove my knife in my belt and get a double-handed grip on my ax, the way they said was best in the gym. "Okay, now." As Maysilee lowers the tarps, I drop the ax back behind my head and then launch it at the porcupine. It makes one rotation before the blade buries itself in the beast's side.

A squeal of pain and indignation rings out. The mutt puts us squarely in line with its butt, but I'm not too worried because we still have ten feet between us. Then it begins to demonstrate some unusual behavior, quivering at first, which leads to it shaking like a wet dog. The quills shoot out in a sunburst, and Maysilee barely has time to yank the tarps back up before a dozen pierce them. One sticks the bulb of my nose and another comes a hair's breadth from my pupil, dangerously close to blinding me. I jerk back and rip the quill from my nose. Tiny bits of my flesh cling to the barbed end, leaving a raw, stinging wound.

Still keeping the tarps aloft, Maysilee removes a spike from her cheek with a wince. "Once again, you were misinformed."

"I'm sorry. Nothing behaves naturally here." She turns the tarps ninety degrees to get the quills away from our eyes, and we peek over the top. I spot my ax lying on the ground, freed by the mutt's shaking. "Think my ax did any damage?"

"Hard to tell," she says.

The porcupine goes on the rampage, stamping its feet and fussing like a toddler having a meltdown. Only, I know it's nobody's baby, just an abomination whipped up in a test tube to murder us. It begins to shake again. We duck below the tarps for cover as another round of quills peppers us.

A cannon sounds, and I know one of the Newcomers has gone. Two remain alive. I don't know what poison the quills carry, but my nose has swelled up like a ripe strawberry. If we give them the antidote, could they recover still? Should I drink some now? Is one quill enough to kill you?

"We need to get to them," I tell Maysilee. "Try the antidote."

"Yes, but I don't think your stick's going to be of much use," she says.

"I don't think anything's going to be of much use since it can shoot those quills." I watch the creature continue its tantrum and think of Sid when he was a little one. "Maybe we're going about this all wrong. Maybe we should try soothing it."

"Soothing it?"

"Yeah, like when you try to calm down a baby. And then just get it to move on."

"Sing it a lullaby maybe?" Maysilee deadpans.

"Maybe," I counter. "Or give it a pacifier."

"I guess you catch more flies with honey than with vinegar." Maysilee unearths the cans from her pack. "Olives or sardines?"

"Well, the olives are easier to throw." I pull one out and chuck it in front of the porcupine, which ignores it. I bounce a few more off its nose. The cries mellow to whimpers as it runs its snout along the forest floor, snarfing up the olives. "Who doesn't love salt?" I lob another one a couple of feet ahead of the mutt, and it lumbers after it. Then another and another, stretching the distance each time, until I've got it ten yards outside the clearing. Out of olives, I throw the empty can as far into the woods as my strength allows and hear the porcupine crashing through the trees like a dog after a bone.

A second cannon fires. Maysilee's in the clearing in a flash, trying to tip the antidote between Hull's lips. I check for Chicory's and Buck's pulses, just in case those cannons were for some unfortunate tribute elsewhere. Nothing. I join Maysilee, who's managed to coax some of the syrup down Hull's throat, and begin plucking quills from his leg to reduce the poison.

"Come on, Hull," she tells him. "You've got to drink this down. Come on, now." He's trying, his throat muscles rippling with the effort, but the antidote's bubbling back and spilling down the side of his face. We continue, her coaxing, me plucking, until the cannon sounds, and even then, for a few minutes more because maybe someone as young and strong and deserving of life as Hull might find his way back to it. But he doesn't and so, finally, we give up.

The hovercraft approaches, a vulture hungry for the remains of our allies. From deep in the woods comes the sound of the porcupine chomping on the olive can, its targets long forgotten. Evening air cools my cheeks and diffuses the creature's musk. Maysilee passes me the bottle and I take a swig of the antidote. I don't know how much poison one quill delivers, but why take a chance? It tastes like somebody mixed chalk bits in buttermilk and forgot to stir it.

Maysilee and I go around and shut each of the dead tributes' eyes and try to arrange their bodies properly so their families' last image won't be of their contorted limbs. On our way out of the clearing, we collect the ax, our tarps, and their supplies. The claw begins its descent as we reach my backpack. We sit smack down in the clump of katniss, side by side, completely done in.

I can barely hear her whisper. "One of us has to win this thing."

My eyes travel up the long stems to the arrow-shaped leaves, the white petals, concealing us from Capitol cameras. "Why's that?" I whisper back.

"One of us has to be the worst victor in history. Tear up their scripts, tear down their celebrations, set fire to the Victor's Village. Refuse to play their game."

Reminds me of Pa. "Make sure they don't use our blood to paint their posters?"

"Exactly. We'll paint our own posters. And I know just where we can get the paint." In a gesture I remember from the schoolyard long ago, she extends her pinkie. "Swear it."

I encircle it with my own and our pinkies lock tight. They will never let me be a victor, not after my attempt to break the arena, but I can swear to try to keep her alive. "One of us paints the posters."

She rises and pulls me up. "Let's check the supplies."

Our allies must have recently received a parachute, because one pack holds crackers and baked beans and an unexpected treat, raisins mixed with nuts and candy. There's a blanket, too, and some more water jugs, one half-full. We decide to save the Cornucopia for tomorrow, so I start a fire. Maysilee heats up the beans, which we dine on in our own fashion, by fork or cracker, and then eat our treat, one morsel at a time.

The anthem plays, and Ringina and Autumn appear, followed by Buck, Chicory, and Hull.

"Five gone, five left," I report.

"You, me, Silka, Maritte, Wellie."

Wellie. Out there as night falls, dealing with all this alone. "We'll find Wellie tomorrow."

"Right. We'll find her," says Maysilee. "It could work for her to win, too. You sleep first, Haymitch. I'll keep watch."

No point in pretending I'm not running on empty. I wrap the blanket around her shoulders, make a hammock bed, and curl up in the mesh. "I sure could use that lullaby right about now."

She gives a surprisingly unladylike snort. "You don't want to hear what's running through my head. Started in the maze and just won't quit."

"Got you an earworm, do you? Well, only cure for that is to pass it to someone else."

"Okay, then. You asked for it." She begins to sing in a low voice.

Ladybug, ladybug fly away home.
Your house is on fire, your children are gone.
All except one, who answers to Nan.
She's hiding under the frying pan.

A grin crosses my face at the silly song from our childhood. "Well, I guess I brought that on myself. Good night, Sis."

I try to fall asleep, but Maysilee's earworm has given me a brainworm . . . ladybug . . . fire . . . the flint striker . . . no, the blowtorch . . . fear . . . fly away. . . . The pieces spin around in a tornado, then cling together like long-lost lovers.

And I know exactly how we're getting through that maze.

The crumbs stick in my throat, so I take another swallow from the bottle to wash them down. What a luxury to wake up to a breakfast of fresh corn bread, buttermilk, and peaches, instead of having to scrounge for stale leftovers. Maysilee had the food all laid out on a tarp, like a party. She folded a pair of handkerchiefs into flowers for napkins and even filled the bowl of the wineglass with some kind of pink blossom, likely poisonous, but undeniably decorative.

Day 6. Somehow I'm still alive. I have no idea why the Gamemakers, under Snow's direction, have not destroyed me already. Could I possibly be so popular that they're keeping me around to please the audience? Are they planning some particularly spectacular ending for me? I don't know, but I do know the arena is still begging to be broken.

The parachute arrived while I slept, which was after Maysilee, as it turned out, because the brainworm cranked me up so I offered to take the first watch. If I can use the blowtorch to burn through the hedge, ladybug, ladybug, what will I find? Hopefully, a generator that's susceptible to fire as well. Perhaps I can burn through the side to some kind of control panel and —

"Do we head for the Cornucopia or search for Wellie?" Maysilee asks.

I help myself to a peach wedge, scooting the final one her way, as I determine the best strategy to get her to support my plan without actually telling her — and all the people watching us — what it is. Any way you slice it, the Cornucopia's no good, since it's southerly. So I reply, "Wellie, don't you think?"

"I do. We can get by on the fish and potatoes today."

"Sure. And thanks for setting out the breakfast so fancy."

"Thought I'd kick off the day with a poster," she says.

I think about it. Her emphasis on manners, her pretty picnics. And I remember her words that first day on the train. *"Listen, Louella, if you let them treat you like an animal, they will. So don't let them."* This morning's poster says, *We're civilized. We appreciate beautiful things. We're as good as you.* It's an extension of her whole campaign to show the Capitol our value. Will they know that she's referring to rebellion? I doubt it. They don't know what Pa told me. A poster could merely be promoting us as tributes. And what harm is there in a few flower napkins anyway?

"Nice paint job," I say, and actually get a smile.

After we pack up our belongings, we survey the woods. "Let's head north again," I say, and start walking. She follows me uncertainly.

"Why?"

"Because I've got a feeling Wellie would want to get as far from that volcano as possible."

"I don't know. We've been all over that area with no sign of her."

"Exactly. It's like Mags said. In the arena, you generally keep moving. And she hasn't been there yet. Let's just give it a try."

Maysilee looks unconvinced, but stays the course. For a mile or so anyway. "I don't think we're going to find her up this way," she says finally.

"Really? I think we're on the right track."

"Why? The arena narrows to a point up north, right? Like it did in the south?"

Never underestimate her observational skills. "Well, not right away."

"But it does. Wouldn't Wellie just feel trapped?"

"Which is exactly why the Careers won't think to look around here. Just what you said." I can feel myself skating on thin ice, but I try to project confidence, adding a little bounce to my step.

Maysilee shoots me a look but trudges along for a while, thinking. Then she stops cold. "No, you're wrong. Wellie would stand a much better chance in the meadow than she would up here. Little thing like her, she could disappear into that grass. It goes on for miles. Lay low and look for food at the Cornucopia. They'd never find her. And even if she did come to the woods, she's too smart to let herself get penned in like that. You know that. But you're taking me north again, Haymitch. Why?" She folds her arms and waits.

I'm going to have to tell her something or it's all over. "The hedge. I think we should give it another look."

She shudders. "Ugh. Even if I had a quart of blood to spare, why on earth would we do that?"

I hold out my hands to indicate the arena. "Because it has to end somewhere, right? The arena can't go on forever."

"What do you expect to find?"

"I don't know. But maybe there's something we can use."

"You mean, like something mechanical? Electrical?"

"Maybe. Or if not that, maybe we can collect those ladybugs to use as a weapon ourselves. Make the maze into a trap for the Careers. Lure them in, drop a tarp of ladybugs on them, get them lost in there. It's not easy to escape. I just think if we're smart, we can use it for our own means." I lift my brows, trying to telegraph that I can't tell her everything, but it's imperative. "I swear, do this and I'll never ask you for anything else as long as I live."

She rolls her eyes. "Well, that's a generous offer."

"Come on, Sis. I need this for my next poster." How quickly that's become our shorthand for defying the Capitol.

She relents. "All right. But it better be a good one."

"Oh, ladybug, it will be," I promise.

My ears feel better today, clearer and more dependable. As we move on, I'm the first to pick up on the high-pitched whine coming from the west, an area I haven't explored this far north. "You hear that?"

"I do now," Maysilee says. "I just thought it was part of the nature sounds here. Like the birds."

"That's what worries me. Think of the size of the mosquito that would generate that." I imagine a four-foot-long bloodsucker that would make the ladybugs seem like pranksters.

"It's a good way off. Let's just keep our distance." She takes a drink from a water jug and hands it over.

There's a confusing moment when the jug bursts, splashing water over both of us, before we make sense of the knife, the fast-approaching boots, and the undeniable truth that we're being ambushed. Caught off guard, we bolt away from the Careers — for it sure isn't Wellie — and straight toward the giant mosquito hum. I'm hoping we can scrape Silka and Maritte off on whatever produces it.

If we could outrun them, it might be worth turning to make a stand, but those girls are so close on our heels, it seems pointless. They'd be upon us before we had time to defend ourselves. At the moment, only the trees we're dodging between protect us from their deadly projectiles. It's all I can do to pull my knife and hope for an opening.

Suddenly, my feet lose traction and I'm on my butt, sliding into a clearing like I've hit a patch of ice. In that moment, my brain tries to make sense of an incomprehensible image. Two young Gamemakers in their signature white outfits hunch over an open berm covered in scarlet poppies. One wears a protective mask and holds some kind of drill, which emits the high-pitched whining. A third Gamemaker leans over a mop. By the look on their faces, I know the surprise is mutual.

I skid to a stop a few feet in front of them in a puddle of something that brings to mind the slime that results when you boil okra. Maysilee whizzes right past the Gamemakers and latches on to a sapling at the edge of the berm, somehow staying upright. For a moment we all freeze, the shock universal. Then Silka bursts into the clearing and goes down, overturning a large bucket and sending a couple gallons of slime back onto the forest floor.

The Gamemaker with the mop, who looks like he's near our age, lets out an indignant "Hey! Watch it!"

I know from experience that mopping's a bottom-of-the-ladder job, so finding a Gamemaker at it seems bizarre. Like watching Plutarch Heavensbee peel potatoes or President Snow clean the hair out of a drain.

Maritte, who apparently sensed some weirdness, comes to a halt at the edge of the clearing. "What's going on? Are you Gamemakers?" she exclaims.

The Gamemaker with the drill raises her mask and straightens up to her full height. "That's right. And all four of you are in absolute violation of the rules. You must immediately withdraw or there will be repercussions."

"That'd be a lot more impressive if you weren't shaking like a leaf," observes Maysilee, fingering her blowgun. "You must be pretty expendable, you three, getting sent in here to tidy up for us."

There's a pause while everybody considers the truth of this. Then all three Gamemakers make a break for the ladder that leads down to Sub-A.

Maritte's arm snaps back and I think I'm a goner, but the trident whistles over my head and lodges in the mopper, sending him into a pillow of poppies. Almost simultaneously, the woman with the drill grabs at the spot beneath her ear and comes away with a dart. She collapses as the final Gamemaker plunges headfirst through the open berm into Sub-A. It takes a few moments before we hear her skull crack on the concrete below. I can picture that floor, having run for my life down it, and find myself preoccupied with imagining the scene.

Silka seems stunned into inertia as well. "What'd you do? Did you kill Gamemakers? They'll never let us win now!"

Maysilee's voice drips honey. "Still chasing that sad little dream, Silka?" She deftly loads another dart and glances at Maritte. "I'm almost sorry to kill you now, Maritte. What's the deal with District Four, anyway? Hooking up with a bunch of Capitol toadies? Seems like you should be on our side."

Maritte hesitates, eyeing her trident with longing, then pulls her knife and begins to back away as Maysilee raises her blowgun.

The hovercraft appears out of nowhere, dropping a bomb into the clearing that explodes in a cloud of dirt and tear gas. I grab Maysilee and we flounder through the woods, branches snapping our faces, stumbling over logs, as we try to escape the stuff. More bombs rain down, releasing more gas, causing our eyes to burn and stream so badly, they're useless. After a while, I can hear the explosions fade a bit. My guess is that the hovercraft could only track one set of tributes, and the Careers drew the short straw.

Some inner compass leads me north and we outdistance the tear gas at the entrance of the hedge. I rip open one of the packs and alternate pouring water in Maysilee's and my eyes.

She's so furious with me she's spitting. "What the hell, Haymitch! Where were you? Why was Maritte the only one who had my back?"

She's right. I froze. Caught off guard by the unexpected encounter, intimidated by the white uniforms, whatever. I choked.

"I don't know what happened, Maysilee. Everything was coming at me so fast and I'm covered in slime and —"

"You're supposed to be my ally! Not her! Not that fish-eating, bootlicking, wished-she-could-pull-off-pin-curls piece of trash! You are!"

Well, I feel terrible, and utterly lack a defense. My knife was in hand, the Gamemakers in easy reach. No one better positioned to kill them. Plutarch's voice taunts me. *"The question is, why didn't you?"* I can't say I'm not a killer anymore. That leaves brainwashed or cowardly. Boy, I sure hope Sid didn't see that. No, of course he didn't. That's one bit of action the audience will never view. They've surely been following Wellie, wherever she is.

"You're right," I tell Maysilee. "You're one hundred percent right and I'm sorry."

"Sorry?" she sneers. "Maybe you should be the victor, Haymitch. That would give you some time to grow a backbone."

Hello again, meanest girl in town. It only hurts because it's true.

She pulls out the can of sardines and yanks off the lid. "I'm eating this whole can. They're mine." She selects a fish and slurps it into her mouth. Boy, she really is mad, to be eating with her fingers.

I let her hog the sardines, even though they smell delicious and my stomach's growling. I've let her down and I need her help with the hedge. Would it matter if she knew about my bombing the tank and the mission to break the arena? Or would my feckless response to having the Gamemakers at our mercy erase it all? I don't know, I just hope that once she has a belly full of fish, she'll give me a hand.

After a few minutes, the slurping stops. Out of the corner of my eye, I watch the can slide into view. Three fish remain. I shake my head. She gives them a nudge in my direction. I'm so hungry I take them.

"Was it because of your poster?" she asks, her voice still tight.

She means, I think, was I avoiding confronting the Gamemakers because of the fabulous statement I'm planning to make. "I wish I could say it was, but no, I don't think it was that. I don't know what it was. Just programmed to be walked all over, I guess. You nailed it."

"No, what I said wasn't fair. You've done your part. With Louella in the chariot. Getting a one in training. And, I suspect, whatever it is you've been up to that you're so cagey about." She dampens a handkerchief and cleans her hands. "You know, if we'd started picking off the Gamemakers before we got in here, we might've stood a chance."

I think of the moment with the knives in training, of the country as a whole, and how we just keep submitting to the Capitol's rule. Why? It's not a conversation I can have in front of the cameras, so I just concentrate on wiping the last bit of oil out of the can. Then I go about scraping the slime off my pants. At least it doesn't smell bad, or burn my skin, or harden, which makes it one of the more benign things I've encountered in here.

Maysilee's breathing has returned to normal. I decide to give her five more minutes to recover before I push for the hedge. I watch as she traces a spiderweb on a bush. "Look at the craftsmanship. Best weavers on the planet."

"Surprised to see you touching that."

"Oh, I love anything silk." She rubs the threads between her fingers. "Soft as silk, like my grandmother's skin." She pops open a locket at her neck and shows me the photo inside. "Here she is, just a year before she died. Isn't she beautiful?"

I take in the smiling eyes, full of mischief, peering out of their own spiderweb of wrinkles. "She is. She was a kind lady. Used to sneak me candies sometimes."

Maysilee laughs. "You weren't the only one. She got chewed out for that." She cups the locket in her hands and examines her. "No one ever loved me more. I always hoped I'd look like her one day. Never going to see myself grow old, I guess."

"Maybe."

"Oh, no. Not after today." She bites her lip. "She used to say, if I was afraid, 'It's okay, Maysilee, nothing they can take from you was ever worth keeping.'"

"I know that song. Lenore Dove sings it."

"It's a song?" Maysilee smiles. "Well, your gal's full of surprises. Guess she got the jump on us after all."

"Doing what?"

"Doing nothing." She snaps the locket closed and stands. "Let's visit your hedge, Mr. Abernathy."

"Well, okay, then, Miss Donner." I break a branch that looks familiar off a nearby tree. "Hold this."

"What do I do?"

I whip out the blowtorch, light her up, and nod at the hedge. "You're my wingman. Anything with wings, you burn. Ready?"

"As I'll ever be."

I charge through the hedge, making a beeline for the site of our previous breakout attempt. Firing up the blowtorch, I cut a straight line from my shoulder to the ground. Ladybugs begin to swarm as the greenery catches fire. Maysilee steps right in, waving her torch over the infestation. The mutts ignite, inflate, and burst open like dried corn kernels in hot grease. I carve another line parallel to the first, a couple of feet to the right. More bugs emerge from along the hedge and fly at us. Maysilee circles her torch, singing as she exterminates them:

Ladybug, ladybug fly away home.
Your house is on fire, your children are gone.
All except one, who answers to Nan.
She's hiding under the frying pan.

I join in as I continue to burn a door in the bushes, sweeping the flame from side to side. The stench of fried insects, chemicals, and burnt sugar surrounds us as the crackling of the holly leaves and bug shells underscores our song. The hedge puts off a prohibitive amount of heat, but we keep on, carving a tunnel through it. A few yards in, daylight peeks through from the other side.

"Almost there!" I shout to Maysilee.

My flame has begun to sputter. I lay on the trigger and the last layer of prickly leaves dissolves into ash. I drop the empty blowtorch to the ground and step out onto an even stretch of parched ground that leads to a dropoff. Maysilee emerges beside me, running her torch around the interior of our tunnel and tossing it in to scorch the last handful of bugs. She beats out the sparks on her shirt.

"So, did we reach the end?"

I walk to the edge of what turns out to be a cliff. A sheer drop of around a hundred feet meets a carpet of pointy rocks. Nestled among them sits a gigantic machine, purring like a contented cat. The generator. Only a stone's throw away, but it might as well be on the moon. A sound leaves my body, something between a moan and a sigh.

"Yeah," I tell her. "This is the end of the road."

Maysilee joins me at the cliff's edge and stares down into the canyon. "That's all there is to the arena, Haymitch. Let's go back."

My latest scheme to disable the generator has led to yet another dead end. Of course it has. The absurdity of it all, the Games, the two failed arena plots, life in general, overwhelms me. Is there a third way to break the arena that I am missing? Maybe. Probably. But I can't think of it at the moment.

The biggest form of resistance I can come up with now is to refuse to go back through that hedge. Maysilee's wrong: This stretch of ground is not the arena; it's not pretty in the least. If the Gamemakers want me dead, they will have to follow me out here into the real world, which would be a victory of a sort. I will have outsmarted them in some small fashion. And at least the air is fresh and the sun is in the right spot. At any rate, I'm not going back into their poisonous cage.

"No. I'm staying here," I tell Maysilee.

There's a long pause. "All right, there's only five of us left. May as well say good-bye now anyway. I don't want it to come down to you and me."

Me neither. And the idea that I would be helping Maysilee or Wellie by continuing to participate in the Games seems laughable. All my allies die while the Gamemakers, apparently, are safe as houses with me. "Okay," I say.

I hear her footsteps return to the hedge.

A cannon fires. My head jerks around, as does hers. We each expected the other to be dead, and neither of us have time to hide the anguish on our faces.

Maysilee swallows hard. "Four of us now."

She looks so lost it totals me. Maybe we two should stick it out together. How do I know? I feel like I constantly demonstrate poor judgment. I don't feel qualified to choose between fried or scrambled eggs. Nothing makes sense in the face of the forty-four dead tributes plus Lou Lou and Woodbine gone from this world.

"You sure you want to split up?" I ask.

She doesn't know either. I can tell, deep down, she's as clueless as me. There's no good rule book on what to do in our situation. No brilliant strategy.

"The only thing I'm sure about right now is I don't want anyone to steal our potatoes," she admits. "I'll get them. Then we'll weigh our options, all right?"

I lift my hands in defeat. "Well, if you're going to drag the potatoes into it, how can I say no?"

Maysilee shrugs and disappears into the hedge. I walk along the cliff, wondering if there's any way I might be able to climb down and reach the generator. My foot inadvertently knocks a reddish pebble over the side, and I listen for how long it takes to hit rock bottom. Too long. I'd never make it. I step away and plunk down on my butt, another plan busted, when suddenly the pebble flies back over the edge and bounces to a stop beside me.

I examine it, confused by its reappearance. Could someone have thrown it back? Doesn't seem likely. I hop up, collect a nearby rock, and toss it at the generator, tracking its descent. A few yards above the machine, it inexplicably bounces back up to me, reversing its trajectory and landing right in my hand, a little warmer than before. It must be, it has to be, some sort of force field positioned over the generator. Easier than stretching a tarp, I guess. A way of protecting it from the elements, wildlife, and, as it turns out, a rascal of a tribute. I suppose it's not impossible that a rebel might try to sabotage the thing, but it seems unlikely they'd make their way to the middle of nowhere. Although, here I am. But even if I dropped a boulder down there, I couldn't touch the thing.

Honestly, my luck's so bad, I can't help laughing.

That's when I hear Maysilee begin to scream. In a flash, I'm on my feet and thrashing through the smoky tunnel in the hedge. I spy bright patches of pink up ahead, hear honking, not unlike Lenore Dove's geese. My ax is out of my belt, drawn and ready as I leave the holly bushes for a whirlwind of feathers.

The two dozen waterbirds remind me of ones I've seen at the lake. Long-legged. Beaks like sword blades — thin, narrow, and deadly. Not cool blue gray, not paper white, but the color of the bubblegum sold at the Donners' sweetshop. They dive again and again at Maysilee, who's kneeling on the ground, trying to use a tarp as protection while she vehemently slices at them with her dagger. A couple of dead birds lie on the ground, but they have taken their toll. Blood blossoms from her cheek, her chest, the palm of her hand. Like Ampert's squirrels, they have no interest in me. Programmed to target Maysilee in a very personal punishment. I hack away at the mutts with my ax, piling up a collection of rosy wings and legs like cattail stems, but they badly outnumber us.

A bird swoops down at a sharp angle, driving its beak through her throat. As it withdraws, I decapitate it, slicing through the skinny neck. I realize Maysilee's beyond recovery when the flock clears out. Falling to my knees beside her, I reach for her sound hand, which grasps mine like a vise. Her wounded one curls up and rests in her nest of necklaces, which lays in a pool of blood. Through the rasping of her breath, she attempts to speak, but the last mutt silenced her voice with its wicked beak. Mine seems silenced as well, as no words of comfort or hope or apology make it out. I just stare into those burning blue eyes, letting her know she's not dying alone. She's with family. She's with me.

In the last moments, she releases her grip enough to lock her pinkie around mine. Looking, I think, for a final confirmation of the promise we made to each other. I nod so she knows I understand and that I will try my best to bring the Capitol down, although I have never felt so powerless in my entire life.

And then she's gone to wherever people go when they die.

She hasn't begged or pleaded; she retained her fury and defiance. Although for me, a person's desperation at the end is not a measure of their life, I know it mattered to her. Maysilee leaves the world the way she wanted, wounded but not bowed. I think about cleaning her up, but this is her final poster, and I won't tidy it up to make it easier for those monsters in the Capitol to sleep tonight.

The hovercraft slides into view and the cannon booms. I remove her blowgun and one of her necklaces — the copper medallion with the flower — as a reminder of her strength.

Too numb to do much else, I scoot back about ten feet and prop myself against a tree, clutching her token to my chest. When the Capitol realizes I'm going nowhere, they lower the claw. I imagine the shot: my stricken face, visible through the metal talons as they lift Maysilee's body up into the sky, leaving me all alone.

If something attacked me right now, I'd let it take me. I know, I know, I just made a deathbed promise to Maysilee to carry on the fight, but I can't seem to rally. I pat her necklace against my pants to wipe off the blood — these black clothes just never stop giving — and hook the fancy clasp behind my neck to hang there with its friends. I've got my own jewelry collection now, what with District 9's sunflower, Wyatt's scrip coin, and Lenore Dove's warring songbird and snake. Why, I'm almost as decorated as Miss Donner herself.

The blowgun seems loaded with a single dart. I dropped the ball not taking the pouch and poison vial, but at least I've got one shot. It makes me feel nervous keeping a poisonous dart so close to my face, so I attach it to my belt with a bit of vine.

Good-bye, Maysilee Donner, who I loathed, then grudgingly respected, then loved. Not as a sweetheart or even a friend. A sister, I'd said. But what is that exactly? I think about our journey — everything from sniping with her in those early days after the reaping to battling those pink birds. I guess that's my answer. A sister is someone you fight with and fight for. Tooth and nail.

A parachute floats through the trees and lands before me. I hope it's not bean and ham hock soup. Pretty sure I couldn't get that down right now. When I open the attached basket, I find two containers. A basin holds strawberry ice cream, which seems like it ought to have some significance I can't pinpoint at the moment. The second, a lidded mug, holds steaming black coffee. Maysilee's beverage of choice. I take a sip, scalding my tongue. Then another.

The ice cream jogs my memory. We're in the kitchen at the tribute apartment and Proserpina's been blubbering about her grade. Her sister, Effie, told her a positive attitude's ninety-seven percent of the battle. And Maysilee . . . Maysilee had said . . .

"I'll try to keep that in mind in the arena. More ice cream?"

Mags and I tried not to laugh, because Proserpina wasn't born evil; she just had a lot of unlearning to do. I'm not sure what Mags is trying to impart now. A directive to stay positive? A reminder of Maysilee's sass? Just a delicious bowl of ice cream? Maybe all three. I pick up the spoon and take a bite. Tears come, and I let them fall, unchecked, while I empty the basin. It's okay to cry around Mags.

The sun closes in on the horizon as I slowly sip the cooling coffee, which helps to clear my head. There's no Maysilee left to protect now. I guess I should return to the cliff for my final poster. I decide to consolidate my remaining supplies in Maysilee's backpack. I add a half jug of water and store the potatoes in the basin for safekeeping. As I tuck in the spare handkerchiefs, I notice a slit in the interior wall of her pack. Wiggling my fingers through the opening, I encounter a bumpy plastic pack. I'd forgotten about the potato-light kit. I guess she didn't reveal it when we inventoried our supplies since it wasn't legal. Not that that much worries me now. So much has gone down with blown-up tanks and dead Gamemakers that a few rogue wires and coins hardly seem worth mentioning.

I start thinking about the Gamemakers we encountered. They were none of them very old. The guy with the mop, early twenties tops. Were their deaths painful? Do they leave people behind? Are their parents, friends, and neighbors weeping for them as ours do when they lose us? Will their loved ones ever know how they really died, or will an accident be fabricated to conceal the Capitol's incompetence? Body doubles probably won't be practical.

As I stow my green pack in the bushes, the oppressive opening notes of the anthem drone from the sky. First there's Maritte, then Maysilee. Doesn't seem random. They've been eliminated swiftly, in punishment for killing their keepers. By abstaining, Silka and I have been rewarded with a few more hours of life.

And what about Wellie? I haven't had time to focus on her much, but she's out there, too. Maysilee indicated that if neither of us survived, it could work for Wellie to carry on the fight. I think about how poised and articulate she was at the interview. She'd be a far better, far smarter, far more convincing victor to represent district rights than a cocky, selfish rascal, even if he had a chance of surviving, which he doesn't. Is that what my final hours should be devoted to? Guarding Wellie from Silka and the Gamemakers' mutts? Making sure that crown winds up on her head, not a Career's? Yes, I'm certain this is what Maysilee would've wanted me to do, if she'd known the whole story.

If I'm going to protect Wellie, I'm going to have to find her. Really, at this point, there's only one way. If I encounter Silka, good. I'll dart her.

"Wellie!" I holler. "Wellie!"

In the fading rays of the sun, I begin my search, heading south toward the meadow. Seems so lonely here without Maysilee. I didn't notice the solitude so much before I had her as a partner, but now the darkness presses in on me, raw and scary.

"Wellie!"

Feels like I'm the only person left alive in the world. Being close to death doesn't help. I reach for Lenore Dove for solace, knowing she must be keeping vigil at her television set, living through my last hours with me. It's much worse for her, really. The helplessness. Thinking of her watching me makes me want to be brave, or at least appear to be. "Wellie! Where are you? It's Haymitch!" I hope Lenore Dove will stay close to Sid when I'm gone, keep teaching him the stars and things, making sure he isn't—

What was that?

My ears have picked up a strange sound behind me, out of sync with the nighttime background noise of the woods. I stand still, listening hard.

Ring, ring!

There it is again. Not natural. Man-made. Decidedly metal on metal. I know that sound from a summer day long ago. I was still young enough to have free time. A bunch of us — me, Lenore Dove, Blair, Burdock, and a couple of the McCoy kids — were playing freeze tag in a field. We stumbled upon a Peacekeeper's bicycle hidden in the bramble bushes by the road. Sometimes they use them to get around town, deliver messages and such. Looked like someone had dropped it quick and was probably coming back for it. But in the meantime, it was ours.

Bicycles are coveted in District 12. A few of the merchants' kids in town have them. I remember Maysilee and Merrilee had matching pink ones, and sometimes rode them around the square to the envy of all. But they were a pipe dream for kids in the Seam. For us to find a Peacekeeper's bike so shiny and unattended was like a litter of kittens rolling smack-dab into a patch of catnip. We swore one another to secrecy, posted guards, and for the next week, every one of us learned to ride. It was a fine machine, well built, smooth, with brakes on the handlebars and a bright silver bell to signal your approach. It disappeared then; probably the Peacekeeper came back to collect it, but it had never been ours to keep.

Ring, ring!

That's a bicycle bell, beyond a doubt. The one Maysilee wove into Wellie's token necklace back in the gym. She's heard my calls and this is her answer. I shut up and follow the bell. It leads back north. I feel like I'm retracing my steps to where Maysilee died.

Ring, ring!

I come to a halt at the base of a large tree. The bell gives a tinny ring from on high. "It's okay, Wellie," I say. "I'm here. You can come down." I wait, but there's no response. No crackling of branches or rustling of leaves. Not a whisper from my ally.

"Wellie? You there?" The only possible alternative, Silka, does not impress me as someone who could scamper up as high as I judge that bell to be. And if Silka had gotten close enough to steal Wellie's token, I'd have seen another dove in the sky. I begin to climb.

Up, up, up I go, so far that I begin to wonder if I have the right tree. The boughs thin out, and I have to plant my boots against the trunk or risk snapping them off. When I do reach her, she's so still that I almost miss her. She lies along a slender branch, belly down, like a possum in the moonlight, her bell tucked under her chin, a child-sized knife clutched in one hand.

"Hey, Wellie."

Her cracked lips move slightly, but no sound comes out. She has the shrunken, glassy-eyed look I know from tough times in the Seam. Another casualty of the Capitol's weapon of choice: starvation. I need to move her down before she rolls right off that branch and get some food into her. But she's so fragile, I don't see how I can manage it, especially at night. I give her a sip of water from the jug, and it spills out the side of her mouth. There's no way I'm getting raw potato down her.

I stay with the water. "Try to swallow it, Wellie," I plead. She manages to get down a few mouthfuls and then drifts off.

The moon slips behind a cloud, leaving us momentarily in darkness, and I hug the trunk for stability until the pale light returns. The air seems to be growing heavier in general; are they prepping a rainstorm? The idea of being trapped up this high in the pitch black while the bark gets slippery scares me, but I can't abandon Wellie. I could get some sparks going with my flint striker, but how would I build a fire up here? I fumble around in Maysilee's pack, looking for something to use as fuel, when I come upon the potato battery kit. Theoretically, I could make my own light. It probably wouldn't produce much if it did, but it might be of some comfort.

A faint rumble of thunder prompts me to try. I wedge myself awkwardly between the trunk and a branch and use the backpack as my worktable. Beetee said that a potato shouldn't be eaten after it was a battery, so I restrict myself to using one, saving the last for Wellie's breakfast. I cut a potato in half, remove each component from the plastic bag, and strain to replicate Beetee's demonstration. Wrap the copper coins and zinc nails in wire, leaving a tail, and stick them in the potato halves. This takes a while given the limited light. There's a bad moment when one of the coins slips through my fingers and escapes to the forest floor. I'm about to give up when I remember Maysilee's medallion and work it out of the woven cord. After more than a few false starts, I attach the final wire to a tiny light bulb and am rewarded with a dim glow. In most circumstances, it would be negligible, but in the gloom of the arena, it feels like life itself. Wellie's eyes flutter open, lock on it, and she gives a little sigh.

The first raindrops patter onto the leaves while I'm looking for somewhere close by to rig a hammock. The branches don't feel sturdy enough. Instead, I position a tarp to keep Wellie dry and wrap Maysilee's blanket around her multiple times. I cut off some strips of tarp and tie them along her legs and midsection, securing her to the branch. She doesn't seem to notice, just fixates on her light.

No moving her until morning, so I arrange a second tarp and a few straps for myself. It rains cats and dogs for a while, turns misty, and then the clouds withdraw. I'm dozing off when something catches in the leaves above my head. The parachute brings a cup of warm vanilla pudding and a packet of balls, each wrapped in crinkly festive paper. Chocolate.

Someone in the Capitol still has a heart.

With patience, I coax the pudding into Wellie, bit by bit. And although we lose half to dribbles, the other half makes it into her belly. Then I break a chocolate ball in two with my teeth and slide a piece into her mouth. She gives a little smack of her lips.

I allow myself a ball or two as well. Chocolate's pricey stuff in the Seam. Definitely for birthdays or special occasions. This stuff's top-of-the-line, creamy and sweet and rich. If it's the last thing I ever eat, I'd be okay with that.

I shake off my tarp to repurpose it as a blanket and have almost dozed off again when I hear Wellie begin to cry. I reach to console her, but she's fast asleep. The weeping comes from far below at the base of the tree. Silka? Who else could it be? She isn't trying to hunt us, just huddled against the trunk. I didn't peg her for a crier. Of course, I've still probably got tearstains on my cheeks from Maysilee's passing. I'm sure Silka has plenty to cry about, too. Even if she's the clear front-runner in the Games, we've all of us got enough dead kids to mourn for a lifetime.

I become intensely aware of the three of us, huddled around this tree, the last trio of human heartbeats in the arena. Sad, desperate, but also a rare moment of district unity in the Games. You know what would make it even better? I drop a handful of chocolate balls into the night. A startled sound. The sobs soften to sniffles. A candy wrapper crackles. Quiet.

Not a bad poster, all in all.

Snatches of sleep breed nightmares, and the dawn finds me weak and weary, like the guy in Lenore Dove's poem. The arena leaves no time to properly grieve anyone and I'm left feeling cheated, shallow, and coldhearted. Louella, Ampert, Maysilee, everybody deserves far better. I just can't generate it.

I check on Wellie, who sleeps peacefully on her branch. No need to wake her yet.

Silka's gone. Not that I expected some grand alliance forming between us. She had a vulnerable moment, accepted the chocolate, and then probably felt ashamed for doing so. I'm guessing District 1 doesn't reward its Careers for being only human. Yeah, Silka's out there and likely nearby unless she's scavenging for food. She could've thought to try the Cornucopia or gone back for Maritte's supplies. But she knows where we are and she'll be back to kill us.

I reach up over my tarp to rub the gunk from my eyes and notice black smudges on my fingers. Not sure where those came from; they didn't really register in the dark last night. I don't think it's the tree bark, though . . . or the tarp . . . something with the potato battery? It doesn't matter really. Unless . . .

Suddenly, a whole bunch of light bulbs turn on all at once. Me working the copper flower medallion out of Maysilee's necklace. The black residue on my hands after I rigged the fuse at the tank. And Beetee's final words to me at the buffet —

"And if Ampert fails to show — we've also replaced the —"

But then Wellie had walked up and I never learned what else besides the District 9 tokens had been replaced. A spare. A backup to Ampert's lone fuse. Is that what I have around my neck in the guise of Maysilee's token necklace? Pretending to focus on the sunrise, I nonchalantly rub a bit of the braided cord between my thumb and index finger, then casually fiddle with the water jug lid. No question. The smudges came from her token.

One last chance. One final opportunity to ruin the Games in a way the Capitol can't conceal. I can't be one hundred percent sure until I can unwind the cord and check for the blasting cap, but if I'm right, I must not waste this good-bye gift.

I lean back against the trunk, trying to look indifferent, while my mind races. What possible targets remain? The tank's blown, the generator's off-limits, access to Sub-A will be hard to finagle a second time. That leaves the Cornucopia. And why not? Isn't it the very symbol of their despicable show? And isn't the gesture left to me purely symbolic, given that the machinery lies beyond my grasp? I could still blow a nice, big hole in the side of their shiny, golden horn. Leave it smoldering and defaced in the center of their pretty little meadow. A twisted and ugly reminder of the history of the Hunger Games. A horn of plenty for the few. Desperation for many. Destruction for all.

Once again, the trick will be to get them to show it on-screen. But with only three of us left, it just might be possible. If I could revive Wellie a bit more, get enough calories in her that I'd be sure she could last, then tuck her somewhere safe, I could stage a showdown with Silka at the Cornucopia. Try and take out her and the Cornucopia in the same explosion. If we were directly beside it, how could they not show it? And then, if I survive, Snow will have the Gamemakers kill me, and Wellie will get the crown.

A peek of her haggard little face gives me pause. Wellie's on the brink of starving to death. Even if she can hang on, the lack of food leaves her vulnerable to a host of other dangers, from physical weakness to dehydration to illness. We've got some chocolate left, but dumping that straight into her shrunken stomach might result in the reverse of the intended effect. There's the last potato — it's good and bland but it needs baking. All right. That's my priority. Bake the potato. Feed up Wellie. Hide Wellie. Lure Silka to the Cornucopia. Blow her up with the Cornucopia. How could anything go wrong?

Well, here's a problem for starters: After the tank incident, if the Gamemakers see me unwinding a token, I'm going to have every mutt in the arena coming at my head. I need an off-camera moment.

No time like the present. As if blocking the sun, I pull the tarp up over my head. With minimal movements, I unclasp Maysilee's necklace and unravel the cord. I get a boost when I expose the blasting cap, securely attached to the end. Perhaps I'm not entirely hopeless. After wrapping the fuse tightly around it, I conceal it in my pocket and rub my hands really good on my pants to clean them. Will the Gamemakers notice the token's disappearance? When Wellie wakes, maybe I should pretend I lost it. It could have gone the way of the brass medallion. Then again, drawing attention to its absence might backfire.

I do an inventory of my equipment. Fuse. Check. Blasting cap. Check. Explosive. Check. Flint striker. Check. I've got everything I need, even a handful of oily candy wrappers for tinder. Eager to get going, I toss off the tarp, give a big stretch, and free myself from the tarp strips.

Wellie's eyes fly open. She takes me in, as if weighing my worth, then frowns.

"Don't leave me again," she whispers.

No doubt I am, from where she sits, the great abandoner of the Newcomers. She's not wrong. I had bigger fish to fry, but she's still not wrong.

I try to sound chipper. "Hey, Wellie. How about I climb down and bake you a potato? Think you could handle that?"

"Don't leave me."

"Well, I'm pretty sure Silka's in the vicinity. Feels like you'd be safer up here."

"No. Can't be alone again." She begins to struggle against her restraints. "I'll follow you."

"Okay, okay!" I settle her back down. "Let me untie you." This is not ideal, but I can't risk her trying to climb down after me; she'd certainly fall to her death. I carefully remove the tarp strips and the blanket and store all our stuff in the pack. "I'm going to need you to hold on. Can you do that?" She nods, but when she puts her arms around my neck, they're as limp as boiled noodles. It will have to be over my shoulders. "Better try the miner's carry," I tell her, tossing the pack to the ground. I gingerly hoist her up and around my shoulders, getting a tight grip on the arm that falls across my chest, the way we're taught to do if we have to haul the injured out of the mine after an accident. There was never much to her, but I doubt she can tip the scale at sixty pounds now. I inch our way down the tree, nearly falling twice as branches snap beneath my boots. When I reach the forest floor, I gently lay her on the pine needles.

Giving her a chocolate ball to gnaw on, I fashion a nest for her out of the blanket. When I check her for fever, her forehead's as cool as marble. "You cold?"

"A little," she says. I note the purple tint to her lips.

"Well, a fire will warm you up. And then we can bake your potato."

A cursory examination of the local brush shows that this will prove a challenge. Last night's rain, while relatively brief, fell heavily, dampening the available fuel. In a few hours, the sun will have lent me a hand, but at the moment, dry fuel seems scarce. Now I'm going to have to forage for some that's been protected by thick overhanging limbs or rock formations.

What to do with Wellie? Carry her? That will be difficult if I'm collecting wood. Cross my fingers and hope that Silka's far off? Too risky. That means trying to hide her. "Wellie, I'm going to have to travel a bit for fuel."

"Don't leave me."

"It won't be for long and I won't go far. I'll make sure you're good and hidden."

"Don't."

"We need fire. It's okay. Look what I've got for you." I hang Maysilee's blowgun around her neck. "This was Maysilee's. It's all loaded. All you do is take a deep breath, blow really hard in this end, and a poisonous dart comes flying out. She killed Panache with this. Saved my life."

"Maysilee left us, too," says Wellie sadly.

"No, she got separated looking for Lou Lou. Couldn't get back to you. She'd want you to have this. She told me she thought you'd be a good victor."

"She did?" Her eyes widen. "What did she mean? A good victor?"

Great question. "It means, I think, that you never stop being a Newcomer."

Wellie tears up, then steels herself with determination. "I can do that. For the others," she says. "Hide me." She reaches out her arms for me to carry her.

Nearby, I discover a tree almost hidden by cascading wild grapevines. Tucking Wellie behind them and arranging the leafy curtain is the best I can do, with the dual pressures of time and geography. She'll await my return, armed with her paring knife and her blowgun. "Remember," I tell her. "You've only got one dart, so make it count. Now, sit tight and I'll be back before you know I'm gone."

I intend this to be true, but as I search in a widening circle, I feel my confidence waning. The available wood would smoke like crazy even if I could get it lit with my handful of candy wrappers, which is doubtful. The whole idea of baking a potato loses its appeal. Perhaps if I slice it paper thin while it's raw, she'd be able to stomach it. What would really help — hello, sponsors! — would be a nice basket full of food. I mean, what are they saving it for? Surely, two of the last three tributes in the arena have enough in their combined accounts for a cup of chicken back broth. I think Mags must read my mind, because as I'm making a beeline back to my ally, a parachute practically brushes my nose as it floats to my boots. I squat down to tear it open and find an ornate picnic basket. A card of thick paper rests atop it with the words COURTESY OF THE CAPITOL. What isn't, in the arena? Inside, nestled in a snowy linen napkin, I find a pitcher. A chill goes through me as I lift it into the sunlight. The white cylinder resting in the spiral staircase. The golden eagle perched on the lid. My thumb depresses its tail, flipping it open, revealing the cool, creamy milk. If this is not the pitcher from Plutarch's library, it's an exact replica.

I stuff the card in my pocket and return the pitcher to the basket to conceal the trembling in my hands. What am I to make of this new arrival? There are only two possibilities, as opposite as day and night.

On the positive-thinking side, this could be a genuine gift from Plutarch by way of Mags. A pint of sustenance, a draft of encouragement. It could mean, *Well done, Haymitch. Through the fog of propaganda, the card-stacking, and the lies, I can see that you succeeded with your mission. You did your bit. And if the tank explosion failed to drown the brain entirely, which is not your fault, it threw everything into a tailspin. Take this milk to Wellie, keep her alive, play out your hand as best you can.*

But on the flip side, maybe Mags had nothing to do with this gift, and the evil message goes like this: *Greetings from your president. You didn't think I saw your little stunt with the milk pitcher in the library, but you were wrong. Because I see everything. Your bombs, your plots, even your flint striker from your pretty little bird. And now you have a choice. Do you drink the milk? Give it to your sickly ally? Pour it into the ground? Because naturally you suspect it's laced with poison. What do you do, Haymitch Abernathy? You must know that the eyes of Panem, and mine in particular, are watching your every move.*

Yes, everyone is watching. If I do not immediately take this milk back to Wellie and attempt to save her, it will look as if I'm playing nice to her but actually trying to kill her so that I can be one step closer to being District 12's second victor. However, I am almost certain that it's poisonous and came from Snow. I don't believe Plutarch would be careless enough to link himself so publicly to me since I bombed the tank. Surely, many people, many Gamemakers on the inside, are familiar with this symbol of the golden staircase that's so often displayed in the Heavensbee mansion. Matchy-matchy. Given that he was assigned to cover the District 12 tributes, it's probably against the rules for Plutarch to back us. Like Proserpina said it was for her and Vitus.

It's from Snow, this milky death. The fate I have been trying to defy ever since I saw that perverse birthday cake on the train has come home to roost like the raven in the poem, forever perched above my chamber door. I am completely in Snow's power and his to manipulate. His puppet. His pawn. His plaything. It is his poster I am painting. His propaganda. I am trapped into doing his bidding in the Hunger Games, the best propaganda the Capitol has.

My pa must be rolling in his grave.

The proud district alliance, the Newcomers, will never be allowed to win. Wellie will die of poisoning, or starvation, or Career. Silka, that Capitol wannabe, will take the crown.

And me? There's only one thing left for me to do if I don't want to die as a traitor to the districts — as Wellie's killer by neglect since I refuse to go poison her — and Snow knows it. He has followed my every move down to this final resolution and awaits my inevitable surrender. I must drink the milk. The time is now. Game over.

I retrieve the pitcher, flip the lid, and examine the contents. Every cell in my body resists capitulating to this end. I'm wondering if I could pretend to trip and drop the pitcher, at least postponing the moment of Silka's victory, when the cannon fires. I freeze, mystified. Was this not the moment for the president to savor my defeat? What's going on? Who has interfered with his game plan?

I hurl the pitcher aside, hearing it crack open on a rock, as I take off for the wild grapevines. As promised, I am not far. I'm hoping against hope that somehow Silka has met a mutty end. That would make everything so much simpler.

Rounding a final clump of saplings, I freeze in horror at what awaits. Silka stands like a statue, her snot-green outfit splattered in bright red. In her right hand, her ax. Her left holds Wellie's head, eyes still open, mouth agape. The only movement, the only sound, comes from the blood dripping into the pine needles on the forest floor. Wellie's body lies crumpled in a heap a few feet away. The shiny silver bicycle bell. The blowgun. The child-sized boots. The tiny knife in her bird claw. Dove-colored feathers. Headless baby chick. I could live ten thousand years and never erase this sight from my memory.

"What did you do?" I hiss.

Silka makes an effort to focus on me. She holds up Wellie's head defensively. "She attacked me."

Now I notice the poison dart hanging harmlessly from Silka's blousy sleeve. Wellie tried to protect herself. Upheld the Newcomer honor. Probably barely had the air to get the dart free of the gun. I abandoned her, as she feared I would. Blinded by my desire to paint my poster, I left the real treasure unattended.

"She had to go. You have to go," Silka continues. "It's the only way I get back to my people."

"We all have people," I say. "You think yours will ever be able to forget this? I know mine won't." Write me off, Sid. Disown me. Spit when you hear my name. Failing at breaking the arena is nothing in the face of this.

"I'll tell how it was, when I get home," she says.

"Oh, you're not going home, Silka." I pull the ax from my belt. We're neither of us going home. I will kill her, and Snow will kill me. These Games will have no victor.

The second Quarter Quell poster.

It helps, the way she tosses Wellie's head aside, with no regard or compassion for her even in death. Helps, too, to see a smear of chocolate high on her cheekbone, where she must have wiped the tears away last night during our one-sided truce. And finally, it helps when she says, "I will be the one to honor the Capitol!"

Ax to ax, we go at it. I wish I could claim greater speed or strength, but we're fairly matched. Her training's superior, but I have an advantage she can never hope for. Those thirty-one allies I boasted of to the Head Gamemaker? I can feel every one of them at my back.

Her first stroke comes straight down at my head, as if to cleave my body into two equal parts. I just manage to block it. My counterattack clips her leg, drawing blood. A flicker of surprise crosses her face. She didn't expect I could get through her defenses. Well, I may not be trained, Miss Silka, but I bet I've spent more time wielding an ax than you have, and I've got the white liquor and clean laundry to prove it. My time chopping up the arena after Ampert's death didn't hurt either. This weapon feels right at home in my hands.

Barbaric. Brutal. Bloody. There's no way to pretty up what follows. As we rain blows on each other, some begin to connect. Our ax heads lock, we grapple, and she knees me so hard I see stars. I dodge an attack that buries her ax into a tree trunk, and as she struggles to free it, my blade bites into the flesh near her hip. A few moves later, she spins toward me and slices my thigh. As our weapons entangle, I bash her in the face with the handle, knocking out a couple teeth. But eventually, Silka's training pays off. When she wields the ax over her head in an intricate looping pattern, I'm distracted. The blade comes down unexpectedly, and before I have time to recoil, she opens a gash across my gut.

I gasp. She strikes again, knocking my ax from my grip. My hands find the damage. It's bad. She's coming at me. I turn to flee and she traps me in a headlock, cutting off my wind. Black flecks pepper the edges of my vision, I can feel myself disappearing when my eyes land on Wellie's decapitated body. I cannot let Silka win. In a last-ditch effort, I yank my knife from my belt and drive it back over my shoulder. A shriek. Neck released, I take to my heels, oblivious to whatever harm I've done her.

Both hands pressed against my wound, I zigzag through the woods, knowing I have to make a stand, certain this is impossible, crazed with pain and fear. Branches whip my face, roots catch my boots as I ricochet from one tree to the next. My one goal is to increase the space between Silka's screams and my being. But she is coming. My legs are beginning to buckle when the smell of burnt insects alerts me and I find myself at the opening to the holly hedge. Ladybug, ladybug, here I am again! But now their home offers both refuge and a chance to regroup. Perhaps that Capitol-loving, rule-abiding, snot-green-wearing Career will be afraid to follow me beyond the established boundaries of the arena.

As the hot air rising from the canyon washes over me, I stagger to the cliff's edge. Unable to run any farther, I turn to face my opponent. Boundary or no, Silka stumbles out of the hedge after me. Now I can assess the damage my knife did, own the empty socket where I gouged out her eyeball. Seems minor compared to keeping my innards contained. Without hesitation, she raises the ax and lets it fly. My knees, already on the verge of giving way, fold like wet cardboard and I collapse to the dirt as the ax whistles over my head into the canyon.

That's when I remember the force field. And what happens to dropped objects. I watch, breathless, for what the love of my life would call poetic justice.

Silka stands there, her hand against her gushing eye socket. Her good eye squints at my gut, estimating the arrival time of my death. Then there's the return of the whistle, her moment of confusion as the spinning ax catches the sunlight, and the dull sickening sound as it lodges in her head.

Now we're both on the ground. I roll on my back, watching the hovercraft that floats above us. Silka's refusing to die — a strangled gurgle seeps from her lips. I just have to wait her out. My hand fumbles in my pocket, searching for a handkerchief to help stem my bleeding. But instead, I unearth the relics of my last, or second-to-last, or I don't know which plan. The tools I needed to blow a hole in the Cornucopia. Well, obviously, that's out. Dying outside the arena will have to be sufficient. Although it seems an awful shame not to try for one more poster. Perhaps there's still a chance to go out with a bang? Yes. It's all become clear now. I know what to do.

It's okay, Pa. It's okay, Ma. Lift up your head, Sid. No one but me will paint this poster.

I can feel consciousness threatening to slip away as I free the sunflower from my neck and place the blasting cap in it. I bite off the fuse with my teeth, leaving a few inches, and toss the remainder aside.

This time it works, Ampert. Loose cannon going off, Louella. Wyatt. Lou Lou. Wellie. I pinkie swear, Maysilee. Pay attention, Panem. Newcomers land on top.

The president's card, courtesy of the Capitol, tears easily. I crumble the pieces and pile them with the candy wrappers. Finally, I pull the flint striker over my head and give it one long kiss.

Oh, Lenore Dove. Oh, love of my life. I am with you before, now, and always. And I will find you. I will find you.

"Haymitch. Haymitch Abernathy. You are to stop all activity immediately."

The quartz settles in one shaky hand, the other closes over the heads of the snake, the songbird. Such fine workmanship. Pretty with a purpose, she said. It has found its true purpose now.

A cannon fires. No victor's crown for you, Silka. Just the claw. Listen, those trumpets must be for me.

A spray of sparks flies to the pile and blossoms into a little flame. A spray of bullets dance around my hands. Ha. Missed me.

"Freeze! Haymitch Abernathy, you have been — Drop that! Drop that now!"

The flame's already dying as I hold out the bomb. It kisses the tip of the short fuse, then hungrily begins to eat up the black cord.

"You don't know what you're doing! Stop! Don't throw it!"

But I do. With my last ounce of strength, I launch the sunflower into the canyon. If nothing else, there should be an impressive boom. But the Gamemaker's panicked voice has allowed me to hope for more. What will happen when the explosion meets the force field? I have absolutely no idea. Only that they seem to fear it. The quartz slips to the ground, blending into the other rocks. I slide the flint striker under my collar, where it can rest on my heart. She'll understand.

The wind scatters the last bits of ash, carrying them into oblivion. Black specks flood my eyes, forming a cloud that blocks the sunlight. A blast rocks the world.

My last sensations are of the slippery coils of my intestines in one hand, the songbird pressing against my skin, and the earth quaking beneath me.

I die happy.

Drip. Drip. Drip.

"Ma must have hung the laundry inside."

Drip. Drip. Drip.

"So cold. Need to put some coal on the fire. So cold. Where's my quilt? Sid, you got my quilt?"

Drip. Drip. Drip.

"Hattie bottling a new batch. Always stinks like this. First part of the run gets tossed. 'Throw out the heads, Haymitch. Stuff will kill you. It'll kill you.'"

Drip. Drip. Drip.

"Too late, Hattie. I'm already dead. Hey, Hattie?"

Drip. Drip. Drip.

"Hattie? Ma?" There's no response. Something bad is happening. "Ma?"

I snap awake. Why is Hattie brewing in my kitchen? Get us all arrested. Why will no one answer me? This isn't the kitchen. What the hell is happening? Why do I hurt so bad?

A greenish tornado sky glow. The sharp alcohol smell married with chemicals lining my nose, coating my tongue. Drip-drip-dripping mixed with a distant murmur, words I cannot quite make out. Cold metal pinning me to cold metal. Fear.

I blink hard and the world comes into focus. Through the swampy light, a high ceiling crisscrossed with pipes. I lick my sand-paper lips, try to swallow. Reach to rub my eyes, but my hands can't make it past my belly. Fingers find the long row of stitches across my gut. Can't make sense of them. A steel table beneath me. No mattress or sheet or pillow. Metal cuffs with short chains on my wrists and ankles. Strap across my chest. Naked as a jaybird. Not a stitch. No, but something left. My flint striker . . .

The memory swoops back into my brain. The cliffside. The bomb. Silka's dying gurgles. The warnings from above. Sparks flying. Fuse catching. The arc of the sunflower against the open sky. Then, that earsplitting sound.

I must be dead. I felt my intestines sliding out. My body shutting down. I wanted to go. The job was done, my poster completed.

What's happened to me?

My flint striker rests on my heart, as it did in my final moment, only now it's fastened to my neck by the leather bootlace. Someone has tied it there, and it wasn't Ma.

Where am I, Lenore Dove? Where are you, my only love?

Tubes sprout from my arms. One in my belly. I twist my head to the right and pain scalds my gut. A few feet away, faces press against a glass wall. Tongueless mouths open. Avoxes, unclothed and dirty, paw the glass, begging me for something I can't give. Terrified, I turn to the left.

A moment of relief as I spot my old friend, the gray rabbit from the arena. My dove in the coal mine, who warned of danger, who led me from the maze. Has it come to save me once again? *Help me. Can you help me?* The green eyes stare unblinking from the tank. It presses into the glass. Why does it tremble so?

From the shadows, something strikes. A six-foot snake swallows up my ally. A lump in the sinewy body.

I slam my eyes shut. This must be a nightmare. Or perhaps I've gone to another world, a bad one. I try to will myself back into unconsciousness, to escape this evil place. But in my heart of hearts, I know it's real. I start shaking as hard as the rabbit.

Harder. Awaiting my snake. Please send the snake and end this.

Muffled footsteps. A tug on my tubes. A woman in a mask swaps a full bag of clear fluid for an empty one.

"Where am I?" I rasp. She ignores me. Just sponges my gut stitches with a foul-smelling liquid, sending shocks of pain across my trunk. "Stop! You're hurting me!" I struggle. She doesn't stop. *I* stop, because moving makes the pain worse.

She leaves. Murmurs again. This time I catch a few words. "Laboratory." "Sepsis." "Disruptive." A coldness surges from the needle planted in my arm. Nothingness.

When I wake again, I have new knowledge. In this place, disruption brings oblivion. Dispensed from afar like the drugs in Lou Lou's pump. I try to be as disruptive as possible for the hours? days? weeks? I am imprisoned here. When I'm conscious, the Avoxes plead. Padded feet bring pain. Grotesque mutts replace the humans. More bunnies die. Nasty concoctions are forced between my lips. No daylight breaches the walls, no ally comforts me. I am utterly alone and defenseless.

Fresh confusion as I surface in a nest of burnt orange. Somehow, I'm back at the tribute apartment. Across the room, Wyatt's bed, bereft of covers, catches me off guard. Still haven't had the space to mourn him.

Gingerly, I wiggle my fingers and toes. All the tubes and restraints have vanished, but a pump identical to Lou Lou's has sunk its teeth deep into my chest, defying me to remove it. I fold back the fuzzy spread, the fine sheets, and examine my gut wound. No stitches, just a puckered, angry scar, like a twisted smile. My thigh has fared better, but I'll carry the mark for life. Still naked. I jump up, only to collapse back down on the bed, gripping the covers as the room spins. I wait for things to settle before a second attempt. With my feet carefully planted on the floor, I slowly rise. My pajamas are still in a jumble on the floor where I left them the morning of the Hunger Games. With no other options, I put them on.

I wobble into the living room and steady myself against the doorjamb of the girls' room. Bedding from our last sleepover drapes the furniture and floor. Dried blood spots from Lou Lou's ear dot her pillow. Maysilee's pajamas sit folded in a neat pile on her bed. Nobody's here because everybody's dead.

"Mags?" I croak. "Wiress?" No answer. The whole building's as silent as a grave. The street outside the apartment, deserted. Locked down. Block barricaded off. I am indeed a dangerous young man. The charming rascal turned deadly rebel. Woodbine Chance has grown up into one of his loose cannon kin, fated to swing by his neck while District 12 looks on. Seized by an impulse to flee, I make for the elevator and press the button repeatedly. No humming, no lights, no escape possible.

In the kitchen, the table's bare, but the refrigerator holds a platter of rolls and a shelf of pint-sized cartons of milk. Snow's diet after the deadly oysters. Though my stomach has shrunk to the size of a walnut, it still craves food. I dip bits of bread in the milk and suck them down. Being poisoned no longer worries me. If the president wanted me dead, why has he gone to so much trouble to keep me alive? He has big plans for me. The camera in the corner reminds me my every move's being watched or at least recorded. No, at this point, definitely watched. Eyes on me, 24/7. I will not be allowed to die. I will be resurrected by the Capitol for their entertainment. Perhaps, I am even being broadcast live now. Perhaps, as a victor, I will never be off camera again. . . .

Exhausted by my excursion, I return to bed and sink into a fitful sleep.

Days pass. My schedule's my own here. Nothing but time to consider the consequences of my actions in the arena. Snow's perfect little showpiece that I undermined every chance I got. I take no pleasure in that now as I wonder who's paying the price for it. Beetee. Mags. Wiress. They're likely all being tortured to reveal the names of accomplices. The rebel sympathizers who crafted sunflower bombs and fuse necklaces. The Gamemakers and Peacekeepers who helped smuggle them in. I hope they've spared the prep team and Effie, who are completely clueless Capitol pawns. I doubt anyone suspects Drusilla and Magno Stift of being sympathizers and I don't care if they do. And Plutarch? I'm still not sure of his role in all this, but he was right about the sun and the berms, and without that knowledge, it would have been impossible to carry out my mission. Is he an ally? A Capitol operative? Both? Impossible to know.

I don't dare think about my loved ones back home. Everything I did, every choice I made, was based on the knowledge that my death protected them from harm. Snow had guaranteed that in the library. *"With you out of the picture, Lenore Dove and your family should be free to enjoy long and happy lives."* Like Beetee said, if he had died, Ampert would have still been alive. Snow wanted him to suffer the horror of watching his son's execution; it was pointless otherwise. But since Snow needed a victor for his perfect Quarter Quell, I guess he changed his mind about killing me.

To make matters worse, Beetee's transgressions were clandestine and mine were televised to the entire country. Or were they? I have no idea how my efforts have been edited, blacked out, and card-stacked. It's possible that nothing significant has been aired, gutting the effectiveness of my posters, but perhaps lightening my punishment.

This I know: I have been publicly challenging Snow and his Quarter Quell since I landed in the Capitol. Even after the private meeting in the library, I flaunted my defiance of him. If he served up poisoned oysters to Incitatus Loomy, the parade master, what feast must he have in store for me and mine?

Maybe a week has gone by, according to the shifting light on the street. Solitary confinement continues. The isolation is almost scarier than the creepy lab. You know when you're starting to miss hanging out with the mutts, you're in trouble, but I long for company.

The rolls harden, the milk begins to turn, but I keep eating, driven by a convalescent's ravenous appetite. I fantasize about food. Fresh plums. Mashed potatoes. Rabbit stew. Stack cake. Will I ever taste stack cake again? Unlikely. If I do make it home, I expect childhood celebrations will be a thing of the past. I won't really be home anyway. I'll have a house in the Victor's Village, with all the niceties Beetee alluded to. Reliable electricity, warm and cool air, flushing toilets, and all the hot water I want at the turn of a faucet. No pumping and chopping required. Like my prison here.

Perhaps my victory celebration has been canceled due to my insurrection. Maybe I'm just being imprisoned for my public execution. One can hope.

I start spending long stretches in the tub. The towel I threw over the camera's been removed and I don't bother replacing it. They'd just drug me and take it away. Might chain me up again. No point. I soak for hours and hours, replenishing the hot water, watching my fingers and toes get pruney as bits of dead flesh float off my scar. Images of the arena consume me. Death upon death. Ones I didn't witness, like the bloodbath, I imagine. I try to recall the other forty-seven tributes plus Lou Lou. Using Maysilee's color system helps a bit, but about half elude me. District 5, District 8. All but forgotten.

Wyatt's absence haunts me in the bedroom, so I take my spread to the couch and make camp there. The television, unresponsive to my attempts with the remote, begins to turn on and off on its own. I'm fed clips from old Hunger Games, curated especially for me. Gory snippets, terrorized children, despair. The early ones, which they rarely feature on Capitol TV, are low-budget affairs with no attempt at the showiness that marks today's extravaganzas. Just a bunch of kids thrown into an old arena with some weapons. No costumes or interviews.

One evening, a haunting melody weaves through my dreams. I startle from sleep, calling Lenore Dove's name. The television glows. On-screen, a girl in a rainbow of ruffles sings a familiar tune with unfamiliar words.

It's sooner than later that I'm six feet under.
It's sooner than later that you'll be alone.
So who will you turn to tomorrow, I wonder?
For when the bell rings, lover, you're on your own.

She performs on a stage with a shabby backdrop before a Capitol audience in old-fashioned clothes. Great-Aunt Messalina and Great-Uncle Silius would fit right in.

Her voice, that accent, the way those fingers command the guitar strings — a Covey girl, for sure. But not mine . . .

And I am the one who you let see you weeping.
I know the soul that you struggle to save.

Too bad I'm the bet that you lost in the reaping.
Now what will you do when I go to my grave?

Sniffles from the audience. Someone shouts, "Bravo!" The crowd goes wild. The girl bows and extends her hand to a figure who's standing just out of the spotlight. A silhouette of a man. Upright, trim. A crown of curls. He waits a moment, as if deciding whether or not to join her. Then takes a step forward as the screen goes black.

The reaping, she said? Must be. Why else would a Covey girl be in the Capitol? Could this girl be District 12's one and only victor? Suddenly, I'm sure she is. No wonder Lenore Dove never wants to talk about her. She knows the story, but it's too secret, or perhaps too painful, to share even with me. I think about the bits of color Lenore Dove adds to her wardrobe, the bright blue, yellow, and pink. Are they scraps from this girl's dress? A way to keep her memory alive? What color name did this rainbow girl carry to the Tenth Hunger Games? What happened to her after? Did she come home? Did she die in the nightmarish lab? What did she do to be erased so completely?

Who was the guy she reached out to at the end of her number? Her district partner possibly, who'd have died in the arena. It was someone she cared about, from the look of it. Or perhaps it was someone else, someone hosting the show. An earlier Flickerman. They'd be forty years older now if they're still alive.

Forty years. Not all that long after the Dark Days. If District 12's forgotten her, it's unlikely she's remembered here in the Capitol. No, wait. Someone here remembers the Covey. Someone who knows how they name their babies and love their birds. Intimate, personal knowledge. The information I attributed to Capitol informers could have an entirely different source. I do the math. Fifty-eight minus forty. Eighteen. President Snow would've been eighteen during the Tenth Hunger Games. The Covey girl would have been no older. The curly-headed man in the shadows that she reached out to . . . was it him?

I recall the library, his knowing smirk . . .

"Bet I know a thing or two about your dove."

"Like what?"

"Like she's delightful to look at, swishes around in bright colors, and sings like a mockingjay. You love her. And oh, how she seems to love you. Except sometimes you wonder because her plans don't seem to include you at all."

Oh, Lenore Dove, what have I done to you? How will you pay for my surviving the Hunger Games?

I lose it, smashing a chair into the window, shattering glass onto a table of china kittens, then pounding at the bars with a heavy lamp. I hammer away until a burst of bullets above my head breaks my focus.

A pair of heavily armed Peacekeepers has materialized, their rifles trained on me. Behind them, my prep team huddles and would likely flee if Effie Trinket didn't have a firm grip on their grooming belts. "Well," she says with false cheeriness, "who's ready for a big, big, big night?"

The Peacekeepers slap on handcuffs and propel me into the center of the room, where my prep team stares at me, aghast. I'm skin and bones, wearing dirty pajamas, and my bare feet bleed freely from the broken glass. Somewhere in the last few weeks, my nails have turned to claws, my hair to fur. I've killed multiple times and preserved no life but my own. I left a simple district piglet and returned as the murderous beast that they always suspected lay in wait.

"Just need a flower for my lapel," I say.

But you can't keep Effie down. She holds up a white rose. "Got it. Why don't we start with a shower? You'll want to look your best for your Victor's Ceremony."

No execution, then. At least, not yet.

Soaped up, rinsed off, trimmed, shaved, teeth brushed, feet bandaged. Revulsion at my scar expressed and dealt with, the team dresses me in another Uncle Silius ensemble.

I finger the champagne bubbles embroidered in the jacket. "Where's Magno Stift?"

Effie's nose wrinkles in disgust. "More toads. He's still recovering, but he's planning to make an appearance tonight since you're the victor."

"I'm going to tell everyone you dressed me."

"Please, don't." She sighs. "He'll only make a scene, and it's hard enough being a Trinket." She arranges my flint striker over my shirt. I try to shove it back under my collar, but she resists. "He said to keep it out, where everybody can see it."

"Magno did?" I ask Effie.

"No." She clips off the end of the rose, slides it into a buttonhole and gives it a tap. "*He* did." She steps back. "You look very presentable. Remember, positive attitude."

Despite my finery, I'm shackled and transported in the van, which feels so dark and desolate without Maysilee, Wyatt, and Lou Lou. No greenroom for me this time. Still rattling my chains, I'm escorted beneath the stage and shoved into a chair, with four guards assigned to me.

Effie, to her credit, stands by me. When the Peacekeepers object, she says, "He's the second Quarter Quell victor. Drusilla and Magno are not available. Someone should be with him to honor his achievement."

"Your funeral," a Peacekeeper says.

I think about the things I did in the arena. Things they definitely would have shown. Killing the pair from District 4. The brutal ax fight with Silka. Maybe they're right to chain me like a beast. I feel grateful to Effie. "I won't hurt you," I mutter.

"I know that," she says. "I've known who you are ever since you helped with my makeup box. And I know your position could not have been easy."

It's surprisingly touching. "Thanks, Effie."

"But they really are for a greater good. The Hunger Games."

And now she's lost me.

The area beneath the stage begins to fill with people and their handlers. The activity centers around five metal plates that will ascend with the featured players of the night. Proserpina and Vitus jitter on one circle in anticipation, tweaking each other's makeup. Drusilla, who appears to be wearing a stuffed eagle on her head, teeters on six-inch heels. Magno reels in, decked in live-reptile fashion, and a few assistants balance him on his spot, with crossed fingers. I crane my neck, trying to find my mentors. Finally, Mags arrives in a wheelchair while a still-mobile but distressed Wiress twitches her head about in a birdlike fashion, a steady stream of words spouting from her lips. Very bad things have been done to them. Mags spots me and tries to rise before she's shoved back in her chair. No reunion for us.

Their torturous treatment makes it impossible to deny my family's certain punishment. Are they already dead? Or will Snow arrange, as he did with Beetee, for a time when I can personally witness their suffering?

The anthem plays and I hear Caesar Flickerman welcome the audience to the second Quarter Quell's Victor's Ceremony.

He calls the Games historic, unparalleled, unforgettable, and as devastating a reminder of the Dark Days as the country has ever witnessed. He begins to introduce my team as a hubbub of shouting and whooping comes from the audience. Up go Proserpina and Vitus, clapping for themselves. Drusilla follows, in a dramatic pose that mimics the eagle's outstretched wings. As his plate rises, Magno almost tumbles off, but catches himself and crawls back aboard. He makes his entrance on one knee, his hands in a victory clasp above his head. The Peacekeepers haul Mags to her feet. She and Wiress, arms encircling each other's waists, lean against each other for support.

Freed of my shackles, I'm held in place on my plate until it begins to rise. What did the audience see during the Hunger Games? Will they boo or applaud for me? And who am I supposed to be? Is it possible I'm still a beloved rascal? Or are they salivating to see the murderous monster from District 12? Effie Trinket, the only one I might ask, has melted into the shadows.

I brace myself, preparing to be pelted with rotten fruit or jeered off the stage. Bright lights partially blind me, and I lift my hand to shield my eyes. When they adjust, I realize the entire audience has given me a standing ovation. Mad cheers and hot tears.

I'm the hero of the moment. The star of Panem. The victor of the Quarter Quell. And that can only mean that President Snow has won the day.

People in the crowd begin to chant a mishmash of sounds that reduce to *"Show it! Show it! Show it! Show it!"*

I turn to Caesar for direction and he draws a line across his abdomen. My scar. They want me to show them my scar. There appears to be no choice. I pull my silk shirt up, unzip my pants as far as modesty allows, and display my scar. The applause lasts for a full five minutes.

Giant screens throughout the auditorium come to life with the anthem playing over a fluttering flag of Panem. Caesar guides me to an upholstered chair positioned in the center of the stage for the recap. It is my first glimpse into how my Hunger Games were broadcast to the public.

The recap opens on the reading of the card, which I watched from home with Ma and Sid in the spring. A little girl dressed all in white, the picture of innocence, lifts the lid on a wooden box filled with envelopes. They widen the shot to include President Snow, who intones, "And now, to honor our second Quarter Quell, we respect the wishes of those who risked all to bring peace to our great nation." He leans over and carefully selects the envelope marked with a 50 and reads the card inside. "On the fiftieth anniversary, as a reminder that two rebels died for each Capitol citizen, every district will be required to send twice as many tributes to the Hunger Games. Two female and two male. In this doubling of reparations, we remember that true strength lies not in numbers, but in righteousness."

Bam! They start drawing the names at the reapings, beginning with District 1. "Silka Sharp!" "Panache Barker!" They machine-gun through the tributes with a quick shot of each and a counter in the corner of the screen that tracks from one to forty-eight. Being the home of the victor, District 12 is allowed a bit more time. Drusilla, yellow hat feathers bobbing, gets in her "Ladies first!" before "Louella McCoy!" My sweetheart marches up. "Maysilee Donner!" There's Maysilee, Merrilee, and Asterid clutching one another in the crowd. One of the tearful good-byes captured by Plutarch. "And the first gentleman who gets to accompany the ladies is . . . Wyatt Callow!" They briefly cover Wyatt, and then Drusilla calls my name. Lenore Dove's refusal to perform has not made this version. Not tearful enough for

Plutarch and too Covey for Snow. But there's no Ma or Sid either. The omission chills me. Why isn't Plutarch's footage here? "Ladies and gentlemen, join me in welcoming the District Twelve tributes of the Fiftieth Hunger Games!" says Drusilla, as if daring District 12 to do anything else. "And may the odds be EVER in your favor!" I'm obliterated by a swirl of confetti.

I want to scream out the truth. A boy's head was blown off! People in 12 were shot! My reaping was rigged! But I just sit there, mute and radiating implicit submission. Snow has me by the short hairs and he knows it.

Incitatus Loomy could not have masterminded a finer parade. The frantic backstage prep never makes an appearance, just a majestic, orderly rollout of the tributes. There's a final aerial shot of all twelve chariots cruising along the route in perfect sync, which ends about fifteen seconds before that blue firecracker exploded, sending the whole event into chaos. This is all the country saw anyway. You had to be there in person to know about the crashing chariots and me holding Snow accountable for Louella's death. Which, as we know, also didn't happen because, look, it's time for the interviews and all forty-eight tributes are in the house.

The Careers have been edited to appear smarter, the Newcomers less unified. Does anyone even notice this besides me? Lou Lou's reduced to a girl wearing live-reptile fashion, Maysilee's and Wyatt's memorable turns are entirely ignored, and I get one snarky exchange with Caesar:

"So, Haymitch, what do you think of the Games having one hundred percent more competitors than usual?"

"I don't see that it makes much difference. They'll still be one hundred percent as stupid as usual, so I figure my odds will be roughly the same."

The audience laughs, and I give them this grin that confirms me as a stuck-up, selfish jerk. No mention of my support of the Newcomers. No silly interplay about making booze for Peacekeepers. The rascal's just a jackass.

Now we're rising into the arena. The opening sequence is a love letter to the Gamemakers as we savor the beauty of flora and fauna. For me, though, it calls to mind the deceptively sweet, brain-clouding smell of the air.

The jackass, meaning me, grabs his gear and hightails it out of there and then we get to watch the bloodbath, where eighteen kids are killed in excruciating detail. The audience before me gasps and cries out in glee, though they've seen it all before. Wyatt dies a selfless hero protecting a bewildered Lou Lou, who manages to scamper off unscathed. Maysilee fights, then follows Lou Lou to protect her. So many Newcomers fall. Two doves, the boys from 7, all of 8 and 9, Lannie and the other girl from 10, Tile from 11. With Wyatt, that makes sixteen. The only Career casualties are a boy and girl from District 5. Eighteen in all.

Oh, hello again, jackass! Sure, take your time. Catch your breath on the rock. Check out your pack. Don't worry about the Newcomers, they've got this. Ooh, look at that pretty woods. Have a nice hike!

A bunch of us sicken as the poisonous fruit and water kicks in. Carat from 1 and Urchin, the boy from 4 who knocked me off the chariot, writhe to death. That accounts for the twenty kids I saw in the sky that first night. The rest of the Careers have formed their pack on the snow-capped mountain.

Up until this point, I think the recap's been a fair record of what occurred in the arena. However, on Day 2, things start to go wonky. At some point, Maysilee, on her own, kills the boy from

District 1, Loupe, which I believe to be true because she told me this. There are a lot of tributes still recovering from the poison and the Career pack's hunting Newcomers. That, too, seems likely. But the recount of what happened in the woods, my tale, begins to deviate almost immediately. Timelines are twisted. Connections misleading. It's less flat-out lying than lying by omission. For instance, I see myself fighting squirrels, although they weren't around until the third day when I fought them to save Ampert. But we haven't even met up yet, so I seem to be trying to save my own life. They show Lou Lou gasping in the flowers, only I'm nowhere in sight. Later, I'm just running from the butterflies without even a glimpse of my fleeing with her body, hiding in the willows, and bringing on the shockers as punishment. What they showed during the actual Games, I don't know, but in the recap, I'm not even attempting to protect any of my allies. Day 3, the squirrels, as if making a second appearance, swarm Ampert, and then there's a reveal of his skeleton on the ground. Again, I'm nowhere to be found. In fact, our picnic, the campout, the bombing of the tank, my rampage, and the arena going haywire — not a bit of that appears.

The horrors of the volcano take center stage. The tributes experience the flame-shooting eruption, asphyxiation by the ash cloud, burns from the chemical lava. Twelve die. The rest barely escape and head across the meadow to the woods.

Cut to me, waking up blanketed by the sparkling ash. I get back to the business of trudging north. With the tank plot erased, my whole agenda seems to have been about getting to the end of the arena, which was, I guess, my cover story. It rains, but they've concealed all the bombing's damage. The arena's as perfect as ever. I get trapped in the hedge, follow the gray rabbit to freedom, and run into Panache and company.

I don't know who that is on the screen, so brutally killing those Careers from District 4. I guess it's me, but I can't own it. I stop thinking of myself as the jackass because it seems too complimentary for the creature I've devolved into. Doesn't help when they show every syllable of my toadying, babbling speech to Panache, who is finally silenced by Maysilee's dart.

"We'd live longer with two of us." Oh, Maysilee. I am mortified to be sitting here.

For a bit, things get back on course again. Maysilee and I look out for each other, and Silka and Maritte take out Ringina and Autumn in combat. But in a mind-bending realignment of events, Maysilee and me drawing off the porcupine mutt and Maritte and Maysilee killing the three Gamemakers at the berm have vanished. Somewhere in time, Maritte and Silka chase us through the woods, and Buck, Chicory, and Hull die from the quills, but it appears the porcupine just wanders off on its own.

Is it Day 4 or 5? Maysilee and my attempts to carve our way through the hedge have merged into one big sequence that involves the ladybugs and blowtorch. We're on the cliff that looks down on the treacherous rocks, but they steer clear of the generator. They've edited out the cannon announcing Maritte's death and with it the part where Maysilee says she's just going back for the potatoes, so it looks like we've really decided to split up. To my surprise, they keep my discovery of the force field. I guess they need it for Silka's death?

The pink birds attack Maysilee and she screams. For the first time, I look like I might be redeemable because I run to her aid. Oh, no. They haven't turned this into a redemption story, have they? Selfish rascal learns to care about others? Please tell me no.

 Day 5 or 6? Who knows? It's just one big, big, big day.

My delivery of milk from Snow has evaporated. As I run through the woods, they've added the sound of Wellie screaming, which didn't happen. I appear to have finally remembered that I belong to a wider alliance so I'm going to the rescue, when the cannon sounds and I come upon Silka, Wellie's head in hand.

Smash cut to the golden squirrels stripping Maritte to the bone. No matter that she's been long dead by this time. But people must know that. Maysilee and Maritte appeared in the sky together. Does no one remember? Do they just not care? Or during the Games, did they show the audience a different sky? Or none at all? And did they intentionally save Maritte's death to increase tension at the end? The Gamemakers must have been scrambling like crazy to control the narrative by this point. Whatever the case, the audience here in the auditorium has embraced this version, cheering and jeering on cue. Their lack of discernment transforms the recap, validating it as truth. I hope those in the districts can still see it as the piece of propaganda it is, but no telling what they've been fed.

We're back to Silka and me facing off, knowing we're the final two. Without words, we quickly engage in battle. Fatal wounds are exchanged. I run to the hedge.

On the cliff, Silka corners me, throws her ax. I drop. They cut to her anticipation and then back to me, convulsing. This must have happened after I lost consciousness.

The ax rebounds and buries itself in her head. And then? — and then?

Silka dies, her cannon fires, and I'm hanging on by a thread. The sunflower bomb, the quartz, the flint striker — there's no record of any of them. All of them gone or tucked away from sight. The hovercraft removes Silka's body. Trumpets declare my victory. A claw closes around me.

Are there rules about breaking out of the arena and using the force field to win? Possibly they are implied, but I have never heard them mentioned. So, what am I? A rascal? A cheater even? Maybe. But clearly I do not rise to the standard of a rebel.

The camera pulls back slowly as they carry me away, for the first time revealing the arena as a whole. It looks like a giant eye. The Cornucopia marks the pupil. The wide circle of spring-green meadow makes up the iris. On either side, the darker green of the forest and mountain terrain narrows to points, forming the whites of the eye. Well, the symbolism has been lost on no one. Even the little kids in the Seam know the Capitol powers are watching us.

I wonder if they ever consider that we're watching them, too.

All eyes on me now, as I rise to my feet before the thundering crowd. The anthem plays as President Snow descends from the heights on a crystal platform, a bloodred rose in his lapel. In his hand, he holds a golden crown.

Some victors bow, some kneel, but I just stand there trying to read his expression as he approaches and places the crown on my head. Heavy. Entrapping. "I guess Snow lands on top," I say under the applause. Utterly guilty on all possible counts, I await his sentence.

He merely smiles and says, "Enjoy your homecoming."

The after-party's held in the ballroom of the presidential mansion. I'm displayed in a giant golden birdcage that dangles from the main chandelier at about eye level. It's supposed to be a joke, I guess; the guests sure seem to get a kick out of it. But it isn't. When I try the little handle at the door, it's locked tight.

My Peacekeeper buddies stand nearby, giving courage to the partygoers. I roll with it, bantering with my sponsors and posing for pictures, painting the best poster I can to convince President Snow that I'm on his team now. His puppet. His plaything. Because my blood's been ice water since his comment about my homecoming. What awaits me? And if I behave, can I alter it?

People bring me tidbits, feeding me by hand like you would a pet dog, and I smack my lips with appreciation, eating until my shrunken belly's like to split open. I'm hoping they're not showing this in District 12. People may forgive but they won't forget such behavior, especially since I won't get credit for all the trouble I've caused, which has landed me in this cage. The shame of this is not the sort of thing a person can live down.

It's all being recorded for posterity, though. Plutarch Heavensbee and his crew, still assigned to me, buzz around, taking footage. He refuses to let me catch his eye. I'm back to doubting if I can trust him — after all, he appears unscathed by the fallout of the rebel plot — but I've got no shortage of questions I'd like to ask him.

I don't see President Snow all night. Or much of my team either. Proserpina and Vitus swing by to congratulate me, tipsy and pink-faced. Drusilla and Magno, who success seems to have reconciled, kiss and coo and briefly pose for photos with me. Magno can't even remember my name and insists on calling me Hamwich, which makes me sound like a ham sandwich. The only person who keeps an eye on me is Effie Trinket. She mingles nearby, watchful, but careful not to take any credit for my success.

It's not until the wee hours, as things are winding down, that Plutarch sidles up to my cage, seemingly focused on an uncooperative camera.

"What's happening with my family? Lenore Dove?" I say under my breath.

"No word on your family. She's still on the base," he whispers.

"What? She said they were letting her go in the morning. Did they arrest her again?"

"No. They never released her."

"What?"

He's moved on, leaving me to dissect those horrible words. *Never released.* That was a lie, theirs or possibly hers. A gift she gave me so I wouldn't worry about her, only myself. And it worked. But now I know that she has been absolutely helpless, completely at their mercy, this whole time while I sabotaged their arena. *Confined. Starved. Tortured. Raped. Murdered.* I grip the golden bars, petrified, as the words I've been refusing to consider pound in my brain.

The woman with the cat ears appears, dangling a shrimp before me. My mouth opens automatically and I chew the delicacy while her friend takes our picture. I cannot quit now. Lenore Dove's life is at stake.

When dawn finally breaks, I'm allowed to relieve myself in a pink marble bathroom with curlicues and rose-scented soap. I'm hoping to be sent to the train station, but instead I'm returned to the apartment. Fresh rolls and milk have been provided. Clean clothes. I'm not going home any time soon.

For the next ten days, I'm carted around the Capitol — to parties and interviews and fashion shoots — to publicly revel in my victory. No greater suck-up exists in the history of the Games. No humiliation is beneath me. I will bear anything to keep my loved ones alive.

Finally, after an all-night party at the Capitol zoo, the Peacekeepers transport me to the deserted train station, which is still hung with the propaganda banners. *NO PEACE, NO PROSPERITY! NO HUNGER GAMES, NO PEACE!* And President's Snow's parting shot, *PANEM'S #1 PEACEKEEPER.*

A doctor, who waits at the door of the train, deftly removes my pump, leaving oozy spots where the teeth secured it to my chest. I can't pretend I'm sad to see it go, although within minutes the drugs wear off and my scar starts to hurt.

No bunk bed with the stiff quilt for me. Back in chains, I'm locked in the room Plutarch once freed me from. He's nowhere to be seen now. I guess the show's over for real. I wrap Great-Uncle Silius's champagne bubble jacket tightly around my body and sit in the corner, feeling the pain blossom across my gut.

The Capitol's got every reason to get rid of me, but the train refuses to budge. I have to get home. I have to know what has happened.

After a couple of hours, a Peacekeeper comes in with a roll and a carton of milk. Still on the Snow diet.

"Why aren't we moving?" I ask.

"Been waiting for your friends," he replies, with a nod to the window, then goes.

My friends? I have no friends here. Does he mean my team? I look out the window of my cell. Three carts are being rolled down the platform. Each carries a plain wooden box. After a momentary confusion, I put it together. They are coffins. Louella, Maysilee, and Wyatt will be riding home with me. I thought them long buried, peacefully resting in their family plots on the hill in District 12. Instead, we will finish this journey together.

I slide back down the wall, shaking uncontrollably. I think of the state their bodies must be in, violated by chariots and blades and birds. I imagine their families, weeping and waiting at the station, turning their backs on me or, worse, turning their faces to me for explanations. Does the Capitol always send the fallen back with the victor? Or is this a parting gift for me in particular?

I can hear the muffled thuds as they load the coffins onto the train. Quite close to me. The next car, I think. Doors slam shut. The train begins to roll. I curl up on the floor, my face against the wall, wishing I'd earned a coffin as well. But no, I have a homecoming to enjoy.

My thoughts turn to Lenore Dove. My Covey girl. What happened to Snow's? The mysterious District 12 victor. She could be alive. He is. And yet she's all but vanished from memory in District 12. Did President Snow have her killed? No, he would only have been a boy. Hardly older than me. He wouldn't have been in power. Not like now. What plans does he have for my dove? I think of the Covey song, the one Maysilee's mamaw used to quote when she was scared. . . . *Nothing you can take from me was ever worth keeping.* The arrogance of those bold words. You can take several things from me — my ma, my brother, my love — that are the *only* things worth keeping.

Another song surfaces unbidden. Also forbidden. Lenore Dove plays it for Burdock sometimes. . . .

Are you, are you
Coming to the tree
Where they strung up a man they say murdered three?
Strange things did happen here
No stranger would it be
If we met up at midnight in the hanging tree.

Are you, are you
Coming to the tree
Where the dead man called out for his love to flee?
Strange things did happen here
No stranger would it be
If we met up at midnight in the hanging tree.

Strange things indeed. A dead man calling out. His ghost. No, Lenore Dove said it was a bird. Birds. Jabberjays. The failed mutts let loose to die in District 12. But they defied the Capitol's sentence of extinction by fathering a new species, mockingjays, before they vanished. Is that what makes the song dangerous? Immortalizing those wayward mutts in a song?

Are you, are you
Coming to the tree
Where I told you to run, so we'd both be free?
Strange things did happen here
No stranger would it be
If we met up at midnight in the hanging tree.

Or is it the Capitol hanging someone who was likely a rebel? That's who died in the hanging tree. I know this tree, it's real, my pa pointed it out to me. We have metal gallows in District 12 now, courtesy of the Capitol, but back in the day, many a rebel died swinging from its branches.

Are you, are you
Coming to the tree?
Wear a necklace of rope, side by side with me.
Strange things did happen here
No stranger would it be
If we met up at midnight in the hanging tree.

Maybe Lenore Dove and I will hang together. Could be easier to find her then, in that next world of hers.

That's as close to comfort as I can get.

We travel through the day, far into the night. Once in a while, there's a stop somewhere to fuel up. Every few hours, rolls and milk are delivered, although I haven't touched a mouthful. My gut aches and the hard floor digs into my unpadded bones. When I manage to doze, dead tributes pay calls. They seem to want me to do something, but it's unclear what that is. The strangest visit involves Louella and Lou Lou, dressed in identical outfits, sitting across the table from me while I peel and eat a bowl of hard-boiled eggs. "Which of us is which?" they ask me. But the Capitol has won. I can't tell them apart.

I jerk awake to find the train has pulled into the District 12 station. I am home. The Peacekeepers come in, remove my shackles, and lead me to the exit. The door opens.

"Get out," says one.

Full of trepidation, I step out onto an empty platform, gritty with coal dust. No one waits for me. No one expects me. It's still dark out and the station clock reads 5 a.m. The Peacekeepers carelessly shove the coffins out after me, damaging a few boards. The train pulls away, leaving me entirely alone except for my fellow tributes. I walk over to them, lay a hand on the nearest coffin. Screwed into the lid's a metal nameplate, not unlike the ones at Plutarch's house, the ones on the berms in the arena. I touch the inscription. *Louella McCoy.*

The smell of death rises through the cracked wood. I turn and propel my stiff body down the platform.

The station's quiet as a tomb. Strange, even for the hour. Perhaps it's early on a Sunday, the one day the mines shut down. With all the drugs, I have no idea what the date is. Didn't think to ask. We must be into August. I push through the heavy glass door, gulping in the night air, warm and moist and laced with coal dust, and for the first time I allow myself to believe that I have really come home.

My heart skips a few beats and, fool that I am, tendrils of hope force their way up through the dirt of my despair. Could it be that within the hour, I might feel Ma's arms around me, ruffle Sid's hair, strip off Great-Uncle Silius's dead man's clothes, and pull on a pair of flour sack shorts? Could Lenore Dove be freed? Are the sweet moments of my previous life, always taken for granted before the Games, once more in reach? Can there be happiness again for a miserable wretch like myself?

As I walk through the lonely streets toward the Seam, I pinch myself to rule out this being a dream. Silly, since I've no shortage of pain. It's just that I was never supposed to return here, arena plot or no. The idea that I might have triumphed in a double

Hunger Games strains belief. But those are my feet, clad in pointed patent leather shoes, kicking up the cinders on the way to my house. My pace quickens. If it is a dream, I want to sustain it until I get to see my family one more time.

I take the glow up ahead for the sunrise, until I realize it's too local, too bright. A whiff of smoke drifts through the heavy, humid air. Fire. But not coal fire. I break into the closest thing I can manage to a run. Withered muscles, screaming scars, swollen feet reduce my efforts to a wild hobble. Maybe I am wrong. Any house can catch fire. What with rusted stoves and unwatched hobs. Maybe it's not mine.

I know it's mine.

Now I can hear the voices, shouting for water, a woman wailing. As I round the bend, it comes into view, fully ablaze against the still-dark sky.

"Ma?" I cry. "Sid?"

I bust through the bucket line, fed by three neighbors' pumps in addition to our own, those slow spurts of water, those pathetic splashes against the inferno. People draw away, startled, frightened by my appearance. Unprepared for the wild-eyed scarecrow in Capitol evening wear.

"Ma! Sid!" I grab the nearest person, one of the Chance girls, no more than eight. "Where are they? Where's my family?" Terrified, she points at the burning house.

Ma and Sid are being burned alive.

My feet dance side to side for a few seconds, looking for a break in the wall of flame, before I charge straight into the inferno. "Ma!"

As I reach the doorway, a beam crashes down and I reflexively jump back in a shower of sparks. Temporarily blinded, I make for the house again, when I'm yanked backward. My patent leather shoes with their slick soles betray me as I'm dragged into the yard and pinned to the ground. With one man on every limb and Burdock on my chest, all I can do is holler. "Let me up! Let me loose, you —"

Burdock's hand clamps over my mouth. "It's too late, Haymitch. We tried. It's too late."

I get some teeth into his palm and he jerks his hand back, but I'm only free enough to yell. "Ma! Sid! Maaaaa!"

Blair, kneeling on my right arm, leans in. Tears cut channels through his soot-blackened face. "We're so sorry, Haymitch. We tried. You know we did. We just couldn't save them."

"No! Let me go!" I fight to free myself, but I'm so outnumbered, still so weak from the long days of recovery, that I'm overpowered. "Let me go with them. Please!" But they don't, they hold on to me tight. I lie there, sobbing, begging, calling for Ma and Sid, until no more sounds come out.

"Can you help him?" I hear Burdock ask.

A cool hand rests on my forehead. The scent of chamomile flowers. Asterid March's face swims into view, pained but surprisingly calm. "Drink this, Haymitch." She presses a small bottle to my lips. "Drink until I say when." Despite my desperation, or perhaps because of it, I follow her orders. Sweetness fills my mouth, soothes my gullet. "One, two, three, four, five — okay, when." She pulls away the bottle. Smooths back my hair. "That's right. That's good. Try to rest now."

My eyelids become leaden. "What . . . ?"

"Just some sleep syrup."

"Ma . . . Sid . . ."

"I know. I know. We'll do what can be done. You go to sleep now. Sleep."

Dead to the world, I am, for over a day. I awake, thick-tongued and groggy, at the McCoys', where Louella's ma stands over me with a tin mug of tea. She does not mince words as she recounts the fire, perhaps because she's so deep in grief herself she knows the last thing I want is sugarcoating. "It was our boy Cayson who spotted it, coming home from his ramblings. The house was already aflame. He shouted to raise the dead. We all started in with the water. But the pump's slow and your cistern's dry."

I'm the reason that cistern's dry. Running off the morning of reaping day, leaving the chores to Sid. "My fault," I mumble.

"I expect you'll think everything's your fault for a long while. But that's got to wait. Today we bury them. You know what your ma would want."

Whether it's shock or a sleep syrup hangover, I can't seem to make sense of anything, so I do what I'm told. Louella's big sister, Ima, has cleaned Great-Uncle Silius's suit and polished his shoes. I've nothing else to wear, my own clothes being ash. It's sweltering out, but I pull the champagne bubble jacket over the shirt to conceal the drug pump bloodstains, faded with washing, but still visible.

"Lenore Dove," I tell Ima. "I got to go to her."

"Cayson knows a Peacekeeper who said she's got a hearing with the base commander today. You showing up won't help her any, Hay. Besides, we're about to head over to the graveyard."

Outside, a plain pine box awaits. "They had hold of each other," Mr. McCoy says. "Thought we'd let them stay that way."

Ma and Sid clinging to each other for eternity.

Burdock, Blair, and a couple of Ma's customers carry the coffin. The McCoys bring Louella's from behind the house and the two groups move forward, side by side. I limp along behind them. The mourners grow as we proceed. Everybody should be at work, but they'll claim they were sick. By the time we reach the graveyard, a couple hundred people have assembled. Seems like a lot compared to Mamaw's burial, but then I realize we're not grieving alone.

Five fresh graves await. One for Ma and Sid. Louella. Maysilee. Wyatt.

"Who's the fifth for?" I hear Burdock ask.

"Jethro Callow," a woman answers, not bothering to lower her voice. "Hung himself yesterday when his boy returned. Couldn't bear the shame."

A Booker Boy's death.

The mayor's come to speak over our loved ones. The words make no more sense than the chirping of birds in the surrounding trees. Sweat soaks through my shirt into my jacket. I want to kneel down and press my face against the cool Abernathy headstone, but I try to stand with dignity, as Ma would want.

There's a bad moment when I look up and see my ally, wearing her District 12 black, and start for her. "Maysilee!" Her face crumples into tears, hides in a handkerchief. Not Maysilee. Merrilee. Like as two peas in a pod. Mr. Donner sobs beside her. I'm led back to my place. Obviously deranged.

Coffins are lowered into the graves. Many shovels work to bury the departed. Dirt's patted down. Some kind soul lays a wreath of wildflowers on each mound. People weep and wail. It's so awful, I want to run away.

Then Burdock begins to sing, in that clear, sweet voice of his:

You're headed for heaven,
The sweet old hereafter,
And I've got one foot in the door.
But before I can fly up,

I've loose ends to tie up,
Right here in
The old therebefore.

The mockingjays, who nest in the surrounding trees, fall silent as he continues:

I'll be along
When I've finished my song,
When I've shut down the band,
When I've played out my hand,
When I've paid all my debts,
When I have no regrets,
Right here in
The old therebefore,
When nothing
Is left anymore.

The mourners have quieted.

When I'm pure like a dove,
When I've learned how to love,
Right here in
The old therebefore,
When nothing
Is left anymore.

The song, suggesting our separation is only temporary, consoles the heart. Lenore Dove would approve, I think. The mockingjays do, because they pick up the melody and make it their own.

As my eyes sweep the crowd, I see person after person press the three middle fingers of their left hand to their lips and then extend it to their dead. Our way of saying good-bye to those we cherished. I follow suit, raising my hand high, because I have so many to honor.

Then it's over. I'm being led away. Even in my confusion, I notice that Cayson, his hands and face bandaged, spits on Jethro Callow's grave. No one reprimands him.

I want to break away, to try to see Lenore Dove on the base, but I'm argued down again. Do I really think my appearance will help her? The best thing is to wait for word. Let her uncles plead her case. With so many kids lost in the Quarter Quell, the districts are in a state of unrest. The base commander won't be looking to throw gasoline on the fire in 12. Lenore Dove may be let go with a stern lecture and time served.

The McCoys take the mourners back to their place, where bowls of bean and ham hock soup are ladled out. I can't stay at the McCoys', though. Their eyes are full of questions about Louella, and I know I owe them answers. I just can't give them yet, not without losing my head again. As soon as I can, I excuse myself.

I go home before I remember I have no home. Just a pile of blackened beams and a pump. I'm standing before the ashes when the clouds in my brain clear enough for me to ask, "What happened?"

Fires are common enough in District 12, where the ever-present coal dust and aging wooden structures invite ignition. From the time I could toddle, Ma had put the fear of stray sparks and sleeping embers in me. No one took more care banking a fire at night. Which is how I know that this was no accident. This was arson, carried out in such a way that my family could not even make it to a window to escape. Ordered by Snow. For my homecoming.

The shards of my heart shift and drive into my lungs, making breathing an agony. "My fault," I say for the second time this morning.

Burdock and Blair catch me as I start to fall and carry me around the bend before they set me on a stump to recover. They try to coax me to their homes, but the thought of their families, when I have none, is unbearable.

"Well," says Burdock grimly, "there's your new house, then."

Only now do I remember the Victor's Village. Desperate to be alone, I let them take me there, to this strange Capitol cage, which I instantly hate. In the bedroom, they lay me down in the artificially chilled air, and I stare at the wall.

"I'm going to find Asterid," I hear Burdock whisper. "See about more syrup."

"I'll watch him," says Blair, leaving the door slightly ajar. "Dig up some clothes, too, can you?"

Hand-me-downs are found. Sleep syrup administered, but not as much, because I wake with a start in the dead of night, mind racing, with one thought only: I must get to Lenore Dove. I must take her away from here. District 12 means death. Through the crack in the door, I make out Burdock and Blair, asleep on the couches in the living room. I climb out a window in the bedroom and flee into the night.

The Covey's house lies dark. The uncles gave Lenore Dove the loft for her own. I climb up the drainpipe, trying to figure if she's made it home, but the whole place seems empty. Were they at the base all night? Have Tam Amber and Clerk Carmine been arrested as well? I doubt they're out giving a show, things being what they are. I don't want to be hanging around the house if they return. If Clerk Carmine didn't approve of me before the Hunger Games, imagine how the rascal's murderous run will have played for him.

I head down to the Meadow, concealing myself behind some bushes. If Lenore Dove gets freed, I know one of the first things she'll do is graze her geese. Unless she goes looking for me at the Victor's Village — in which case, she'll cut across the Meadow on the way.

Sitting on a fallen log, barefooted and in the worn miner's clothes, I feel safer than I have in weeks. I like being hidden here in the dark, where no one can find me. Out of the view of the Capitol, but also away from the pitying eyes of District 12. I try to figure out a plan for me and Lenore Dove. We can't stay here. But where is there to run? Only Snow's "ghastly wilderness." I love it, but I don't live in it. I'm no Burdock, with his trusty bow and knowledge of plants. I'm not even a bona fide bootlegger yet. I'm nothing. And while Lenore Dove's at home in the woods, she's no more capable of surviving out there than I am. Maybe I'm just being selfish, wanting her to run with me when the truth is she'd be fine here without me. Snow would have no cause to target her if I was dead or gone. The right thing to do is take off on my own and leave her to lead her life.

She won't want to let me go and I sure don't want to let her go. But what is the alternative? I'll wait and see her one more time, go back to the Victor's Village, and ask Burdock for a bow and some fishing line. If I die out there, so be it. Lenore Dove will be safe.

The sky takes on the soft glow that precedes the sun's arrival. The first birds begin to sing in the day. They're joined by a chorus of honking, then angry voices. I lift my head to see the rare and radiant Lenore Dove herding her gaggle into the Meadow.

"You're not to go running off!" Clerk Carmine says from the edge of the Meadow. He's agitated, shaking a finger at her.

Tam Amber stands with him, a little more stooped than I remember. "He's right, Lenore Dove. This is stretching house arrest to its limits already." The base commander must have given a hard-line directive. Tam Amber's the easy parent, the one she goes to with a questionable request, so if he's worried . . .

"I know! I heard you the first ten times!" she hollers back in exasperation. "I just want five minutes to myself. Is that possible around here? Or am I still in prison?"

"Fine. Five minutes. Then I want you back in the house for breakfast, you hear me?" says Clerk Carmine.

She gives him a Peacekeeper's salute. "Yes, sir. Understood, sir. You can count on me, sir."

Clerk Carmine takes a step forward, but Tam Amber lays a hand on his arm, and he just resigns himself to a parting shot. "Don't make us come down to fetch you, young lady." The uncles head back to the house.

Suddenly, I feel a burst of affection for Clerk Carmine. We both really want the same thing: for Lenore Dove to be safe and happy. And he was right. About his concerns over me, I mean. A boy from a rebel family who brews white liquor and disappears for hours with his niece in the woods does not spell security. Plus, I'm not even musical. I think I would have won him over eventually, if I'd had the chance. But now, it consoles me some that when I run away, he will be here guarding her. I guess I'll never have a chance to tell him so, but it's true.

As I wait to be sure the coast is clear, I soak up the loveliness of Lenore Dove. She spins around, head back, arms lifted to the sky. It must have been hell for her being locked up. She can't stand for anything to be confined. Especially wild things, which, of course, she is. The geese run around, chewing her out for being gone. She just sweet-talks them and strokes their necks. She's about to roost on her favorite rock when she gives an exclamation of surprise and scoops something up.

It's my bag of gumdrops. The ones I had Sid deliver to her after the reaping. I guess she left them here before she went to perform that night. She presses the candy to her heart and twirls around, grinning, then breaks into the little white bag. I can't wait another second. As I take off across the Meadow, she catches sight of me, cries out my name, and runs to meet me. I sweep her into my arms and spin her around and we're both laughing and kissing like crazy.

"Oh, Lenore Dove. Oh, my love," I say.

"You came back," she says, tears streaming, but happy tears. "You came back to me. In *this* world!"

"And you managed not to get hung!" I crow back.

We hold each other so tight it's like we're one person. Which we are, for real.

Her hands run over my face. "Are you okay? Are you really all right?'

"As right as rain," I promise her. I don't care, I can't leave her. She'll want to run away with me, and I'll let her. We'll figure out a way to live. Because I don't think either of us can live without the other.

We sink into the Meadow grass, hands clasped. She reaches for the bag of gumdrops that she dropped in our reunion. "Thanks for the candy. Gosh, look how hard I'm shaking!"

"Here," I say, taking the bag, not that I'm any steadier. I pluck a sweet from the bag and pop it in her mouth.

She laughs. "Now you're home, I guess I can eat the others."

"What others?" I feed her another gumdrop.

"The ones Sid brought me. I put them under my pillow."

"But . . ." I look down at the bag. It's a normal bag, with the Donners' label. Then I notice the gumdrops. Not a variety of colors. Not a rainbow. They're all a deep bloodred. I remember Snow's rose, his final words to me, and the pieces fall into place.

"Spit it out!" I order her, cupping my hand before her mouth. "Spit it out now!"

Her face registers shock as she spits a half-chewed gumdrop into my palm. "What? It's fine."

"Where's the other? Where's the first one?" I give her a shake.

"I swallowed it, I guess. Why?"

"Throw it up! Get it out of your stomach!"

She's panicking now. "What's going on, Haymitch?"

I think of the arena. "Do you all have any charcoal tablets at the house?"

"Charcoal tablets? No, I don't think so. Why would —" I see her put it together. She leans over, sticks a finger down her throat, and tries to gag the thing up. "I can't do it. I've barely eaten in days. There's nothing to throw up!"

"Come on," I pull her to her feet. "Come on." I begin to call for help. "Clerk Carmine! *Clerk Carmine!*"

"Haymitch, I —" A perplexed look crosses her face and she presses a hand to her chest. Her knees give way. "I can't stand up."

I pull her back to her feet. "You've got to! Just get to the house." I throw back my head and scream, "Clerk Carmine! Help! Help us!" She collapses into my arms. I kneel back on the ground, her body across mine. "Lenore Dove . . ." I plead. "Don't. Don't." A blood-flecked foam bubbles up over her lips. "Oh, no . . . no . . ."

Her eyes fixate on something in the distance. "See that?" she says hoarsely.

I turn my head and see the sun, just peeking over the horizon. "What? The sun?"

"Don't you . . . let it . . . rise . . ." she gets out.

Tears choke me. "I can't stop it. You know I can't stop it."

Her head jerks a bit to the side. ". . . on the reaping," she whispers.

Oh, no. Don't leave me with that. Don't leave me at all. "Lenore Dove? Please try and hold on, darling. Lenore Dove?"

"Promise." Her eyelids flutter shut.

"Okay, okay, I promise. But you can't go. You can't leave me. Because I love you like all-fire."

"You, too." I think that's what her lips said.

"Lenore Dove?" I press mine against hers. Willing her to stay with me. Refusing to say good-bye.

But when I pull back, I taste the poison and know she is gone.

The nightmare always starts with me feeding her that gumdrop. We're in the Meadow, holding fast to each other, her face shining with tears of joy. And I don't check the bag. I never check the bag. Why can't I remember to check the bag? I just lift that bloodred gumdrop to her lips, and there's no stopping what follows. My realization, her terror, the bloody foam, my pleading with her to stay, her making me promise. Then the uncles are there. Clerk Carmine ripping her from my arms, trying to restart her heart while he calls her name. Tam Amber standing stiffly over them, his head shaking as he mumbles, "Not again. Oh, not again."

That's when the music kicks in, her name poem, her song, careening around my brain like a runaway train.

Once upon a midnight dreary, while I pondered, weak and weary,
Over many a quaint and curious volume of forgotten lore —
While I nodded, nearly napping, suddenly there came a tapping,
As of some one gently rapping, rapping at my chamber door —
"'Tis some visitor," I muttered, "tapping at my chamber door —
Only this and nothing more."

Ah, distinctly I remember it was in the bleak December;
And each separate dying ember wrought its ghost upon the floor.
Eagerly I wished the morrow; — vainly I had sought to borrow
From my books surcease of sorrow — sorrow for the lost Lenore —
For the rare and radiant maiden whom the angels name Lenore —
Nameless here *for evermore.*

The raven. The unforgiving songbird. Repeatedly reminding me of President Snow's crystal-clear message to me on my homecoming. That I will never get to love anyone ever again. Nevermore. Because he will make sure they end up dying a horrible death.

And so, I drive away anyone and everyone who could ever have been considered dear to me. Old neighbors. Hattie. Customers. Schoolmates. Blair and Burdock hang on the hardest. Blair finally acknowledges the truth of my position, gives me one final hug and leaves sobbing. Even then, Burdock insists on showing up, sometimes along with Asterid, who bears bottles of sleep syrup. Defiant. Deaf to my pleas. I resort to throwing rocks, hard, at them. It takes one hitting Asterid on the forehead, blood pouring down her perfect face, to finally get them to leave me alone. Hurting her that way feels worse than anything I did in the arena.

And the silken, sad, uncertain rustling of each purple curtain

Thrilled me — filled me with fantastic terrors never felt before;
So that now, to still the beating of my heart, I stood repeating
"'Tis some visitor entreating entrance at my chamber door —
Some late visitor entreating entrance at my chamber door; —
This it is and nothing more."

Presently my soul grew stronger; hesitating then no longer,
"Sir," said I, "or Madam, truly your forgiveness I implore;
But the fact is I was napping, and so gently you came rapping,
And so faintly you came tapping, tapping at my chamber door,
That I scarce was sure I heard you" — here I opened wide the door; —
Darkness there and nothing more.

The world goes silent. I see no one. I have never really been alone before, always with my family. Or my friends. Or my love.

A Peacekeeper slides an envelope of money, my victor winnings, under my door every week, and leaves a food parcel on the porch. On the envelope, meat and bread and milk and various supplies have been meticulously deducted. Who has arranged this service? The president? Is he still insisting on keeping me alive?

I would welcome death, if it wasn't for my promise to Lenore Dove that I would somehow keep the sun from rising on the reaping. The impossibility of it adds to my despair. I drain the bottles of sleep syrup to escape reality, only to feed her gumdrops in my dreams.

Deep into that darkness peering, long I stood there wondering, fearing,

Doubting, dreaming dreams no mortal ever dared to dream before;
But the silence was unbroken, and the stillness gave no token,
And the only word there spoken was the whispered word, "Lenore?"
This I whispered, and an echo murmured back the word, "Lenore!"
Merely this and nothing more.

Back into the chamber turning, all my soul within me burning,
Soon again I heard a tapping somewhat louder than before.
"Surely," said I, "surely that is something at my window lattice;
Let me see, then, what thereat is, and this mystery explore —
Let my heart be still a moment and this mystery explore; —
'Tis the wind and nothing more!"

I go looking for her one night, searching for freshly overturned earth and a new headstone in the graveyard on the hill. The others are there — Ma, Sid, my fellow tributes — but not Lenore Dove.

The Covey's crooked house stands dark and silent in the moonlight. I roam around the yard like a stray dog, curl up under her window, yearning for her ghost to find me. It must be three in the morning when the fiddle begins, soft and low, playing her song.

Does Clerk Carmine somehow know I'm there? Is this his attempt to drive me stark raving mad? I pound on the door, screaming at the top of my lungs, "Where is she? Where is she?"

The fiddle falls silent. But it's too late. The earworm has awoken.

Open here I flung the shutter, when, with many a flirt
and flutter,
In there stepped a stately Raven of the saintly days of yore;
Not the least obeisance made he; not a minute stopped or
stayed he;
But, with mien of lord or lady, perched above my chamber
door —
Perched upon a bust of Pallas just above my chamber
door —
Perched, and sat, and nothing more.

Then this ebony bird beguiling my sad fancy into smiling,
By the grave and stern decorum of the countenance it wore,
"Though thy crest be shorn and shaven, thou," I said, "art
sure no craven,
Ghastly grim and ancient Raven wandering from the
Nightly shore —
Tell me what thy lordly name is on the Night's Plutonian
shore!"
Quoth the Raven "Nevermore."

The sleep syrup runs out and in desperation I begin to visit old Bascom Pie, loading a sack with bottles of rotgut, clinking all the way home. Some nights I find the oblivion I seek, others I wander through the dark. One morning, as I awake half-naked on the green outside my house, covered in mosquito bites, I realize where she must be. That her uncles would not have laid her to rest in the District 12 graveyard but taken her somewhere she loved. That they all loved. The woods.

I am a man on a mission. For weeks, I wander through the trees, circle the lake, examine the soil under the apple trees, looking for any sign of her. Entreating the mockingjays for a clue to her whereabouts. Calling her name into the wind. The leaves turn scarlet and gold, crunching beneath my feet. "Lenore Dove! Lenore Dove!" I cry, but she doesn't reveal herself.

Burdock comes, though, appearing out of the mist. His leather jacket fastened against the frost, his bow in hand, a brace of wild turkey at his hip. He has not forgiven me, will never, but is not beyond pity. Perhaps because he knows what it is to love. "If you want her, come on" is all he says. And I do want her, just as long ago I wanted the apples he promised, and so I follow him far, far into the woods. Beyond the lake, beyond my ken, to a hidden grove no normal human eye could detect. And here he leaves me.

A small, secret graveyard with beautifully carved headstones. Covey. Each marked only with a snippet of their name poems.

Among them, on a creamy white stone:

"Lady," he said, — "Maude Clare," he said, —
"Maude Clare": — and hid his face.

On a mossy slab of slate:

— Yet some maintain that to this day
She is a living child;

That you may see sweet Lucy Gray
Upon the lonesome wild.

And on a gray rock, speckled with pink and purple:

But the silence was unbroken, and the stillness gave no token,
And the only word there spoken was the whispered word, "Lenore?"
This I whispered, and an echo murmured back the word, "Lenore!"
Merely this and nothing more.

I lie on her grave and remain there as night falls, dawn breaks, and blackness descends again. I tell her everything and beg her to return to me, to wait for me, to forgive me for all the ways in which I have failed.

When dawn breaks on the second day, she has not come. I bury the flint striker, snake and bird, in front of her headstone. I ask her to free me from my final promise. I ask her to let me come to her now. I ask her for a sign. Then I somehow make my way home and fall asleep . . . where I feed her another gumdrop.

Much I marvelled this ungainly fowl to hear discourse so plainly.
Though its answer little meaning — little relevancy bore;
For we cannot help agreeing that no living human being
Ever yet was blessed with seeing bird above his chamber door —
Bird or beast upon the sculptured bust above his chamber door,
With such name as "Nevermore."

But the Raven, sitting lonely on the placid bust, spoke
only
That one word, as if his soul in that one word he did
outpour.
Nothing farther then he uttered — not a feather then he
fluttered —
Till I scarcely more than muttered "Other friends have
flown before —
On the morrow he *will leave me, as my Hopes have flown*
before."
Then the bird said "Nevermore."

I hit the bottle even harder. Drinking, disappearing into the night, regaining consciousness in the forgotten places of District 12. One morning, at the crack of dawn, I snap awake, shivering, in a back alley in town. I'm staring at a message sprayed in bright orange paint. *NO CAPITOL, NO HANGING TREE!* It's a rebel play on the Capitol's propaganda. *NO CAPITOL, NO REAPING!* Tucked away in this alley, a rallying cry beyond the Peacekeepers' radar.

A memory tugs at me . . . Maysilee in the arena . . . after she killed the Gamemaker . . . spider silk and her mamaw's song . . .

"Well, your gal's full of surprises. Guess she got the jump on us after all."

Full of surprises. Full of secrets, even from me. But Maysilee had put it together. Orange paint on her fingernails. This is Lenore Dove's work. Her sign. Her message to me now. Her reminder that I must prevent another sunrise on the reaping.

And it says, *"You promised me."*

With that, she condemns me to life.

Startled at the stillness broken by reply so aptly spoken,
"Doubtless," said I, "what it utters is its only stock and store
Caught from some unhappy master whom unmerciful Disaster
Followed fast and followed faster till his songs one burden bore —
Till the dirges of his Hope that melancholy burden bore
Of 'Never — nevermore.'"

But the Raven still beguiling my sad fancy into smiling,
Straight I wheeled a cushioned seat in front of bird, and bust and door;
Then, upon the velvet sinking, I betook myself to linking
Fancy unto fancy, thinking what this ominous bird of yore —
What this grim, ungainly, ghastly, gaunt, and ominous bird of yore
Meant in croaking "Nevermore."

Now that Lenore Dove has said her piece, other ghosts, filled with hate and rage, visit me in the night. Panache seems to have little to do but hunt me down and Silka thinks I owe her a crown. The terror bleeds into my waking hours. I start sleeping with a knife in my hand.

It's Effie Trinket who finds me thus, the morning of the Victory Tour. I come to, startled, to discover she's taken possession of my knife. "I'm so sorry about your family's accident, Haymitch. And then your girl's appendicitis right after? Tragic. But this just won't do. We have a responsibility to carry on."

My family's accident? Lenore Dove's appendicitis? She's right. I do have a responsibility to carry on. But how can I?

I let Effie pour coffee down me. Send me to the tub until Proserpina and Vitus can stomach me. Button me into a paisley suit that Great-Uncle Silius never had occasion to wear, and somehow make me presentable as I board the train to District 11.

"Word got out. Magno was fired for negligence and Drusilla broke her hip falling down an escalator," Plutarch tells me in confidence. "It seems Maysilee was right about those heels. Anyway, I pitched Effie last-minute and they jumped on the idea. Especially since she brought the depraved uncle's wardrobe with her."

"How are you here, Plutarch?" I ask. It's a question that could be answered on many levels. He chooses the most superficial.

"I'm here to record your Victory Tour. It's in my contract. Hey, you look like you could do with a sandwich. Tibby!"

A different train than I rode before. Fancier. Lots of steel and chrome. Dove-colored velvet upholstery, lest I forget. Trying to forget is my full-time job now.

Effie does her best to keep me sober, but the train's loaded with booze.

This I sat engaged in guessing, but no syllable expressing
To the fowl whose fiery eyes now burned into my bosom's core;
This and more I sat divining, with my head at ease reclining
On the cushion's velvet lining that the lamp-light gloated o'er,
But whose velvet-violet lining with the lamp-light gloating o'er,
She *shall press, ah, nevermore!*

Then, methought, the air grew denser, perfumed from an
unseen censer

Swung by seraphim whose foot-falls tinkled on the tufted
floor.
"Wretch," I cried, "thy God hath lent thee — by these angels
he hath sent thee
Respite — respite and nepenthe from thy memories of Lenore;
Quaff, oh quaff this kind nepenthe and forget this lost
Lenore!"
Quoth the Raven "Nevermore."

In District 11, I stand on the steps of their Justice Building facing the grief-stricken families of Hull, Tile, Chicory, and the other girl, Blossom. I search the wider sea of faces for Lou Lou's kin and come up empty.

The party begins. I drink my way through the festivities, which run far into the night. When the Justice Building finally sleeps, Plutarch spirits me up multiple stairways and into the attic.

"Respite and nepenthe," I mutter into my bottle.

Plutarch yanks it from my hand. "Listen, Haymitch, we don't have long. This attic is the only spot in the entire Justice Building that isn't bugged."

Well, he might be right about that. The place looks like it hasn't been disturbed in a hundred years. There's a coat of dust so thick you could comfortably sleep on it. Why you'd sneak off to this place for privacy instead of stepping outside the Justice Building, I don't know and I don't care. There's nothing left they can do to me. Unlike Plutarch.

"How is it you're looking so well, Plutarch? Wiress and Mags were tortured, right? And I'm guessing Beetee's dead."

"Beetee's too valuable to kill."

"I thought he'd have killed himself."

"He can't. His wife's pregnant. Besides, he wouldn't let Ampert down that way."

"Oh, I see. He's going to overthrow the Capitol, is he?"

"Maybe one day. But we can't any of us do it alone. You demonstrated a lot of nerve and intelligence in that arena. We need your help."

"Me?" I say in disbelief. "I am living proof that the Capitol always wins. I tried to keep that sun from rising on another reaping day, I tried to change things, and now everybody's dead. You don't want me." And I don't want him. I don't want help from anybody in the Capitol ever again. I could never trust them.

"We do want you. You shook up the Capitol, both figuratively and literally, with that earthquake. You were capable of imagining a different future. And maybe it won't be realized today, maybe not in our lifetime. Maybe it will take generations. We're all part of a continuum. Does that make it pointless?"

"I just don't know. But I do know, you need someone different from me."

"No, Haymitch, we need someone exactly like you."

"Just luckier?" I say.

"Luckier, or with better timing. Having an army at their back wouldn't hurt."

"Sure, that would've helped. Where're you going to get an army, Plutarch?"

"If we can't find one, we'll have to build one. But obviously, finding one's easier."

"And then we can all kill one another, like back in the good old Dark Days?"

"Well, you know better than anyone what we're up against

with Snow. If you think of another way to stop that sunrise, you let me know."

"Prophet!" said I, "thing of evil! — prophet still, if bird or
devil! —
Whether Tempter sent, or whether tempest tossed thee here
ashore,
Desolate yet all undaunted, on this desert land enchanted —
On this home by Horror haunted — tell me truly, I
implore —
Is there — is *there balm in Gilead? — tell me — tell me,*
I implore!"
Quoth the Raven "Nevermore."

"Prophet!" said I, "thing of evil! — prophet still, if bird or
devil!
By that Heaven that bends above us — by that God we
both adore —
Tell this soul with sorrow laden if, within the distant Aidenn,
It shall clasp a sainted maiden whom the angels name Lenore —
Clasp a rare and radiant maiden whom the angels name Lenore."
Quoth the Raven "Nevermore."

I avoid speaking to Plutarch for the rest of the Victory Tour. Through all the districts, where I stand on stages looking down at the families of the dead tributes. Through all the parties that culminate in the Capitol, where I'm returned to my comfy cage. Through all the strained festivities in District 12.

My team heads to the train. Plutarch and his crew do a style piece on my new house and tape a parting shot of me in the yard.

As I stand there, staring at my prison, unwilling to cross the threshold and resume my sentence, he joins me.

"All right there, Haymitch?"

"I have nothing to live for." I say this without even a note of self-pity. I am simply stating a fact.

"Then you have nothing to lose. That puts you in a position of power."

I would like to kill him at that moment, but what would be the point? Instead, I say, "You think you're a good person, don't you, Plutarch? You think you're a good guy because you told me about the sun and the berms. When what you really did is help create the Capitol's propaganda and broadcast it to the country. Forty-nine kids died for it, but you gave it the old Heavensbee spin and, in that propo, you're some kind of hero."

Plutarch takes a moment to answer. "I'm nobody's idea of a hero, Haymitch. But at least I'm still in the game."

"Be that word our sign of parting, bird or fiend!" I shrieked, upstarting —
"Get thee back into the tempest and the Night's Plutonian shore!
Leave no black plume as a token of that lie thy soul hath spoken!
Leave my loneliness unbroken! — quit the bust above my door!
Take thy beak from out my heart, and take thy form from off my door!"
Quoth the Raven "Nevermore."

And the Raven, never flitting, still is sitting, still *is sitting*
On the pallid bust of Pallas just above my chamber door;
And his eyes have all the seeming of a demon's that is
dreaming,
And the lamp-light o'er him streaming throws his shadow
on the floor;
And my soul from out that shadow that lies floating on the
floor
Shall be lifted — nevermore!

And so I remain, forever trapped in my chamber.

I am so desperate to forget. To escape the grief, the aching loneliness, the loss of those I love. There are no mementos of them; all are burned or buried. I work on forgetting their voices, their faces, their laughs. Even in my head, my language becomes dull and flat, stripped of the color and music of yesterday.

The only human contact I allow myself arrives by way of Capitol News, which I play on my television set 24/7. That way, if Lenore Dove's ghost ever comes to me, I can tell her I'm working on a strategy to keep that sun from rising.

I make no plans, have no hopes, keep no company, speak to no human being except old Bascom Pie when my nepenthe runs low. But I can't say I have no future, because I know that every year for my birthday, I will get a new pair of tributes, one girl and one boy, to mentor to their deaths. Another sunrise on the reaping.

And when I remember that, I hear Sid's voice, waking me the morning that raven first tapped on my chamber door.

"Happy birthday, Haymitch!"

EPILOGUE

When Lenore Dove comes to me now, she's not angry or dying, so I think she's forgiven me. She's grown older with me, her face etched with fine lines, her hair touched with gray. Like she's been living her life beside me as the years passed, instead of lying in her grave. Still so rare and radiant. I fulfilled my promise about the reaping, or at least lent a hand, but she says I can't come to her yet. I have to look after my family.

I first saw the girl at the Hob when she was just a baby. Burdock was so proud of her, he toted her around everywhere. After he died in that mine explosion, she started coming alone, trading the odd squirrel or rabbit. Tough and smart, her hair in two braids then, reminding me for all the world of Louella McCoy, my sweetheart of old. And after she volunteered for the Games, that nickname couldn't help but slip out. I didn't want to let them in, her and Peeta, but the walls of a person's heart are not impregnable, not if they have ever known love. That's what Lenore Dove says, anyway.

I didn't want to have anything to do with their memorial book after the war. What use? What point? To relive all the loss. But when Burdock's page came up, I had to mention him showing me the grave. And I felt compelled to tell them about Maysilee Donner, former owner of the mockingjay pin. And how Sid loved the stars. Before I knew it, they all came tumbling out: family, tributes, friends, comrades in arms, everybody, even my love. I finally told our story.

A few days after that, Katniss showed up with an old basket filled with goose eggs. "Not to eat, to hatch. I raided a few different nests, so they can breed all right." Never mind that we had roast goose for dinner. She's not an easy person; she's like me, Peeta always says. But she was smarter than me, or luckier. She's the one who finally kept that sun from rising.

Peeta fashioned some kind of incubator, and when the eggs hatched, mine was the first face those goslings saw. Sometimes they just graze on the green, but on fine days, we've been known to wander on over to the Meadow. Lenore Dove likes it best there, and I'm content where she's content. Like the geese, we really did mate for life.

I'm not sure I'll be here in the old therebefore much longer. My liver's wrecked and I only dry out when the train's late. I drink differently these days, though, less to forget, more out of habit. When my time comes, it comes, but I've no idea when that will be.

I know one thing, though: The Capitol can never take Lenore Dove from me again. They never really did in the first place. Nothing you can take from me was ever worth keeping, and she is the most precious thing I've ever known.

When I tell her that, she always says, "I love you like all-fire."

And I reply, "I love you like all-fire, too."

THE END

acknowledgments

My dear friend and creative collaborator, James Proimos, passed away on July 8, 2024, as I was finishing up this novel. Both an amazing artist and writer, his delightfully funny and inventive books encourage his audience to consider building a kinder and gentler world, one cupcake at a time. My personal favorites include *The Many Adventures of Johnny Mutton*, *Joe's Wish*, and *Paulie Pastrami Achieves World Peace.*

I'm pretty sure The Hunger Games wouldn't exist without Jim (which is why the first book is dedicated to him). We met on *Generation O!*, an animated TV show that he cocreated. Jim thought I should be an author and repeatedly encouraged me to give it a try. He said to write something, anything, and then he'd do a few drawings for it and his agent, Rosemary Stimola, would have to look at it. So that's how it started. Neither the ABC or counting books we attempted ever found a home — although Jim's art was fantastic. But they gave me enough of a connection to Rosemary that on the morning I woke up in a state of excitement with the idea for *Gregor the Overlander*, I felt comfortable calling her at an inappropriately early hour and pitching it. The rest unfolded from there. It seems unlikely that I would've found my way to books without Jim, and I will always be grateful to him for opening that door and quietly and persistently nudging me through it.

Jim was one of the truly original thinkers it has been my privilege to work with. We collaborated on a number of TV projects, but only one other book. I had been struggling to find a way to transform my memories of the year my dad was deployed to

Vietnam into a picture book. Over a casual lunch, I started telling Jim the story. As he responded, I began to see it come to life with his art, not dark and heavy-handed but through the eyes of a six-year-old. *Year of the Jungle* was a tough story for me to tell, far more personal than my usual writing, and having an empathetic and trusted friend by my side gave me the courage to explore it. His incredible art, which transforms the jungle from a magical playground to a terrifying nightmare while maintaining a child-like visual style, made the book possible.

For the encouragement, for the jungle, and for the many years of your kindness, humor, patience, talent, and friendship, thank you, Jim. At this point, I think it's safe to say, "We will never drift apart."

In addition, I'd like to thank my gander and first reader, Cap Pryor; my son, Charlie; and my aforementioned agent, Rosemary, for their impactful early response to this book. Good friends Richard Register and Michael Arndt also gave invaluable support and input on the story.

Coming home to Scholastic is always a joy. Deep appreciation once again for my editorial director, David Levithan, who has always been so generous in sharing his extraordinary authorial expertise; my first and always editor, Kate Egan, who has beautifully advised me from the first Gregor book; the responsive Emily Seife, whose heartfelt emotional notes gave me a much needed boost when my batteries were running low; our terrific copy editor, Joy Simpkins, for catching what the rest of us do not; and Elizabeth Parisi and Tim O'Brien for another gorgeous cover.

A big shout-out to the rest of my fabulous publishing family: the late, great Dick Robinson, Iole Lucchese, Peter Warwick, Ellie Berger, Rachel Coun, Lizette Serrano, Tracy van Straaten, Katy

Coyle, Madeline Muschalik, Mark Seidenfeld, Leslie Garych, Erin O'Connor, JoAnne Mojica, Melissa Schirmer, Maeve Norton, Bonnie Cutler, Nelson Gómez, Lauren Fortune, Paul Gagne, Andrea Davis Pinkney, Billy DiMichele, and the entire Scholastic sales force.

A note about the songs: "The Raven" by Edgar Allan Poe was first published in 1845. "Ah! Sun-flower" by William Blake appeared in his *Songs of Experience* in 1794. "The Goose and the Common" was written by an unknown author in the seventeenth or eighteenth century. "Ladybug, Ladybug" is a District 12 variation of a centuries-old nursery rhyme. I wrote both "Wiress's Arena Song" and "The Harvest Song" for this story. "The Happy Birthday Song" and "Gem of Panem" first appeared in the novel *The Ballad of Songbirds and Snakes*; James Newton Howard wrote the music to the latter for the screen. "The Hanging Tree" lyrics originated in the book *Mockingjay*, and the film version was composed by Jeremiah Caleb Fraites & Wesley Keith Schultz of the Lumineers and arranged by James Newton Howard. "Nothing You Can Take From Me," "The Ballad of Lucy Gray Baird," and "The Old Therebefore" all first appeared in the *Ballad* novel and Dave Cobb wrote their music for the film. Much gratitude goes to all these artists, from long ago to the present, whose brilliant, whimsical, and soulful works have enriched Panem.

Managing this fictional world is a complex and ever-growing job. To Rosemary; my entertainment agent, Jason Dravis; legal experts Eleanor Lackman, Diane Golden, and Sarah Lerner; and my daughter, Izzy, who keeps the District 12 office in shape — thanks for the super job you do making sure everything runs smoothly.

I wish my dad was here to see that our discussions on David Hume inspired *Sunrise on the Reaping*, and I hope my English-major mom, who shares her love of literature with me, enjoys this story. Much love always to you both.

To all my wonderful readers, thanks for once again returning to Panem and investing in these characters and their struggles, even when you know the eventual outcome. The snow may fall, but the sun also rises.

ABOUT THE AUTHOR

Suzanne Collins is the internationally bestselling author of the Hunger Games series, which also includes the novels *The Hunger Games*, *Catching Fire*, *Mockingjay*, and *The Ballad of Songbirds and Snakes*. Together, the books have sold over 100 million copies and were the basis for five popular films. Her other books include the acclaimed Underland Chronicles series, which begins with *Gregor the Overlander*, and the picture book *Year of the Jungle*, illustrated by James Proimos. To date, her books have been published in fifty-three languages around the world.